TH
KINGDOM

AMANDA
STEVENS

MIRA®

MIRA®

Recycling programs for this product may not exist in your area.

ISBN-13: 978-0-7783-1277-2

THE KINGDOM

Copyright © 2012 by Marilyn Medlock Amann

For questions and comments about the quality of this book please contact us at Customer_eCare@Harlequin.ca.

www.Harlequin.com

Printed in U.S.A.

First printing: April 2012
10 9 8 7 6 5 4 3 2 1

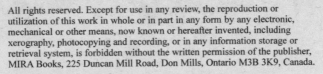

THE
KINGDOM

Praise for

AMANDA STEVENS

and
The Graveyard Queen Series

One

The breeze off the water carried a slight chill even though the sun had barely begun its western slide. It was still hours until twilight. Hours until the veil between our world and the next would thin, but already I could feel the ripple of goose bumps at the back of my neck, a sensation that almost always signaled an unnatural presence.

I resisted the temptation to glance over my shoulder. Years of living with ghosts had instilled in me an aberrant discipline. I knew better than to react to those greedy, grasping entities, so I leaned against the deck rail and stared intently into the greenish depths of the lake. But from my periphery, I tracked the other passengers on the ferry.

The intimate murmurs and soft laughter from the couple next to me aroused an unexpected melancholy, and I thought suddenly of John Devlin, the police detective I'd left behind in Charleston. This time of day, he would probably still be at work, and I conjured up an image of him hunched over a cluttered desk, reviewing autopsy reports and crime scene photos. Did I cross his mind now and then? Not that it mattered. He was a man haunted by his dead wife and daughter, and I was a woman who saw ghosts. For as long as he clung to his past—and his past clung to him—I could not be a part of his life.

So I wouldn't dwell on Devlin or that terrible door that my feelings for him had opened. In the months since I'd last seen him, my life had settled back into a normal routine. Normal for me, at least. I still saw ghosts, but those darker entities—the Others, my father called them—had drifted back into their murky underworld where I prayed they would remain. The memories, however, lingered. Memories of Devlin, memories of all those victims and of a haunted killer who had made me a target. I knew no matter how hard I fought them off, the nightmares would return the moment I closed my eyes.

For now, though, I wanted to savor my adventure. The start of a new commission filled me with excitement, and I looked forward to the prospect of uncovering the history of yet another graveyard, of immersing myself in the lives of those who had been laid to rest there. I always say that cemetery restoration is more than just clearing away trash and overgrowth. It's about *restoration.*

The back of my neck continued to prickle.

After a moment, I turned to casually glance back at the row of cars. My silver SUV was one of only five vehicles on the ferry. Another SUV belonged to the couple, a green minivan to a middle-aged woman absorbed in a battered paperback novel, and a faded red pickup truck to an elderly man sipping coffee from a foam cup. That left the vintage black sports car. The metallic jet paint drew my appreciative gaze. In the sunlight, the shimmer reminded me of snake scales, and an inexplicable shiver traced along my spine as I admired the serpentine lines. The windows were tinted, blocking my view of the interior, but I imagined the driver behind the wheel, impatiently drumming fingers as the ferry inched toward the other side. To Asher Falls. To Thorngate Cemetery, my ultimate destination.

Brushing my hand against the back of my neck, I turned again to the water, mentally rummaging through the tidbits I'd gleaned from my research. Located in the lush Blue Ridge foothills of South Carolina, Asher Falls had once been a thriving community, but in the mid-eighties, one of the town's most prominent citizens, Pell Asher, had struck an unsavory bargain. He'd sold acreage to the state to be used as a reservoir, and when the dam opened, the area flooded, including the main highway leading into Asher Falls. Already bypassed by a new freeway system, the town sank into oblivion. The only way in and out was by ferry or back roads, and the population soon withered. Asher Falls became just another statistic in a long line of dying rural communities.

I'd never set foot in the town, even to conduct a preliminary assessment of the cemetery. I'd been hired sight unseen by a real estate agent named Luna Kemper, who also happened to be the town librarian and the sole administrator of a generous donation made anonymously to the Daughters of our Valiant Heroes, a historical society/garden club for the beautification of Thorngate Cemetery. Luna's offer couldn't have come at a more perfect time. I needed a new project and a change of scenery, so here I stood.

As we approached the dock, the engines powered down and we came to a near standstill. The heavy shadows cast by towering trees at the shoreline deepened the water to black. At no point could I see the bottom, but for a moment, I could have sworn I saw something— *someone*—just below the surface. A pale face staring up at me....

My heart took a nosedive as I leaned over the railing, searching those blackish depths. People without my ability would have undoubtedly wondered if the play of light and shadow on the water had tricked them. Or worse, if they might have spotted a body being washed ashore in the ferry's wake. I thought instantly of a ghost and wondered who on board might be haunted by the golden-haired apparition floating underneath the water.

"I believe this is yours."

A man's voice pulled me back from the railing, and I turned reluctantly from the lake. I knew at once he belonged to the sports car. He and the vehicle had the same dark, sleek air. I thought him to be around my age—twenty-seven—with eyes the exact shade of a tidal marsh. He was tallish, though not so tall as Devlin, nor as thin. Years of being haunted had left the magnetic police detective hollow-eyed and gaunt while the stranger at my side appeared to be the picture of health—lean, sinewy and suntanned.

"I beg your pardon?"

He extended his hand, and I thought at first he meant to introduce himself, but instead he uncurled his fingers, and I saw my necklace coiled in his palm.

My hand went immediately to my throat. "Oh! The

chain must have snapped." I plucked the necklace from his hand and examined the links. They were unbroken, the clasp still securely closed. "How strange," I murmured, unlatching the claw fastener and entwining the silver strand around my neck. "Where did you find it?"

"It was lying on the deck behind you." His gaze slid downward as the polished stone settled into the hollow of my throat.

Something cold gripped my heart. A warning?

"Thank you," I said stiffly. "I would have hated to lose it."

"It's an interesting piece." He appeared to study the amulet intently. "A good luck charm?"

"You might say that." Actually, the stone had come from the hallowed ground of a cemetery where my father had worked as caretaker when I was a child. Whether the talisman retained any of Rosehill's protective properties, I had no idea. I only knew that I felt stronger against the ghosts when I wore it.

I started to turn back to the water, but something in the stranger's eyes, a mysterious glint, held me for a moment longer.

"Are you okay?" he asked unexpectedly.

"Yes, I'm fine. Why do you ask?"

He nodded toward the side of the ferry. "You were leaning so far over the railing when I came up, and then I saw your necklace on the deck. I was afraid you might be contemplating jumping."

"Oh, that." I gave a negligible shrug. "I thought I saw something in the water. Probably just a shadow."

The glint in his eyes deepened. "I wouldn't be too sure. You'd be surprised at what lies beneath the surface of this lake. Some of it occasionally floats to the top."

"Such as?"

"Debris, mostly. Glass bottles, bits of old clothing. I even once saw a rocking chair drifting to shore."

"Where does it all come from?"

"Flooded houses." As he turned to stare out over the water, I studied his profile, drawn by the way the late afternoon sunlight burnished his dark hair. The coppery threads gave him an aura of warmth that seemed to be absent from the midnight-green of his eyes. "Before the dam was built, the lake was half the size it is now. A lot of property was destroyed when the water rose."

"But that was years ago. You mean the houses are still down there?" I tried to peer through the layers of algae and hydrilla, but I could see nothing. Not even the ghostly face I'd spotted earlier.

"Houses, cars…an old graveyard."

My gaze shot back to him. "A graveyard?"

"Thorngate Cemetery. Another casualty of the Asher greed."

"But I thought…" Uneasiness crept over me. I was good at my job, but recovering an underwater cemetery wasn't exactly my area of expertise. "I've seen recent pictures of Thorngate. It looked high and dry to me."

"There are two Thorngates," he said. "And I assure you that one of them does rest at the bottom of this lake."

"How did that happen?"

"The original Thorngate was rarely used. It was all but forgotten. No one ever went out there. No one gave it a second thought…until the water came."

I stared at him in horror. "Are you telling me the bodies weren't moved before they expanded the lake?"

He shuddered. "Afterward, people started seeing things. Hearing things."

I fingered the talisman at my throat. "Like what?"

He hesitated, his gaze still on the water. "If you look for this basin on any South Carolina map, you'll find the Asher Reservoir. But around here, we call it Bell Lake."

"Why?"

"In the old days, coffins were equipped with a warning system—a chain attached to a bell on the grave in case of a premature burial. They say at night, when the mist rolls in, you can hear those bells." He glanced over the railing. "The dead down there don't want to be forgotten...*ever again.*"

Two

A tremor shot through me a split second before I saw the gleam of amusement in the stranger's eyes.

"Sorry," he said with a contrite smile. "Local folk-lore. I couldn't resist."

"It's not true then?"

"Oh, the cemetery is down there all right, along with cars, houses and God knows what else. Some claim they've even seen coffins float to the surface after a bad storm. But the bells…" He paused. "Put it this way. I've fished on this lake since I was a boy, and I've never heard them."

What about the face I'd seen under the surface? I wondered. Was that real?

His lingering gaze made me uneasy, though I had no idea why. His eyes were just a little too murky, a little too mysterious—like the bottom of Bell Lake.

He leaned forward, resting his forearms against the railing. He wore jeans and a black pullover sweater that hugged his toned torso. An unexpected appreciation skimmed along my nerve endings, and I glanced quickly away because the last thing I needed was a romantic complication. I wasn't over Devlin, might never be over him, and an attractive stranger could do nothing more than momentarily ease my intense longing. Assuage an almost physical ache that had settled deep inside my chest since the night I'd fled the house Devlin had shared with the very beautiful and the very dead Mariama.

"So what brings you to Asher Falls?" the stranger asked. "That is, if you don't mind my asking. We don't get a lot of visitors. We're pretty well off the beaten track."

His voice was pleasant enough, but I detected a slight edge to the question. "I've been hired to restore Thorngate Cemetery. The high and dry one."

He didn't respond, and after a moment, his silence drew my reluctant gaze. He was staring down at me, his eyes still gleaming, though not with amusement or even curiosity, but with a spark of what I could only name as anger. The emotion faded, but I knew I hadn't imagined his irritation.

I tried not to read too much into it. I often encountered local opposition. People were protective and sometimes overly superstitious about their graveyards. I started to reassure him that I knew my business. Thorngate would be in good hands. But then I decided that might be a job best left to the woman who had hired me. She would know how to address the concerns of her community far better than I.

"So you're here to restore Thorngate," he murmured. "Whose idea was that?"

"The name of my contact is Luna Kemper. If you have questions, I suggest you direct them to her."

"Oh, I will," he said with a tight smile.

"Is there a problem?" I couldn't resist asking.

"Not yet, but I can foresee some tension. Thorngate—the high and dry Thorngate—used to be the Asher family cemetery. After the original graveyard flooded, the burial site was donated to the town, along with enough land for expansion. A lot of people still have strong feelings about it."

"The Ashers gave away their family cemetery? That seems a bit extreme. Why didn't they just donate land for a new one?"

"Because a gesture was needed after what the old man did." The green eyes darkened. "An atonement, if you want to know the truth. The irony, of course, is that the ostentatious memorials and family mausoleum only serve to highlight the divide between the Ashers and everyone else in town."

"Is Pell Asher still alive?"

"Oh, yes. Very much so." I saw another flicker of emotion before he glanced back at the water.

"What do you do in Asher Falls...if you don't mind my asking?" I mimicked his earlier question, but he didn't seem to notice.

"I drink," he said. "And I bide my time." He turned with a look that sent another shiver skittering along my backbone. There was something in his voice, a dark undercurrent that made me think of drowned cemeteries and long-buried secrets. I wanted to glance away, but his heavy-lidded eyes were disarmingly hypnotic. "I'm Thane Asher, by the way. Heir apparent to the shriveling Asher Empire, at least until Grandfather rewrites his will. He tends to go back and forth between my uncle and me. I'm the fair-haired child this week. If he kicks the bucket before next Thursday, I'm golden."

I didn't know how to respond to that, so I merely extended my hand. "Amelia Gray."

"A pleasure." He took my hand and squeezed. His was the warm, smooth palm of the privileged, un-marred by the calluses I'd acquired over the years from clearing brush and lifting headstones.

My thoughts turned to Devlin once again, and I imagined the stroke of his long, graceful fingers down my back.

Suppressing a shudder, I tried to pull away from Thane Asher's grip, but he held me for a moment longer, his gaze locked with mine until the ferry docked with a slight jolt and he freed me.

"Here we are," he said cheerfully. "Asher Falls. Welcome to our kingdom, Amelia Gray."

Three

Disembarking behind the minivan, I pulled to the side of the road to reset my navigation system. My windows were down, and a cool wind swept through, carrying the verdant, piney scent of the Upcountry. The dog days had extended into September, and the bee balm and hedge nettle were still blooming, carpeting the meadows in lavender. Rising above the gentle hills of the Piedmont, the area was beautiful, but the landscape of looming mountains, deep shadows and the green-black forest of pine and hemlock was foreign to me. My beloved Lowcountry, with its steamy marshes and briny breezes, seemed a long way from here.

The roar of an engine drew my attention from the scenery, and I glanced at the road as the black sports car zoomed past my window, leaving a thin cloud of dust and exhaust in its wake.

"Welcome to our kingdom," I muttered as I watched Thane Asher take a sharp curve without slowing. It was an impressive maneuver of reckless abandon, squealing tires and shimmering metallic paint. Then with a whine of the powerful motor, he was gone, and the quiet that settled around me seemed heavy and ominous, as if weighted by some dark enchantment.

I glanced in the rearview mirror at the ferry, mentally retracing my route to Charleston. To Devlin. But I was here now, and there was no turning back.

Pulling onto the road, I trailed Thane Asher into town.

Asher Falls had once been a picturesque town of cobblestone streets and classic revival-style buildings situated around a formal square shaded and shrouded by live oaks dripping with Spanish moss. Quaint was the word that came to mind, and it was only on second glance that one noticed the deteriorating vital signs of a dying community—boarded windows, sagging gutters, the stopped clock in the beautiful old tower.

I saw no one as I drove around the square. If not for a few scattered vehicles, I might have thought the place deserted. The streets were as silent as a tomb, the storefronts dark and lonely. The whole town had the quiet, forlorn air of the abandoned.

I pulled into a parking space and got out. Luna had emailed me the address of her real estate office, and I located it easily. But the door was locked, and I saw no sign of life through the window. Pecking on the glass, I waited a moment, then headed next door to the library, an impressive three-story structure with arches and columns reminiscent of some of my favorite buildings in Charleston.

A girl of about sixteen stood behind the counter sorting through a stack of books. She glanced up as I stepped inside but didn't offer a smile or a greeting.

Instead, she went back to her work, the pixie cut of her silver-blond hair revealing an anemic-looking face.

I took a moment to enjoy the familiar library scent before approaching the counter. I'd always loved the smell of old books and records and could happily immerse myself for hours in musty archives. Proper research was vital to a successful cemetery restoration, and as I took in the sagging bookshelves and shadowy alcoves, I felt a pulse of excitement at what I might discover—in the library and in Thorngate Cemetery.

The ancient floorboards creaked beneath my boots as I walked over to the counter. The blonde lifted her gaze but not her head. Her eyes were crystalline-blue, the clear, rinsed cyan of a spring sky. She was very slight, but I didn't think her fragile. She had a presence about her, a subtle gravitas that seemed unusual and a bit unsettling in a girl of her age.

She still said nothing, but I didn't take her silence for insolence. Rather, she seemed guarded and wary, like those of us who spend too much time in our own little world.

"My name is Amelia Gray. I'm here to see Luna Kemper. She's expecting me."

The girl spared a brief nod before finishing with the books. Then she turned and strode to a closed door, rapped once and slipped inside. A moment later she reappeared and motioned me around the counter. As she stepped aside to allow me to enter the room, I saw that her eyes were focused—not on me—but on a point just beyond my shoulder. I had the strangest feeling that if I followed her gaze, I would find nothing there. It was a disquieting sensation because, with few exceptions, I'm the one who sees what others cannot.

Before I had time to ponder her odd behavior, Luna Kemper rose, shooing aside a gorgeous gray tabby as she came around her desk to greet me. The scent of wildflowers suddenly filled the room as though she exuded the fragrance through her very pores. A vase of purple foxglove—Papa called them witch's bells—sat on the corner of her desk, but I didn't think the smell came from them. I'd never known that particular flower to have such a pungent perfume.

Luna looked to be in her early forties, a sensuous brunette with a lustrous complexion and eyes the color of a rain clouds. "Welcome, Amelia. I'm so happy to finally meet you in person." She extended her hand and we shook. She wore a charcoal pencil skirt and a lavender sweater accentuated with a large moonstone pendant. Her easy smile and friendly demeanor were a welcome contrast to her subdued assistant, who was dressed similarly to me—black T, jeans and a light-weight jacket.

"How was your trip?" Luna asked, leaning a shapely hip against her desk.

"It was great. I haven't been up this way in a long time. I'd forgotten how beautiful the foothills are this time of year."

"You should take a trip up to the falls if you get a chance. It's the most beautiful spot in the whole state, though, I expect I'm biased. I was born and raised in the foothills. My mother used to say I'd wither away without the mountains and the woods to roam in, but I love the occasional weekend jaunt to the beach. I have a cousin who has a place on St. Helena. Do you get down that way much?"

"No, not really. I stay pretty busy."

"I sympathize. Running a business doesn't leave much time for play. I can't remember the last time I had a real vacation. Maybe next summer...." She trailed off, her gaze moving to the door where the blonde still lurked. "Sidra, this is Amelia Gray, the cemetery restorer I told you about. Sidra Birch. She helps out in the library after school and sometimes on weekends."

I glanced over my shoulder and nodded. "Hello, Sidra."

She still said nothing but tilted her head and studied me so intently I grew uncomfortable. There was something about that girl. Something at once familiar and off-putting. She had the air of someone who knew dark things. Like me.

I suppressed a shudder as I turned back to Luna.

"I'm sure you're anxious to get settled in," she said briskly. "I've arranged for you to stay in Floyd Covey's house while he's in Florida tending to his mother. She's laid up with a broken hip so I expect he'll be gone for a couple of months at the very least—"

A sound from the doorway drew both our gazes. Sidra was staring at Luna with an expression I couldn't begin to fathom.

"What's wrong?" Luna asked.

"Why'd you put her way out there?"

"Why not?" Luna asked with a note of irritation.

Sidra's blue gaze fell on me, then darted away. "It's creepy."

"Nonsense. It's a lovely place right on the lake and the location is perfect. It's halfway between town and the cemetery," Luna explained. "I think you'll be very comfortable there."

"I'm sure I will be." But Sidra's comment, along with

Thane Asher's tale of restless souls beneath Bell Lake had planted an insidious seed.

Luna straightened from the desk. "Why don't you make yourself at home while I run next door and fetch the key? We can go over the contracts and permits and then I'll take you out to see the house."

Sidra had already disappeared, and I assumed she'd gone back to her work behind the counter. After Luna left, I wondered if I should go out there and ask the girl what she'd meant about the Covey place. Then I decided it was probably best to wait and form my own opinion.

Killing time, I glanced around Luna's office. It was one of those eclectic, overstuffed places that I'd always been drawn to. So many interesting and unusual treasures to admire, from the hand-carved pedestal desk to the brass ship's bell mounted over the doorway. I hadn't noticed the bell before, but now I detected the faintest ting, as if a draft had stirred the clapper. There was a second, narrow door with an arched top and an ornate keyhole plate that made me wonder where it led to.

Slowly, I circled the room, admiring the bric-a-brac in mahogany cabinets, everything from blown-glass figurines to antique pocket watches, from fossils and shells to an assortment of oddly shaped knives. Framed photographs covered the walls, most of them local historical buildings, but the people shots interested me more. One in particular caught my attention—a picture of three young women, arms entwined as they stared dreamily into the camera. I recognized a teenage Luna, and one of the other girls bore an uncanny resemblance to Sidra, but I knew it couldn't be her. A good twenty-five years separated their ages, and besides, the hairstyles and clothing screamed the eighties. Sidra wouldn't have even been born then.

A fourth girl hovered in the shadowy background, her wavy hair floating about her in a breeze as she glared into the lens. I felt an odd tightening in my chest as I studied that stony face, and for the longest time, I couldn't seem to catch my breath, couldn't tear my eyes from that fiery glower.

"Are you all right?"

I took a step back, Sidra's voice breaking whatever hold the photograph had on me. I turned to find her watching me from the doorway. Light from the window picked up the silvery threads in her hair, creating an ethereal illusion that, along with her paleness, made me wonder if she might be a ghost. I'd been fooled before, but since Luna could interact with her, too, the likelihood seemed slim.

"Why are you staring at me like that?" she asked with a frown.

"Was I staring? I'm sorry," I managed to say calmly. "I was just thinking how much you resemble the girl in this picture."

She came over to stand beside me. "That's my mother, Bryn." Pointing to the redhead on her mother's right, she said, "That's Catrice, and, of course, you know Luna. The three of them were best friends in high school. Still are, I guess."

"Do they all live here in Asher Falls?"

She hesitated. "You heard what Luna said. She'd wither away if she left the mountains. My mother would, too, I think. None of them would last long out in the real world."

"This isn't the real world?"

"God, I hope not," she said with a shiver.

"You don't like it here?"

"Like it? This place is a ghost town," she said, and something in her voice made *me* shiver.

"Sounds as if Luna manages to stay busy."

"Oh, yes. Luna is a very busy woman."

We were both staring at the photograph, and I could see Sidra's pale refection in the glass.

"I like her name," I said. "It's unusual but it suits her. And yours is unusual, too."

"I'm named for her. Sidra means 'of the stars,' and Luna means moon, so…" She shrugged. "Kind of cheesy, but they've always been into that mystical stuff."

"Who's the fourth girl?"

I heard her breath catch and glanced over to find her in the grip of some strong emotion—eyes wide, hand pressed to her heart—but then she swallowed and tried to recover. "What girl?" she asked in a thin voice.

"The one in the background. Her." I put a finger over the glass and felt a rush of something unpleasant go through me.

Sidra said nothing. In the ensuing silence, I heard the bell again, so faintly I wondered if my imagination had supplied the sound.

"There's no one else in the picture," she said. "I don't know what you're talking about."

I could clearly see an angry countenance in the background, but suddenly I understood. Whoever she was, she'd already been dead when the picture was taken. The photographer had captured her ghost.

It was the clearest shot of an entity I'd ever seen.

But…if I was the one who saw ghosts, why was Sidra so distressed?

"It's just a shadow or some trick of the light," she insisted. "There's no one else in the picture."

Our gazes met and I nodded. "Yes, that must be it," I agreed, as icy fingers skated up and down my spine.

Four

As I followed Luna's Volvo through town a little while later, I couldn't stop thinking about the look on Sidra's face when I mentioned the fourth girl in the photograph. I'd always assumed my ability to see ghosts was a rare thing, and because of Papa's warnings, I'd lived a solitary existence. I had no close friends, no confidante, no one other than Papa with whom I could share my secret. I'd spent most of my life behind cemetery walls, cloistered and protected in my graveyard kingdoms. And at times I'd been unbearably lonely.

But now I had to wonder if Sidra could see them, too, and I wasn't sure how I felt about that possibility. The ghosts were a heavy burden. I didn't wish such a dark gift on anyone.

My mind drifted back to my first encounter. I could remember that twilight so well…the glimmering aura beneath the trees in Rosehill Cemetery and the peculiar way the old man's form had become clearer to me as the light faded. Somehow, I'd known he was a ghost, but I hadn't been so frightened until Papa had sat me down and grimly explained our situation. Not everyone could see them, he'd told me, and it was important that we do nothing to give ourselves away. Ghosts were dangerous to people like us, because the one thing they craved above all else was acknowledgment, so they could feel a part of our world again. And in order to sustain their earthly presence, they attached like parasites to the living, draining away energy and warmth in much the same way a vampire fed on blood.

Papa had spent a lot of time teaching me how to protect myself from the ghosts. He'd given me a set of rules by which I had always lived my life: never acknowledge the dead, never stray far from hallowed ground, never associate with those who are haunted and never, ever tempt fate.

And then I'd met John Devlin. I'd lost myself in Devlin, lost all sense of reason. I'd allowed his ghosts into my world, strayed too far from hallowed ground and, because of my weakness, because of our passion, a door had been opened.

If only I'd listened to Papa's warning....

If only I'd followed his rules....

But I'd foolishly let down my guard, and now I could not unsee what I'd witnessed the night I fled Devlin's house.

He was still my weakness, and if I'd learned anything in the past few months, it was the necessity of shoring up my defenses against him...and his ghosts. No matter what I had to do.

As I kept pace with the Volvo, I caught a flash of metallic jet paint and vintage lines out of the corner of my eye. Thane Asher's car was parked in front of a place called the Half Moon Tavern, and I thought in-

stantly of what he'd told me on the ferry. "I drink," he'd
said. "And I bide my time." I couldn't imagine a more
depressing existence, but I knew nothing of his family
or his background, and it wasn't my place to judge.

As the tavern receded in my rearview mirror, I tried
to purge Thane Asher—and Devlin—from my thoughts
by concentrating on the passing scenery. Edged by the
forest on either side, the road narrowed and the quaint
gingerbread houses I'd noticed earlier disappeared. For
the longest time, I saw no sign of humanity other than
an abandoned grain elevator and the occasional dilapi-
dated shed. I rolled down my window, and a faint but
ubiquitous smell of mildew and compost seeped in.

Up ahead, Luna turned left onto a single-lane trail
that led straight back into the woods. Where the trees
had been thinned, I could see the points of a roof.

A moment later, I pulled up beside her and got out
of the car as my gaze traveled over the arched windows
and steep gables of the house. Luna waited for me on
the front porch, key in hand, but I took my time join-
ing her. I needed to orient myself to the surroundings.

Hugging my arms to my body, I let the deep silence
settle over me. We were sheltered by woods and the
looming mountains in the distance, but there were no
bird calls from the trees, no scampering feet in the underbrush. I heard no sound at all except for the faint
whisper of a breeze through the leaves.

I turned back to Luna. She stood watching me with
the oddest expression, her thumb caressing the moonstone cabochon she wore at her throat. She looked…
bemused, as though she couldn't quite figure me out.

"Well?" She folded her arms and leaned a shoulder
against a newel post. "What do you think of the place?"

"It's so quiet."

She smiled dreamily, lifting her face to the sky. "That's what I love about it."

Her voice held a husky timbre I hadn't noticed before, and she looked very different to me now. No, not *different,* I amended. She looked...*more.* Her figure appeared fuller, her skin creamier, her hair so darkly lush I had to wonder if she'd donned a wig in the car. Everything about her—the sparkle of her eyes, the enigmatic curve of her lips, that earthy sensuality—seemed heightened by the natural setting.

For some reason, I was reminded of that photograph in her office and the furious visage lurking in the background. And then I heard, very faintly, the wind in the trees again as I glanced up at the house.

"Was this place once a church?"

She cocked her head in surprise. "How did you know that?"

"The architecture—carpenter Gothic, isn't it?—was commonly used for small churches in the nineteenth century." I couldn't help but wonder about the selection for my temporary quarters. The hallowed ground of churches and some cemeteries offered protection from ghosts. But how would Luna Kemper know about that?

"What happened to it?" I asked.

Those gray eyes gave me a curious appraisal. "Nothing sinister. The congregation dwindled until it became more feasible to attend one of the larger churches in Woodberry. The place stood empty for a number of years, and then Floyd Covey bought it and gave it a complete renovation. All the modern amenities. You should be quite...cozy here."

I noted the slight hesitation as I nodded and followed her into the house, pausing just over the threshold to allow the peace of a hallowed place to envelop me. I *would* be cozy here, but more important, I would be safe from ghosts. Which once again begged the question as to why Luna Kemper had picked this particular house for me.

"You mentioned something on the phone about an anonymous donation," I said as I watched her move gracefully about the room. She seemed to bask in the late-afternoon sunshine pouring through the pointed arched windows. She reminded me of the gray tabby in her office—sleek, exotic and a bit superior. "I was just wondering how involved this person was in making the arrangements. I'm not the only cemetery restorer in the state. Was the decision to hire me yours or the donor's?"

She smiled. "Does any of this really matter?"

"I suppose not. But I am curious how it all came about."

"There's no big mystery. It really is as simple as I explained it," she said.

"And this house…was that your idea, as well?"

"I'm the only real estate agent in Asher Falls. Who would know the available property better than I? But if you're dissatisfied with the accommodations—"

"No, it's not that. This place is perfect, actually."

Her smile seemed knowing. "Then let me show you the rest."

Once again, I obligingly followed her lead. The bedrooms and bath were located on one side of the house, the living room and large eat-in kitchen on the other. A screened porch had been added to the back, and already I looked forward to having my morning tea out there watching the sunrise.

We walked single file down a flagstone trail to the water and strolled along a private dock. As the sun dipped below the treetops, I felt a familiar bristle of apprehension, that eerie harbinger along my backbone that preceded every twilight. The veil was lifting. Soon, the ghosts would come through.

A boat bobbed in the gentle waves at the end of the pier, but I saw no other movement. Heard nothing at all. In that in-between moment of light and dark, the night creatures hadn't yet stirred.

The air turned chilly, and I was glad for my jacket as I stood contemplating the water. I saw something float to the surface and thought it might be an apparition before realizing in relief it was my own reflection.

I turned to say something to Luna, then stilled as I caught sight of something out of the corner of my eye. A scrawny brown mutt—part German shepherd—stood at the end of the wooden dock gazing down at us. The dog was so emaciated, the outline of his ribs was clearly visible beneath the coarse fur. But what disturbed me even more was the wretched creature's deformity. His ears were missing, and his snout and mouth were horribly scarred from some trauma.

"What happened to that poor dog's face?" I kept my voice soft so as not to spook the animal, but he started when Luna whirled.

She scowled in distaste. "Looks like a bait dog."

"A what?"

"Do you know anything about dog fighting?"

My stomach turned over. "I know it's illegal. And it sickens me."

She nodded absently. "Bait dogs often have their ears cut off to avoid unnecessary injuries, and their jaws are wired shut so they can't bite the fight dogs. When the owners have no more use for them, they turn them loose."

A wave of rage washed over me. "How could anyone be that cruel?"

"This isn't Charleston," she warned. "You're apt to see a lot of things around here you don't understand."

"What's not to understand?" I asked in disgust. "Someone has abused this dog and we need to get him to a vet."

"A vet? There isn't one for miles. Best just to leave him be. He'll go back into the woods eventually."

"But he needs help." When I would have started toward him, Luna caught my arm.

"I wouldn't do that. He could be rabid for all you know."

"He doesn't look rabid, he looks hungry."

"For God's sake, don't feed the creature!"

Her vehemence startled me, and I glanced at her as a rush of fresh anger warmed my cheeks.

Before I could stop her, she clapped loudly, scaring the poor dog. "Get out of here! Go on, get!"

"Don't do that!"

Now it was I who caught her arm, and she spun, eyes blazing. We faced off, the malicious curl of her lips chilling me to the bone. I almost took a step back from her, but I caught myself. Our gazes clashed for the longest moment, then her expression softened so rapidly

I thought I might have imagined the whole troubling confrontation.

"Strays are common around here, I'm afraid." She gave a regretful shrug. "You can't feed them all, nor can you allow yourself to get overly sentimental. But I expect you'll have to learn the hard way."

I didn't care to argue, so I let the matter drop. The dog had already retreated to the edge of the woods where he watched warily from the shadows. He observed us for a moment longer before slinking back into the trees.

Luna glanced at her watch. "I should be getting back to town. I have a meeting tonight."

We walked around the house to the driveway.

"If you need anything, you have my number." She opened her car door, anxious to be on her way. "Tilithia Pattershaw is your nearest neighbor. Everyone calls her Tilly. She's been keeping an eye on the place while Floyd is away. I asked her to come by yesterday to clean the house, and she left some food in the refrigerator. She's just down that path." She waved toward the woods. "She may drop by now and again to check up on you. Don't be alarmed. She's a little peculiar, but she means well."

"I'll be on the lookout for her."

Luna smiled as her eyes strayed to the woods. "Oh, you won't see Tilly until she's ready to be seen."

I followed her gaze to the trees. Was the woman out there right now? I wondered.

"The cemetery is a mile or so up the road," Luna said. "There's a turnoff just after you round the first curve. You'll see it."

"Thanks."

She climbed into her car, started the ignition and waved as she drove off. The sound of the engine faded, the silence deepened, and I turned once again to scour the trees.

Five

After Luna left, I carried my bags into the house, then made one last trip to the car to make sure I had everything. As I turned from the vehicle, I felt that warning tingle again and realized that twilight was upon me. The evening was still but no longer silent. I could hear the trill of a loon somewhere out on the lake and, even more distant, the eerie howl of a dog. I thought about the mutt that had crept out of the woods earlier and wondered where he'd gone off to.

Inside, I headed straight for the bedroom where I unpacked my clothes and toiletries, and then I made another trip through the house, familiarizing myself with all the nooks and crannies while making sure all the doors and windows were secure. Ending my tour in the kitchen, I checked the refrigerator to see what Tilly Pattershaw had left for dinner. Peeling back the foil on a mysterious casserole, I sniffed, grimaced and quickly recovered. Thankfully, the crisper yielded enough fresh vegetables to assemble a salad, and I settled down to eat my dinner at a small table that looked out on the lake. I also had a view of the woods, and I could just make out the path to Tilly's house that Luna had mentioned. The stir of the low-hanging branches over the trail caught my attention, and my scalp prickled a warning. It wasn't that I saw anything specific, but more a gnawing suspicion that something was out there. Tilly?

I didn't want to stare directly into the forest for fear that the watcher might not be of this world. So I pretended to admire the last shimmer of light on the water while I studied the woods from my periphery. A few moments later, a shadow detached from the black at the tree line and moved toward the house.

My heart thudded until I realized it was the battered dog. Evidently, he had retreated into the woods, waiting for Luna to depart before making another cautious foray into the yard. He sniffed the ground and rooted through dead leaves, then finding nothing of interest, plopped down in my direct line of sight between the house and the lake. Even in the fading light, I could see the protrusion of his rib cage and the mutilated head and face. And yet, despite everything he'd been through, he carried himself with great dignity, with great soul.

I got up and searched through the refrigerator again, throwing together an unappetizing bowl of casserole and rice, and carried it outside. Ever aware of the gathering dusk, I moved carefully down the steps and placed the food halfway between the porch and where he lay. He didn't move until I'd retreated behind the screen door, and then he trotted over to smell the contents. Within a matter of moments, the bowl was licked clean, and he stood staring at me with dark, limpid eyes.

Without thought to the danger—from him, from the twilight—I opened the door and eased down the steps.

He looked at the empty bowl, gave a little whine, then finally came over to nuzzle my hand. I rubbed behind the nubs where his ears should have been and cupped his scarred snout in my hands. He whimpered again, this time more in contentment, I thought, as I ran my hand along his side, feeling his bones.

"Still hungry? Well, don't worry. There's plenty more where that came from. We'll wait a bit, though, so we don't make you sick. Tomorrow I'll drive into town and get you some proper food."

His nose was cool and moist against my hand.

"What's your name, I wonder. Or do you even have one? You look like an Angus to me. Strong and noble. Angus. Has a nice ring to it."

I prattled on in a soft voice until he plopped down at my feet, and I had to lean over to scratch him. We stayed that way for the longest time until I felt him tense beneath my hand. The hair along his back quilled as he emitted a low, menacing growl.

I continued to pet him even when he rose warily and slanted his head toward the lake. Beneath my lashes, I glanced past him and saw nothing at first. Then my own hair lifted as my eyes adjusted to the twilight.

She was there at the end of the dock, a diaphanous form wavering like a reed in a current. I kept my expression neutral even though my heart had started to pummel my chest. Somehow I managed to soothe the dog even as he whirled toward the water and bared his teeth. Animals—both domestic and feral—are highly attuned to ghosts. They not only see them, but also can sense them. That was one of the reasons Papa had never allowed me to have a pet. I'd had a hard enough time learning to ignore the ghosts, let alone an animal's reaction to them.

"What's the matter?" I asked Angus. "You're not afraid of the dark, are you? Nothing out there but squirrels and rabbits and maybe a possum or two."

And a ghost.

I couldn't see her face, but I had the impression she'd been young when she died. She had long, wavy hair that blew over her shoulders in a nonexistent breeze, and she wore a black dress that seemed much too austere for her willowy frame. But she was exactly how one might want to envision a ghost—ephemeral and lovely, with no outward sign of any physical distress she might have suffered in life.

And then she turned her dead gaze on me. I wasn't staring at her but I could *feel* it. Like an icy command. *Look at me!*

Which was crazy because she couldn't know that I saw her. I'd done nothing to give myself away. And yet I felt something inside my mind, a nebulous tentacle that gave me the blackest of chills. I'd never experienced anything like it, even with Devlin's ghosts. Shani, the child entity, had made contact on at least two occasions, and Mariama's specter had tried to manipulate me in Devlin's house. But nothing like this had ever happened. What I felt now wasn't a possession, but some strange telepathic link that allowed me to sense the ghost's bewilderment. The connection terrified me, and I had to use all my willpower not to jump to my feet and dart inside the house. But I knew better. The most dangerous thing I could do was acknowledge the presence of the dead.

Angus, meanwhile, had placed his quivering body

firmly between the apparition and me. Strong and noble, indeed. I couldn't have loved him more at that moment had we been lifelong friends, because I was pretty sure he would have liked nothing more than to turn tail and run for the woods.

"Good boy," I whispered.

A light wind rippled through the leaves and the trees began to whisper. *Who are you? Why are you here?*

Presently, I got up to go inside. The ghost was still there at the end of the pier, staring after me. Angus whimpered, and I opened the screen door so that he could come up on the porch. As I turned to secure the latch, another breeze sighed through the trees.

Is it really you?

For almost as long as I could remember, ghosts had been a part of my world. Papa used to take me out to the cemetery on Sunday afternoons, and I would help him tidy graves as we waited for twilight, waited for the veil to thin so the ghosts could come through. At first, I'd tried to avoid the excursions, but then I realized it was Papa's way of teaching me how to live with our gift. After a while, I grew so accustomed to those floating specters I never reacted to their presence even when I felt the chill of their breath down my back or their wintry fingers in my hair. I could even walk among them and not give myself away.

But then Devlin had come along, and Papa's rules could no longer protect me. My defenses had been breached by his ghosts. And now another phantom had entered my world, one with an ability that had allowed me to sense her confusion as I suspected she could sense mine. This intuitive connection was new and frightening because I not only had to guard my physical reaction but also now my thoughts. What would I have to protect next...my soul?

I lay awake that night for the longest time, dwelling on all the old questions. I'd never understood my place in this world or the next. Why had I been given this gift if not for some larger purpose? Papa never had answers. He didn't like to talk about the ghosts. It was our secret, he would say. Our cross to bear. And we must never, ever tell Mama. She wouldn't understand.

Looking back, I could see how easily he'd put me off...about the ghosts, about my birth, about everything. He and Mama had taken me in when I was only a few days old, but I still knew nothing of how I had come to them or of my biological parents. All my queries had been met with a wariness that had made me so uncomfortable I'd finally stopped asking. But I knew there were things they hadn't told me. Especially Papa. He'd never even mentioned that realm of unseen ghosts—the Others—until it was too late, until I'd already fallen for Devlin. Now I had to wonder what else he'd kept from me. What other terrors lay in wait for me?

My thoughts churned on and on. Eventually, I drifted off, only to be awakened by the distant toll of bells. In my hazy, half-asleep state, I wondered if the faint tinkle might be a wind chime somewhere in the woods—at Tilly Pattershaw's perhaps. But each peal was separate and distinct, as if from a chorus of ringers. Far from melodic, however, the notes were random and discordant, almost angry.

I got up and padded barefoot through the darkened house, glad that I'd taken the time to familiarize myself with the layout. I moved easily from room to room with only the moonlight to guide me.

Pausing at the kitchen window, I glanced out on the back porch where I'd left Angus. He, too, had been roused by the bells. Or by something. He'd planted himself in front of the door, and I almost expected to see a ghost peering in through the screen. But his maimed head was lifted as he looked out over the yard and down the stepping-stones to the lake where a thick mist had fallen over the water. Or had it risen from the underworld?

The bells were muffled by that mist. I could barely hear them now. Only a faint peal every so often until the sound faded entirely.

I stood there shivering on my little piece of hallowed ground as I watched the lake. The night was very still, but some infinitesimal breeze stirred the mist. Through that swirling miasma, I thought I detected a humanlike form, the writhe of some restless spirit.

And I realized then that the underwater graveyard lay just beyond my doorstep.

Six

The light was still gray when I arose the next morning, but a golden aura hovered just above the horizon. If dusk fed my fears, dawn brought a sense of anticipation, and I luxuriated in the knowledge that the whole day stretched before me without ghosts.

After a quick shower, I carried a cup of tea out to the porch to watch the sun come up. Ribbons of mist hung from the treetops, but most of the haze had already burned off the lake. The air was crisp and clean, like the smell of line-dried laundry, and for the first time, fall seemed inevitable. Overnight a patchwork of crimson and gold had been woven into the dark green backdrop of the woods.

I coaxed Angus off the porch with the rest of the casserole and left him to enjoy his breakfast while I packed up my gear and headed for the cemetery. It was so early I had the road to myself. Although, for all I knew, there was never any traffic. Like the town, the countryside appeared deserted, but I wasn't completely alone. As I rolled down the window, I caught a whiff of wood smoke from someone's chimney. It was such a beautiful day. I didn't want to sully my mood with midnight doubts. A fresh project was a time for renewal. A time for restoration.

As I came out of the first curve, I spotted the turnoff. The cemetery was nestled on the side of a steep, craggy hill and half-hidden by a thicket of cedar, an evergreen long associated with coffins and funeral pyres because of its spicy aroma and resistance to corrosion.

The trees were so thick in places the sun was almost completely blocked, but every now and then a shaft of light would angle just right through the feathery boughs to blind me. I found myself creeping along so that I wouldn't hit a bounding rabbit. The grove teemed with wildlife. I even saw the dart of a fox between two hemlocks, and as I came to a stop in front of the entrance, the flutelike trill of the wood thrushes filled the air.

Armed with cell phone, camera and sketch pad, I got out of the SUV. There was a gate, but it wasn't locked. Luna had told me the day before that the cemetery used to close after dark, but no one bothered with it anymore. However, she'd supplied me with copies of permits and other pertinent paperwork just in case anyone challenged my presence. I wondered if she knew of any specific objections to the restoration. Thane Asher had hinted at trouble.

I closed the gate behind me and then glanced around. Thorngate was smallish for a public cemetery but large for a family burial site. It was easy to spot the delineation between the two. The terrain nearest the gate had been flattened and the markers placed flush to the ground to accommodate lawn mowers. There were no fences or walls to separate the plots, no excessive adornment on the stones, though I did spot personal mementoes on some of the mounded graves. It was a modern, space-saving cemetery that did little to inspire the self-reflection and tranquility of my favorite old graveyards. By contrast, the original family site was lush and Gothic, clearly influenced by Victorian perceptions of romance, death and melancholy.

The first order of business was to walk the grounds, recording any special features and anomalies that would be included on the new site map. As I wandered through the public area, I spotted a couple of markers with familiar names—Birch and Kemper. I also saw a fresh grave near the fence. The dirt was mounded and covered with dying flowers.

As I passed through the old arched lych-gate into the Asher section, the sparse landscaping gave way to mossy stepping-stones, curling ivy and the remnants of what I thought might be a white garden inside a circle of magnificent stone angels. The heads tilted eastward, toward the rising sun, and the hanging branches of a cedar dappled the early-morning light that fell upon their faces. But the expressions were neither serene nor forlorn as I'd come to expect from cemetery angels. Instead, I found them arrogant. Maybe even defiant. And these statues marked the resting places of the lesser Ashers. The remains of the immediate family were interred in a large mausoleum decorated with elaborate reliefs and stained-glass portals.

The door was unlocked, and I shoved it open to peer inside, noting at once the absence of wall crypts. The mausoleum was a façade for an underground tomb, but I would save that inspection for later when I was better equipped to deal with any snakes that might be looking for a place to hibernate. Burial chambers were notorious lairs—not to mention a breeding ground for spiders. A childhood encounter with a black widow had left me with a nasty infection and lingering arachnophobia, an inconvenient anxiety for someone in my field, but I'd learned to cope.

Backing out of the mausoleum, I closed the door and turned as I brushed imaginary cobwebs from my hair. Then I froze. A man stood just inside the fence, staring across the headstones at me. He reminded me of the old man's ghost that haunted Rosehill Cemetery. From a distance, he had a similar appearance—tall, withered, dressed in black. But this man's hair was gray and fell in limp hanks past the shoulders of a heavy wool overcoat. I'd already shed my lightweight jacket, so I thought his choice of outerwear on such a warm day a bit peculiar.

I didn't think him a ghost, but the rules had changed since I met Devlin. This man's lack of an aura didn't make him human any more than his strange appearance or statuelike stillness made him a specter.

As I hovered indecisively on the mausoleum steps, he did something that was neither human nor ghostlike. He dropped to the ground and slithered underneath the fence where he rose on hands and feet to scurry like a spider into the thicket.

I stared after him in astonishment, my skin crawling in distaste. How bizarre and utterly unnerving that he should mimic my thoughts about snakes and spiders. I shuddered. A coincidence, surely. But coming on the heels of the ghost I'd seen on the pier last night, I was thoroughly shaken and couldn't get the man's grotesque behavior out of my mind. It left me with a terrible feeling, as if a message had been sent, but I didn't know how to interpret it.

The premonition lingered as I finished my walk. All the while, I kept a constant vigil and a can of mace handy, just in case. I was always careful in isolated cemeteries, but more so now than ever. My experience with a killer a few months earlier had left me wary and cautious. And now the appearance of that strange man. I couldn't help shivering every time I thought of him.

Working well into the afternoon, I used colored flags to stake a grid that would help me keep track of the graves once I started to photograph. Hunger finally drove me back to my car. After a bite to eat, I decided to head into town to do a little research at the library. I also thought now might be a good time to drop in at the police station and make my presence known. Apart from my own safety, an introduction was common courtesy. In these small communities, people often became apprehensive when they saw a stranger poking about in a graveyard, and suspicion could often be averted by developing a cordial relationship with local law enforcement.

As I drove down the hill, I saw the gray-haired man again. He walked along the side of the road, pulling a rusted toy wagon behind him. His coat was so long it dragged the ground, and the tail billowed in the slight breeze. He turned to stare at me as I drove past, and though I didn't return his scrutiny, I had the impression of pale eyes, jutting cheekbones and a hawklike nose. My window was down, and I caught the scent of rotting flesh a split second before I saw the animal carcass in his wagon. I couldn't tell what it was, but the body looked to be the size of a possum or raccoon.

Quickly, I raised the window, trapping a fly that pestered me all the way into town.

As I entered the town proper, I noticed yet again the empty streets. A few cars were parked around the square, but I didn't see anyone as I crossed over to the library. Inside, silence enveloped me. It wasn't the usual library hush, but the deep stillness of an abandoned place. Which was crazy because I'd met Sidra and Luna in there yesterday. I assumed Sidra was still in school and Luna was probably next door at the real estate office. I told myself there was nothing sinister about their absence, but I found myself wincing at those creaking floors.

I had no idea where to look for the cemetery records, but I decided to do a little browsing. The color-coded signs tacked to the end of the bookshelves led me past fiction, nonfiction and biographies to the religion and history aisles where I scanned titles searching for something local. Alongside copies of *The South Carolina Travel Guide* and *Wildflowers of the Blue Ridge Mountains* were more esoteric titles: *Mountain Magic, Folklore of the Appalachians* and Frazer's *The Golden Bough,* which I'd read in one of my anthropology classes for extra credit. As I pulled it from the shelf to skim the introduction, I heard someone laugh—a low, throaty female chortle that gave me goose bumps.

Turning, I glanced behind me. Nothing. I walked around to the next aisle. No one.

Then I glanced up. The gray tabby I'd seen in Luna's office blinked down at me from the top shelf.

I went back to my reading, and now I heard a man's voice, taunting and furtive. The library was empty, but

I wasn't alone. I walked along the wall, gazing down each row of bookshelves. When I got to the end, the voices grew louder, and my gaze dropped to an ornate grill that covered an old vent. Someone was in another room, and the air shaft carried their sound straight to me. Had I been standing in another part of the library, I probably wouldn't have heard them at all.

Should I say something? I wondered. Or at least clear my throat to alert them of my presence?

As I stood there contemplating the proper etiquette, the murmurs turned to moans. Husky, sexual and extremely aggressive.

I backed away from the vent, but the sound followed me. Quickly, I shelved *The Golden Bough* only to dislodge another book. To my dismay, the heavy volume fell to the floor with a bang that sounded to me as loud as a shotgun blast.

"What was that?" The masculine voice sprang out of the air shaft, and I jumped. "I thought you said no one comes in here this time of day."

"No one does," the woman replied. "It was probably a bird flying into a window."

"That does seem to happen when you're around."

"A lot of things happen when I'm around."

"Yes," he said. "And not much of it good."

I was pretty sure the woman was Luna, but I didn't wait around to hear her response. As quietly as I could, I exited the building and closed the door behind me. I'd recognized something in the male voice, too, and that familiarity niggled at me. I found myself looking up and down the block for a flash of metallic black paint. If Thane Asher's car was parked nearby, I couldn't spot it. Not that it mattered. If he had a relationship with Luna Kemper, it was none of my business.

But the echo of those feral moans followed me as I hurried away from the library.

I found the police station a few blocks over, housed in a grand old building that had been the county courthouse in more prosperous times. Despite an overall air of decay, there was still something dignified and a little awe-inspiring about the carved motifs and towering columns. As I approached the front entrance, my gaze rose to the scene depicted in the entablature—an eagle with a palmetto branch in its clutches. A popular sentiment during Reconstruction and one that appeared on a number of public buildings all over the state.

Inside, I followed the signs down a long corridor and through a set of tall wooden doors marked Police Headquarters. No one manned the front desk, nor did I see anyone milling about in the tiled lobby. I didn't want a repeat of the library situation, so I called out, "Hello?"

Someone appeared in the doorway of one of the back rooms, the light hitting him in such a way that I could see little more than the silhouette of an average-size man. "Can I help you?"

"Yes, hello. I just wanted to stop by and introduce myself. I'm Amelia Gray. I'll be working in Thorngate Cemetery for the next few weeks, and I thought it a good idea to let you know in advance in case you get calls or complaints."

"What are you doing in the cemetery?" The voice coming from that featureless face was curiously unsettling. He spoke in a pleasant enough tone, but I detected a disagreeable edge.

"I'll be restoring it," I told him.

"Restoring it? You mean, clearing away brush, that sort of thing?"

"More or less..." I trailed off as he walked out to the counter, and I got my first good look at him. I judged him to be in his mid-forties, with dark hair swept back from a wide forehead and deep-set blue eyes fringed with thick lashes. No doubt, those eyes had once been the focal point of a ruggedly handsome face, but now the gaze was drawn to the scars—five jagged ridges that ran from the lower right eyelid back into the hairline and all the way down to his neck. Claw marks, I thought at once. Something had very nearly taken the side of his face off. *Sweet Jesus.*

Accepting the premise that the exceedingly attractive always had an easier path, I had to wonder what this man's life had been like before and after the attack. Given his natural good looks, it couldn't have been a painless adjustment. But this passed through my mind in a flash. I'd had years of practice in schooling my expression, and I knew none of my shock showed on my face as our eyes met across the desk.

"By whose authorization?" he asked.

"Luna Kemper contacted me."

"Luna's behind this? I might have known." The contempt in his voice took me by surprise.

"I beg your pardon?"

"Where's the money coming from?" he demanded.

I didn't see how the financial arrangements could possibly be any of his business. "I'm sorry. You seem a little concerned about this project. Is there some problem, Officer…" I glanced at the name tag clipped to his uniform pocket. Wayne Van Zandt.

"It's chief," he said in a cool tone.

"I assure you, all of the permits are in order…Chief Van Zandt."

He made a dismissive gesture that was at once graceful and oddly menacing. "I'm not concerned about permits. What I do care about is how people are going to react. Feelings still run strong about that cemetery."

"So I hear. And that's why I came to see you. I don't want to cause any problems for you or the community. I'd just like to do my work in peace."

His mouth tightened, emphasizing his disfigurement. "It might help me keep the peace if I know who's behind it."

I thought about that for a moment and nodded. Maybe he had a point. "The local historical society is funding the project."

"Historical society?"

"The Daughters of our Valiant Heroes."

He stared at me for a moment. "You think Daughters is a historical society?"

"Isn't it?"

He laughed.

I didn't get the joke. Chief Van Zandt obviously had a chip on his shoulder, and considering what he must have been through, I was empathetic enough to cut him some slack. "I won't take up any more of your time. If you do get calls or have any questions, you know where to find me. Oh, and one more thing." I stepped back up to the desk. "I saw a man in the cemetery this morning. He was acting pretty strange."

"Like how?"

"When he saw me, he slithered under the fence and crawled off into the bushes."

A brow rose. "Slithered?"

"Slithered, wiggled, whatever you want to call it. I saw him later hauling a dead animal down the hill in a child's wagon."

He shrugged. "Sounds a mite peculiar, but these mountains are full of odd folk. Mostly, they just want to be left alone. Some of them don't see another living soul for months at a time, and when they finally emerge, they don't know how to act."

"You think he's a hermit?"

"I think some weirdo with a little red wagon is the last thing you need to be worried about in these hills." His pleasant voice was now edged with something that sounded very much like a warning. Or was it a threat?

"What do you mean?"

"The woods around here are full of wild animals…" He let his words trail off, a deliberate lingering as he traced a finger down one of his scars.

"What kind of wild animals?"

"Mountain lions, coyotes…" Another hesitation. "Been a lot of black bear sightings this year, too."

I glanced at his facial scars. I couldn't help myself. "Black bears don't normally attack humans, do they?"

"Animals are unpredictable. You ask the experts, they'll tell you wolves have been gone from this part of the country for decades, but they're still out there. I've seen them."

I thought about that eerie howl I'd heard last evening. "Speaking of animals," I said, "I'm staying in Floyd Covey's house. A stray came out of the woods last night. He'd been horribly abused. Luna called him a bait dog."

"She did, did she?" He stroked another scar. "Best you forget what she said. Best you forget about that stray, too."

"I can't forget about dog fighting," I said indignantly. "I assumed if it's going on in your jurisdiction, you'd want to know about it."

He shrugged. "I'll ask around, see if I get wind of any kennels. About all I can do. People tend to be close-mouthed about that sort of thing around here, even if they're not directly involved. They don't want any trouble. And they don't cotton to a lot of questions, especially from strangers."

The warning note in his voice was unmistakable now. "I'll remember that," I said coolly.

"In the meantime…" His gaze swept over me. "You want me to come out there and take care of that problem for you?"

"What problem?"

"The stray."

"Take care…you mean put him down?" I asked in horror.

A muscle twitched at the corner of one eye. "Think of it as a kindness."

I wanted to tell him that Angus didn't need his brand of kindness, and how would he like it if someone had tried to do the same to him?

But I kept my mouth shut because I didn't trust Wayne Van Zandt. Not in the slightest. It was instinct, like an animal's hackles rising when danger was near.

"Thank you, but that won't be necessary," I said. "I'm sure that dog is long gone by now."

Seven

On my way home, I stopped by a small market I'd
spotted earlier to stock up on fresh produce for me and
dog food for Angus. There wasn't much of a selection
for either of us, but we'd just have to make do until I
found time to take the ferry across the lake to shop.

When I came out of the store, I saw Sidra and another girl standing near my car. They were dressed in
identical school uniforms, but the resemblance ended
with the plaid skirts and navy blazers. The other girl
towered over Sidra. Her hair was dark and sleek and she
eyed me with sullen curiosity through a long curtain
of bangs. I nodded and said hello as I went to put my
bags in the back. When I came around the car, she was
leaning against the fender, smoking. I noticed then the
smudged liner around her eyes and the pale lip color
on her sulky mouth. It looked very dramatic against
her tanned skin. Despite the prim uniform, she looked
cool, edgy and bored, the kind of girl that would have
terrified me in high school had I not been so preoccupied with ghosts.

"Can you give us a ride?" she drawled, releasing a cloud of blue smoke that curled up into her thick lashes.

"Sure. If you don't mind putting that out."

She discarded the cigarette with a deliberate flick.

I glanced at Sidra, who seemed to shy away from her dominant companion. She didn't look intimidated or cowed, but her demeanor was definitely anxious, as if she wanted to extricate herself from an awkward situation but didn't know how.

"Where do you want to go?" I asked.

"You can drop us at Sid's place."

"I already told you…my house is out of her way," Sidra said.

"I really don't mind." It wasn't like I had a clock to punch or someone to go home to. Besides, the company of two teenagers might be just the thing to dilute the bad taste left by my visit to the police station. "Hop in."

"Merci beaucoup." The dark-haired girl sent me a treacly smile as she strode around the car and climbed into the front. Sidra reluctantly got into the back, and as I slid behind the wheel, I glanced in the rearview mirror, hoping a smile would reassure her that a lift wasn't a problem. But she'd turned to the window and sat motionless, making me wonder yet again if she could see something outside that I couldn't.

I started the ignition. "I'll need directions."

"Head north, take a right at the first intersection and then keep going until I tell you to stop," the dark-haired girl instructed. "I'm Ivy, by the way."

"Amelia."

"I know who you are." She turned to give me a frank assessment between narrowed lids. "Sid says you work in graveyards or something."

"I'm a cemetery restorer."

"Sounds...interesting."

I smiled politely. "It is to me."

"You don't get spooked?"

"Sometimes. But mostly I find cemeteries peaceful. Some of the really old churchyards were built on hallowed ground." I shot a look in the mirror to gauge Sidra's reaction, but her eyes were still riveted on the window.

"Thorngate isn't," Ivy said. "Built on hallowed ground, I mean."

"How do you know?"

"Because it's built on Asher ground and everything that family touches is cursed."

"Ivy."

The warning note in Sidra's voice startled me, but Ivy just shrugged.

I gave her an uneasy glance. "What do you mean by cursed?"

She waved a hand toward the window. "Look around you. See all the boarded-up buildings? All those caved-in roofs? And that stink in the air? That's the smell of the damned," she said with calculated nonchalance as she unzipped one of her boots to examine what appeared to be a fresh tattoo on her ankle.

When she saw that I'd noticed—which I had a feeling was her intent—her smile turned smug. "You don't know what that is, do you?"

"I can't really see it from here."

"It's one of the symbols carved into the cliff at the falls. No one knows where they came from or what they mean, but I think this one makes a pretty cool tat, don't you?"

She didn't give me a chance to respond.

"I had to sneak over to Greenville to get it. Mother would have a cow if she knew. Which is so hypocritical since she has one herself. But she thinks I'm too young and I think she's too old." She admired the ink for a moment longer before rezipping her boot.

I glanced in the mirror, startled to find Sidra staring back at me this time. What was she thinking? I wondered. And why had she tried to silence Ivy about the Ashers?

Ivy fell back against the seat. "Personally, I find the whole idea of hallowed ground laughable."

It took me a moment to redirect my train of thought. "Why?"

"How can a place be sacred just because people died there or because some priest sprinkled a little holy water over it? If you're really into spiritual places, you should go up to the falls."

"I hear it's really beautiful up there."

"It's more than beautiful. People say it's a thin place."

I turned in surprise. "A thin place?"

"Don't tell me you don't know what that is, either."

She seemed to enjoy her superiority, so I allowed her to keep it. "Why don't you tell me?"

She lowered her voice. "It's where the living world and the dead world connect. It's where…well, never mind. Anyway, people used to go up there because they hoped to catch a glimpse of heaven. Now they stay away because they're afraid of—" She broke off and turned to glance at Sidra in the backseat. I watched the girl in the mirror and saw her shake her head.

"They're afraid of what?" I pressed.

"Nothing. Speak of the devil," Ivy muttered as she sat up in the seat.

I followed her gaze to Thane Asher's car parked at the curb. He was hunkered in front of the rear wheel well changing a flat tire, and my mind shot back to the library. I could still hear those animalistic moans in some back recess of my mind.

"We should stop," Ivy said.

"I thought you said the Ashers were cursed."

She slanted me a withering look as she lowered the window and called out to him. When he glanced over his shoulder, there was nothing I could do but pull up beside him and stop.

He rose and came over to the car, bending slightly to glance in the window. He wore a dark green shirt that deepened his eyes to moss and a brown leather jacket that had cracked and faded over the years. His car also showed signs of wear and tear that I hadn't noticed on the ferry. Looking past the dazzle of metallic paint, I could see a dent here and there and the odd speck of rust.

"Hello," he said.

"Hello," I responded with a noncommittal smile.

Ivy gaped at him. I suspected she had a crush, which explained why she'd so easily tossed aside the notion of a curse. I could empathize. Hadn't I done the same thing with Devlin? Thrown caution aside for passion? And Thane Asher did look ridiculously attractive in that leather jacket. Not darkly handsome like Devlin, of course, but there was something about him that I could appreciate. For one thing, he didn't have ghosts hovering nearby. That was a definite plus. But then I reminded myself that I couldn't know whether or not he was haunted until I saw him after twilight.

"Having car trouble?" Ivy drawled.

"A flat. Must have picked up a nail somewhere."

"We thought you might need a ride."

"Thanks, but I'll have it changed in no time."

Ivy tossed her hair over her shoulder and gazed up at him through those thick, curly lashes. "Are you sure you don't need help with the lug nuts? They're always so hard to get off."

I didn't know how she managed to pack so much sexual innuendo into two simple sentences, but she did.

Thane looked bemused...and wary. He glanced at his watch. "Shouldn't you girls still be in school?" His tone was devoid of inflection, but I had a feeling the question was a conscious attempt to put Ivy in her place. A valiant effort, but one that seemed to sail right over the girl's head as she twirled a dark strand of hair around one fingertip.

"We left early," she said. "We had better things to do, right, Sid?" The two exchanged another glance, and Ivy grinned.

Thane's gaze was on me, those green eyes gleaming with something dark. Something just for me. I didn't know how to feel about that look. I was just as wary of him as he was of Ivy but for a very different reason. "And what part did you play in these shenanigans?"

"None at all. I'm just giving them a lift home."

"Let's hope the truant officer sees it your way," he said ominously, but his eyes were still teasing. "How goes the cemetery restoration?"

"I've hardly begun. It's only been one day."

"Maybe I'll drop by sometime. I haven't been up there in years."

Ivy's grin faded, and she gave me a hard stare. She wasn't the type of girl who would be comfortable sharing the spotlight, let alone relinquishing it to someone like me. "What is so fascinating about a bunch of old headstones?" she asked with an eye roll.

"It's history," Thane said. "How can you know who you are if you don't know where you come from?"

How strange that his question should mirror the doubts and the uncertainties of my adoption that I'd pondered just last night. The insight made me uneasy.

I put a hand on the gearshift. "We should let you get back to that tire."

His eyes lingered as he nodded. "You ladies take care."

He stepped away from the curb, and as I drove off, I refused to look in the mirror. But I had a feeling he was staring after us. I was almost certain of it.

Ivy whirled. "How do you know Thane Asher?"

"I don't really know him. We met yesterday on the ferry."

"Why didn't you say so earlier?"

I shrugged. "There was no reason to."

She folded her arms. "I wouldn't go getting any ideas if I were you. Thane would never choose someone like you."

"Someone like me?"

"An outsider," she said with disdain.

"I guess it's lucky I'm not here to socialize, then. I just want to finish my job and go home."

"You should do that. Go home, I mean."

The whole conversation was starting to make me

feel very uncomfortable. I couldn't wait to drop them off and drive back to the Covey house. Although at that moment, I would have liked nothing more than to heed Ivy's advice and head home to Charleston.

Something was seriously amiss in this town. I'd felt it the moment I crossed Bell Lake. The shadows seemed deeper, the nights longer, the secrets older. Even the wind felt different here. And I couldn't forget the repugnant man in the cemetery who had mimicked my worst fears or the ghost who had somehow let me sense her confusion.

According to Ivy, Asher Falls was located near a thin place. Could that explain the bizarre nature of the town and the people who inhabited it? Maybe there was hyper supernatural activity in the area. I'd have to ask Dr. Shaw next time I went home. He ran the Charleston Institute for Parapsychology Studies and usually had answers for all my questions, whether or not they were the ones I wanted.

With an effort, I turned my attention back to the road. As we passed a gray stone building shrouded in vines, I noticed several girls dressed in the same uniform as Ivy and Sidra ambling out a side door.

"Is that your school?" I asked.

"Oh, damn!" Ivy slid down in her seat. "Hurry and get past before someone sees us. We're supposed to be home sick."

"Both of you?"

"There's a bug going around. They were sending kids home all day. We left after lunch."

"Pretending to be sick?"

"It's easy enough to fake illness when the school nurse is half-blind." She laughed at her own cleverness.

"So where did you go?"

"We've just been hanging out. But if Sid's mother finds out we didn't go straight home, we're dead."

"She probably already knows," Sidra said gloomily. "I can't believe I let you talk me into leaving school, much less going up *there*—"

"Shush." Now it was Ivy who issued a warning look. "At least *you* won't get expelled."

"I almost wish I would," Sidra muttered.

"Why would one of you get expelled and not the other?" I asked.

"Sid's mother is the headmistress at Pathway," Ivy explained. "A real *witch,* if you know what I mean. She'd like nothing better than to get rid of me. I'm such a bad influence and all."

"And you left school, anyway? That was brave." I glanced in the mirror to gauge Sidra's reaction to such a harsh critique of her mother. She looked agitated, but I didn't think the name-calling had much to do with it.

"It wasn't brave, it was *stupid,*" she said.

Ivy shrugged. "No one twisted your arm. And, anyway, I don't care if I do get expelled. I'll just call my father. He's a very important man. One of the most powerful lawyers in the state." The last was said for my benefit, I was certain.

"Pathway is a private school?" I asked.

"Private and *très exclusif,*" Ivy said. "The local kids who can't afford the tuition have to ride the ferry across the lake and catch the bus into Woodberry."

So there was no public school, no veterinarian clinic and no supermarket in Asher Falls, but the withering town could support a private school for children of the privileged. The place was getting stranger and stranger by the minute.

We rode in silence after that until Sidra said from the backseat, "That's my house on the corner. The white one."

I pulled up to the curb in relief, and as the girls climbed out, I lowered my window to admire the three-story Victorian with spindle-work trim along the veranda. The garden was still lush and green, but the witch hazel had started to turn, and I could see squirreis foraging for fruit in the silver bell tree that grew at the corner of the porch. As my gaze lifted to the front gable, I saw a blonde woman in one of the upstairs windows a split second before the lace curtain fell back into place.

Uh-oh. The girls had been made, it seemed.

After a muttered thank-you, Ivy strode up the walkway without a backward glance, but to my surprise, Sidra came over to my window. Her eyes were very clear and very blue, her alabaster skin almost translucent in the afternoon sunlight. She wore no makeup, nor did she need any. Cosmetic enhancement would have only detracted from the ethereal quality that made her so arresting.

"Did you forget something?" I asked.

"No…I need to tell you something."

Her gaze met mine and I felt a prickle of foreboding. "What is it?"

"You've seen the old clock tower in the square?"

"Yes. It's very beautiful."

"It's built on hallowed ground. A battle was fought there or something. Anyway, I thought you should know." She turned to scurry off.

"Wait! How do you know the ground is hallowed?"

Pausing on the walkway, she glanced over her shoulder, her expression enigmatic. I would never know what she intended to reveal, though, because just then the woman I'd seen at the upstairs window came out on the front porch and called to her.

Sidra froze.

"Is that your mother?"

"She's home early. Now she knows we didn't come straight home."

"Will you be in much trouble?"

"I don't know. I'd better go in."

The girl looked terrified and no wonder. As the woman's gaze met mine, I felt an awful chill go through me.

Eight

Could Sidra see ghosts? Why else had she felt compelled to tell me about the clock tower? And why else would she have waited until Ivy was out of earshot? If she could see ghosts—or something—that required her to seek hallowed ground for protection, she might not want anyone else to know, especially her mother, given everything I'd observed. That I could understand. The fact that she'd shared the knowledge with me should have been a comfort, but instead I felt uneasy and more out of my element than ever.

And yet as I drove back through town, I had a vague sense of familiarity, of destiny, as if maybe I'd been brought here for a reason. Which didn't really make sense because I'd never been to Asher Falls, and I'd never met anyone from here. It was a lonely place, isolated by a haunted lake. Was it any wonder the people were so strange?

As I turned onto the highway, my gaze lifted to the distant mountains where a dark cloud had formed against the blue haze. As I watched, the cloud drifted lower, swooping down over the treetops until I realized it wasn't a cloud at all but a flock of blackbirds flying south for the winter.

There was a nip in the wind that blew in through my open window. Despite the warm days, fall was just around the corner, and I dreaded the loneliness that winter always brought. I wouldn't look ahead, though. What was the point? Right now, it was still hours until twilight, the road was empty and I was free to let my mind wander.

I forced my thoughts back to Sidra and Ivy. What an odd pair—Sidra, with her cropped, silver-gold hair and waiflike demeanor, and Ivy, with her hard edges and exaggerated ennui. I wished now that I'd pressed them for more information about the falls. I really wanted to know why people were afraid to go up there, especially since Luna had recommended that I make the trip. Was that where they'd gone today? I wondered.

I knew all about thin places, of course. Those in-between times and landscapes where the veil between our world and the spirit world was at its thinnest. The Celts believed those places were not only passageways for ghosts but also for demons. On the night of Samhain, they donned horrific masks to placate the forces of chaos. As I dredged up all those old legends Papa used to tell me, I had a sudden image of Wayne Van Zandt's scarred visage. I seriously doubted he'd clawed his own face in order to mollify evil spirits and yet—

My thoughts shattered as something hit the windshield with a sickening thud. I shrieked and automatically threw a hand up to protect my face. Then I realized what it was. A bird had flown into the glass. I glanced in the mirror and saw a pile of feathers in the middle of the road. A blackbird or a crow, by the looks of it.

Pulling to the shoulder, I got out and approached slowly. The feathers weren't moving, but I held out hope that the bird might just be dazed. I'd seen them drop like stones after hitting windows, only to rally a few minutes later and fly off. But colliding with a moving vehicle would have a lot more impact than flying into a static pane of glass.

Still, I couldn't see any blood, and the neck didn't appear to be broken. I didn't know what else to do but carefully lift the tiny body from the road and carry it to the shoulder where I nestled it in a bed of clover. I sat there with it for the longest time until something drew my gaze upward where dozens of crows had silently lit on branches and power lines. I caught my breath at the eerie sight, and then I thought of that dark cloud swooping down from the mountains. There were more of them out there. Hundreds more. I wasn't afraid of an attack, but the fact that they were gathering to watch me made my heart jerk uncomfortably.

Slowly, I got to my feet and eased back to the car. I started the engine, rolled up the windows and pulled onto the road. Thankfully, the birds didn't follow.

As I neared the turnoff, I took myself sternly to task. I was letting my imagination get the better of me. The crows had probably been there all along. I just hadn't noticed them. And if I were wise, I wouldn't place too much importance on the old wives' tale that claimed birds were not only harbingers of death but also of insanity. I wouldn't try to connect a murder of crows to all the strange things that had happened since my arrival in Asher Falls. I wouldn't dwell on the disturbing behavior of the man at the cemetery or Chief Van Zandt's warning of dangerous animals roaming the woods. I wouldn't obsess on why I'd been chosen for this job or why Luna Kemper had arranged accommodations for me in a hallowed place.

Above all, I wouldn't give a second thought to that random meeting with Thane Asher.

Late that afternoon, I called my mother, but she didn't feel well enough to talk after her chemo session. Since her diagnosis last spring, she'd spent most of her time in Charleston with my aunt Lynrose so that she could be near the hospital for her treatment. I'd been a little hurt that she hadn't wanted to stay with me, but given my long hours and travel, this arrangement made more sense. Lynrose was retired and could devote herself completely to my mother's recovery. And truth be told, the two of them were closer than my mother and I would ever be, though I loved her dearly.

I chatted with my aunt for a few minutes, then afterward Angus and I had dinner on the back porch. He didn't seem concerned about the quality of his dog food any more than I minded the overripe banana in my fruit salad. He cleaned his bowl, and later we sat out on the back steps to watch the sunset. Despite all the disturbing things that had happened since my arrival in Asher Falls, it was a moment of deep contentment. I'd bonded with Angus in a way I rarely connected with humans. He was the perfect companion. Noble, loyal and I didn't have to hide my secret from him. He already knew about the ghosts.

I said his name softly, testing his hearing. He turned at the sound of my voice and rested his snout on my knee, giving me that soft, soulful stare. I scratched behind his severed ears and then lay my cheek against his head. His coat was rough and matted, and he wasn't the sweetest-smelling dog in the world. But I wanted to earn his complete trust before I drove the dark wedge of a bath between us.

We sat there for the longest time, my hand absently stroking his back as I admired the shifting patterns of light and color on the lake. But by the time dusk fell, I was already inside, safe and sound from the ghosts. I listened to music and read for a while, then turned in early, falling asleep without much trouble. If the bells pealed beneath the lake or a ghostly face peered into my window, I wasn't aware of them. But I dreamed about both.

Nine

The next morning I took Angus with me to the cemetery. After my conversation with Wayne Van Zandt, I wanted the dog close by so that I could keep an eye on him. I also thought he could serve as an early warning system in case that strange man or anyone else showed up.

Considering everything the poor mutt had been through, I'd assumed it would take weeks if not longer to build up his strength. But I was amazed at how frisky he seemed when I let him out of the car that morning. While he chased squirrels, I began the time-consuming task of photographing each grave and headstone from every angle in order to create a prerestoration record for the archives. It was a tedious job for one person. The new part of the cemetery went quickly, but once I moved into the Asher portion, the shade from all the trees and shrubbery slowed me down. Where lichen and moss obscured the inscriptions, I had to use a mirror to angle light onto the stones. Ideally, this was a two-person job, but I'd learned to make do alone.

I worked steadily all morning and broke for lunch around one. I opened the back door of the SUV and sat on the bumper munching an apple while I tossed treats to Angus. He gobbled them with unseemly gusto. I gave him fresh water, and then he found a sunny spot to snooze while I went back to work. The afternoon passed uneventfully, and I became so engrossed in shooting all those strange, angelic faces that I lost track of time. The sun had already started to dip below the treetops when I packed up my equipment and headed back to the car. I had just stepped through the gate when I heard Angus barking. The sound came from somewhere in the woods.

Alarmed, I stored my equipment in the back of the SUV, then walked over to the corner of the fence to call for him. His barking grew even more frantic when he heard my voice, but he still didn't come.

The tree line lay in deep shadows. I would have preferred not to explore any farther, but I couldn't leave Angus. Something was keeping him from me. Maybe he'd treed a squirrel or a possum. Or a mountain lion or a bear....

"Angus, come!"

I heard a howl then and couldn't tell if it came from the dog or something else. One of those elusive wolves perhaps. The eerie wail completely unnerved me. I had my cell phone and that tiny container of mace in my pocket, but I shuddered to think how close I would need to be to someone—or some*thing*—to use it.

A narrow trail led back into the woods, but I had to constantly veer off to avoid fallen branches. The smell of rotting leaves and damp earth mingled with the woodsy aroma of the evergreens. As I began to descend on the other side of the mountain, the cedar and hemlocks thinned, and I found myself tunneling through a heath bald where rosebay rhododendron and mountain laurel grew so dense it was easy to become disoriented. Papa had told me once about getting lost in such a thicket. Laurel hell, he called it. The maze hadn't been more than a mile square, he said, but it had taken him the better part of a day to find his way out. And this from a man who'd been born and raised in the mountains.

As I picked my way along, the stunted rhododendrons tangled in my hair and pulled at my clothing. The canopy hung so low that very little light seeped through the snarled branches. It was very eerie inside that place. Dark and lonely. As I stopped and listened to the silence, a feeling of desolation crept over me. I heard no birdsong from the treetops, no rustling in the underbrush, nothing at all except the distant rush of a waterfall. I wondered if there was a cave nearby, because I could smell the sulphury odor of saltpeter.

To break the quiet, I called out to Angus again, and his answering bark filled me with relief. Scrambling down a rocky ridge, I finally spotted him. His gaze was fixed on the cliff behind me, and I turned, hoping to come face-to-face with nothing more menacing than a cornered raccoon, although they could be vicious creatures when threatened. As I scoured our surroundings, I didn't see anything at first, just a straggly stand of purple foxglove that had managed to survive in the hostile environment. Then I noticed the patterns of stones and seashells on slightly mounded ground, and I realized I was looking at a grave, hidden and protected by a rocky overhang. I had no idea how Angus had managed to find it. I didn't think the grave was fresh. Other than the odor of saltpeter, I couldn't detect a smell.

I walked over for a closer look, noticing at once that the surrounding soil had been scraped, not recently, but frequently enough in the past to discourage growth. The banishment of grass was a burial tradition that had fallen out of favor—though I had seen it recently in the Georgia Piedmont—and the meticulous upkeep was yet another curiosity.

Carefully, I cleared away dead leaves and debris to reveal a marker. The stone had been sunk into the earth, making it nearly invisible unless one knew where to look. I pulled a soft-bristle brush from my pocket and gently dusted off a thick layer of grime so that I could read the inscription. But there was no name, no date of birth or death. The only thing etched into the stone's surface was a thorny rose stem with a severed bloom and bud, a symbol sometimes used for the dual burial of mother and child. But why had they been laid to rest out here in such a lonely location?

The isolation, as well as the north-south orientation of the grave, might once have been an indication of suicide, but the tradition of remote burials for those who had taken their own lives had also been obsolete for years. Judging by the condition and modern style of the marker, I didn't think the grave was that old, twenty or thirty years at most. Well within the timeframe when the custom had mellowed, even within the Catholic Church. So why this desolate spot when Thorngate was so nearby?

As I traced a finger along the severed stem, my chest tightened painfully, and I felt a terrifying suffocation. Gasping for air, I put a hand out to steady myself as a wave of darkness rolled over me. The next thing I knew, Angus was nuzzling my face with his wet nose. I opened my eyes and looked around. I was lying flat on my back on the ground. I had no idea what had happened, but it must have been only a momentary blackout. I wasn't the least bit disoriented. As soon as I opened my eyes, I knew exactly where I was.

But the air had changed. I could feel a shift in the wind, as something cold and dank and ancient swept down from the mountains.

An angry gust swirled the dead leaves over the grave, and I could have sworn I heard the whisper of my name through the trees. The hair on my nape bristled as my heart started to hammer. I scrambled to my feet and glanced around in dismay. I hadn't been confused when I first opened my eyes, but now I couldn't seem to pinpoint the trail I'd followed into the bald. The shrubbery was too dense, and I felt hopelessly trapped.

Then I called Angus's name, and he came to my side at once. "Run!" I commanded, and he bounded around me to take the lead. Even in his weakened state, he could have easily outpaced me, but he measured his stride, slowing when I stumbled and pausing now and then to growl at that thing at our backs.

As we fought our way through the laurel and rhododendron, I began to have serious doubts we would ever get out of that awful place. It was like swimming through mud. By the time we emerged, my legs had gone wobbly and my lungs felt ready to explode, but the woods offered only a brief respite. Here, roots and dead branches tripped me up, and the dense leaf covering blocked the sun so that the landscape lay in premature twilight.

On and on we ran. When we finally burst from the trees, I gave a sob of relief. But the wind didn't let up. It swirled dirt in front of us, a gritty dust-devil that nearly blinded me. As we sprinted for the car, I dug the remote from my jeans and hit the unlock button. The moment I opened the door, Angus sailed past me into the front seat. I climbed in behind him and slammed the door. Somehow my shaky hand started the ignition, and I pressed the accelerator to the floor, sending a shower of gravel over the fence to pepper nearby graves.

The heavy SUV trembled in the wind. For a moment I thought we might be blown off the road, but I tightened my grip on the steering wheel and hardened my resolve. We were getting out of there one way or another.

By the time we hit the highway, the wind had died away. The setting sun peeped through the treetops, and the countryside looked as pastoral as I'd ever seen it.

I glanced at Angus. He was riding shotgun, eyes peeled on the road.

"I didn't imagine that back there, did I?"

He whimpered and settled down in the seat. I put my hand on his back. We were both still trembling and no wonder. Something had been after us in the bald. An amorphous evil that I dared not put a name to. It hadn't been my imagination. Angus had sensed it, too. And he was still just as shaken as I was.

My inclination now was to keep driving until we were far, far away from this place. I needed to be home in Charleston, in my own sanctuary where I would be protected from whatever had driven that wind to me. But I couldn't bring myself to leave. I had a job to do here and a dire sense of purpose that I didn't yet understand. I would stay for now, and I would manage my fear. I'd had years of practice, after all. As a child, I'd learned to quickly settle myself after a ghostly encounter because I knew of no other way to survive such a burden.

I drew on that experience now as I touched the amulet at my throat. Something had protected me in that thicket. Whether it had been the stone from Rose-hill Cemetery that I wore around my neck, or Angus or even my own strength, I didn't know. But I was safe and, except for a few nasty scratches on my arms, no worse for the wear.

As we neared the turnoff to the Covey place, my heart rate slowed and I began to calm. The closer we got to hallowed ground—my temporary sanctuary—the stronger I felt.

"It's okay," I whispered, more to myself than Angus.

Ten

Thane Asher was waiting for me on my front porch when I got home. As I opened the car door to climb out, Angus shot past me before I could grab him. I called to him sharply, but I needn't have bothered. After a warning bark and a wary sizing up, he settled right down and allowed Thane to scratch the back of his neck.

Some guard dog you are, I thought. But then I remembered how he'd placed himself between me and the ghost on that first night, and how just minutes ago, he'd matched his stride to mine as he guided me back to the car. What would I have done without him? I might still have been stumbling around in that thicket, hopelessly lost.

"Who's this?" Thane asked as I approached the porch.

"Angus." Hearing his name—or perhaps my voice—he trotted over to my side, and I leaned down to pet him.

"What happened to him?"

"Luna Kemper said he'd probably been used as a bait dog."

Thane's expression never changed, but I thought I saw something dark and vicious fleet across his face, making me wonder if there might be a layer of razor wire beneath that smooth, impenetrable façade. He looked straight at me then, an electrifying glance that caught me completely off guard. Without another word, he knelt beside the dog, running a gentle hand down the emaciated rib cage as he murmured something reassuring to Angus. I had no idea what he said, but Angus nuzzled against him appreciatively.

I picked at one of the scratches on my arm. The sting was oddly reassuring. "I told Chief Van Zandt about the dog fighting. I thought he'd want to know."

"What did he say?" Thane examined the dog's ears, then cupped the snout to check his teeth. Angus endured the examination without so much as a whimper.

"He said he'd keep a lookout for any kennels in the area, but I don't know if I believe him."

"Don't worry about it." Thane stood and dusted his hands on his jeans. He had on the same black sweater he'd worn when I first met him, and I couldn't help but notice how tautly it pulled across his broad shoulders. I couldn't help but wonder how formidable he might be if crossed. "If there's dog fighting in the area, I'll find it and put a stop to it."

"How?"

He glanced at me again, his eyes vividly intent. "Best not to concern yourself with the details."

Something in his voice alarmed me, a miniscule crack that exposed the razor wire. I'd been angry, too, when I found out about Angus, but Thane Asher was a man of unlimited resources in these parts. I had no idea how he might unleash his fury.

I buried my hand in Angus's fur so that he wouldn't see how badly I still trembled. I'd had a bad scare in the thicket, and I wasn't yet over the shock. But I was good at hiding my feelings, and I didn't flinch as Thane's gaze lingered on my grimy appearance. I thought I detected a softening of his features, but it may only have been my imagination.

"What happened to you?" he asked.

I had no intention of telling him anything. If he'd never had a supernatural encounter, he wouldn't understand. My description of an evil wind would undoubtedly elicit laughter or pity, and I didn't like opening myself up to ridicule. I was a private person, and my ability to see ghosts was by necessity and desire a very personal thing. Nor was I ready to reveal the discovery of the grave. Not quite yet. Not until I'd had time to think it through calmly.

So I ran a hand through my gritty hair and shrugged. "I tangled with a briar patch. Occupational hazard."

"You should probably go in and put something on those scratches."

"I will later," I said with a shrug.

"And by later, you mean after I'm gone."

I smiled thinly. "You'll have to excuse my manners. I just got home from work and I wasn't expecting company."

My own subtle rebuke had the intended effect, and for a moment he looked suitably contrite. "I apologize for just dropping by this way, but I won't take much of your time." He motioned to the porch. "If we could just sit for a minute?"

I hesitated. The sun was well below the treetops. It would be dusk soon, and even though I knew how to protect myself from ghosts, I'd never lived so close to a desecrated cemetery before. I had no idea what might rise from that lake. It was best not to take any chances.

"I promise I won't stay long," he said. "I'd like to talk to you about Thorngate."

I gave an inward sigh. All I wanted at that moment was a hot bath, a soothing cup of chamomile and Angus keeping watch from the back porch. But I was my mother's daughter, and the Southern social graces were as deeply ingrained in my nature as my father's rules. I nodded and smiled politely as I moved over to the steps.

The air had chilled as the sun had gone down, and the woods crowded in on us. I could smell the evergreens as they loomed thick in the fading light, rank upon rank of towering sentinels. I drew Angus close as Thane and I sat side by side on the porch.

"What's this about Thorngate?" I asked.

He paused for a moment as his gaze scoured the landscape. I had a feeling he was searching for something to say. "I haven't been up there in years. How bad is it?"

"I've seen worse." I gave him a puzzled glance. He faced straight ahead, and I could divine nothing from his profile. But instinct told me that the cemetery was the furthest thing from his mind, and I began to feel a little apprehensive. Why was he really here?

He turned suddenly and caught me staring. I glanced away as warmth stole up my neck. "I'll tell you a little secret about Thorngate," he said. "The only way to fully appreciate it is by moonlight. There's an area near the mausoleum that was specifically designed for night-time viewing."

I thought about the stone angels with their strange,

upturned faces and the silvery overgrowth of sage, wormwood and moonshine yarrow. "I recognized the remains of a white garden," I told him. "I have one at home so I can well imagine how beautiful the cemetery would be in moonlight. Especially with all those stat-ues. The faces are extraordinary."

"Yes," he said dryly. "We Ashers have always been very good at erecting handsome monuments to ourselves."

"What's wrong with that?"

"Nothing, I suppose, except our ego has taken os-tentation to a whole new level. I sometimes wonder if all that money spent on the dead might not have been put to better use on the living."

"But cemeteries are for the living," I said. "And those who pay tribute to the dead usually have a commensu-rate respect for life."

He gave me a look that I couldn't begin to interpret. "You really don't know very much about us, do you?"

A brittle edge in his voice made me wonder again about his relationship with his family, but I merely shrugged.

Angus had planted himself in the middle by this time so that neither of us had to reach too far to pet him. He was no fool. I scratched behind one of the ear nubs while Thane ran his hand along the sharp ridge of his backbone. The rhythmic motion was very soothing, and I began to relax.

"How did you get involved in the cemetery busi-ness?" he asked.

"My father was a caretaker for many years. He taught me early on an appreciation for old Southern grave-yards. When I was a kid, I used to think the cemetery by our house was enchanted. It was my favorite place to play. I called it my kingdom."

"Is that why you're known as The Graveyard Queen?"

"How in the world did you find out about that?" I asked in surprise.

"I looked you up."

"And?"

"You're accomplished for someone so young. Undergraduate degree in anthropology from the University of South Carolina, a master's in archeology from Chapel Hill and you spent two years in the State Archeologist's office before opening your own business. All very impressive."

"It seems you've gone to a great deal of trouble to check me out," I said coolly.

"Not really. It was all there on your website."

"Oh. Right."

He grinned, and I couldn't help noticing how young and appealing he looked when he smiled. He should do more of that, but then…the same could undoubtedly be said about me.

"Were you worried about my credentials?" I asked.

"No. I was curious about *you.*"

That silenced me. I wasn't looking at him, but I knew his eyes were on me. I could feel that gaze just as surely as I felt the sting of all those scratches.

"Actually, I did a little more than read your website," he confessed. "I came across a newspaper account of the cemetery restoration in Charleston last spring."

"Oak Grove," I said and felt the familiar hitch in my breath when I remembered.

The knife scar from my struggle with a killer tingled on my upper arm even though the cut had healed months ago. But the wounds on the inside ran deeper. The fear had subsided, at least during daylight hours, but the memory of my entrapment would fester for years, gnawing at me relentlessly on nights when sleep was hard to come by.

Thane must have sensed my reluctance to dredge up that particular nightmare because he said nothing else on the subject. But his gaze on me was soft and so gently inviting that I found myself wanting to confide in him. I suddenly had an intense need to let everything that had happened all those months ago come pouring out, but I barely knew the man. I couldn't talk to him about personal things. Especially not about Devlin.

We didn't speak again for several long moments. Thane continued to stroke Angus's back, and I felt myself slide even more deeply into relaxation. Maybe after the ordeal in the thicket, I was simply too bone tired to fight it. Had it not been getting on dusk, I would have been content to remain as we were, but it was long past time I learned the real purpose of his visit.

"You didn't come here to talk to me about Thorngate, did you?" I asked. "Why are you really here?"

The hand stilled on Angus's back and he glanced up. "I need a favor."

I frowned. "What kind of favor?"

"What are your plans for the evening?"

I hadn't anticipated that question. The amity I'd felt moments before vanished, and I found myself pulling away. "Early dinner, early bedtime," I said stiffly. "I get up at the crack of dawn."

"Could you make an exception just this once? I'd like you to come to a small dinner party at Asher House tonight. We have them every so often. My grandfather started the tradition a long time ago when the community first fell on hard times. Jobs were drying up, people were moving away. He wanted to find a way to show solidarity with the townspeople. A noble enough sentiment, I guess, but over the past few years, the evenings have degenerated into the same handful of guests. It's become tiresome. We're in dire need of fresh blood."

The chill in the breeze made me shiver. "Thank you, but I'm not much on dinner parties. And even if I were, I don't have anything suitable to wear. I packed mostly work clothes."

His gaze drifted over me. "You can come as you are as far as I'm concerned."

I gave an awkward laugh to cover my uneasiness. "I think I could at least manage a shower."

"Is that a yes, then?"

I shook my head. "Sorry. I'm really not in the mood for a party. It's been a long day." And I needed time alone to digest everything that had happened in the laurel bald.

"Then I guess I'll just have to be a little more persuasive," he said slowly.

"Meaning?"

"I believe I have something you want."

My pulse quickened at his ominous tone, even though I suspected he was teasing me. "And what would that be?"

"A lot of the old cemetery records are stored at Asher House. I could arrange for you to have a look at them."

"Luna told me the records were stored at the library in town."

"Some of them are, but not the ones you'll want to

see. If you come to dinner, I'll make sure you have full access."

"That sounds very much like a bribe," I accused.

He grinned. "Would it pique your interest to know there are pictures—actual photographs—of the cemetery from the late 1800s? The original site map should still be around, too, and who knows? We may even be able to dig up the family Bible."

I thought about that hidden grave once again and wondered if any record of it might be included in the Asher family archives. I wanted to know who was buried there. In fact, I had to know. Unidentified graves were anathema to me.

"You drive a hard bargain," I said with a sigh.

The green eyes gleamed. "Shall I pick you up at quarter of eight?"

"No, thank you. I'd rather drive."

He gave me a knowing look. "So you can leave whenever you want?"

I shrugged.

He nodded. "Fair enough. I'll see you at eight, then. You can't miss the house. It's just past the cemetery. Cross the creek and you're there."

Eleven

If the cemetery statuary was a tribute to Asher ego, then I could only surmise the house must pay homage to the family's hubris. The place was massive, a towering cliff-top behemoth with three stories of verandas and half a dozen gleaming columns that seemed at least a mile high. I had expected something large but nothing quite so grand. Nor was I prepared for the floating illusion created by moonlight and clever illumination.

A circular drive swept me up and around to the front of the house, and my first inclination was to make the arc and keep going. For some inexplicable reason, I found myself intimidated, and I didn't understand why. Status meant nothing to me. I'd been brought up by a gentle mother who embodied the more refined qualities of a Southern belle, but also by a father who came from the mountains of North Carolina and worked with his hands. I was a product of both and proud of it.

So why the nervous hesitation? Why that foreboding that warned me to stay away from this house and the Ashers?

My gaze traveled up the mansion's façade as I climbed out of the car. The ground floor veranda was well lit, but the upper balconies lay in darkness. Even so, I fancied I could see a shadow way up high staring down at me. A ghost? I wouldn't be surprised. Not in this house. Not in these hills. The whole area seemed afflicted by some dark spell, some evil enchantment. I knew how daft that would sound to anyone other than my father, but I couldn't discount my instincts. Too many strange things had happened in the short time I'd been in Asher Falls.

I climbed the steps and rang the bell, feeling a little underdressed. The only decent outfit I'd brought with me was a plain black sheath that I often wore when invited to speak or give interviews. If I'd been back home in Charleston, I could have accessorized it with pearls and pumps, but tonight I had to make do with flats and a cardigan.

A uniformed maid answered the door and gave a little curtsy as I relinquished my bag. I had only a brief impression of crystal chandeliers illuminating a magnificent double staircase before I was ushered down a spacious hallway. As I walked along behind her, my gaze was drawn to the faded paintings on the walls— generations of Ashers, I presumed—and I couldn't help but notice the curl of the brocade wallpaper and the water-stained ceiling. Despite its grandeur, the house smelled old and musty, and the air had the damp chill of a tomb. A place where time had stood still. A home more suited to the dead than the living.

The maid waved me through the arched doorway, and the room fell silent as I entered. I hastily searched the small crowd for Thane, and my gaze lit upon Luna

Kemper, breathtakingly lovely in lavender chiffon. She smiled and nodded, but I had the distinct impression she was shocked to see me. She was flanked by two women. I recognized Sidra's mother from the day before and the redhead from the photograph in Luna's office. The picture had captured a hovering ghost in the background, and I searched the window behind them now for that scowling countenance. But I saw nothing more menacing than reflected candlelight.

Sidra's mother wore a white sheath with coils of silver chain around her throat and the redhead, a vintage brocade cocktail dress in emerald-green. They watched me warily, the way one might observe something suspect in a petri dish, and I saw Sidra's mother touch Luna's arm and murmur something in her ear. I grew even more anxious and wished that I'd followed my initial inclination to circle the drive and head back home. Or that I'd at least taken a little more care with my makeup. Done something different with my hair. Then I told myself I was being ridiculous. When had the way I looked become such a pressing concern? Like my father, I worked with my hands. I had no need of frills in my wardrobe. As lovely as those dresses were, they wouldn't suit me at all. But I knew the tension that knotted my stomach really had little to do with my appearance. The worry over my plain attire was merely a manifestation of some darker uneasiness that plagued me.

The three women had grouped themselves around a tall, broad-shouldered man who had his back to the door. He was the only one who hadn't turned when I arrived. There was a fourth woman, but she blended so seamlessly into the background I nearly missed her. She

was slight and nondescript, and her unfortunate choice
of brown velvet all but swallowed her. She looked
uncomfortable and so out of her element that I felt an
instant kinship.

All of this was but a brief assessment before Thane
materialized at my side, handsomely bedecked in a
charcoal suit with a narrow green tie that complemented
his eye color.

"You found us," he said warmly.

"Of course, I did. Your directions were perfect. And,
anyway, it would be hard to miss this house." I glanced
around. "I'm not late, am I?"

"Right on time. But I admit, I was starting to worry
you might have had a change of heart."

"I almost did. Several times."

"Lucky for us you didn't. Come along, then. Let's
get the introductions out of the way and I'll see about
getting you a drink." Weaving my arm through his, he
led me across the room to the others. A set of French
doors stood open to the cool night air, and the scent of
wildflowers drifted in. Or was that Luna's perfume?

Detaching herself from the group, she came forward
to greet us alone, the airy fabric of her dress swirling
gracefully in the breeze. I couldn't help but admire the
one-shoulder cut and the contrast of dark hair against
creamy skin. She was beautifully and meticulously
groomed—hair, makeup, nails, everything perfect—
but there was something feral in her eyes and in the way
she walked that reminded me of a jungle cat straining
at a jeweled leash.

I thought back to her transformation at the Covey
house that first afternoon and how everything about
her had seemed so enhanced by our natural surround-

ings. And then I also remembered her attitude toward Angus, and my esteem for her quickly vanished.

"You know Luna, of course," Thane was saying.

I nodded with a polite, if forced smile. I suspected her greeting was just as strained.

"Lovely to see you again, Amelia, although I never expected to run into you here." Her inquisitive gaze flicked to Thane. "I didn't realize you two even knew each other."

"We met on the ferry," he said.

"That explains it." Her smile settled back into place, her expression as benign as the evening breeze. But now I was remembering something else about Luna Kemper—that flash of rage when I'd dared stand up to her about Angus. She was not a woman to be crossed. Certainly, not someone I'd want for an enemy.

"How do you like your accommodations?" she asked. "Not too far from town, I hope."

"No, everything's fine. Thank you for making the arrangements. Although…"

She tilted her head and regarded me with that same bemusement, as if she still couldn't quite figure me out. "Yes?"

I wanted to ask her why she hadn't told me about the proximity of the original Thorngate, but I didn't dare mention it without providing some alternate explanation as to how I'd come by the knowledge. I couldn't tell her about the bells, after all. Or the swirl of restless souls in the mist.

"Never mind," I murmured. "It's not important."

"If you say so." Annoyance flashed in her eyes, but she quickly shrugged it aside. "By the way, has Tilly been by since you arrived?"

"Not that I know of."

She sighed. "And I specifically asked her to keep an eye on you…in case you needed anything. I thought she might even be able to help you in the cemetery. She's always on the lookout for odd jobs."

"That's not a bad idea," Thane said. "Tilly's a hard worker. I'll speak to her myself if you like."

The blonde glided up beside Luna with a frown. "Forgive me…I couldn't help overhearing. You're referring to Tilly Pattershaw, I assume. She may be a hard worker, but I'd worry about her mental stability if I were you."

"Bryn," Luna admonished.

"Don't *Bryn* me. I'm just saying what we've all thought for years. The woman is strange. Living out there in the woods for so long has affected her mind. When was the last time anyone saw her in town? I shudder to think what she lives on."

"She's not hurting anyone," Thane said. "So I really don't see the problem."

"She may not be a problem *yet,* but that doesn't negate the fact that she hasn't been right since—"

"My goodness, where are my manners?" Luna interrupted. "Here we are going on and on, and you two haven't even been formally introduced yet. Amelia, I'd like you to meet one of my oldest and dearest friends, Bryn Birch. You met her daughter, Sidra, at the library the other day."

Before I could offer my hand, Bryn lifted her head, giving the effect of gazing down her nose at me. "Actually, I feel as though we've already met. You brought my daughter home yesterday. She and Ivy couldn't stop talking about you." She glanced at Luna. "They pretended to be sick so they could leave school early."

"That doesn't sound like Sidra," Luna said.

"It's that *girl*," Bryn said scathingly. She turned back to me. "I'm certain you weren't in any way complicit in their little scheme."

"All I did was offer a ride. I drove them straight home." I hated that I sounded so defensive, but Bryn Birch had a way about her. She was beautiful, cold, haughty and aloof—the embodiment of every quality I found intimidating. The perfect headmistress.

"Where did you pick them up?" she asked.

"At that little market off Main Street."

"You don't know where they'd been all afternoon?"

"They never said."

She exchanged another glance with Luna, and at that moment, I wasn't so certain I would have told her of their whereabouts even if I'd known. Both professionally and personally, she had every right to be concerned, but there was something very disturbing about her third degree. I wasn't getting apprehension so much as suspicion.

The redhead joined us then and thrust out her hand. "Amelia, welcome! I'm Catrice Hawthorne." Her handshake was warm and firm—a relief from the frostbite of Bryn's interrogation—and her soft brown eyes sparkled with good humor. "Ever since Luna told us you were coming, I've been dying to meet you."

"Oh...well...thank you." Her effusive greeting caught me off guard.

"I've been reading your blog," she said. "Digging Graves...such a clever name. You're quite the celebrity, it seems."

"Hardly. It's just something I do in my spare time."

"Well, I'd say it's a very successful hobby. One of the videos you posted has over a million hits."

"That's from an interview I did in Samara, Georgia," I said. "The camera captured reflected light over the cemetery and the footage made the rounds on ghost-hunting sites. It really had nothing to do with me."

"Cat is something of a celebrity herself in these parts," Luna said. "She's a noted ornithologist and a very talented artist."

"Translation—I'm a bird-watcher who paints," Catrice said with a charming touch of self-deprecation.

"You're far too modest." Luna turned back to me. "One of her paintings hangs in the governor's mansion. That's quite an honor."

"I'd love to see some of your work," I said.

"Drop by my studio one of these days and I'll give you a tour. But enough about me," she said with a wink. "You haven't met Hugh and his lovely wife."

I felt Thane's hand on my elbow then, and he gave it a little squeeze as he propelled me forward.

"Amelia, I'd like you to meet my uncle, Hugh Asher."

I'd been aware of the man lurking in the background during the introductions, but I hadn't gotten a proper look at him until now. I tried not to stare, but it wasn't easy. He had the smooth, sophisticated looks of an old-timey movie star. Dark hair, dark eyes—a middle-aged Adonis with an easy smile and a restless virility that made me instantly wary.

"Welcome to Asher House," he said graciously, and I almost expected him to lift my hand to his lips. I was grateful that he didn't.

"Thank you for having me." His features were so unnervingly perfect I felt compelled to search for a flaw as we shook hands. I found one in the softness of his jawline, another in the infinitesimal puffiness beneath his eyes that suggested a propensity for drink.

"My wife, Maris," he said, moving aside to include the tiny woman who hovered behind him. The first thing I noticed was how much younger she was than her husband, closer to Thane's age than Hugh's. The second thing that caught my attention was the way she anchored herself to his side, her gaze flitting birdlike from me to the other women as if she felt threatened from all sides.

"Would you excuse us?" Thane asked, taking my arm again. "Amelia hasn't met Grandfather yet."

"Good luck with that," Hugh Asher muttered as he lifted his drink.

"What did he mean by that?" I asked as we walked away.

"Don't mind him," Thane said with a shrug. "He and my grandfather have a difficult relationship. Come to think of it, I guess we all do—"

He broke off, his gaze going past my shoulder a split second before I felt a strange tingle at the base of my spine. I turned instinctively to the open French doors. Something had drifted in on the breeze. A whisper of that same evil....

Twelve

I saw nothing at first as I searched the outside shadows. Then a slight movement drew my gaze downward, and I could just make out the silhouette of a wheelchair. I wondered how long he'd been sitting out there in the gloom. Had he been watching us this whole time?

He glided in, the wheels making the faintest swish on the hardwood floor. Even seated, he looked tall and regal, immaculately attired in a dark suit that set off his silver hair. His face was thin and deeply lined, his eyes as black as soot. I could detect a faint resemblance to his son, but unlike Hugh, this man was far more imposing than handsome. And despite his age, there was no softness in the jawline, no weakness of any kind other than the withered legs half-hidden by a cashmere throw.

"Grandfather, I'd like you to meet Amelia Gray," Thane said.

I went forward to greet him. "How do you do, Mr. Asher?"

He had been clutching a leather-bound book, and as he laid it aside, I caught a glimpse of gold tooling on the cover, an emblem that triggered some distant, elusive memory. Then it was gone as he took my hand in his, and that strange quiver traversed slowly from the base of my spine all the way up to the back of my neck. It was all I could do not to pull my hand from his.

"Leave us," he commanded.

"I beg your pardon?"

"He means me," Thane said.

"Oh…"

"How about that drink?" he asked cheerfully, unruffled by his grandfather's bluntness. "What would you like?"

"Some white wine?"

He glanced down. "Grandfather?"

The older man answered with an imperious wave, and Thane sauntered off. I was then summoned to a seat next to the wheelchair, and I perched on the edge, as uneasy as a rabbit caught in a snare.

"So you're the restorer I've been hearing so much about," he said. "The one who's come to save our little cemetery."

I glanced at him sharply, searching for evidence of animosity or sarcasm, but I found nothing in those black eyes but a mild curiosity. "I don't know about that. I'm just here to do what I've been hired to do."

"Have you seen the cemetery yet?" His voice, more than the wheelchair, gave away his frailty. It had a brittle quality that couldn't be masked with a throw.

"As a matter of fact, I spent the day there photographing headstones."

"And what did you think of it?"

It was the same question Thane had asked earlier, and like then, I had a feeling Thorngate was merely a blind. The man was after something else. But then I wondered if my uneasiness—more than his words—had created the suspicion. "I was just telling Thane earlier how much I admire the statuary. The faces are so expressive. They remind me of some of the statues I saw in a Paris cemetery once."

"Père Lachaise?"

"Yes," I said. "Have you been there?"

He nodded. "You have a good eye, my dear. Many of the statues in our cemetery were sculpted by European artists. They're priceless."

"Then it's lucky there's been no vandalism," I said. "You can't imagine the kind of damage that can be done with a can of spray paint."

"No one would dare."

The comment was so offhand I almost missed the supreme arrogance, but it was there in the haughty glitter of those obsidian eyes, in the thin, mirthless smile that sent another shiver up my spine. I hadn't come here expecting to like Pell Asher. His greed had destroyed a cemetery, and in my eyes, that was an unforgiveable sin. But despite his past deeds, despite the pomposity, I was strangely intrigued by the man. I'd fallen victim to his mystique even as his very nature repelled me.

"Tell me more about your travels," he said smoothly. "As you can imagine, I don't get out much these days. I tend to live vicariously. You mentioned Paris. Do you travel abroad often?"

"Whenever I can. But Paris was some time ago. A high school graduation gift from my aunt."

"A very generous one, I'd say." His smile was now warm and inviting, almost eager. I couldn't help responding.

"Too generous, according to my father," I found myself telling him.

One dark brow rose in sympathy. "He didn't want you to go?"

"He's always been…protective." And I would say no more on the subject. My relationship with Papa was a private matter, but that brief conversation had stirred a hornet's nest of memories. He'd been so dead set against that trip. I'd rarely seen him so angry. Looking back, I understood why. The notion of my straying so far from the hallowed ground of Rosehill Cemetery must have terrified him. He'd always kept such a watchful eye. But Mama and Aunt Lynrose had been relentless. They'd had their own worries about me. They didn't know about the ghosts and so couldn't understand why a girl of my age was all too content to sequester herself in an old graveyard with only her books for company. It was high time I had an adventure, they'd said. A bit of culture. So off to Paris I'd gone. And while my aunt toured the Louvre and Notre Dame, I'd slipped off by myself to wander the pathways of Père Lachaise where the likes of Chopin and Jim Morrison and Édith Piaf had been laid to rest. I'd had a wonderful time despite the ghosts—Paris had been full of them—and when we returned, the chasm between Papa and me had grown even wider. To this day, I didn't understand that distance. I still didn't know why that first sighting of a ghost had changed our relationship forever.

The old hurt flitted away as Thane placed a glass of wine in my hand. I looked up with a smile. "Thank you."

His gaze on me was attentive. "Everything okay?"

"Yes, fine."

"You sure?"

I nodded.

"You need to see about Maris," his grandfather said darkly. "She's started to drink, and you know she can't hold her liquor. Go head her off before she makes a fool of herself."

"I'll see what I can do," Thane murmured.

I took a sip of the wine—a dry, crisp Riesling—and savored the acidity on my tongue as I watched Thane over the rim. He'd gone straight over to Maris and bent to say something in her ear. She looked up with a grateful smile and nodded, her hand fluttering to his sleeve. I was reminded of the way Angus had nuzzled against Thane earlier. It seemed he had a way with strays, and I wondered if he regarded me as such.

Hugh had drifted out to the veranda with Luna. I could see the two of them out there talking through the open doorway. There was nothing inappropriate about the way he stared down at her. Nothing particularly intimate about her answering smile. But it hit me like a thunderbolt that Hugh Asher was the man who had been with her in the library. I thought now of the laughter and whispers, those animalistic sounds of pleasure. His voice was nothing like Thane's, but they had a similar accent, a certain inflection in the long vowels that had caused me to jump to the wrong conclusion.

My gaze shot back to Maris. Did she suspect? Maybe that was why she'd clung to Hugh so proprietarily during my introduction. But allowing her husband's mistress into the house? I couldn't imagine a more cutting humiliation. However, it wasn't my place to judge her marriage or her forbearance. I couldn't help feeling sympathy for her, though, and a deepening appreciation for Thane, who had managed to coax a smile and some semblance of animation from her.

Pell Asher said something at my side, and I turned with an apologetic murmur. "Sorry. I was just admiring this room. The whole house is incredible. A far cry from my modest place."

He adjusted the throw over his legs. "Thane tells me you're from Charleston."

"I live there now, but I grew up in Trinity. It's a small town just north—"

"I know where Trinity is," he said. "A very good friend of mine lived there for years. After she died, I used to drive down every so often to visit her grave."

"Where was she buried?" I inquired politely.

"Rosehill Cemetery. Do you know it?"

My brows shot up. "My father was the caretaker at Rosehill for many years. I grew up in that white house near the gate."

He gave me another of those strange smiles. "I remember that cemetery very well. It was always so beautifully maintained. I used to marvel at the grueling hours it must have taken to keep all those graves so pristine."

"And that was only one of several cemeteries he cared for," I said proudly. "But Rosehill was by far the largest."

"I recall seeing him during some of my visits," Pell Asher reminisced. "Tall, stoop-shouldered, hair as white as cotton. We spoke on occasion. A very dignified man."

"Yes, that's Papa," I said with a pang of loneliness.

"He sometimes had a little girl with him. A solemn,

golden-haired child who seemed quite at home among the dead."

What an odd way of putting it, I thought. And how unnerving to catch a glimpse of my childhood self through the eyes of this stranger. The whole conversation edged toward the surreal…to think of such a happenstance meeting with Pell Asher all those years ago.

"Are your parents still living?" he asked softly.

"Yes. My father's retired, but he still helps out in the cemetery from time to time."

"It must be a comfort to them to have you nearby. Charleston is what…an hour's drive from Trinity?"

"If that. But I don't get back home as often as I'd like. Even when I'm working in Charleston, the hours are long."

"You should make the time. Without the touchstone of family, one leads an imbalanced life."

"I suppose that's true."

"Of course, it's true," he said. "The strongest ties are blood and land. They are constant. Romantic love is all too fleeting."

I didn't necessarily agree, possibly because I had no blood ties, and the only land I'd ever been attached to was hallowed ground. But I knew about love. The bond I'd felt with Devlin had been so swift and irrevocable that even now, months apart, I couldn't stop thinking about him. Couldn't stop wanting him. It was a constant ache.

I glanced at Pell Asher. His gaze was hard upon me, and I felt that odd little shiver again.

"Blood and land," he repeated. "That's why we treasured our cemetery. Alive or dead, Ashers are compelled to return home."

The cemetery—I noticed he refused to call it Thorngate—had been so valued, in fact, that he'd given it away as atonement for his sins. I had no idea if the family was still involved with the upkeep, but it occurred to me that Pell Asher could very likely be the secret benefactor. Who else in town would be so inclined to make such a large donation to the Daughters of our Valiant Heroes for the purpose of a restoration? And who else would find discretion necessary in order to avoid poking any lingering resentment?

"It's a lovely resting spot," I murmured, for lack of anything better to add.

"Have you been inside the mausoleum?"

"I took a peek. I didn't go down into the tomb, though. I've found it best not to explore underground chambers alone. One never knows about the stability." Among other dangers.

"It's perfectly sound," he said. "But if you're worried, get Thane to go with you. You'll want to see the vaults. Julia's, my wife, is especially beautiful. And he'll want to show you the Sleeping Bride."

"Is that another statue?"

"No, my dear, the Sleeping Bride is my great-aunt Emelyn Asher, my grandfather's youngest sister. She died on her wedding day, trampled by a team of runaway horses. The family had her body sealed in a glass coffin where she remains to this day as perfect as the day she died. Thane can tell you the rest of the story. He was fascinated by it as a boy."

I could imagine. "Did he grow up here?"

"He came to me when he was seven. His mother was married to my son Edward for a time. After she passed, Thane stayed on with my son because he had nowhere else to go. But Edward wasn't long for this world, either." I heard the sharp edge of grief in his voice. "After his diagnosis, he brought Thane here, and in time, I grew to love the boy as if he were my own flesh and blood. God knows, he's done more to restore the family's holdings than my son."

My gaze strayed back to Thane. His grandfather had painted a very different picture from the image I'd formed on the ferry. But Thane's own words had led me to believe him a shallow, aimless man given to drink while awaiting his grandfather's passing. Now I was starting to see him in a different light.

"He's been through a lot for someone his age."

I sipped my wine without replying. We were straying into territory I had no wish to explore. None of this was any of my business, and I would be horrified to learn that Mama or Papa had ever spoken to a stranger about my personal affairs. Not that they would. We Grays were a private lot even with one another. But in spite of my discomfort, I found myself listening attentively.

Those black eyes gleamed, as if he sensed—and enjoyed—my uneasiness. "Thane lost his mother and the only father he'd ever known in a very short period of time. He recovered, of course, because he is nothing if not a survivor. But then he lost Harper…"

He had purposefully trailed off to make me curious. He knew exactly what he was doing and so did I, but I took the bait, anyway. "Harper?"

"The girl he wanted to marry. They were inseparable for a time, but it was a match that was never meant to be."

Such a high-handed proclamation. I felt resentment on Thane's behalf. "What happened to her?"

"She was killed in a car accident. Driving too fast in a rainstorm…missed a turn…" He sighed. "She'd been up here to see Thane that night, and he blamed himself for allowing her to leave in such terrible weather. But Harper was headstrong and that is putting it kindly. Truth be told, the girl was unstable. So reckless and out of control she was a danger to herself and to others. Thane refused to see it, of course, and her parents were useless. They could have gotten her help years earlier, but they preferred to bury their heads in the sand. It was easier to let someone else clean up her messes. I'm just grateful she didn't take Thane with her that night."

"It sounds like you knew her well."

"I knew her only too well," he muttered, or at least, that's what I thought he said.

He watched me with those dark eyes. I had the unsettling notion that he was trying to plumb my deepest thoughts. I had no idea why he'd spoken so frankly about something so personal, but I suspected he did nothing without premeditation. What he wanted from me, I couldn't imagine.

I was relieved when Thane materialized before us. "You've monopolized Amelia enough for one night," he said and reached for my hand. "I promised to show her the library."

"I'm afraid it'll have to wait." Pell Asher's gaze shot to the doorway where a split second later, the maid appeared to announce dinner.

Thirteen

Candlelight masked the water stains and peeling wallpaper in the dining room, but that faint scent of mildew followed us through the arched doorway. The table, however, showed no sign of the deterioration that plagued the rest of the house. Antique china and crystal gleamed on a bed of ivory lace, while silver candelabras flanked a centerpiece of purple wildflowers in shades so complimentary to Luna's dress, one might assume she'd had a hand in the selection. Surely, no woman in her position would be so brazen, but Luna was an enigma. I wondered if, like candlelight, her luminous façade veiled some deeper flaw.

The table display was lavish for such a small gathering, and I was reminded of Thane's earlier comment about the extravagance of cemetery statues—money that might be better spent on the living. I was no expert, but I had to think that even one or two of those exquisite place settings may have netted enough at auction to fix a leaky roof. Why, then, had Asher House been allowed to fall into such a state of disrepair?

Handwritten cards designated the seating arrangement, and with a little shuffling, we all found our places. Pell Asher dominated the head of the table, and Maris nervously took a seat at the other end. I was sure she would have preferred to be nearer to her husband, but etiquette and tradition dictated her position. When we were all settled, I noticed that Luna had somehow ended up next to Hugh, making me wonder if she'd engineered a last-minute switch. I didn't dare glance at Maris to confirm my suspicion. It was hard to look at her knowing what I knew, but my awkwardness paled in comparison to her situation.

I was seated to her right, Catrice Hawthorne to her left. At the other end of the table, Luna and Bryn bookended the elder Asher while Thane and Hugh claimed the middle chairs, directly across from one another. Despite poor Maris's discomfort, it was the best possible arrangement for me, with Bryn Birch on Thane's other side. I would have hated to spend an entire evening next to her.

Regardless, I wasn't looking forward to the meal. The library beckoned, and I was itching to get started, particularly if the records turned out to be the treasure trove Thane had promised. As a restorer, I tried to remain as faithful to the original vision and layout of a cemetery as was humanly possible, which was why I spent hours scouring old newspapers and church books before I ever removed so much as a thistle. But it wasn't often that I had the opportunity to examine photographs from the late 1800s. The prospect of studying those historic images excited me almost as much as the possibility of uncovering information about the hidden grave.

That grave. I was self-aware enough to know that I wouldn't have peace of mind until I could put a name to it. Until I made sure it was given proper respect. The site was so remote and lonely. I couldn't imagine why someone had been laid to rest in such a desolate spot. It made me sad to think of it.

As I contemplated how best to go about finding my answers, I realized the most fruitful resources might not be the cemetery records at all, but someone seated at this table. The grave wasn't that old. Interment had probably occurred during the lifetime of everyone present, with the possible exception of Thane. And me, of course.

Earlier I'd been hesitant to reveal my discovery, but now I couldn't see the harm in asking a few questions. After all, it wasn't as if someone had used the grave to hastily dispose of a body. The site was sheltered, but nothing had been done to disguise the appearance. Quite the contrary, the mound had been decorated with pebbles and shells and marked with a headstone. And at one time, someone had taken great pains to remove the grass and weeds.

"You're very quiet," Thane observed as we began the first course—a delectable acorn squash soup flavored with a hint of curry. "Grandfather didn't say anything to upset you, did he?"

"Why would you think that?"

"He can be difficult."

"Really? I found him charming."

Thane grinned. "I can't tell if you're being facetious or not, but I suspect that you are."

I shrugged. "Maybe a little, but he was fine. We talked about graveyards."

His green eyes glittered in the candlelight. "And that's all?"

"Mostly."

He gave me a curious look, but let the matter drop and turned to engage Bryn. I tried to make small talk with Maris, but after a couple of feeble attempts, I crawled back into my shell and allowed Catrice to carry the conversation. She seemed only too happy to oblige, chatting away about the migratory patterns of the local bird population as she nibbled on a generous helping of crispy pork shoulder.

The bird talk made me think of the poor crow that had flown into my windshield the day before. It still unnerved me to think of that motionless body, not to mention all those birds watching me from the treetops. I wondered if Catrice would take that gathering as some sort of omen or if her knowledge could provide a logical explanation for their odd behavior.

"I blame it on so many outsiders moving into the area," she said. "The natural balance is off-kilter."

I glanced up, wondering for a moment if I'd spoken my mind. But then I realized she'd segued from bird migration to people migration, in particular those flocking to Asheville, North Carolina, where she apparently owned part interest in an art gallery.

"Don't get me wrong. The influx is great for business, but I find it creatively disruptive." She sampled a roasted beet. "They call it the new Sedona, you know. Mystics claim the area has more geological vortexes than any other part of the country."

"What's a vortex?" Thane asked.

"A gateway, if you believe in that sort of thing."

"A gateway to what?" I could hear amusement in his voice.

"To the other world," Bryn put in. "The realm of the dead."

Catrice's eyes sparkled as she watched me from across the table. "Have you been lately?"

"To…Asheville, you mean? Not since I was a child. My father's people are from around there. I remember driving through once when I was a child."

"Did you experience the transformation?" she asked.

"Transformation?"

"That feeling of utter lightness as you drive through the passages. It's like flying," she said dreamily.

Pell Asher glared from the end of the table. "Utter lightness? Utter nonsense, if you ask me."

Undaunted, Catrice leaned forward and smiled. "Now, Pell, you know as well as I do these mountains are full of secrets. Just look at them." She waved a hand toward the tall windows behind me.

I couldn't help glancing over my shoulder, but all was dark outside. I had to imagine the distant escarpment rising majestically out of forest and mist.

"Cat is right," Bryn said. "The Appalachians are ancient. Older even than the Himalayas and just as spiritual."

I found the whole conversation vexing. I had the strangest feeling they were somehow testing me, but I couldn't imagine why.

Then I remembered what Ivy had said about the waterfall being a thin place. People used to go up there because they hoped to catch a glimpse of heaven. Now they stayed away because they were afraid.

Afraid of what? I wondered. Whatever evil had been carried on the wind today?

"Speaking of secrets." I reached for my wineglass. "I stumbled across something interesting today."

"Really?" Catrice politely inquired.

"I found a hidden grave."

Had I flung off all my clothes and danced naked on the tabletop, I don't think I could have elicited a more stunned response. A hush fell over the room, broken only by the sharp intake of someone's breath. I happened to be looking down the table at Luna and saw a shadow fleet across her face, a flutter of something in her eyes that might have been fear. For a moment only, her mask slipped, and I found myself staring at the gray, weathered visage of a much older woman. The illusion was transitory and undoubtedly a trick of the flickering candlelight because in the next instant, she looked exactly the same. But I was reminded again of that first afternoon when she'd taken me to the Covey house, how she'd seemed to change—*transform*—before my very eyes.

Thane turned to me. "You found a hidden grave in the cemetery? Where?"

I tore my gaze from Luna. "No, not in the cemetery. On the other side of the hill, in the laurel bald."

The emotional undercurrents in the room were strong enough now to raise the hair at my nape, making me wonder if I'd made a dangerous miscalculation. Maybe I should have gone with my initial instincts and kept silent about that grave.

"What were you doing on the other side of the hill?" Pell Asher demanded. "Did no one warn you about that place?"

I glanced up, alert now for the slightest nuance. "What do you mean?"

"He's talking about the laurel bald," Thane said. "Those places can be tricky to navigate. It's easy to get turned around."

"Oh...I'm aware of that. As I said, my father grew up in these mountains."

"Then why would you knowingly enter one?" Hugh asked. Of all the people at the table, I found him the hardest to read, maybe because his face was so surreally handsome.

But...how to answer his question? After my conversation with Wayne Van Zandt, I didn't want to mention Angus. The fewer people who knew about him, the better. And, oddly enough, I found myself feeling a little defiant in the face of all their disapproval.

"I wanted to do some exploring. I thought the waterfall was nearby. Luna mentioned the other day that I should see it while I'm here." I flashed a smile, but she didn't return it.

"There's a much easier way to get to the falls," Thane said. "I can show you if you still want to go. But about that grave..." His expression sobered. "Why didn't you tell me about it this afternoon?"

"You caught me by surprise. I guess it slipped my mind."

"Did you call Wayne Van Zandt?"

"I never thought of it as a police matter." I glanced from face to face. All eyes were still on me, reminding me yet again of those birds staring down from the treetops. "Maybe I should clarify. The grave isn't so much hidden as it is secluded. It even has a headstone."

"Is there an inscription?" Thane asked.

"No, unfortunately. No name, no date of birth or death. But there is some symbolism—a rose and a rosebud. The inclusion of both sometimes signifies a dual burial of mother and child. And the presence of the severed stem may indicate a sudden or unexpected death."

I paused but no one said a word. Their silence seemed like a held breath. "Even more interesting is the layout," I continued. "The traditional placement, especially in the South, is for graves to face the rising sun. Feet to the east, we call it. There was a time when a north-south orientation was reserved for outcasts and undesirables—those ostracized for their moral shortcomings."

"Like wearing a scarlet letter for all eternity," Bryn said, and I thought I heard a mocking note in her voice.

"I guess you could put it that way." I scoured the table. "No one knew about that grave?"

"Why would we?" Hugh's shrug was a little too casual. "You said yourself it's secluded. Probably been there for ages. You walk far enough into these hills, you're apt to stumble across any number of old graves."

"But this one isn't historical," I said. "I'd guess it's no more than twenty or thirty years old."

He looked skeptical. "And how can you possibly know that? You said there isn't an inscription."

"I'm going by the style and condition of the marker. And I'll tell you something else about that grave... someone does know about it. The site has been cared for over the years."

"Cared for...how?" This from Luna.

"The ground has been scraped. Which is another curiosity, because that's a tradition you don't often find around here."

"Fascinating," Bryn said.

Maris stood abruptly, and the grate of her chair legs on the hardwood floor jarred me because I'd forgotten all about her.

Catrice touched her arm. "Are you all right? You look so pale."

Maris's hand fluttered to her forehead. "You'll have to excuse me…. I feel a migraine coming on…." She barely got the words out before she turned and fled the room.

There was an awkward pause, but I felt some of the tension deflate with her departure. I didn't think it had much to do with Maris, though. Any disruption would have been welcomed.

"Well? What are you waiting for?" Pell Asher snapped at his son. "Go see about your wife."

Hugh looked as if he would have rather faced a firing squad, but he nodded and graciously excused himself from the table. My eyes were glued to Luna. I didn't know her well enough to read her expression, but if I had to hazard a guess, I would have said she looked quite pleased with herself.

Thane used the interruption to make our excuses. "It's getting late, and I did promise Amelia that tour of the library."

"You'll come again," said Pell Asher.

It wasn't a question or an invitation, but a foregone conclusion that once again put me on the defensive. *We'll see,* I thought.

I inclined my head and murmured good-night. As we walked out of the room, I couldn't help glancing back. Luna, Catrice and Bryn had all gathered around the old man much the way they'd done with Hugh earlier.

I saw one of them stroke his arm while another replenished his wineglass. It was an odd, troubling scene, and I glanced away quickly, afraid of seeing too much.

Fourteen

The library smelled of dust, leather and old books, a scent that had comforted me since childhood. I paused just inside the door as I waited for Thane to turn on the light. Directly across the room, French doors opened into a garden, and I found myself searching for a pale face among the silhouettes of statues and topiary, even though I had no evidence that Asher House was possessed. Ghosts were drawn to people, not places. Entities craved the warmth and energy emanated by a living being, not the cold memories of a dying house. But if I'd learned anything during my brief time with a haunted man, it was that ghosts were no more predictable than humans.

The light came on, and I glanced around curiously. No specters, but plenty of shadows. And spiders, I thought with a shiver, my gaze lifting to the glimmering cobwebs hanging from the vaulted ceiling.

The space was large—cavernous, by my standards—but still seemed overly crowded with massive bookcases carved out of oak, and heavy furniture upholstered in distressed leather. There was a desk in the center of the room, a huge affair that rose on claw feet to face the fireplace. Several old hatboxes had been stacked at one end, and a brass reading lamp occupied the other. As my gaze slowly traveled the room, I saw globes, maps and a gigantic painting over the mantel of a proud and pampered bluetick coonhound. I crossed to the fireplace to have a closer look.

Thane came up behind me. "That's Samson."

"He's beautiful," I said, admiring the mottled coat.

"Was. He's no longer with us."

"Oh…I'm sorry. Was he your dog?"

"Grandfather's." He moved up beside me, his gaze still on the painting. "They were quite a pair. Samson was never far from Grandfather's side. He was like a shadow. And then one day he up and disappeared."

"Your grandfather must have been heartbroken."

"Heartbroken?" He frowned. "I don't know about that. But he was certainly livid. I don't think I've ever seen him so angry."

"Angry with whom?"

"With me." He glanced away but not before I saw the dart of warring emotions, the remnant of an old shame. "It was my fault."

A chill feathered along my spine at that look on his face. I told myself to leave it alone, but, of course, I didn't. "What happened?"

The green eyes darkened under a furrowed brow. "I took the dog into the woods one day without Grandfather's permission. It was right after I first came here. I suppose he told you about that?"

"About the dog?" I deliberately misunderstood.

"No. About how I came to live with him."

"He mentioned that your mother died when you were young." I had no intention of telling him everything his grandfather had revealed to me about his past. It was just too awkward.

But he knew. I could hear a trace of bitterness in his voice despite the ghost of a smile. "You're very diplomatic. I'm sure he gave you an earful. He makes no bones about the fact that I'm an Asher in name only."

I remembered his grandfather's insistence that blood and land were the strongest ties, and I wondered how many times Thane had been made to feel an outsider by that outdated sentiment. For some reason, I felt the need to reassure him. "He spoke very highly of you."

"Oh, I'm sure he did." He glanced back up at the painting, but the air between us was charged with something unpleasant. Obviously, his place in this household was a thorn that still pierced deeply. I could understand that feeling of displacement. I'd come to my parents as a baby, and even though I always knew they loved me, I'd sensed a detachment, a wall that I never quite managed to scale. The only place I ever felt truly at home was the cemetery. My graveyard kingdom.

I could feel Thane's gaze on me. When I turned, he gave me a speculative smile, as though wondering where my mind had drifted. "Anyway, we were talking about Samson."

"Yes." I didn't know why I suddenly felt breathless. He had a way of looking at me that, despite my own walls, made me feel vulnerable and a little self-conscious.

"We'd gone pretty far into the woods that day. He caught a scent and just took off. I called and called, but he wouldn't come. He vanished and I never even heard a sound. I walked those trails for days and didn't find anything more than a few drops of blood."

"Samson's blood?"

He shrugged. "We'll never know. But if he was attacked, I can only assume it was something large enough to drag the body off without leaving a trace."

I thought of the scars on Wayne Van Zandt's face and that eerie howl I'd heard in the woods earlier. And suddenly I was very glad that I'd left Angus on the back porch. "Is it possible someone took him?"

"I've always wanted to believe that. Samson was a purebred, highly coveted in these parts. Someone could have taken him, but without making a sound? I don't know…" He bent to light a fire. The kindling caught, and the flames began to crackle. I put out a hand, but the flickering warmth did little to chase away the chill of his words.

He straightened. "We should probably get started," he said briskly.

"Yes. It's getting late and I really do have to get up early."

"The crack of dawn, I believe you said."

I was glad to hear a more lighthearted tone in his voice. "When you work outside in the South, you learn to beat the heat. Although the weather these days is perfect."

"You have a hard job," he said. "You don't hire help?"

"Sometimes, if the cemetery and the budget are large enough. But I don't mind doing the work myself." I glanced down at my calloused hands. "I'm particular about the way things are done. People tend to get a little slapdash if they don't know what they're doing or haven't a vested interest. Breaks my heart to see a hundred-year-old rosebush chopped down out of carelessness."

He searched my face. "You're not afraid to be alone in a cemetery after what happened?"

He was still curious about Oak Grove. I couldn't blame him. It was a bizarre story. The discovery of an underground torture chamber beneath an old city cemetery had caused quite a sensation in Charleston. The notoriety eventually died down, but last spring, after it first happened, I couldn't leave my house without being accosted by a reporter. I wondered now if I'd come to Luna's attention through the news.

"I always take precautions. Besides, once I'm immersed in a restoration, I forget about everything else. It's very therapeutic."

"You're brave," he said, and there was something in his eyes that hadn't been there a moment before. "I admire that."

I tried to laugh off the compliment. "I'm not so brave. Just prepared."

"Even better. Brave and sensible."

I was reminded of something Devlin had once said to me. *Strange and practical,* he'd called me as we walked through the killer's tunnels.

Devlin.

I didn't want to think about him just now or of that night in his house when our passion had opened a terrible door. When the Others, drawn by our heat, had crept through the veil, and I'd had to face the nightmarish reality of our union. I'd seen firsthand the consequences of associating with a haunted man, and now there was no going back. No closing that door.

I drew a breath and turned away. I couldn't deny that

I was drawn to Thane, maybe because I sensed something in him that I recognized in myself—that feeling of not belonging.

Before tonight, I hadn't known much about him beyond that charming smile and those beguiling green eyes. I wished for that ignorance back. He was a little too real to me now. A little too appealing for someone who needed to forget.

"Where should we start?" I asked awkwardly, looking everywhere but into those eyes. "You mentioned old photographs. And maybe a site map?"

"About that." He scratched the back of his neck. "I probably should have warned you…it's going to take some digging to find that stuff. Everything was moved up to the attic years ago. I brought down a bunch of boxes earlier so we'll just have to go through all of them until we find what you need."

"The attic?" There was a note of horror in my voice. "Even the photographs?"

His nod was grim. "I know. A lot of them have historical significance so it's a shame they haven't been properly stored or cataloged. I've always meant to get around to it, but never found the time or patience."

Said the man who'd once led me to believe he had nothing but time on his hands.

"I can see how it would be a daunting task," I murmured, but I would have relished such a project. Photography was a hobby of mine and old photographs, a passion. As a child, my favorite pastime on rainy days was going through the family albums. Even though I'd always known of my adoption, I'd spent hours searching through those pictures in hopes of finding someone who looked like me.

We walked over to the desk, and Thane blew a cloud of dust from one of the hatboxes before lifting the lid. I tried to hide my dismay at the jumble of photographs inside, so many of them faded and creased from age and careless handling. I shouldn't have been shocked by the condition. The whole house was a testament to neglect.

"Have a seat." Thane motioned to the chair behind the desk while he perched on the corner. He handed me one of the boxes and took another for himself.

"So…did you go to school in Asher Falls?" I asked as I began to sift through the photographs.

He looked up in surprise. "For a while. Why?"

"No reason. I drove by the school the other day with Ivy and Sidra. It seems a little odd that a town this size has a private academy but no public school."

"It's really not that odd. Asher Falls had a public school years ago. When enrollment dropped, they consolidated with Woodberry."

"Didn't the enrollment drop at the private school, as well?"

"No, because Pathway is also a boarding school. Kids from all over attend."

"What's Pathway like?"

"Like any school, I guess." But there was something in his voice that made me wonder. "It's a prep school, really. If you can find a way to fit in there, you can adapt to places like Emerson."

My head came up. "Emerson University in Charleston? You went there?"

He looked bemused. "Yes. Is that a bad thing?"

"No, it's just… I knew someone else who went there."

"Oh?"

"Actually, I've known a few people who attended Emerson. A friend of mine used to be a professor there…Rupert Shaw. But he was probably before your time."

"The name sounds familiar, but I can't place him."

"Nowadays, he runs the Charleston Institute for Parapsychology Studies."

"Parapsychology? As in paranormal goings-on?" His eyes gleamed in the lamplight. "Don't tell me you had a ghost problem."

"Doesn't everyone?" I smiled benignly before bowing my head to my work.

We fell silent after that, and I was soon so absorbed in the photographs that I barely noticed when Thane got up to stretch. The parade of Ashers enthralled me. I found the faces so intriguing…the nearly identical shape of their noses, the same jaw and chin line. But the familiarity of those features also unsettled, like the nag of a restive memory. Then it came to me. The circle of statues in the cemetery—all those angelic faces— had been sculpted in the likeness of long-dead Ashers. Thane had been right. Apparently, the family was very good at erecting handsome monuments to the collective ego.

He hadn't returned to his place, but instead ambled over to the fireplace to gaze pensively into the flames. It was awkwardly apparent that he'd already grown bored with the project—bored with me, perhaps—so I decided it was time to call it a night. We'd barely made a dent in the boxes, but I didn't want to outstay my welcome, and Angus would need to go out soon, anyway.

I was just sorting through one last batch when I happened upon a photograph that reminded me of the one hanging in Luna's office—a teenage Bryn, Catrice and Luna smiling dreamily into the camera. A young man stood with them in this shot. An Asher, judging by his features, but he wasn't handsome enough to be Hugh. And just like in the other picture, a fourth girl hovered in the background. Even though she was hidden by shadows, she seemed more substantial here, making me wonder if she'd still been alive when this picture was taken.

Ghost or human, I had a visceral reaction to her. As I gazed down into her face, a tremor coursed through me, an almost electrical vibration that jolted a memory. It was as if a shutter had clicked, and in place of this image, another came into focus. The ghost on the pier. It was her. It was the same girl.

I dropped the picture like a hot coal. There was something truly creepy and maybe a little sinister about the way she skulked about in the shadows. About the way she glared into the lens, as if staring straight through the camera, straight through time and space at me.

Thane must have seen something on my face because he came over to see what I'd found. "Oh, look there," he said as he gazed down at the picture. "The Witches of Eastwick. Or I should say Asher Falls."

"What?"

He grinned. "Haven't you noticed a certain…eccentricity about those three?"

Those *three.* Could he not see the fourth girl? "Sidra said they used to be into some sort of mysticism, hence her celestial name. I guess they still are, judging by the conversation at dinner." I glanced up at him.

He didn't react. He was still frowning down at the picture.

"Who's the young man?" I asked.

"My stepfather, Edward," he said absently as he picked up the image. "Did you see the girl in the background?"

Cold fingers danced along my spine. "Do you know who she is?"

"She looks familiar, but I can't seem to place her." His voice had an almost trancelike quality. "I've seen this picture somewhere before, I think."

"Luna has a similar one hanging in her office. Maybe you've seen it." I held my breath, waiting to find out if he'd been able to see the ghost captured in Luna's photograph.

"I've never been in her office, so that can't be it." His face suddenly cleared. "I've got it, though. It was a picture I found stuck in a book after my mother died." He shivered, as though seized by a violent chill. "Whoa. It's weird how vividly that came back to me just now. I've never given it a second thought before tonight."

"This girl was in it?" I asked more anxiously than I meant to.

"In the background, just the way she is here. I don't even know why I remember her so well. She's not exactly beautiful, is she? But there's something mesmerizing about her. I think it's the eyes. It's like she's looking right at you…" He trailed off, then seemed to shake himself. "Anyway, I remember something else odd about that picture. It had been ripped apart and painstakingly taped back together. When I showed it to Edward, he turned completely white, like he'd been confronted with a ghost almost. He said she was just a girl he'd known a long time ago, before he met my mother. But considering his reaction, I think she must have been a good deal more than a casual friend. And later, when he thought I'd gone to bed, I saw him in his study staring at that picture."

"He never said who she was?"

"No, but there was a name scribbled on the back. Freya." He pronounced it Free-a.

Freya. I said the name to myself, and those icy fingers skated along my spine again.

"It wasn't until I came here to live that I actually heard the name," he said. "Tilly Pattershaw had a daughter name Freya."

"Had?"

"She died years ago. Probably not long after this photo was taken." He placed it carefully, almost reverently on the desk.

I thought again of that ghost on the pier, of that curious telepathy I'd felt in her presence. And now here she was, turning up in old photographs, almost as if my very presence had conjured her. "What happened to her?"

Thane shrugged. "A fire, I think. No one ever wanted to talk much about her."

A shudder of dread went through me, though I had no idea why Freya Pattershaw's fate should affect me so strongly. "Why does Bryn think Tilly is mentally unstable?"

Thane looked annoyed. "She's exaggerating. Tilly's a little strange, but she's not dangerous. I wouldn't have suggested she help you out in the cemetery if I thought otherwise."

"Do you really think she'd be interested in a job?"

"Couldn't hurt to ask. But I don't think we should mention Freya. Tilly's a tough old gal—she's had to be—but there's also something fragile about her."

I looked up, surprised at the protective note in his voice. "I wouldn't do that."

But I had so many questions, and I knew I wouldn't rest until I found answers. I still couldn't shake the troubling premonition that I'd been brought here for a reason. Everything that had happened, all these strange events, were somehow connected to my arrival in Asher Falls.

"She doesn't have much use for strangers," Thane was saying. "It might be best if I go with you to see her. Just let me know when you're ready."

I gave a noncommittal nod. "Thanks. But right now, I think it's time for me to be getting home." I pushed up from the desk. "Do you want me to help you put everything away?"

"Just leave it. No one ever comes in here, and like Grandfather, I'm hoping you'll come back."

My smile was also noncommittal.

We went into the foyer where the maid waited by the door with my bag. Thane walked me outside. The night was clear and very, very still, the forest a looming darkness all around us. But where the tree line was broken at the bottom of the hill, I could see the faint glimmer of moonlight on Bell Lake, so lovely and serene from this distance. Not even a ripple betrayed the stir of restless souls beneath. I shivered, thinking of that rising mist, and pulled my sweater around me as I drew in the crisp, pine-scented air.

Thane took my arm as we walked down the drive, and I was surprised to feel my pulse jump at his touch.

When we reached my car, I turned to say good-night, but the words died on my lips. He was staring down at me, eyes glistening like tidal pools in the moonlight. I could see the curve of his lips, too, and the thick shadow of his lashes. We were standing very close, and I fancied I could hear the drum of his heart, though I knew that was only my imagination.

He wanted to kiss me. I could sense his desire as surely as I felt the night air on my face, and I didn't know what to do about it. I wasn't ready for anything more than a friendship.

As we stood in that loaded silence, my gaze moved past him and lifted. I could just make out a silhouette on one of the upper balconies. Not a ghost this time, but Pell Asher staring down at us.

Uneasy, I tore my gaze from that shadow.

"I should be going—"

Before I could protest, Thane bent and brushed his lips against mine. I didn't respond or reject, but my eyelids fluttered closed, and the nervous excitement that quivered in my stomach was more than a little disconcerting. I didn't want this, and yet I didn't *not* want it enough to pull away.

But Thane had picked up on my reluctance, and he broke the kiss, putting a hand briefly to my face. "Soon," he promised, and I nodded vaguely even though I had no idea what he meant.

As I drove away, I glanced in the rearview mirror and saw him at the top of the drive, illuminated by starlight. He stood there seeing me off, and as I felt an ever-so-slight quickening of my heartbeat, two things occurred to me. Despite his guilt over Harper's death, he had no ghost.

And secondly, I hadn't thought of Devlin at all when Thane kissed me.

Fifteen

When I got home, I went straight to the back porch to see about Angus. He was waiting at the door to greet me. I gave him a little extra attention before I let him out, and he rewarded me with a tail wag, which I hadn't yet seen from him. He was looking so much better, and I thought his coat even had sheen in the moonlight. That may only have been wishful thinking, but I wasn't imagining his response to my TLC. He pressed up against me, those dark eyes shining with appreciation.

"It'll soon be bath time for you, mister," I told him. "I've mollycoddled you long enough. Who knows? You may even enjoy it."

He responded by nuzzling his cold nose against my chin. "Enough of that now. Let's get on with this so I can go to bed."

I smothered a yawn as I followed him outside and stood at the bottom of the steps while he prowled the moonlit yard. He took his sweet time, sniffing at every bush and occasionally pawing at something in the dirt.

I hated to rush him. From everything I'd read about dog fighting, he'd probably spent most of his life in cramped cages and filthy kennels before being dumped in the woods to starve. Now that he had the luxury of a full belly, I wanted him to enjoy his freedom. But the hour was late, and I was ever mindful of that lake. As I turned to skim the glimmering surface, the moon withdrew behind a cloud, shrouding the landscape in deep shadow. The night fell silent, so deadly still I could hear the whisper of a rising breeze through the leaves and the sudden hammering of my heart in my ears.

The ghost was there, somewhere behind me in the dark. I could feel the chill of her presence creeping up my spine. For a moment, I thought she might even have touched me....

Freya.

The name came to me so sharply, I was jolted by my certainty. I didn't move, of course, didn't outwardly react at all. I remained rooted to the spot, my gaze fixed on the lake as my pounding heart sent a surge of blood to my temples. I felt a little light-headed from the strain of a suppressed shudder. Why such a strong reaction to *this* ghost? Why was she so different from the others?

Somewhere off to my left, Angus growled, and I knew that he'd seen her, too. Or at least sensed her. His reaction gave me an excuse to turn, and I whirled toward the sound of his snarl, calling to him in a voice steadied by years of ghost sightings.

"What is it, boy? What do you see?"

She was right there. Directly behind me.

So close, dear God, my breath frosted on the night air. The cold that emanated from her nebulous silhouette was almost unbearable. It took everything in me to silence my chattering teeth.

I wanted to ask why she had appeared here, of all places, and what she wanted from me. But I blocked those questions from my mind. I'd broken my father's rules to dire consequences, so I knew better than to acknowledge the dead.

As if sensing my resistance, she floated closer. Was she drawn to my warmth? My energy? Like the other specters that came through the veil, did she crave what she could never have again? I desperately wanted it to be that simple, but I could feel the icy tentacles of that strange telepathy curling around me. She wanted to communicate. She was doing everything in her power to make me acknowledge her.

This, of course, was only my interpretation. She didn't speak or try to touch me, but I suddenly had images in my head that didn't belong there. Jumbled, dreadful visions that didn't make any sense to me. And so much darkness. So much loneliness. It was like getting a peek through the veil. And that glimpse was terrifying...yet somehow seductive....

I think I may actually have taken a step toward her when I heard Angus's warning growl. I glanced past the ghost to where he crouched at the corner of the porch.

"Angus! Come, boy!"

He growled again, cutting a wide swath around her wavering form to come up beside me. I pressed against him because now I craved his warmth.

And still she drifted closer, hovering for the longest time right before my face. I no longer sensed confusion from her, but some darker emotion. The force of it, as she started to fade, was like a physical blow.

Leave now!

I sprinted up the porch steps with Angus at my heels.

Something awakened me that night. My eyes flew open, and I lay shivering under the covers, straining to hear whatever sound had roused me. All was silent in the house, but I rose, anyway, and pulled on a sweater over my nightgown as I padded down the hallway. The glimmer from the long windows guided me to the front door where I checked and rechecked the lock. Then I went through the kitchen to peer out the back door.

I could see the sparkle of moonlight on water and the feather-edged outline of the pines against the night sky. The forest beyond the lake was a solid blackness, blending seamlessly into the distant silhouette of the mountains. As my gaze skimmed those starlit peaks, something Catrice had said at dinner came back to me. *You know as well as I do these mountains are full of secrets.*

Secrets…and hidden graves, apparently.

Nothing seemed amiss outside, so I'd just decided to go back to bed when gooseflesh rose on my arms and at my nape, as if an icy draft had seeped in through a crack. I turned back to the window. Something *was* amiss. Angus would have come to the back door the moment he heard me stir. I called to him through the glass as my gaze went to his empty makeshift bed. Where was he?

I opened the door and stepped out into the chilly night air. "Angus?"

He wasn't on the porch, but I told myself not to panic. He'd obviously found a way out. Dogs were good at that.

But there was a quality to his absence that once again made the hair rise up at the back of my neck.

And then I saw the hole that had been cut in the screen, large enough for a hand to reach in and unfasten the latch. Someone had let Angus out—or taken him—and I hadn't heard a sound.

Flinging back the door, I clamored barefoot down the steps, only to pause at the bottom, head cocked toward the woods. Something came to me. A faint, but chilling whimper. So tepid, I wanted to believe that I'd imagined the cry. It was only the wind riffling through the trees or the boat moored at the end of the pier scraping against the pilings. Then I heard it again, the high-pitched keen of an animal in distress. *Angus.*

I whirled toward the sound, my heart flailing like a startled robin against my chest, but even in that first moment of panic, I checked the impulse to rush blindly into the woods. Instead, I ran back into the house and grabbed my boots, struggling into them as I armed myself with flashlight and mace. I didn't consider myself brave. I'd learned to live with ghosts out of necessity, not courage. But I moved through the house now with unhesitating determination. If Angus was lying hurt in the dark—and, oh, the images going through my head—I had to find him.

Hurrying down the back steps, I made my way across the yard and followed the footpath into the woods, using those desperate whimpers to guide me. But I didn't call out to Angus again. I had no idea what might lie in wait for me in those trees. Stealth was my only friend. I kept the flashlight lowered to the ground as I slipped along the trail. Beyond the reach of the beam, the forest was a black, silent abyss. I would have welcomed the hoot of an owl or the patter of leaves to help mask my foot-steps, but even the breeze had died away.

About a hundred yards in, the trees thinned, and up ahead, I could see the pool of moonlight in a small clearing. In the center of that circle, a dark form waited. I told myself it was nothing more than a shadow or a bush. When it moved, I stumbled in shock, the hard kick of my heart snatching my breath. Then I played the light into the clearing and saw the familiar gleam of soulful eyes.

"Angus." I said his name on a gasp of relief. He'd been lying on the ground when I came up, but he rose when he heard my voice and rushed toward me, only to be jerked back so sharply he yelped in protest. An instant later, I saw why. He'd been tethered to a tree with a rope.

Icy panic stopped me in my tracks as if I, too, had been bound. My limbs went watery, and no matter how much I wanted to go to Angus, I simply couldn't make my muscles obey. Because in that moment, I was as afraid as I'd ever been. Which might sound strange coming from someone who had seen ghosts since childhood and who had been the target of a killer not so long ago. I'd known my share of fear, but the terror I felt now wasn't for my physical safety or even for Angus. I was afraid of something…inside me. Some unknown part of myself that I was only now discovering. The puzzle piece that connected me to this strange, disturbing place.

Drawing a shaky breath, I quieted my racing pulse and forced myself toward Angus, only to freeze once more, not in fear this time, but from the warning bristle of my every nerve ending. I didn't know what had set off that alarm. Angus's piteous whimper. Something in the wind. A dormant instinct come suddenly to life. Whatever the trigger, I paused there, one foot in front of the other as I slowly angled the beam along the path in front of me.

I almost didn't see the thing, the camouflage of leaves and pine needles was so clever. It was only by pure luck that the light caught the gleam of metal. So complete had been my absorption in the metaphysical that I'd lost track of the real menace. Someone had taken Angus from my porch and tied him to a tree in the woods. This was no random act of cruelty. There was a very dark purpose behind the action.

Grabbing a stick from the forest floor, I swept aside the debris on the path to reveal the jagged teeth of a steel trap. An enormous one, much bigger than the size needed for a human leg. But in that first moment, I had no doubt about the motive. It had been placed at the end of the path directly between Angus and me. Someone had brought him here to lure me into the woods.

But why?

Instantly, I thought of that hidden grave and the reaction my revelation had provoked. I hadn't imagined the tension at dinner, nor Hugh's overly casual attempt to explain it away. I hadn't imagined Luna's response, either. I'd dropped a bombshell at that table and now someone felt threatened.

I eased toward the trap as if sidling up to a coiled snake. Using the sharp end of the limb, I poked at the spring until the metal jaws snapped shut with a clatter that shook me to my core. The sound reverberated through the woods like the shock of an unexpected thunderclap, startling roosting birds from the treetops.

I didn't glance skyward. Instead, I peeled my gaze on the clearing and the surrounding woods. Was the perpetrator nearby, waiting to hear that sound?

I felt vulnerable and exposed, armed with only that can of mace. The thought crossed my mind that I should take cover and wait to see who came out of the woods. But I had to get to Angus, and besides, whoever had set the trap might be long gone. For all I knew, the intent was to leave me until morning, giving wild animals a chance to pick up the scent of my blood.

Taking a deep breath, I aimed the light across the clearing where the path resumed to Tilly Pattershaw's house. Nothing stirred on the trail, so I shifted the light, only to jerk my hand back, fixing the beam on a telltale mound of leaves and pine needles where another trap had been concealed. I stepped into the clearing and turned in a slow circle with the flashlight. The traps were all around us.

It hit me then. I wasn't the quarry. Angus was being used as bait to lure something out of the woods. Something that could come from any direction. *Something big enough to drag a body off without making a sound.*

I felt it in the wind then, that terrible dankness. The bone chill of an ancient evil. All around me, the leaves began to whisper and sigh, like the release of a pent-up breath. *Amelia...Amelia...*

Everything went deathly still except for that whisper and the roar of rushing blood in my ears. And then the breeze gusted, swirling dead leaves across the clearing, and somehow I was released from the grip of my paralysis. I rushed to Angus and dropped to the ground beside him. He didn't appear to be hurt, but when he pushed his nose against me, I smelled an odd chemical scent on his breath and wondered if he'd been drugged. That would explain how he'd been taken without rousing me.

But…no time to worry about that now. The wind brought a fresh terror. A howling from deep inside the woods. I saw the hair rise up on Angus's back as he turned to growl at the darkness.

"It's okay," I whispered over and over as I worked to free him. The rope around his neck had been tied with multiple knots, none of which I could loosen. The wind was cold, but sweat trickled down my back from fear and tension, and I cursed myself for not having had the foresight to grab the utility knife from the pocket of my discarded cargoes. "Come on, come on." I worked until my fingernails were in shreds, but I still couldn't budge those knots.

Behind me, one of the traps sprang shut, and as I jerked around in shock, I lost my balance and went sprawling to the ground. I watched in terror as a shadow detached from the deeper darkness of the woods and rushed into the clearing. Angus whirled and crouched, but he didn't try to attack.

As the shape took form, I thought the wraithlike creature before me must surely be a ghost. But as she moved into the moonlight, I glimpsed an aged face framed by a mane of unkempt gray hair and somehow I knew who she was. Tilly Pattershaw.

Like me, she wore boots and a white nightgown topped with a heavy wool sweater. She was slight— frail, I thought at first—but in her gloved hand she wielded a knife, some long, fearsome thing that she swung over her head as she simultaneously grabbed the tether and pulled it taut. The knife slashed, cutting clean through the rope. I was so astonished by her sudden appearance and behavior, I hadn't moved or uttered a sound. But now I scrambled to my feet as the howling grew louder.

Her gaze went past me to the trees, and I thought I saw her shudder. "Get out of the woods, girl!" The wind whipped at her long, wiry hair and tore at the hem of her gown.

"What about you?"

Her eyes were luminous in the moonlight, her face like the wizened visage of an ancient shaman. But her speech was pure mountain folk. "It don't come for me."

I turned to follow her gaze, my eyes scanning the woods. Even the trees were shivering, and the air hummed with the oddest vibration.

"Go!" she screamed.

"Angus, come!"

He was right at my heels as I tore across the clearing.

"Keep to the path!" I heard her call after us, but the sound died away quickly in the wind.

I bolted blindly down the trail, tripping over a root that almost took me down. A nauseating fire shot up my leg, but I wouldn't let a twisted ankle slow me. Not with that howling thing at our backs. Gritting my teeth against the pain, I raced along the path with Angus now at my side.

Something swooped across the trail in front of us—a bat, I thought—and then I heard what sounded like the flap of bird wings, hundreds of them, but I didn't dare look up even as a cloud passed over the moon.

As we neared the edge of the woods, I grabbed the rope that still dangled from Angus's neck, preparing for that final dash across the open yard. Instead, I drew up short and gazed in horror out over the water.

Whatever had been lured down from the mountains had stirred the restless souls at the bottom of the lake. I could hear the bells—that hair-raising chorus of the dead—tolling from those murky depths. The discordant peals were muffled by water and a thick, writhing miasma that crept shoreward, up the stepping-stones and into the yard where Angus and I stood trembling.

And from that wall of mist, diaphanous arms reached out for me. Exactly like the recurring nightmare of my childhood. Hands thrusting through walls to grab me. I knew in my dream, as I knew now, not to let them touch me. They would draw me into that mist, drag me underwater, pull me down, down, down to that sunken graveyard....

The howls were getting closer. Over the frantic batter of my heart, I swore I could hear the ragged breath of some fierce creature racing up the path behind us.

Entwining the rope around my hand, I gave it a tug. "Run!"

I didn't have to tell him twice. Spurred by fear and instinct, Angus leaped forward with so much power, the momentum nearly wrenched me off my feet. I found my balance and kept going. I didn't glance back at the mist, but I could feel the abnormal chill as we sprinted across the yard, up the porch steps and into the house. Slamming the door, I slid to the floor and wrapped my arms around Angus, pulling him close as I waited for the cold to seep in through the cracks. But the house protected us. The hallowed ground on which it had been built gave us sanctuary. After a while, I got up to peek out the window. The mist had receded, and the trees were silent now that the wind had died away. The sparkle of moonlight on water was as lovely as I'd ever seen it.

Fetching the utility knife, I hacked through the rope around Angus's neck and tossed it in the trash. Then I checked again for wounds, but aside from that odd scent on his breath, he appeared no worse for the wear. I gave him some fresh water but decided to wait until morning to feed him in case of an upset stomach.

"You're sleeping inside tonight," I told him.

He whimpered gratefully and followed me down the hallway where I grabbed a blanket from the closet and spread it on the floor at the end of my bed. He lay down facing the door. I kicked off my boots and climbed under the covers, but even with Angus keeping watch, I didn't sleep until daylight.

Sixteen

Except for a sore ankle and the slit in the screen door, last night's drama might never have happened. I slept in and arose to sunshine. Angus was already awake and prowling through the house. When he heard me stir, he started to whine to let me know he needed to go out.

I took a closer look at the damaged screen as we exited the porch, wondering how on earth I'd slept so soundly through the break-in. Angus must have been sedated or otherwise subdued because he surely would have alerted me to a prowler. I remembered now the way he'd sniffed the ground when I let him out after dinner and wondered if someone might have tossed a chunk of drugged meat into the yard. Still recovering from near-starvation, the poor dog likely would have gobbled it up despite a strange smell or taste.

I checked the area for clues but found nothing other than a heel print in the dirt that I thought might be my own.

A trio of squirrels foraging for acorns kept Angus entertained while I found a sunny spot on the steps where I could sit and keep an eye on him. He seemed perfectly fine this morning, but the sooner I took him in for a checkup and shots, the better I would feel.

I'd already decided to make a trip back to Charleston soon, anyway. My mother hadn't felt well enough to come to the phone the last two times I'd called, and I was starting to worry that the chemo might be taking too much of a toll. Aunt Lynrose had tried her best to reassure me, but I wouldn't have peace of mind until I saw for myself. Maybe I would also drop in on Papa. Since my mother had been staying in Charleston for her treatments, I rarely saw him. I couldn't even remember the last time we'd spoken, but that wasn't unusual. Even though he was the one person I could talk to about the ghosts—we would always have that bond—I no longer tried to bridge the gulf between us. I had finally accepted that, for whatever reason, he needed his distance.

Absently, I plucked a stem of bee balm that grew near the steps and lifted the purple blossom to my nose. The morning was impossibly peaceful, the lake a quiet mirror reflecting nothing more sinister than sun, sky and the wavering images of the evergreens. I got up and walked down the stepping-stones to the pier where I leaned over the rail to gaze into those still depths. I could see nothing, of course. The water was too cloudy. But it wasn't hard to imagine the ruins of Thorngate Cemetery at the bottom. There was a faint hum in the air that I thought might be the echo of those bells. But when I listened closely, I heard only the gentle lap of water against wood pilings and the occasional thump of the boat.

Tossing the flower into the lake, I went back up the steps to the yard where Angus sat watching the squirrels. I was tempted to pack him up and head back to Charleston today. Just abandon the restoration regardless of my contract and business reputation. I needed to get out of this place. Something very alarming was happening in Asher Falls, and somehow I'd become a part of it. Might even be the reason for it. I didn't understand why or how, but I couldn't help but think my role here was preordained. The anxiety I'd felt last night in the clearing—the fear of my own destiny—had left me shaken.

And yet...I didn't leave. I sat there in the lemony scented sunshine as if I hadn't a care in the world. Because somehow I knew that whatever—*whoever*—had led me here in the first place would find a way to bring me back.

Alive or dead, Ashers are compelled to return home.

Why that particular snippet popped into my head at that precise moment I couldn't imagine. I tried to ignore it because I didn't want to dwell on Pell Asher this morning. Despite his charisma, my time with him had been very disconcerting. How odd to think that our paths had crossed so long ago, and I'd never even known it. How stranger still that he'd seen me playing in Rosehill Cemetery as a child and remembered it after so many years.

On the heels of that reflection, my own memory surfaced, hazy with time and distance and invoked, no doubt, by a combination of concern for my mother and the strange events that had unfolded since my arrival. Reacting to the stimuli, the shutter in my brain clicked once more, and an image slowly came into focus.

I could see myself on the floor of our living room, legs drawn up, arms wrapped around my knees as I listened through an open window to Mama and Aunt Lynrose on the front porch, lulled as always by the lovely cadence of their Lowcountry drawls. I had been six or seven at the time and had yet to learn of the ghosts. But my world had always been guarded and insular, and those accents had given me a glimpse of the lush and exotic. My mother and aunt were very beautiful women, exuding a bygone femininity that smelled of honeysuckle, sandalwood and fresh linen. Papa, by contrast, smelled of the earth. Or was that me? To Mama's horror, I often had little half moons of dirt beneath my nails, the odd leaf or twig stuck to my hair. Even wearing my Sunday best, a bit of the graveyard seemed to cling to me.

I'd been sitting with my cheek resting on my knees, drowsy in the warm breeze that stirred the lace curtains. I even remembered the incessant drone of a bee trapped against the screen and the smell of freshly mown grass. It was a typical summer afternoon, dreamy and hypnotic, until the sudden anger in my aunt's voice brought my head up. I'd never heard her speak to my mother in that tone.

"Do you have any idea what I would give to be in your shoes? You have a husband and daughter who love you. What more do you want?"

"You don't understand—"

"Oh, I understand. You always imagined yourself having the perfect life, the perfect husband, the perfect child. It was what everyone else expected of you, too. But dreams go awry, Etta, and life gets messy. What's done is done. You need to forget about the past."

"I thought I had," Mama said wistfully. "But then I found myself driving up there the other day."

My aunt gasped. "After all these years? Why would you do such a thing?"

"To visit the grave."

There was a long pause, during which I'd held my breath. I didn't understand much of that conversation, but I knew it was serious because my aunt never raised her voice. She doted on Mama. Only a year or so separated them in age, but Aunt Lynrose had always seemed both younger and older to me. Younger because she still had the coquettish quality of a girl while my mother grew more solemn with each passing year. And older because she was so fiercely protective of Mama. Their closeness had always filled me with deep yearning because they shared secrets I could never be privy to. Sister secrets.

"And?" Lynrose asked softly.

My mother paused. "It was a very strange moment."

"What do you mean?"

"I can't explain it any more than I can put into words how I felt driving through that town." Her voice dropped. "It's as if the soul of that place has been eaten away. The people, the houses…even the very air seems befouled. I can't stand to think of my little girl in such an awful place."

"You don't have to. She's right here with you. Exactly where she belongs."

"For now." In the ensuing silence, I could imagine my mother's hand going to her throat, plucking nervously at the gold cross she always wore. "Oh, Lyn. I've been so weak. I've never let that child fully into my heart because I was so afraid someone would come for her."

"They won't. How *can* they?"

"You know how."

"Too many years have passed. She's ours now, Etta. Just accept it as a blessing and let that child into your heart," Lynrose murmured, but I had heard something in my aunt's voice—a palpable fear—that made me shudder now in memory.

The images fluttered back into the shadows of my past, leaving me deeply troubled by what I'd overheard. But had I really overheard it? Maybe that conversation was nothing more than a remembered dream or a false recollection planted by my own fears. I had so many memories of my mother and aunt. Over the span of my childhood, I'd spent hours and hours by that open window as they reminisced and gossiped on the front porch. Why would I have buried that particular memory?

Even if it was real, I wouldn't have been able to recall everything in such detail. Not after so many years. I must have embellished an impression. Besides, it was too much of a leap to assume the town in question was Asher Falls. What could possibly have driven my mother all the way up here? Whose grave had she felt compelled to visit? And why had she always feared that someone would come for me when even the woman who gave birth to me hadn't wanted me?

As if drawn by my disquiet, Angus came over to plop down at the bottom of the steps. I rested my chin on my knees as I reached down to scratch behind the ear nubs, but my thoughts were still on that conversation. *It's as if the soul of that place has been eaten away. The people, the houses...even the very air seems befouled.*

That was a near perfect description of Asher Falls, but I still couldn't believe my mother had been talking about this town. I certainly couldn't picture her here. In some ways, she'd lived an even more sheltered existence than I had. She knew nothing of the ghosts and had scoffed at any mention of the paranormal, especially the stories Papa had told me of his childhood in the mountains.

The sun was warm on my shoulders, but I found myself shivering. The longer I stayed here, the more convinced I became that my restoration business had not been picked randomly from a phone book or the internet. My arrival was part of a design, a grand scheme that went back to those days in Rosehill Cemetery when Pell Asher had watched me play among the dead.

After I loaded up my tools, I came back around the house to collect Angus. A woman stood at the end of the pier tossing something into the water, and my heart lurched until I reminded myself a ghost wasn't likely to appear before dusk. And, anyway, even though she had her back to me, I recognized Tilly Pattershaw's slight form.

Angus still lay in the shade watching the squirrels, and I thought it odd that he hadn't barked when she came up. He didn't seem the least bit alarmed by her presence. In fact, he looked half-asleep. I bent to give him a pat before I started down the stepping-stones, coughing discreetly so as not to catch her unaware. But she paid me no mind even when my boots clattered on the wooden planks of the pier.

"Ms. Pattershaw?" I said softly as I approached.

"I'm called Tilly," she said, without turning.

"Good morning. I'm Amelia."

"I know who you are, girl."

"I guess Luna told you that I'd be staying here for a while. Thank you for getting everything ready for me. And thank you especially for your help last night." I moved up beside her at the railing. "I don't know how I would have gotten my dog free if you hadn't come along when you did."

"I'm not here for thanks," she said stoutly.

"I never thought you were. Still…I'm very grateful." I motioned toward the house. "Someone cut a hole in the screen and took Angus off the porch last night. You didn't see anyone else in the woods, did you?"

"I saw no one but you, girl." Her gaze darted over me, and I felt the oddest quiver at the base of my spine. I wasn't afraid of Tilly Pattershaw…far from it. I was genuinely happy to see her. But there was an undercurrent in her voice, the shadow of something dark in her eyes that made me grip the railing until my knuckles whitened. It was only with some effort that I was able to relax my fingers.

"You did notice the traps that were set all around the clearing, didn't you?"

"Don't you worry none about that." She tossed another handful of crumbs into the water and then turned, her assessment once again quick and sharp. Contrary to Bryn Birch's assertion, the woman seemed in complete control of her faculties. "I took care of them traps."

"That's good to know." I had so much more I wanted to ask her about the episode in the woods, but I remembered Thane's caution that she had little use for strangers, and I didn't want to frighten her away.

We fell silent as I watched her feed the fish. She was a plain woman, but I found great beauty in the movement of her hands, encased though they were in a pair of cotton gloves. She wore her gray hair scraped back in a bun at her nape, a harsh style for such a careworn complexion, but the wind-loosened tendrils gave her face an unexpected sweetness that belied her gruff demeanor and shadowy eyes. She was a woman of contrasts, I thought, and I liked that about her.

I made a slight movement, and she glanced up, her eyes revealing a flutter of emotion before she quickly returned her attention to the water.

"Luna said your house is down that path," I said. "Is it close by?"

"Close enough."

"Do you come here often to feed the fish?"

"I come here to visit the cemetery."

"The cemetery? You mean…the one down there?" I glanced into the murky depths and shivered. "You had family in Thorngate?" I asked carefully.

"Most of my people are buried in Georgia," she said.

What about Freya? I wondered. "Thane Asher told me that the bodies weren't moved before the water rose. Is that true?"

"He told you right. They're still down there. Right under our feet. The Fougerants and the Hibberds and those poor little Moultrie boys. My girl knew every last one of them."

I glanced at her, startled. "What do you mean?"

She hesitated, but the motion of her hand was steady. "She used to come here to read the headstones when she got lonely. She knew all the names by heart. They were her friends, she said. And the graveyard was her hideaway. Her special place."

I felt that tingle along my spine again. "I had a place like that when I was a child. Rosehill Cemetery. It was my special hideaway. My sanctuary. The only spot I ever felt truly safe."

She nodded. "My girl's gone now, but I reckon she'd still come here if she could."

I didn't trust myself to speak at that moment. My heart had quickened, and I felt a little breathless as I envisioned Freya's ghost hovering on this very pier. I wanted to tell Tilly about her, but I knew better than to acknowledge the dead. And I knew, too, that the restless spirit of a loved one rarely offered comfort. It was far better for Tilly to think of her daughter at peace.

Still, I couldn't help wondering if she could sense Freya's presence here, if she somehow knew that her daughter lingered. Was that why the ghost had told me to leave so vehemently? Was I intruding on her peace… her sanctuary?

I didn't think so. It had been my experience that places were rarely haunted. *People* were haunted.

I turned back to Tilly. "You say your family is from Georgia?"

"Union County," she said. "I was born and raised in the shadow of Blood Mountain."

"How long have you lived here?"

"Since I was a girl. I was fifteen when I left home. I came here to study with a midwife. When she died, she left her place to me, so I stayed on."

"You've been here most of your life, then."

"I reckon I have."

"It's beautiful country," I said.

Her eyes lifted to the mountains, and she shivered.

"Are you still a practicing midwife?"

"I gave that up years ago." She glanced down at her

gloved hands. "Just as well. Not many babies being born around here these days."

"I guess when businesses started to close a lot of people left town."

Her gaze went back to the mountains. "The lucky ones."

"What do you mean by that?" When she didn't answer, I touched her sleeve and felt a slight tremor go through her. "Why did you come into the woods last night, Tilly? How did you know I needed help?"

"Sound carries at night," she said.

"Did you hear the howling?" I asked urgently.

"I heard your dog. I could tell he was in trouble."

"But you told me to get out of the woods. You said something was coming." I studied her face. "What was out there last night?"

Her voice hardened. "You ask too many questions, girl."

"Because I need to know what's going on! Strange thing have been happening ever since I came to town. What's out there in those woods? What lives up on that mountain?"

She turned with a scowl. "It don't live in the woods, girl, or up on that mountain. It don't live anywhere because it's not any*thing*."

The hair at my nape lifted as I looked into her eyes. "But I've felt it in the wind. I've heard the howling. It's out there. I know it is. It's cold and evil—"

Her hand whipped out to grip my wrist, her fingers digging into my flesh until I jerked away. "Go home, girl. Go back to where you came from. Best not meddle in things you don't understand."

I massaged my wrist, shaken. "I can't go home. I

have a job to do here." And I needed this job. I had a living to make, a business to run. My professional reputation was on the line.

"Best not be so stubborn."

"I'm not being stubborn, I'm being practical. I signed a contract. I can't just walk away. And, anyway…" I watched her warily. "Why does it matter? If it's not any*thing,* how can it hurt me?"

Her voice lowered to a desperate whisper. "Don't you understand? It's not what's out there you need to be a-feared of." She placed a gloved hand over her heart as she leaned in, and for the first time, I thought there might be a hint of madness in her eyes. "It's what's in *here.*"

Seventeen

The black sports car was parked near the cemetery entrance when I arrived a little while later, but Thane was nowhere in sight. Normally, I would have left Angus to his own devices outside the fence, but today I brought him in with me because I didn't dare leave him alone. He shadowed me down the pathway, as if he didn't want to let me out of his sight, either.

The day was so warm I stripped off my jacket and tied the sleeves around my waist as we moved through the lych-gate into the Asher section. I could smell sage in the unseasonable heat and every now and then a whiff of rosemary until the trail led us far enough into the cemetery where shade and neglect bred the gloomier scents of ivy and dead leaves. Through breaks in the evergreen canopy, I caught glimpses of white fleece hanging motionless over the mountains, the dark edges hinting at rain.

I spotted Thane coming from the direction of the mausoleum, and as I paused at the circle of angels to wait for him, my gaze lifted to those eerie, otherworldly faces. It was easy now to pick out the Asher qualities I'd noticed in the old photographs. The high cheekbones. The finely sculpted noses and lips. As I studied those familiar features, something came to me. The angels faced east, not to await the rising sun, but to gaze upon the mountains.

The foreboding conjured by that revelation skittered away as I turned to watch Thane weave his way through the gravestones. He wore a pair of faded jeans with a gray cotton shirt rolled up at the sleeves, and I found myself inadvertently comparing his casual outfit to the more formal attire favored by Devlin. His elegant wardrobe had been well beyond the means of a police detective, but Devlin was no ordinary cop. He came from old Charleston money, and I imagined his dead parents had left him quite well-off so that he never had to worry about extravagances even after his grandfather disowned him. I still found it more than a little ironic that Devlin had turned his back on everything Thane now strove so hard to reclaim for the Ashers. But even though Devlin had shunned tradition and his grandfather's expectations, he was still very much a product of his upbringing. He was a private, graceful, sometimes old-fashioned man given to aloofness and brooding. Thane had a little of that reserve, too, but I suspected in him it was self-preservation.

I berated myself for the constant comparisons. Thane was his own man, and maybe it was high time I heeded Aunt Lynrose's advice to my mother and stopped living in the past. Stopped yearning for what couldn't be.

"Good morning," he called.

Almost begrudgingly, I lifted my hand to wave at him.

He came up on the shadowy side of the angels, so that I didn't notice anything amiss straightaway. What I did take in was last night's stubble on his chin and the fatigue lines around his mouth that hadn't been there at dinner. His gaze went straight to the angels, and I saw a frown fleet across his features before the pleasant mask dropped smoothly back into place.

Then he turned to me, and the force of his gaze drew an uneasy shiver. The turmoil in those green depths didn't match the placid expression or the easygoing demeanor. No shade or mask could hide the violent intensity of those eyes.

"I hope you don't mind my dropping by like this," he said.

"No…no, of course not." I recovered my poise and shrugged. "Why would I mind? It's a public place. You have as much right to be here as I do. Especially considering this is your family's cemetery."

Angus sidled up to Thane, and as he bent to give him a pat, a shaft of sunlight struck the side of his face, highlighting a cut at his left temple.

"What happened to you?" I blurted.

His eyes flickered, a brief darkening. "A miscalculation. It won't happen again."

I was dying to know the particulars of that miscalculation, but something told me this was as much information as I'd likely get. Something also told me that in this instance, ignorance might be bliss.

He straightened and glanced around the cemetery. "This is the first time I've been up here in years. I had no idea it was so overgrown. You can barely see some of the monuments for the ivy and brambles."

"It's not as bad as it looks. Most of the headstones

are in good shape, and I've seen no trace of vandalism. Defacement is usually a big problem in older cemeteries."

"Vandals can be caught," he said. "Time and neglect are stealthier culprits."

I looked up at him. "Meaning?"

He shrugged. "Defacement is defacement in my book."

"Are you saying the cemetery has been deliberately neglected out of disrespect?"

"It's like I told you on the ferry. Thorngate still inspires strong feelings." He spoke in a hushed tone, not solely out of reverence, I suspected, but also from habit and instinct. This was not a place for harsh voices. He would have been taught that as a boy, given his grandfather's veneration for the family cemetery. "Over the years, this place has become a symbol of everything the town lost because of Asher greed."

"Your family didn't make provisions for the upkeep when ownership changed hands?"

A flicker of impatience suggested that I'd failed to grasp some elemental aspect of that exchange. "That would have defeated the whole purpose of Grandfather's grand gesture. What good is atonement without sacrifice?"

I had a feeling there were nuances and subtleties to Pell Asher's "grand gesture" that an outsider like me would never be able to comprehend. "If the neglect is deliberate, why am I here?"

He squinted into the sun. "Evidently, someone thought it time for a restoration."

"And you wouldn't know anything about that?"

One brow rose ironically. "Me? Hardly. You know my feelings on cemetery expenditures. No offense."

"None taken." I had a feeling he might be a little more interested in the restoration than he let on, though. "I saw you by the mausoleum just now. Did you go inside?"

"Just a quick look around. Why?"

"Your grandfather thought you might be willing to go down into the tomb with me. He said the vaults are not to be missed. He also said when you were a boy you were quite taken with the Sleeping Bride."

He grimaced, but I could see a twitch at the corner of his mouth, and he seemed to relax. "I was a ghoulish little bastard, all right. Did he explain that the Sleeping Bride is, in fact, some great-great-great-aunt perfectly preserved under glass?"

"Yes, and I guess I'm ghoulish, too, because I'd love to see her."

"She's quite a spectacle. As fine a testament to Asher arrogance as you're likely to find anywhere."

I slanted him a glance. "And here I thought the angels were impressive. Particularly after I discovered the family resemblance."

"So you noticed." I caught the ghost of another smile as he turned back to the statues. "Personally, I prefer dear Aunt Emelyn. At least she had the grace and humility to die with a peaceful expression. The angels, on the other hand, are a little too self-satisfied for my taste. Although there is something haunting about the one in the middle. I've always wondered about her..." His voice trailed away on a curious note.

"What is it?"

He turned to gaze down at me, and I could have

sworn I saw something ominous pass swiftly across his non-Asher features before he shook it off. "Nothing. Nothing at all," he murmured, his gaze lingering on my lips.

I wondered if he was thinking about last night because I certainly was. When I'd first seen his car outside the gate, I told myself I would act as though the kiss had never happened. I wasn't so conceited as to think he'd come here to see me, anyway, and I certainly wasn't going to place undue importance on such an innocent buss. But try as I might, I couldn't get it out of my head. Like Thorngate Cemetery, that kiss was symbolic of everything that had been lost to me.

"You okay?" He was still gazing down at me very intently, head cocked as if I were some great mystery he intended to solve.

"I'm fine," I said in my best pretend-you-don't-see-that-ghost voice. "Why?"

"You seemed to drift off there for a minute, and I can't help noticing that you look a little tired this morning."

"Oh, that. I slept badly last night. In fact, I didn't sleep at all until sunup."

"Strange bed?"

"Strange everything." I didn't know how much I wanted to tell him. Encounters with the supernatural always complicated confidences. "Someone cut a hole in the screen door and took Angus off the back porch. I found him tied up in the woods surrounded by steel traps. Big ones. I think they were bear traps."

"*Bear* traps?" I saw a flash of that razor-wire temper before he knelt beside Angus.

"If Tilly hadn't come to our rescue, I don't know what would have happened."

"Tilly Pattershaw?"

"She came out of nowhere with a huge knife. It was pretty amazing. She cut Angus loose and then…" I trailed off.

"And then what?"

I thought of that terrible wind, the howling…and Tilly's warning not to meddle in things I didn't understand.

"And then nothing. We went home."

He ran his hands along Angus's ribs. "Did they hurt him?"

There was an undercurrent of aggression in the question that worried me. My gaze went inadvertently to the cut at his temple, and then I noticed the bruised and swollen knuckles on his right hand. Just what the devil had he been up to the night before?

"He seems fine. I thought the traps had been set for me at first."

He glanced up sharply. "Why would you think that?"

"It seemed obvious Angus had been used to lure me into the woods. And it occurred to me that someone might have gotten nervous over my discovery."

"The hidden grave?"

"Yes. But then I wondered why someone would place traps all around the clearing when I would be coming from only one direction."

"They were probably after coyotes," he said. "The packs have been unusually troublesome this year."

"What about wolves? Wayne Van Zandt said he's seen some around here."

"I've heard other people say that, too, but I've never

spotted one." He glanced up, the hard gleam of suppressed violence still taking me aback. "You didn't hear
or see anything last night?"

"No, but I think someone must have been in the yard
earlier when I let Angus out before bedtime. When
I found him in the woods, I could smell something
chemical on his breath. I think he was drugged."

Thane rose. "Did you call the police?"

"No."

"Why not?"

"Because I don't trust Wayne Van Zandt." I told him
about my conversation with Van Zandt at the police station and his callous offer to come out and take care of
my stray. "He's the only one other than you and Luna
who even knows about Angus."

Thane was silent for a moment. "You're assuming
no one else has seen you with the dog, but you had him
here at the cemetery with you yesterday, didn't you?"

"No one else was around, though. Not yesterday."

"Just because you didn't see anyone doesn't mean
you weren't seen."

I thought about the old man who had appeared in the
cemetery on my first day. I hated to think of anyone
watching me while I worked, but that man's repulsive
behavior had been so unnerving, the memory of him
was a shiver up my spine. I lifted my gaze to the statues and for an instant—the way the sun hit them—the
ethereal faces twisted into something ugly and sinister. Something…demonic. It was only my imagination,
of course, but I saw that hideous man's features—the
pale eyes, the jutting cheekbones, the hawklike nose—
superimposed on the faces of those angels.

I shook off the illusion and turned back to Thane.

He was still staring down at me, and in that moment, I was very glad that he didn't look like the Ashers.

"I don't understand why they had to use Angus as bait," I said. "Why go to the trouble of drugging my dog and taking him from my porch?"

"To get rid of the evidence," Thane said. "You've been asking questions about dog fighting. That makes people jumpy."

I paused. "Is that what happened to your face and hand? You asked too many questions?"

He said nothing as he glanced down at Angus.

"You found the kennel, didn't you?" I asked softly.

The silence stretched, punctuated by the stillness of the day. It was strange how the quiet roused my drowsy senses, like a gentle hand waking someone from a deep sleep. I could still remember the peaceful feel of dappled sunlight on my face and the comforting fragrance of earth, ivy and moss, that fecund perfume so peculiar to old cemeteries. In the distance, draped in the ethereal blue haze of the pine forest, the ancient mountains beckoned.

A thorn pricked the idyllic setting, and I suddenly felt very frightened. Not of Thane. Not even of that bizarre man with the wagon. I was afraid of those mountains, fearful of something inside me that had responded to the siren call of those seductive peaks.

Don't you understand? It's not what's out there you need to be a-feared of. It's what's in here.

A breeze shuddered through the trees, and as Thane's gaze met mine, I felt an odd little thrill shoot through me, almost like a premonition. A sign.

Destiny.

"Keep Angus close," he said. "And stay out of the woods after dark."

Eighteen

The fear I'd experienced a moment ago was already starting to fade as we walked back through the lych-gate into the public section of the cemetery. But I was glad enough to turn my back on those looming hills. The sun was warm on my face, and I could hear the pleasant trill of the wood thrushes in the trees outside the entrance. A more peaceful setting, I could hardly imagine, and yet…I couldn't resist glancing over my shoulder where mountain met sky in that timeless union.

"Will you take me to that grave?" Thane said at my side, and had I not been so adept at schooling my reaction, I might have jumped. For a moment, I'd forgotten all about him as I contemplated the mystique of those distant blue walls.

I turned back around. "There isn't much to see. I gave you a thorough description at dinner. A north-south oriented grave decorated with seashells, pebbles and a headstone without an inscription."

"Yes, I know. But I need to see it for myself." He

surveyed the woods with a frown. "That's still Asher land. Now that you've brought it to my attention, I can't just ignore that grave. It's my responsibility to find out who's buried there."

His responsibility. Not Hugh's. Not his grandfather's. *His.*

I remembered at dinner how Hugh had shrugged aside my discovery, claiming the mountains were full of such remote burial sites. And Pell's main concern had seemed to be that no one had warned me about the laurel bald. I wondered what either of them would say about Thane's interest.

"Unless someone comes forward with a name, it'll be difficult," I warned him. "Unmarked graves are hard enough to identify in old graveyards, but at least one has the help of site maps and descendant recollections. Here, there's not even an inscription to go by. Without the guideline of year of birth and death, you'll have to wade through thousands of records, and that's even assuming a death certificate was filed. The process could take months. Years even."

"The old courthouse has boxes of files stored in the basement. I guess we could have a look through those. Although I would think vital records are computerized these days."

"Not the old ones, especially in rural counties. But..." I glanced up at him. "You said *we.*"

He held the gate for me, then closed it behind us. When he turned, I saw worry lines between his brows. "I'd like your help with this. You know more about these kinds of searches than I do."

I said flatly, "Your best bet is to ask around. In a

town this size, someone has to know who's buried there."

"People around here don't like answering questions. They're too afraid of stepping into someone else's business."

Did that reticence explain the reaction to the hidden grave at dinner last night? And Tilly's warning about meddling in things I didn't understand?

I pushed a strand of hair back from my face. "I'd love to help, but I'm committed to the restoration. My first priority has to be the cemetery. That won't leave a lot of free time for tracking down records." It was a cursory excuse at best because I already knew I would help him. An unmarked grave, no matter how old or remote, couldn't be allowed to stand. Whoever was buried there deserved a name. Deserved to be remembered.

"Will you at least take me to the grave? I can find it on my own, but it'll save time if you show me the way."

I decided not to remind him that he'd just warned me to stay out of the woods. Besides, it was hours until dark, and I had a feeling nothing would happen with an Asher along.

"All right. I'll show you."

"Should we take Angus with us?" he asked.

"We'll have to. I'm not leaving him here by himself."

He glanced down at me. "You're really spooked about last night, aren't you?"

"Can you blame me?"

"No. But try not to worry. I'll find out who set those traps."

"The same way you found the kennel? What did you do to them, Thane?"

His gaze dropped again to Angus. "Not nearly as much as I wanted to," he muttered, and I decided it was best to leave it at that.

We paused at my car just long enough to allow Angus to lap up some fresh water, and then the three of us entered the woods together, our footsteps silent on the mossy floor. It was cool and dim inside the trees, the air spicy with pine and cedar. As we walked along in that perpetual gloom, I thought again of Papa's mountain stories, but why should I waste time worrying about mythical creatures like vampires and werewolves when my world was full of ghosts? And now I had entered a new world, one of hidden graves, strange winds and whispering trees.

And Thane Asher.

He seemed distracted as we walked along, head slightly bowed, eyes on the ground. It seemed to me that the temperature had been steadily dropping the deeper we walked into the woods, and I stopped to put on my jacket. Thane automatically reached over to help me, and I felt a little tingle where his fingers brushed the back of my neck. If he noticed my slight withdrawal, he said nothing.

"Can I ask you something?"

He nodded without lifting his gaze from the path.

"At the risk of sounding insensitive, what happened to Wayne Van Zandt's face?"

He shrugged. "I can only tell you what I've heard. It's one of those things that people tend not to talk about."

"There seems to be a lot of forbidden topics around here," I murmured.

I caught the edge of a smile. "You catch on fast.

Anyway, it happened a long time ago, before I came here, so what I'm about to tell you is second- and third-hand information. Take it with a grain of salt. The story goes that he went up to the falls to meet someone one night. A girl he'd been seeing. He was found unconscious the next morning by the pool. He'd been badly mauled and nearly died from blood loss and infection. When he finally came around in the hospital, he didn't remember a thing."

"Not even the attack?"

"Nothing. But the wounds were consistent with a bear attack."

"He warned me about wild animals when I saw him the other day. I thought he was just trying to frighten me, but maybe his concern was genuine."

Thane swatted a gnat from his face. "I wouldn't assign too much nobility to Wayne Van Zandt's motives. He's had a chip on his shoulder for as long as I've known him."

"With good reason, it would seem."

"Yes, but remember, he's the same guy who offered to take care of your dog. And he would have probably derived a great deal of pleasure from doing so."

I glanced over my shoulder where Angus plodded along behind us on the trail. When he noticed my attention, he gave a little whine and came up between us, nudging Thane off the path. "Hey!"

I laughed and bent to give his mangled head a pat.

Thane good-naturedly fell into step behind us. "You've got yourself quite a companion," he said.

"I know. He's wonderful."

"Will you take him with you when you leave here?"

I answered without a second thought. "Of course."

"He's lucky he found you, then. I'd like to think Samson happened upon someone like you."

"Maybe he did." But neither of us sounded convinced.

Angus soon grew bored of my pace and loped ahead. I called him back because I didn't want him out of my sight in the woods.

"Now that I know what happened to Wayne Van Zandt, I understand something that Ivy said to me the other day."

Thane had moved back up beside me, and our shoulders kept brushing even though I hugged the edge of the path.

"What was that?" he asked carefully.

His wariness amused me. "You do realize she has a crush on you."

When he didn't say anything, I glanced at his scowling face. "Come on. It's just a crush."

"Ivy's not like other girls," he said. "There've been some incidents."

My smile faded at his tone. "Like what?"

"Stalking," he said grimly.

"Stalking? As in following you?"

"Yes, and breaking into my car. Stealing some personal items."

"How do you know it was her?"

"Trust me, I know."

"What did you do?"

He shrugged. "Not much I could do. I couldn't prove it and I thought it best to just ignore her rather than to make a big deal of it. I figured she'd outgrow it in time."

"Has she?"

"I'd hoped so. Until the other day, I hadn't seen her

around much." He paused. "So what did she say to you?"

That you would never choose an outsider, I thought. "We were talking about the waterfall. She said it was a thin place. A location where the living world and the Other world connect."

"Like vortexes," he said. "What did Bryn call them?"

"Gateways to the realm of the dead," I said evenly. "According to Ivy, people used to go up to the falls because they thought they could glimpse heaven, but now they stay away because they're afraid. Sidra cut her off before she could finish, but I have a feeling she was talking about Wayne's attack."

Thane shrugged. "You never know. These hills are full of folklore and superstition. Even the educated aren't immune. You heard the way Catrice and Bryn talked about the mountains."

"They do seem to hold them in reverence. Luna, too, I think. She told me her mother used to say that she would wither and die if she left this place."

"I somehow think Luna would survive," he muttered, and I wondered if he knew about her relationship with Hugh. "Actually…" he said slowly, "she was the girl Wayne went up to the falls to meet that night."

I swung around in surprise. "Luna Kemper?"

"There's only one Luna around here," he said. "She and Wayne were close back then. Inseparable, people say. Then my uncle came back from Europe and…well, you've seen him."

"Wayne is an attractive man, too. I'm sure before the accident he was a real heartbreaker."

"But he's not an Asher." Thane's voice was so matter-of-fact, I wondered if I might have imagined a slight edge.

"That certainly explains Wayne's attitude," I mused. "He was very contemptuous when I mentioned that Luna was the one who made all the arrangements for the restoration. I had the distinct feeling there was bad blood, at least on his end. But you said his accident happened years ago before you came here. That's a long time to hold a grudge."

"Grudges are like superstitions. You know they don't make sense, but you cling to them, anyway."

We walked along in silence for a moment, and I became overly aware of the forest sounds. The scurry of tiny feet through the underbrush. The rustle of leaves in the treetops. I glanced up, almost expecting to see hundreds of birds staring down at us, but the branches were empty.

"When did Maris come into the picture?" I asked.

"A few years ago. She was in town visiting a cousin and someone introduced her to Hugh."

"Was he still with Luna?"

"They were together off and on for years. But by that time, Maris had a certain attraction that Luna could no longer offer. Namely, youth. Her money was a bonus."

"That sounds—"

"Cold? Mercenary? I told you we Ashers are a self-serving lot," he said grimly. "Grandfather was the one who pushed for the union. Hugh had turned forty without producing an heir, and God forbid the Asher bloodline die out."

"And yet there's been no baby."

"Ironic, isn't it?"

"What about Edward?"

"He and my mother had no children. I can't speak to his past before they married. Although I think he and Bryn were together for a time. That was long before she had Sidra, though."

"Bryn and Edward...Luna and Hugh. What about Catrice?"

"Odd woman out, I guess." He shrugged. "There's been no Asher offspring for a whole generation, so you can imagine Grandfather's impatience."

"Blood and land," I murmured.

"Aw." He slanted a glance down at me. "So he shared his philosophy with you."

"Yes, and it all sounds so archaic. So seventeenth century."

"It is archaic," Thane agreed. "And I've always thought it resembled the Fisher King myth. Grandfather's visions of the family and himself are nothing if not grandiose. In his eyes, land and family are inexorably entwined."

"Restore the bloodline, restore the kingdom."

"Something like that."

"Who's the Grail knight in his story?"

"Well," Thane said softly. "They do call you the restorer."

I tripped over a root and would have gone down if Thane's hand hadn't shot out to steady me. "I restore old cemeteries the hard way," I said and held out my palms. "See? I have lots and lots of calluses. There's nothing mystical or mythical about what I do."

His eyes glinted. "I was teasing."

"Oh." I tried to take it as such, but something niggled at the back of my mind. That same feeling of destiny that had plagued me in the clearing. That unsettling notion that I had been brought here for a reason.

They do call you the restorer.

"Anyway," Thane was saying. "I suppose Grandfather still has hope of an heir, but I'm not so sure the marriage will last that long."

A divorce would probably make Luna happy.

I thought of that overheard rendezvous, the intimate murmuring and animalistic moans of pleasure....

I drew a sharp breath. That day at the library, I couldn't leave those sounds behind fast enough, but now I found the voyeuristic memory titillating. And that in itself was disturbing.

As we neared the summit, I felt something in the air, an odd vibration that thrummed through my veins and teased like a feather along my nerve endings. The breeze lifted my hair and stroked my face like a lover's caress. I closed my eyes on a shudder. Then slowly I turned my gaze upon the man beside me. For a moment, his face seemed to morph into...

Thane scowled down at me. "Are you okay?"

"Do you feel something in the air?" I asked, pulling my jacket tightly around me.

The frown deepened. "Rain, maybe. I noticed storm clouds moving in earlier."

That could explain the vibration, couldn't it? The electrical shock that had pulsed through my body when I looked up and saw Devlin's face?

Thane's gaze lingered. "Are you sure you're all right? Maybe this wasn't such a good idea. Why don't you wait here for me? I'm sure I'll be able to find the grave on my own."

"No, I'm fine. Something strange just happened."

"What?"

How could I explain what I'd experienced when I didn't understand it myself? Maybe it was all the talk of bloodlines and fertility, but the vibration seemed to stir something deep inside me, almost akin to a sexual excitement. "It was..." I paused and started again. "For a moment, when I looked at you...I saw someone else..."

He studied me curiously. "Who?"

I glanced away, unable to hold his gaze. "No one. It doesn't matter."

"Lack of sleep," he pronounced. "Fatigue can play strange tricks on the mind."

I willed my heartbeat to slow. "I guess you're right. Kind of like a waking dream. Anyway, I'm okay now."

He cocked his head. "Listen."

"What is it?"

"You can hear the falls from here."

We were silent, heads turned toward the summit. Over the distant rush of water, another sound came to me. A whisper that undulated like a gentle wave through the trees.

Amelia...Amelia...

Nineteen

We crested the hill and started down the rugged incline toward the laurel bald, the sun at our backs. We were not that far from Thorngate and the highway, but it felt as if we'd been transported a million miles into nowhere. I saw a lizard sunning on a rock, and high overhead, a lone hawk floated serenely on an air current. But no other living creature stirred as we made our way down the slope.

I was favoring my ankle now, though it didn't really hurt. But an uncomfortable stiffness in the joint made me wary of a misstep, and I didn't mind when Thane offered a hand over some of the more treacherous terrain. The vibration had stopped, and I'd regained my equilibrium. I could view him now as a pleasant, attractive man whose company I had come to enjoy. Nothing more.

As we reached the bald, I realized it was a very good thing we'd brought Angus along. In my mind's eye, I'd pinpointed the exact spot where I had entered the thicket, but now that we were here, the breaks in the wall of scrubby growth looked exactly the same. Without Angus to once again guide me through that maze, I would have been hopelessly lost. Papa was right. The sameness of the landscape played tricks on the eyes and on the senses. I wasn't able to pick out a familiar landmark until we scrambled down the overhang that sheltered the grave.

Angus had bounded ahead, and now he sat facing the mound, tail thumping excitedly as he waited for us to catch up.

"This is the place?" Thane asked.

"Yes. The grave is up there, underneath the overhang. See the foxglove? They didn't grow there wild. Someone planted them. But if you were just passing by, you'd never notice."

Thane glanced around. "Hell of a place to bring a body. Must have been torture getting it through all that mountain laurel. Unless…" He trailed off, but I knew where his mind was headed.

"Unless the body was still mobile? I know. I've thought of that. But the mounding of the dirt is deliberate and there's a headstone. Anyone trying to cover up a crime would never be so brazen. And, anyway, I don't think the grave is hidden. I think it's protected."

As we stood there talking, Angus got up and ambled over to the grave to paw at some leaves. Then with an odd whimper, he came over to nuzzle my hand. A moment later, he returned to the grave and repeated the ritual.

"What's he doing?" Thane asked.

"I have no idea. There's something about this place that excites him. He's the one that led me here. He kept barking and barking until I followed him through the woods, and when I found him, he was just sitting there with his gaze fixed on the grave."

"He must smell something," Thane said.

"I don't think so. The grave is too old for that."

"Dogs have a more developed sense of smell than we do. He's probably picking up on a scent that's undetectable to us. Maybe one that's lingered here for years."

I thought suddenly of that overheard conversation between my mother and aunt. Was it possible this was the grave they'd been referring to? Had Angus somehow picked up the scent of my mother here and on me?

It seemed too far-fetched. That conversation had taken place years ago. Even if this was the same grave, Mama's scent would have long since been washed away. And if I couldn't imagine her in Asher Falls, I certainly couldn't picture her climbing down a rugged hillside and trudging through a laurel bald.

But Angus's behavior was intriguing. Obviously, he knew something about this place that I didn't.

A nosegay of wildflowers had been placed near the headstone, and I knelt quickly to inspect them. "These weren't here yesterday."

"They look fresh," Thane said. "Someone must have been here early this morning."

"I told you at dinner, this grave has been taken care of for years. See the way the grass and weeds have been scraped away? In the Southern folk cemetery, that's a sign of respect, leaving the bare earth exposed that way. It's mostly an archaic tradition and rarely see in this area, but at one time, people spent hours and hours hoeing every scrap of grass from gravesites. It takes a lot of work and patience to keep it so clean."

"Why the seashells?" he asked. "The ocean is miles from here."

"It's another custom, sometimes symbolic of a watery passage. You'll see whole graves covered in cockle shells, especially here in the South."

"And the roses on the headstone…you said a full bloom and a bud symbolize a dual burial."

"That's one interpretation and used to be indicative of a mother who died in childbirth and was buried with her stillborn baby. But gravestone art can be subjective. The same symbol can mean different things in different areas and different time periods." I studied the grave for a moment, trying to sort out the messages. "There are a lot of clues here, but I think they speak as much to the caretaker as to the deceased. Whoever visits this grave puts a lot of value in tradition. This site has been cared for with love and respect."

I placed my hand flat on the headstone and felt again that strange jolt, that overwhelming feeling of suffocation. My head swam as my ears started to buzz, and I jerked back with a gasp. If my mother had somehow stumbled upon this site, I understood why it had troubled her. The place seemed charged with some dark emotion.

Thane glanced up. "You okay?"

"I just need to get a little air."

I stood and moved away from the grave, uneasily scanning our surroundings. It was so quiet here, and the sun streaming down through the skeletal limbs of the laurel and rhododendron seemed unusually bright. I was only a few feet away from the grave, but the glare in my eyes was so brilliant and the shade beneath the overhang so deep that Thane had all but disappeared. I might have been alone. Forsaken in that desolate land-scape.

A terrible heaviness pressed down like a stone upon my chest. The suffocation I felt now was loneliness, so intense I could scarcely draw a breath.

An image came to me suddenly. A ghost in a dark dress, wavering reedlike on the pier as she gazed up the stepping-stones…willing me to see her.…

A shadow fell across my face, and I glanced up into the sun. For a moment, I could have sworn I saw a sil-houette poised at the edge of the overhang staring down at me. But when I lifted a hand to shade my eyes, it was gone. Dissolved like Freya's ghost back into the mist.

Freya's ghost.

An incessant dread had been tap, tap, tapping at my subconscious for a while now. The fear that I was being haunted by Freya Pattershaw. Was it only a matter of time before my energy began to wane? Before I grew pale and gaunt and hollow-eyed? Before I became like Devlin?

My knees went weak. Not a good sign. I found a place near the overhang where I could lean back against a warm rock while I tried to recover my strength.

By the time Thane emerged from the shade, I was feeling almost normal. "Do you think this could be Freya's grave?"

He glanced at me in surprise. "Freya Pattershaw? Why would you think that?"

I shoved my hands into my pockets. "You said no one likes to talk about her death. Maybe she was buried out here so that people could forget about her."

"Freya was buried in Thorngate," Thane said.

My gaze shot to his. "Which one?"

"The new one. She died after the old one was flooded."

I leaned back against the rock and closed my eyes for a moment. "You know this for a fact?"

"For a fact, no. But when I was a kid, I used to see Tilly in the cemetery. I always assumed she was visiting her daughter's grave." He scratched the back of his neck. "Am I missing something here? What does it matter where Freya Pattershaw was buried?"

"You want to know who's buried here, don't you? Unless someone comes forward with concrete information, it'll be a process of elimination."

He frowned. "You weren't kidding, then, when you said identification could take a long time."

"No. But it would go a lot faster if we could just find out who left those flowers."

"I'll ask around," he said. "In the meantime, we're close to the waterfall. If you still want to see it, I'll take you up there."

The sun was warm and pleasant on my face, but I found myself shivering at the prospect. What if the falls really was a gateway to the realm of the dead?

Twenty

I had to shed my jacket again by the time we reached the waterfall. The trek had taken us up and around the laurel bald, through a mountain meadow carpeted with goldenrod and along a rocky stream. As the hillside gave way to a more treacherous climb, we skirted the base of a sandstone cliff, eventually arriving at a natural archway that led us into a fern grotto shaded with sugar maples.

The waterfall was directly in front of us, the upper portion a series of cascades that merged into a single thirty-foot drop before plunging into a deep pool at the base of the cliff. All around us, craggy walls honeycombed with clefts rose at least fifty feet.

The beauty of the place was breathtaking, but already I could feel a spiny tickle at the base of my neck as I walked through the archway, Angus at my heels. I didn't like the claustrophobic feeling of being hemmed in. I could imagine a little too vividly the scenario with Wayne Van Zandt. Once he'd entered the enclosure, he would have been trapped by whatever had followed him through the arch.

Near the base of the falls, the mouth of a cave opened into darkness. Above the entrance, three circular symbols had been carved into the face of the rock. A slight breeze swept in behind us, and a whisper ran through the trees as my gaze fastened on those marks. I inhaled sharply at the sight. "Ivy told me about those symbols, but I never imagined they'd be so large."

"You want to take a closer look?"

My gaze traveled up the side of the cliff. "You're joking, right?"

Thane grinned. "It's not as dangerous as it looks. It's actually an easy climb."

"I'll have to take your word for that."

"You sure? You can't see them from here, but there are some smaller drawings up near that ledge." He pointed to a narrow shelf about ten feet from the top of the cliff.

"Like these?"

"I think so."

I squinted up at the symbols. "Ivy said that no one knows what they are or who carved them."

Thane shrugged. "All I can tell you is that they've been here for a long time. Up close, you can see where they've started to erode. You can also see chisel marks."

"I know what they are," I said a little breathlessly.

He turned in surprise. "You've seen them before?"

"Yes, on old gravestones. They're hex signs. And despite what Ivy said, I'm willing to bet I'm not the only one around here who knows what they are."

"Hex signs? What do they mean?"

"They're not as ominous as they sound. Mostly,

they're used to ward off bad luck or evil spirits. Kind of like the evil eye. You see them a lot in cemeteries that are in or near old Germanic communities, especially in Pennsylvania. I've also seen them on gravestones in Texas and North Carolina. It's a little unusual to find them in this area, though. And why *here?* Why over *that* cave?"

My fascination seemed lost on Thane. His attention had already been caught by a red-tailed hawk that had landed on another ledge at the top of the cliff.

"I wish I'd brought my camera." I moved more deeply into the enclosure to get a better look at the signs. "I wonder how long they've been here. There must be some information about them in the library. Surely someone has written about them."

"I wouldn't know," Thane said, his gaze tracking the hawk as it took flight. He walked over to the pool and knelt to skim his fingers through the water. "Ice-cold. It always is, no matter the time of year. Makes for an invigorating swim."

That got my attention. "You've been swimming in this pool?"

"When I was a kid. I wasn't supposed to come up here alone, so naturally I snuck away every chance I got."

Light struck the cut on the side of his face, making him seem both tough and vulnerable. An appealing dichotomy, I was coming to discover.

"You're braver than I am," I told him.

"You're the one who works alone in cemeteries."

"Most cemeteries aren't the least bit scary."

"How would you rate Thorngate?"

"Verdict is still out," I said lightly. My gaze lifted

again to the symbols. Something tugged at the edge of my memory, and I struggled to recall what I'd read about them.

"What's wrong?" he asked.

"I'm trying to remember what I know about hex signs. You almost always see them in multiples of at least three," I said. "The one on the outer edge, nearest the falls is the most common. It's called a sun wheel. The one in the center is a compass star. See how the points are rounded like flower petals?"

Thane rose and walked back to where I stood. "I've always thought the third one was a pentagram."

"It's called a *Drudenfuss*. A witch's foot. According to German folklore, it has the power to stamp out demons." And then suddenly I had it. I knew what had been worrying me about that symbol. "Do you notice anything strange about it?"

"They're all strange to me," Thane said.

"No, this one has an anomaly. One of the lower points of the star has an open end. See how the tip is blunted?"

He tilted his head. "Are you sure that's not just erosion or a characteristic of the rock?"

"No, I'm pretty sure the end was opened on purpose."

"For what reason?"

"Some people believe that an open point on a pentacle is a way for evil to enter our world. And in order for it to exit, another point must be opened or the whole star destroyed."

"So if only one point is open…"

"Evil is still here." The breeze stirred again, arousing

a murmur from the trees. Leaves peppered the surface of the pool, then floated serenely away.

"But it's only a legend," Thane said. "More mountain lore."

"I know that. But in all the cemeteries I've visited, I've never once seen a pentacle with an open point. It's a little unsettling to find one here."

"Why? Because this place is supposed to be some sort of gateway or vortex?"

"That's part of it." I wrapped my arms around my middle as I gazed around. "And because it's so closed in. It feels a little claustrophobic to me. I keep thinking about what happened to Wayne Van Zandt here. If something followed him in here that night, he never stood a chance. There's only one way in and one way out."

"Unless you go up," Thane said, his gaze lifting.

I pictured the marks on Wayne's face, those five raised scars where claws had slashed across his cheek, stealing his good looks and almost taking his life. Whether it was the vision of that attack or Ivy's insinuation about a thin place, I didn't know, but I began to experience the same light-headedness I'd felt in the laurel bald. I could feel that odd thrum, too, pulsating along my every nerve ending.

I turned to Thane. "Do you feel that?"

"What?"

"A vibration. I felt it earlier before we entered the thicket."

Thane was silent for a moment. "I don't feel anything except mist from the waterfall."

"There's no transformer or power plant around here?" I asked anxiously.

"Not for miles." He paused. "Do you still feel it?"

"Yes. And I can hear it, too, if I listen closely enough. It's like…"

"What?" He was staring down at me very intently. He made no move to touch me, but I was suddenly so aware of his presence, I could feel the heat of his flesh as surely as if he were pressing into me.

I took his hand and put it on my chest. "Can you feel it?"

His eyes darkened. "I feel your heartbeat."

"No, it's *there*. It's inside of me…" I started to tremble. "It's like this place is somehow a part of me…."

My vision clouded, and an image came to me of two naked bodies entwined and straining toward climax in this very glade as the vibrations pulsated all around them, calling the dead, calling forth creatures from out of the cave and holes and up from the deepest, coldest depths of the pool to witness the union. They were everywhere, red-eyed and leering.

I felt myself sway toward him, and something in my eyes seemed to startle him. He held me at arm's length for a moment before he swore and pulled me roughly against him.

The next thing I knew we were kissing, and I told myself I should push him away…this was all happening too fast. It wasn't real. It was this place. It was that strange vision, that strange vibration.

I could do nothing but melt into him. Something at the core of my being had been awakened. Whatever had drawn me here, whatever was keeping me here, had also driven me into Thane Asher's arms.

His tongue slid into my mouth, and the hum grew louder and louder until my whole body pulsated with need. I'd never felt anything like it. It was like a heart-beat, like the throb of blood through my veins, but it was coming from the mountains and from the cave and from the very land on which we stood. And it was coming from inside me.

The vision came back to me and I saw the woman rise over the man, her head thrown back in carnal aban-don. As their cries and moans melded in that dark glade, I could have sworn it was Devlin and his dead wife, Mariama. Then the woman turned with a seductive smile, and I saw that it was…me.

As if in the throes of his own orgiastic dream, Thane drew me closer, one hand on my back crushing me to him, the other hand tangled in my hair, tilting my head back. He buried his face in my neck, pressing his mouth to my pulse as if he could devour my very essence. And there was nothing, *nothing* I could do to stop him. Be-cause I didn't want him to stop.

Something intruded—a sound, a ripple, a whisper of fear—and he jerked back very quickly, looking stricken. For the longest moment we stood there with ragged breath and raging emotions, until he glanced away and broke the spell. "Damn. What just happened?"

The buzzing subsided, and I stared up at him in con-fusion. "I don't know."

"Are you okay?"

"Yes." I couldn't meet his gaze. "That was…unex-pected."

"I know. I'm sorry."

"It wasn't just you." I glanced around with a shudder. "It's this place. It makes you think strange thoughts."

He lifted a hand to push back a lock of hair. "It never has before. But just then…I thought…"

"What?"

He shook his head. "Nothing." But his gaze clouded. "Are you sure you're okay?"

"I'm fine—" I broke off abruptly. "Where's Angus?"

Thane glanced around, too. "He can't have gone far. He was here a minute ago."

I started to call to him, but Thane put a hand on my arm. "Shush. Listen." He cocked his head.

In the silence, I heard the distant echo of a bark. "Oh, no. Thane, he's gone into the cave."

We were still standing face-to-face, and I hadn't realized that my hand had crept to his chest. When I noticed, I quickly dropped it to my side.

"I'll go in and get him," he said.

"I'll come with you."

"No, you stay put. I know that cave. I explored every inch of it as a kid. It dead-ends about a quarter of a mile in, so he can't go far."

"But you don't even have a flashlight."

"I have a penlight on my key chain and I have my cell phone. Don't worry. I'll find him."

I glanced anxiously at the opening in the cliff. "What if he's cornered something in there?"

"All the more reason I should go in alone." When I would have protested, he said, "I'm not trying to be all protective. Like I said, I'm familiar with the cave. Alone, I can move a lot faster if I need to get the hell out."

It seemed foolish to argue with that logic. I watched him slip through the opening into darkness, then I waited by the cave for a moment, trying to pick up the sound of Angus's bark. I heard Thane call to him, and then all was silent. I told myself they would be fine.

Thane was more than capable of taking care of himself and Angus's instincts would keep him safe. It did no one any good for me to stand there working myself up into a panic.

Nor would I dwell on that kiss. I had no idea what had happened, how I had let myself get carried away so quickly because that wasn't at all like me. I was the cautious, reserved type. Or at least…I had once been. Before Devlin.

Moving away from the entrance, I knelt by the pool and dipped my fingers in the water. Thane was right. The water was as cold as a melted glacier, the spray from the falls like the chill of a winter rain. As I stared down into those dark depths, a leaf dropped into the water, and my reflection wavered in the tiny spirals. But even as the leaf floated past me, the ripples continued as though the water had been disturbed by some underwater eruption. Once again, I heard a hum, like the ghostly vibration of a tuning fork.

I was still staring down into the pool, watching the tiny undulations, when a reflection appeared over mine in the water. I thought it was Freya's ghost at first, but then I realized that someone stood at the top of the cliff gazing down into the glade. Even as I lifted my head, the spirals intensified, and the reflection quivered into nothingness.

She had been there, though. I hadn't imagined her any more than I'd invented the silhouette in the laurel bald. Someone was following us. And for that split second the face had appeared in the water, I could have sworn it was Ivy.

A sound came to me from the cave. A bark and then Thane's voice. Thank God, they were coming back.

I was still staring up at the top of the cliff when they emerged from the cave a few moments later. Angus must have caught the girl's scent because he began to bark excitedly.

Thane frowned. "What's the matter with him? He was perfectly fine in the cave."

"Someone was up there." I pointed to the top of the cliff.

Thane glanced up. "Just now?"

"Yes. I saw a reflection in the pool, but when I looked up she was gone."

"She?"

"It was a girl."

He shrugged. "Probably just some kids camping out in here. I saw the remnant of a fire in the cave. Maybe that's why she disappeared so quickly. This is Asher property. She was probably afraid of being caught trespassing."

"Is there another way to the top of the cliff besides scaling the wall?"

"Yes, there's a path a little farther on."

"If someone was coming from the laurel bald, would they have had time to get up there by that path?"

A brow lifted, but all he said was, "Assuming they know the area."

I started to mention Ivy, but then I wondered if what he'd told me earlier had planted the idea in my head. That cliff was at least fifty feet above the pool. An accurate identification from a wavering reflection didn't seem all that plausible even to me now. And maybe that silhouette at the gravesite had been nothing more than a shadow. The sun had been in my eyes, after all.

But I hadn't imagined those traps last night. I hadn't imagined being lured into the woods.

"You want me to climb up there and take a look around?" Thane asked.

"You don't need to do that. It was probably just a camper like you said."

"You still look upset. Are you sure you're okay?"

"Yes, I'm fine. But I'm ready to get out of here."

"Let's head back, then."

As we walked through the archway, I glanced back into the glade, my gaze lifting to the symbols and then to the top of the cliff. I couldn't be sure, but I thought I glimpsed a shadow moving stealthily along the edge, as if trying to keep pace with us.

Twenty-One

It was noon by the time we started back. The sun was directly overhead, but dark clouds hung suspended over the mountains, and I could hear thunder rumbling through the hills. The storm was a long way off, though, and I had no idea if it was even headed our way. Still, I felt an electric tingle along my scalp and in my fingertips, and as the breeze died away, the air felt heavy with portent.

The path around the cliff was narrow, so we walked single file. Thane led the way, with me in the middle and Angus bringing up the rear. I wasn't much in the mood to talk. I was still too preoccupied by what had happened in the glade between Thane and me. And I couldn't shake the notion that someone—possibly Ivy—had been following us. I found myself glancing back now and then to see if I could spot her.

Thane had gotten a bit ahead of me, and as we neared the forest, he waited for me to catch up before entering the trees. The path widened, and we were able to walk side by side, shoulders brushing. I welcomed his nearness even as I shied away from any physical contact.

He lifted a pine bough that drooped over the path, and as I ducked under, he said, "I need to tell you something."

I straightened and looked at him. "Yes?"

For a moment, he seemed oddly at a loss, as if he didn't quite know where to start. "Yesterday, I told you that I'd gone to your website to look you up, but that's not altogether true. I did go to your website, but I already knew about you. I knew that day on the ferry."

I was still on edge so my tone sharpened. "How?"

"I remembered seeing your picture in the paper last spring after everything came out about Oak Grove Cemetery."

"Why didn't you say anything?"

"I wasn't one-hundred-percent certain. That's why I looked you up. I started searching back through some of the internet articles until I found the photograph. You were standing outside the cemetery gates with a man. A cop. He had his arm around you. You were both looking away from the camera, but I had the feeling the photographer had captured an intimate moment." He paused. "None of my business, of course, so feel free to tell me to go to hell. But...you know what I'm asking, right? And why I'm asking?" He turned to stare down at me, and I thought he seemed tense. "It isn't just about what happened at the waterfall."

My heart gave a painful kick. "I know."

"Well?"

I drew a quick breath. "His name is John Devlin. He was the police detective in charge of that case. I was a consultant for a time."

"And more?"

"Yes."

"How much more?"

"It doesn't matter. We're not together now."

"Why not?"

I couldn't tell him about Devlin's ghosts. Even if he would have believed me, it wasn't something I could share. Devlin didn't even know about them, and confiding in Thane somehow seemed a betrayal to him. "It's complicated." I turned and walked past him up the path. When he caught up with me, I said, "He lost his wife and daughter. He wasn't ready to move on."

"What about you? Are you ready to move on?"

I closed my eyes briefly. "I don't know. I'm not over him, if that's what you're asking. I'm not sure I'll ever be."

"Is that why you came here? To nurse a broken heart?"

"I came here because I was offered a job," I said flatly.

His expression was guarded, the eyes deeply shadowed. "For what it's worth, I know what it's like to lose someone you love. I know that emptiness, that awful helpless feeling."

"Your grandfather told me about Harper," I said softly.

He frowned. "What did he say?"

"He said she was the girl you wanted to marry. She died in a car crash, and you blamed yourself for allowing her to go out in a storm."

Anger flared. "Did he also mention how he'd done everything in his power to keep us apart?"

"No." But I remembered his grandfather's comment

about the girl's mental instability. "Why did he try to keep you apart?"

"Because she wasn't part of his grand design." A muscle pulsed at his temple. "And her family didn't meet with his approval."

"Why not?"

"She didn't have money or connections, the right kind of pedigree. None of that mattered to me, of course. I only wanted Harper. If not for the accident, we would have been married that spring despite Grandfather's objections."

"I'm sorry."

He was silent for a moment. I heard the rumble of thunder in the distance and the rustle of leaves overhead as the breeze picked back up, bringing the scent of rain and the promise of bad weather.

Thane looked up through the breaks in the canopy where the sun still shone brightly. "It was a long time ago and who knows if it would have lasted. We were young, and I can look back now and admit that part of the appeal of our romance was bucking Grandfather's wishes. Don't get me wrong," he said quickly. "I did love her. And I'm also grateful to Grandfather for taking me in when I had nowhere else to go. I'll never be able to repay him for all that he's done for me. But—"

"He never quite lets you forget that you're not a true Asher."

He gave a little laugh. "When you say it like that, it sounds pretty petty."

"No, it doesn't. At best, it must be awkward and at worst, soul-crushing."

He reached out briefly to touch my cheek, his fingers

as light as a dragonfly skimming across a pond. "He's a fool, you know."

We were no longer talking about Pell Asher.

It's not his fault, I wanted to tell him. *It's hard to let go of the ghosts of your past when they won't let go of you.*

I didn't want to look at him, didn't want to read too much into his eyes, so I focused instead on Angus, sitting on the path patiently waiting for us.

But my mind was in turmoil. I hadn't expected this, nor did I want it. I wasn't looking for romance with Thane Asher, and yet I couldn't deny a connection that was starting to frighten me.

"Thane—"

"Don't say it. Don't say anything."

"I have to."

He put a fingertip to my lips. "Life's too short to live in the past, Amelia. Let him have his ghosts."

When we arrived back at the cemetery, I turned to say goodbye at the gate. I needed to work for as long as I could before the storm moved in, and I really wanted some alone time to sort things out. That kiss at the falls had left me confused and emotionally shattered. I felt the inevitable tug-of-war: the desire, always, to return to Charleston, to Devlin. The need, for now, to stay here with Thane.

"I should get to work," I said briskly.

The old grin flashed. "You're not getting rid of me that easily. I think it's time for you to meet the rest of the family."

"I'm sorry?"

"Dear old Aunt Emelyn. You did say you wanted to

see her." Thunder rumbled closer, and he looked out over the cemetery toward the mountains. "You're not going to get any work done this afternoon. That storm is moving down fast."

And with his words came a gust of wind that swept a flurry of dead leaves across the graves. Along the edge of the forest, the tops of the pine trees started to dip and swell like waves in a dark green sea, and a sheet of rain raced toward us, the patter on the leaves and on the ground like the whisper of a thousand ghosts. On the heels of the rain came rolling thunder and flash after flash of lightning. And just like that, the storm was upon us.

Thane took my hand. "Come on. Let's make a run for it."

We could just have easily backtracked to the cars, but instead we raced through the maze of monuments and headstones, through the lych-gate and past that circle of angels with their faces upturned to the storm.

Shoving open the mausoleum door, Thane stepped aside for me to enter. Angus came in behind me, shaking water droplets from his coat. It was dim inside, but I could see lightning flashes through the stained-glass windows and the shimmer of cobwebs from the corners. The stone walls were cold and felt damp to the touch, and the whole place reeked of mildew and neglect. In the middle of the stone floor, a long set of stairs led down into the dead-dark shadows of the tomb.

Thane wedged something underneath the door to keep it open so that what little light was left outside filtered in. I welcomed the fresh air, too, that storm-charged breeze that tangled my hair and stirred the cobwebs.

"What do you think?" he asked. "You still want to see her?"

"Yes, only..."

His eyes glinted. "Not afraid, are you?"

"Of Aunt Emelyn, no. I'm not crazy about snakes and spiders, though."

"What kind of restorer are you, anyway?"

"The cautious kind. Do you still have your pen-light?"

He dangled the key chain. "But I seem to remember candles from before and, hopefully, matches. Should I go down alone?"

"That's okay. I've learned to deal with my phobias. You can go first, though."

"Thanks." He descended into the gloom. "Stay close and watch your step. These stairs are steep."

Angus, I noticed, didn't follow. He wanted no part of that tomb.

I was right on Thane's heels. When he stopped halfway down, I almost smashed into him. "What's wrong?" I asked breathlessly.

"Just trying to remember where the sconces are." He went down another few steps and played the light over the stone walls. "Ah. Here we are." I heard the strike of a match, and then light flared, animating giant shadows on the walls. Cupping the flame, Thane lit the candles, then plucked one from the sconce and handed it to me as he pocketed his penlight. Then he took another candle for himself.

We went down the rest of the steps, and he lit more candles at the bottom. The tomb was larger than I would have expected, with walls of crypts and vaults that vanished into darkness. I saw the glitter of more cobwebs, the glint of reflected light on sterling-silver markers and plaques. The smell of mildew grew stronger, and I could well imagine the creep of black mold in every corner and crevice.

"This is incredible," I said, and the stone walls threw my breathless voice back to me.

"Too bad we don't have proper lighting," he said. "We'll have to come prepared next time. Some of the carvings and scrollwork on the vaults is extraordinary."

"Was that the tiniest bit of pride I heard in your voice just now?" I teased him.

He glanced over his shoulder, his face eeric in the flickering light. "I've never disputed the family has taste," he said. "My quibble is with the overindulgence. And speaking of which…" He held the candle high. "Emelyn's coffin is this way."

He led me through an arched doorway into a small chamber where the glass coffin rested on an ornate pedestal. As he turned to place his candle in a nearby holder, I came up beside him, which is how I happened to make the discovery first. The candlelight reflected in the glass so that I couldn't see anything at first. But as I repositioned, I got my first glimpse of her. And gasped.

Thane whirled. "What is it?"

I held my candle over the coffin. His gaze dropped, and he said on a breath, "Jesus."

Air must have gotten into the container through a fracture or a seam because the body had started to wither and shrink. The wrinkled skin had turned gray, and the eye sockets were empty, the lips shriveled back into a hideous grin. And even more grotesque, somehow, were the bridal trappings in which the corpse had been displayed.

"How long since you were down here?" I asked.

"Years. I wonder how long she's been this way."

"Who knows? If there's even a hairline fracture in the glass, I imagine decomposition would have happened quickly." I paused on a shiver as I glanced down at the corpse. "Will you tell your grandfather?"

"I see no reason for him to know. It would just upset him and he'll never come down here again. Not until—" He broke off as a cold wind swept down into the tomb, snuffing the candles a split second before the door slammed closed upstairs.

In that utter blackness, I felt the chill of dread creep along my backbone.

"Thane?" As I breathed his name, I felt his hand on my arm.

"It's okay. The wind blew them out. Let me find the matches."

I sensed his body close to mine, and in the deep silence of the tomb, I swore I could hear his heartbeat. Or was it my own? His arm came around me as he fumbled for the matches. I could feel his breath against my cheek, the whisper of his lips in my hair.

"Thane?"

He pulled me back against him, an arm around my waist holding me still as he lifted my hair and licked my neck at the pulse point. *As if trying to devour my essence.*

I jerked away in shock. "What are you doing?"

"Trying to find the damn matches." His voice came from the bottom of the stairs. He was no longer in the chamber with me. But the arm was still holding me....

In the paralyzed moment before I could react, I felt the hand slide up to my breast, another down to my thigh. A raspy voice whispered in my ear, *"Soon."* And then I heard the scrabble of claws on the stone floor a split second before Thane appeared in the doorway with a candle.

I whirled but no one was there. I was alone in the chamber with Emelyn Asher's withered corpse.

Twenty-Two

The storm blew over quickly, and the sunset that evening was spectacular. I sat out on the back steps with Angus at my feet as the sky over Bell Lake ripened from a rosy blush to a deep apricot, then faded to smoky lavender shot through with gold.

Up in the hills, the nocturnal creatures began to stir as twilight gathered. I would need to go inside soon, but for now I allowed myself a moment to enjoy the deep respite of the in-between, that bated breath of half-light before darkness descended.

A moth lit, with quivering wings, on the bee balm beside the steps. Out on the lake, a loon called to its mate, the melodic wail thin and haunting and a little unnerving as night sounds tend to be. Somewhere deeper in the forest, I heard the faint yip of coyotes and what might have been the scream of a "painter," the elusive black panther from my father's stories of his childhood in the mountains.

I was restless and lonely and still frightened by what had transpired in the tomb. I wanted to believe that terrible presence had been my imagination, a conjure of my fear, but I couldn't forget the feel of that hot breath on my face, the whispery promise in my ear....

I drew a trembling breath. Any sensible person would turn tail and run. There was no shame in it. I could head out now and be home in Charleston in a matter of hours. Fix a cup of chamomile in the kitchen. Browse through the mail on my desk. Sleep in my own bed. Be nearer to Devlin.

Another tremulous breath.

But would I be any safer there? In all those agonizing months of avoiding Devlin, I'd somehow managed to convince myself that I would be fine so long as I kept my distance. But now I had to wonder if everything happening to me in Asher Falls was a direct result of my wanton disregard of Papa's rules. My love of a haunted man had not only opened a door, but it had also weakened me, made me susceptible to the dark forces at work in this town and in these mountains.

Was that too fantastical? I didn't think so. Not anymore.

I thought again of that old man who had appeared in the cemetery, his grotesque behavior neither animal nor human but the embodiment of every strange thing that had happened to me here.

Catrice was right, I thought. The natural balance was off-kilter in these mountains. The axis had tilted in Asher Falls. Cemeteries had been drowned, hex signs had been altered and now nature had been reordered. And somehow I was a part of it all. I had been brought here for a reason.

I glanced down at my calloused palms and thought again of my father. He'd always tried to shelter me.

From the moment I saw the ghost of the old white-haired man in Rosehill Cemetery, Papa had given me those rules so that I would be protected. But he had kept things from me, too. They all had. He and Mama and Aunt Lynrose. They had information about my birth. I was convinced of it. Whatever they knew, whatever dark secret bound them, had closed Mama's heart to me and made Papa retreat so deeply inside himself, I could scarcely remember the man who had told me those mountain stories, who had instilled in me a reverence and love of old cemeteries. Their secrets and silence had shut me out and made me retreat into my own little world.

Devlin had managed to penetrate that world to dire consequences. And now there was another threat knocking at the gate. Thane Asher.

I closed my eyes on a shudder. I was drawn to Thane in a way that I didn't understand because it wasn't just him, the man. The pull came from this place, this town, the very earth beneath my feet.

Pell Asher's voice seemed to echo down from the hilltop. *The strongest ties are blood and land. They are constant. Romantic love is all too fleeting.*

I glanced toward that hilltop. I thought if I stared hard enough, I might be able to see the lights of Asher House. I might be able to will some answers. But the silence only deepened.

Dusk dropped swiftly and still I sat there. The gray sky shimmered above the treetops where the moon would soon rise, but beyond the forest, the blue haze of hill and mountain darkened into a seamless shadow.

And I held my breath, waiting. Somewhere in that twilight, the veil had thinned, and I imagined Freya's ghost drifting through. Would she come to me tonight? Drawn by my warmth and energy? My life force? Did she crave what she could never have again?

Or did she haunt me for another reason?

I should seek sanctuary. I knew that. By acknowledging the dead, I was once again tempting fate. But the door had already opened, and I needed to know why I had been brought here. I needed to know the secrets of my birth, the secrets of my destiny. I needed to know why I was so drawn to Thane Asher.

Soon, the trees whispered, and I shivered.

Freya's ghost didn't appear to me that night, although I may have missed her. I went inside before full dark and curled up in bed with my laptop. I'd been neglecting my blog shamelessly since I left Charleston, and now I spent some time moderating the comments from my last entry and outlining a new article about hex signs.

I also checked my in-box. There was an email from Devlin.

The mouse hovered indecisively. Should I click or should I let sleeping dogs lie? Move on from the past? Leave Devlin to his ghosts?

In the end, I couldn't resist. I opened the email and devoured the one-sentence message. Then I read it again, scowling: *Where are you?*

Was it my imagination—my wishful thinking—that a hint of desperation had crept into that brief missive?

I closed the in-box, shut down the laptop and slid under the covers. As I lay there in the darkness, night sounds invaded my sanctuary, and Devlin once again invaded my dreams.

Twenty-Three

The warm weather held over the next few days, and I spent long hours at Thorngate, armed with rake, shovel and machete as I hacked and chopped and dug my way through the vegetation that had crept from the old cemetery into the new. The physical labor lifted my spirits, and I threw myself into the work, ignoring Devlin's email and Thane's kisses and the havoc they had wreaked on my peace of mind. But as absorbed as I was in the task at hand, I never once turned my back on the mausoleum.

When I thought of that hot breath on my neck, the flick of that phantom tongue, I slashed even harder at the brush until blisters formed beneath the gloves. By the end of the week, my energy was spent, and I decided to take a long overdue library break. I hadn't been able to locate Freya's grave, and I could only conclude that it had yet to be uncovered in the tangle of vines and brambles that had overrun a section of the cemetery. Until I could clear it all away, I would need a site map to identify the graves.

Stopping by the house for a quick shower and change of clothing, I made sure Angus was settled in with plenty of fresh water and food, and then I left him snoozing in a patch of sunlight in front of my bedroom window. I hated to lock him inside, but I couldn't take him into town with me, and I certainly wasn't going to leave him alone in the yard.

Ivy stood at the counter talking to Sidra when I entered the library a few minutes later. They both wore their school uniforms, so I assumed neither had been expelled.

"Hello," I said with a friendly nod.

"If it isn't The Graveyard Queen," Ivy drawled. "That is what they call you, isn't it?"

"Sometimes."

"Creepy."

What I found creepy was the fact that she must have looked me up to know my nickname. What I found even creepier was the possibility that she'd been spying on Thane and me at the falls that day. *Ivy's not like other girls,* he'd said. *There've been some incidents.* "I guess it depends on one's perspective," I said, carefully.

Her gaze was slightly contemptuous. "If you say so."

I turned to Sidra. "Is Luna here?"

She shot a warning glance at Ivy. "No, but she'll be back soon."

"I guess that's my cue." Ivy straightened. "See you later, Sid. Don't forget what we talked about."

Sidra frowned. "I already told you, I'm not going up there again."

"Never say never," Ivy said and gave me a knowing smile.

Sidra waited until the door closed behind Ivy, then turned back to me. "Can I help you with something?"

"Is everything okay? You look a little anxious."

"I'm fine. It's just..." She shrugged. "Nothing."

"Are you sure? If you need someone to talk to—"

"I don't," she said, dropping her gaze to the counter.

"Okay, then maybe you can help me." I told her what I needed, and she led me through the library to a long table stacked with books and records. "Luna gathered up all this stuff for you days ago. We were wondering when you'd be back."

I almost told her that I'd been in once before, but then I remembered the circumstances of that visit and decided to hold my silence.

"If you don't find what you're looking for here, I can always check the archives," Sidra said, thumbing through one of the file folders. "And I'm sure we have more reference books that mention Thorngate."

"Thanks. Whatever you can find will be a big help. Oh, and speaking of reference books, I'd like to find out more about the hex signs up at the waterfall. I tried an internet search, but nothing turned up."

Her eyes widened, and I saw something surface in those blue depths that might have been fear. "Hex signs?"

"I've seen similar ones on old gravestones. I'm curious how they came to be carved into the side of that cliff."

She hesitated. "You won't find any information in here or anywhere else about those symbols. And I wouldn't mention them again. People around here are funny about those things."

"Superstitious, you mean?"

Her gaze darted away. "I just wouldn't say anything if I were you."

I was puzzled by her behavior, but I let the matter drop.

A door closed somewhere in the library, and she looked a bit alarmed. "Luna must be back. I'll let her know you're here."

She hurried away, and I settled down at the table to work, but I'd barely had time to shuffle through the first stack of papers when Sidra returned with a couple of books. "Should be something in here about the cemetery," she said. "It lists all the graveyards in the county."

I glanced up. "You sure found that fast."

"I know just about every book in this library. I've spent most of my life in here."

"You must enjoy your work, then." I smiled. "I love libraries, the older the better. Just like cemeteries."

She said almost shyly, "I like cemeteries, too. I could help you go through some of this stuff if you'd like."

"Luna wouldn't mind?"

"I don't have anything else to do," she said and pulled out a chair. It had occurred to me while she'd been gone that she might know something about Freya. The girl had died before Sidra was born, but in a town this small, she was bound to have heard something. And she'd certainly reacted to the photograph in Luna's office.

We worked in silence for a few minutes before I casually remarked, "I met your mother at Asher House the other night."

"I heard."

"She told you?"

"My mother never tells me anything, but I always manage to find out what I need to know."

The hint of superiority sounded more like Ivy than Sidra. "After dinner, Thane and I went through some old boxes. I came across a photograph that reminded me of the one hanging in Luna's office—that group photograph of her and your mother and Catrice. There was another girl in the background. Thane said her name was Freya Pattershaw."

Sidra didn't glance up, but I could sense a sudden tension and remembered her strong reaction that day in Luna's office. I'd suspected then, as I did now, that she'd seen Freya's ghost in that photograph.

"Have you ever heard that name?"

Her blue gaze lifted to mine, and something in those crystalline pools made me shiver. It was the dichotomy of light and dark, I realized. "I've heard the name," she said. "She was the bird woman's daughter."

"The bird woman?" I asked in confusion.

"Tilly Pattershaw. That's what we call her."

"Shouldn't that nickname belong to Catrice? She's the ornithologist."

"Catrice studies birds," Sidra said. "Tilly takes care of them. She's a rescuer. And she probably knows as much or more about birds than anyone around here, including Catrice. You should see her yard. Sometimes they flock to her by the hundreds."

I had a sudden vision of all those crows staring down at me. "Do you go out to her house often?"

Sidra gave a wary glance over her shoulder. "I'm not supposed to go out there ever. But I like birds. The little ones especially and the songbirds. Catrice studies predators."

I tried to keep my voice mildly curious. "Why aren't you allowed to go out there?"

Another pause. "Tilly's not one of us."

"What do you mean?"

"She's not from Asher Falls."

"But she's lived here most of her life."

"She's still considered an outsider by people like my mother and Luna."

Ironic, considering she'd probably lived here longer than they'd been alive. "Do you know what happened to Freya?" I asked.

"She died."

"Yes, I know, but how?"

She hesitated with another cautious glance over her shoulder. "No one likes to talk about it, but…I've heard people say it was a fire. That's how Tilly burned her hands. They say she tried to go in after her daughter."

"That's why she wears gloves," I said.

"Always. I've never seen her without them even when she feeds the birds."

"Where was the fire?"

"I don't know. Some abandoned building in town. There was a party or something. That's all I know. Except…" Her eyes were very cool and very blue but filled with something I couldn't put a name to. Something that unsettled. "I don't think they liked her much."

"They?"

"My mother and Luna and Catrice."

"Why didn't they like her?"

"Maybe you should ask Luna."

"Ask me what?"

My gaze shot to the end of the aisle where Luna stood holding her cat. She wore a deep purple dress the exact shade of a twilight sky. Silver cuffs circled her wrists and I could see the milky glow of the moonstone at her throat. She bent, and the tabby leaped from her arms to dart under one of the shelves, claws scratching at the hardwood floor.

"He's after a mouse," Sidra said.

"Yes, he's a bloodthirsty little thing," Luna said. "It's a natural instinct, though, so one can hardly begrudge him. Besides, rodents are the bane of old libraries. Traps can only do so much." She smiled as she leaned a shoulder against the shelf and folded her arms. "Now, what was it you wanted to ask me?"

Sidra had her back to Luna. Her head was bowed to the book, but her gaze was lifted to mine, and I saw an almost imperceptible shake of her head. For some reason, she didn't want me to mention Freya, maybe because she wasn't supposed to know anything about her.

I said evenly, "I'm trying to find a site map for the cemetery. Thane said there might be one at Asher House, but it never turned up. Have you seen one in the library archives?"

"Should be one somewhere in all those records." She walked over to the table, her hand sliding up Sidra's back to rest on her shoulder, and I saw the girl close her eyes, as if suppressing a shudder. "At least for the new section. But the site map for the original cemetery could very well be at Asher House. I'll have a look myself next time I'm there."

"Thank you."

She stared down at me for a moment, and then before I could react, she reached out and grasped my chin, turning my face to the side, as if to study my profile. I jerked away in shock.

She smiled. "Sorry. Didn't mean to startle you. I thought I saw a spider in your hair.

And now it was I who suppressed a shudder. In that brief moment that we were so close, I noticed a fan of lines around her eyes, the crepey skin at her neck, the shimmer of gray hair in her dark mane. She didn't seem quite so vital or lush as I'd first perceived her, and for some odd reason, I thought of that withering corpse in the Asher mausoleum.

She straightened. "Sidra, don't forget you're locking up tomorrow."

The girl's gaze was on me. "I won't."

To me Luna said, "Is there anything else I can do for you, Amelia?"

"No, thank you," I said a little too quickly. "Sidra has been kind enough to help me sort through the records."

"Yes," Luna said, "Sidra can be quite the helpful girl." And with that, she turned and disappeared.

Sidra let out a breath. "Thanks."

"For what?"

"Not mentioning Freya. I don't like to make Luna angry."

"Why would that make her angry? Regardless of what she and the others felt for Freya back then, the poor girl has been dead for years."

"You don't know Luna very well," she murmured. Then she leaned in, her voice lowered to a whisper. "There's something you need to see."

"What is it?"

"Not now. Meet me here tomorrow after Luna leaves."

"I don't know if I can make it—"

"It's about those hex signs," she said. "Come back tomorrow and I'll show you."

Twenty-Four

~∘≪∘≫∘~

When I left the library a little while later, I found Wayne Van Zandt nosing around my car. He had his hands cupped to his face, peering in through the back window. When he heard my approach, his head came around, but his smirk told me he wasn't unduly concerned that I'd caught him snooping.

"Are you looking for something?" I asked coolly. My gaze tried to stray to those scars, but I forced myself to focus on his eyes. Still, I couldn't help but think of everything Thane had told me about the attack. Apparently Wayne had no recollection except that he'd gone to the falls to meet Luna.

I felt an odd tug and glanced over my shoulder, expecting to find Luna glaring at me. Instead, I saw Ivy standing in the shade of the clock tower staring at us. As our gazes collided, I felt a chill creep up my spine. Wayne noticed her, too, and muttered under his breath.

"Were you looking for something in my car?" I asked again.

"Just waiting for you," he said.

"Why?"

"I thought you might be interested to know that I found a kennel up in the hills."

"Did you make an arrest?" I asked anxiously.

He stroked a finger down one of the scars as if deliberately trying to bait my gaze. "No need to," he said. "Someone was there before me. The dogs were all gone and the kennel was torched. The owner got himself roughed up, too. He wouldn't talk, of course." His eyes narrowed as he searched my face. "Don't suppose you'd know anything about that incident."

"Me?" I asked in surprise, even as I visualized the cut at Thane's temple and the bruises on his knuckles. "How would I know anything about it?"

He turned his head to observe the street. "That stray still hanging around the Covey place?" His tone was casual, almost distracted, but I had the impression of a cold calculation behind the question.

If he meant to catch me off guard or provoke a reaction, he had no idea who he was dealing with—a woman who had been disciplined by the presence of ghosts since childhood. "I told you the other day, he's probably long gone by now."

"That is what you said," he agreed.

"Wayne, what do you think you're doing?" a voice demanded from the sidewalk. We both turned as Catrice Hawthorne stepped off the curb and headed toward us, her shabby attire a far cry from the elegant cocktail dress she'd worn to Asher House the other night. Her floppy hat and shapeless capris reminded me of the garb favored by the tourists who flocked to the Battery in the summer, the ones who avidly snapped pictures of the mansions and bartered for souvenirs at the Market.

Annoyed, Wayne said, "This is none of your business, Catrice. Go back to your vultures."

Her eyes sparkled with good humor. "Vultures are scavengers. Hardly my area of expertise."

"Maybe I wasn't talking about birds," he muttered.

She laughed as she turned to me. "I'm so glad I ran into you, Amelia. My car is on the fritz and I wonder if I could trouble you for a ride home. I'm right on your way."

"Of course. No trouble at all."

"You're a lifesaver. And if you have time, I'll give you that tour of the studio I promised."

Her genuine warmth once again took me by surprise. She was so much more personable than either Bryn or Luna, or anyone else I'd met in Asher Falls, for that matter—with the possible exception of Thane.

She shook a finger at Wayne. "I know it's asking a lot, but try to work on that attitude. You'll give Amelia a bad impression, and we don't want to scare her off."

He merely glared as we climbed into the car, and I pulled away from the curb.

Catrice glanced back with a chuckle. "I hope this isn't too much of an imposition."

"Not at all."

"I thought you looked as if you needed rescuing. Wayne can be a little overbearing at times, especially with strangers. He's been through a lot, though, so we try to cut him some slack."

"You've known him a long time, I take it?"

"We grew up together...all of us...Wayne, Luna, Bryn, Edward, Hugh and myself. We were thick as thieves as children." She removed her hat and placed it on the console between us. Sunlight streaming in through the windshield set fire to her red hair as she ran fingers through it. "Then Hugh and Edward were shipped off to boarding school, Wayne's family moved to Woodberry for a time and we three girls were left to our own devices."

"You and Luna and Bryn?"

She smiled. "Blood sisters, we called ourselves. We were quite the explorers. There was a time when we knew these hills as well as our own backyards."

"What about Freya Pattershaw?" I kept my gaze on the road, but from the corner of my eye, I saw Catrice turn to study me.

"How do you know about Freya?" she asked after a moment.

I'm being haunted by her ghost. "I saw a picture of you and Bryn and Luna at Asher House. Freya was in the background."

"How did you know who she was?"

"Thane told me."

"How would *he* know?" I heard the frown in her voice. "She was dead long before he came here."

"It's a small town. I'm sure he's heard of her. Maybe he's even seen other pictures of her," I said with a shrug.

She sighed and turned to stare out the window. "Poor Freya. She was always lurking in the background, always trying to fit in where she didn't belong. I always suspected her insecurities came from not having a father."

"What happened to him?"

"No one knows. Tilly was never married, you see. Her past is a little mysterious, to say the least, and she seems to like it that way. She's always kept to herself, always been the eccentric. Freya was the exact opposite.

She wanted more than anything to belong. She would have done anything to fit in." Idly, Catrice studied her hands. "But for all her indiscretions, she had a way about her. An innocence. Men loved her, women hated her."

"Did you hate her?"

She swung around. "Me? No, I liked her. As I said, she had a naive charm that I found endearing."

"How old was she when she died?"

"Just seventeen."

My chest tightened. "That young? I had no idea."

"Yes. We were all still in high school. It happened the weekend of prom. *Our* prom. Not hers."

"She went to a different school?"

"She attended the public school before it closed. I'm sure she would have transferred to Woodberry with all the others if she hadn't—"

I flashed a glance. "What?"

"It was just so sad and tragic. Poor Tilly never got over it. She was always such an odd duck, but Freya's death pushed her over the edge. I suppose one of these days she'll have to be put in a home."

I thought about the knife-wielding woman who had come to my rescue in the woods the other night. The same woman who had warned me away from Asher Falls. Mad she might be, but she was also very, very capable. "Freya died in a fire, didn't she? That's how Tilly burned her hands."

"Yes." Catrice massaged her own hands, as if in deep pain. "It still distresses me to think about it after all this time."

"Were you there?"

"We were all there. We all saw what happened." She

turned back to the window, deliberately shutting me out, and I knew she wouldn't say anything else. Thane was right, it seemed. People were reluctant to talk about Freya Pattershaw's death, and I couldn't help wondering why.

We drove in silence until Catrice said, "It's just ahead. See that red mailbox? Turn there. I'm down the road a piece."

Like the Covey house, her place was sequestered from the main road by the forest. She lived in a quaint cedar cabin with cane rocking chairs on the porch and a hammock strung between two oak trees in the front yard. I could imagine myself spending lazy summer afternoons in that hammock, watching the clouds. Waiting for twilight and the ghosts.

The studio was in a separate building at the back of the property, accessed by a well-worn footpath. As I followed Catrice along the rough trail, my gaze lifted now and then to a trio of hawks circling overhead, their piercing screams raising a chill even in broad daylight. The afternoon was cloudless, and the sun shimmering down through the evergreen boughs was warm on my face. But the deep shade of the woods pressed in on me, and the scent of the pines somehow seemed ominous. I was glad when the trail broke away from the trees, and we descended toward the studio.

The structure itself was inelegant, a large, mishmash of a building perched at the water's edge, but inside the rustic charm of stone walls and floors complemented the magnificent view of lake, forest and mountain. An easel with a covered painting stood in front of the tall windows, while finished canvases were stacked at least a dozen deep against the back wall, as if they had been accumulating there for years. Most of them were wild-life and landscape scenes, but I noticed a few portraits that intrigued me.

"Have a look around," Catrice invited. "I'll make us some tea."

"Thank you, but I wish you wouldn't go to the trouble. I really can't stay long."

She smiled. "It's no trouble. I won't be a minute."

After she was gone, I browsed through the paintings. The landscapes were beautiful, but I naturally gravitated to the portraits. She'd painted them all— Luna, Bryn, Hugh and a man I recognized as Edward. I thought they must have been done a long time ago because the subjects were very young and Catrice's technique still crude. But even then she'd managed to tap into an uncanny essence in all of them—that feral quality in Luna, the ice maiden in Bryn and the almost perverted perfection of Hugh. But it was the portrait of Edward that fascinated me the most. His features were unmistakably Asher, but I thought there was a hint of the neurotic in his eyes. I couldn't stop looking at him.

"Those are really old," Catrice said as she came to stand beside me. "And not very good. I was still a novice back then."

"No, you captured them beautifully," I said. Eerily so. "Do you still paint portraits?"

"Now and then but only for fun. The landscapes are my bread and butter. I'm lucky they've done so well at the gallery."

"I don't think it's luck. You're very talented."

She shrugged. "It's a gift. I can't take credit."

"But you've developed that gift."

"You have one, too," she said, and for a moment I

thought she meant my ability to see ghosts. "Your restorations are every bit as inspirational as my paintings. More so, perhaps."

I lifted a brow in surprise. "You've seen my work?" Was *she* the anonymous donor?

"I mentioned the other night at dinner that I've been to your website. I browsed through your gallery and read your blog. I'm fascinated by what you do. You have a calling," she said softly. "A purpose. We all do."

A swooping shadow drew my attention to the window. "What was that?"

"Come see," Catrice said, and as we gazed out on that magnificent vista, a hawk glided down, talons extended, and snatched something from the grass, winging skyward with a triumphant scream. I was jolted by the scene even though it was perfectly natural. Survival of the fittest.

Catrice said in amusement, "That one didn't last long."

"I beg your pardon?"

"The mouse." She turned to me, eyes gleaming. "Hawks are such marvelous hunters, aren't they? They can spot something as small a rodent from above the treetops. They rule the skies, too. Other birds fear them. Did you notice how quiet the forest was when we walked through?"

I said slowly, "How did you know it was a mouse?"

She smiled and cocked her head. "I hear the teakettle," she said and disappeared.

I stared after her. In her own way, Catrice was every bit as off-putting as Luna and Bryn, and I was suddenly reminded of how Thane had referred to the three women after dinner the other night. The Witches of Eastwick, he'd called them. *Or I should say Asher Falls.*

I tracked the hawk for a moment longer, and then as I moved back into the room, I suddenly had the uncanny sensation that *I* was being watched. I decided that it must be the painting. Edward Asher's eyes. Even on canvas, his face unnerved me. But as I moved about the studio, I could have sworn an invisible gaze followed me. It was all I could do not to glance over my shoulder.

Somewhere to my right came a very faint click—like the stealthy closing of a door.

Catrice had gone through a doorway near the windows, but this sound had come from the opposite side of the room where three arched niches had been cut into the stone. As I moved in for a closer look, I saw that one of the arches was actually a door. Had someone been standing there watching me while my back was turned?

I stepped into the alcove and pushed on the latch. The door silently opened, and I heard the distant murmur of voices. I didn't know why I felt so compelled to discover who else was in the studio. I told myself to let it go. I shouldn't go snooping through someone else's private space. My mother would be appalled by my bad manners.

But despite that internal censure, I slipped through the opening and followed a dim hallway until it curved around to another partially open door through which I spotted Catrice.

"—I'm telling you, it's *her*," she insisted.

"I pray you're wrong," someone else said, and I thought I recognized Bryn's voice. "Because that would mean—"

"Oh, God, don't say it." Catrice shuddered. "It's too horrible to contemplate."

"I'll tell you what it means," Luna said softly. "Someone knows."

When Catrice came out of the kitchen a little while later, I was back at the windows. I turned with an apologetic smile. "I'm sorry you went to so much trouble, but I really have to be going."

"Oh, you have to at least try the tea," she said anxiously. "It's my own special brew."

My gaze fell to the steam rising from the porcelain cup, and I suppressed a shudder. After what I'd just overheard, I didn't trust her. And I certainly didn't want to drink her tea. "I really do have to go," I said, edging toward the door. "I'll try it next time."

"I'll hold you to that." She set aside the tea tray to walk me to the door. Her eyes lifted as she stepped outside, and I knew that she was watching the hawks. For some reason, her rapt expression frightened me.

"You can find your way back up to the house?" she asked.

I forced a smile. "No problem. I'll just follow the path."

She stood outside until I was out of sight. I never glanced back, but I could feel her eyes on me. The others watched me, too. I had a terrible thought that they had all gathered at the studio to observe me, but how could that be? How could they know that I would give Catrice a ride home...unless it had somehow been prearranged?

But why?

As I hurried along the path, my nerve endings tingled with an awareness I didn't understand. It was as if some long-dormant instinct had suddenly come alive, and I could feel the forest reaching out to me, hear the leaves whispering to me once again. Even the screams of the hawks somehow seemed familiar.

I was so attuned to my surroundings that even the miniscule sound of a snapping twig brought me to an abrupt halt. I told myself it was nothing, just an animal rustling in the underbrush. A bird flitting in the tree-tops. I didn't believe it, of course. Someone was out there.

The silence seemed palpable as I stood on the trail holding my breath. My heart began to hammer, and I could feel the blood pulsing in my ears. So many things rushed through my head. Wayne's warning about wild animals. The face wavering in the pool at the water-fall. The chill of the wind, that awful howling. I had the sense that I was being stalked, but was the tracker human, animal…or something from the other side?

I took a few tentative steps along the trail and heard the rustle of leaves as the pursuer moved with me. Now I really was scared. I considered turning and making a run for the studio, but how could I be sure it wasn't one of *them?*

Swallowing hard, I willed my pulse to slow. The last thing I needed was to succumb to a full-blown panic. My father had grown up in woods like these. I tried to remember everything he'd told me about wild animals. *The moment they sense your fear, you become prey.*

Prey.

The very word sent a shiver of dread up my spine. I hadn't understood before, but it came to me clearly in that moment. I'd been watched at the cemetery, lured into the woods, followed to the laurel bald and now something was stalking me up this trail. I'd been prey ever since I arrived in Asher Falls.

And with that thought, I gave up all pretense of calm. I whirled and plunged headlong up the path, my footsteps pounding in time to my heartbeats. I didn't know if I was pursued. I had the sense of something rushing through the woods, but I didn't look back until I rounded the corner to Catrice's house, and even then I spared only a brief glance over my shoulder.

He came out of nowhere.

In the split second my attention was diverted, he appeared on the path in front of me and put out his hands to stop me.

If not for years of suppressing fear, I would have shrieked louder than the hawks, but instead I gulped back the scream and wrenched myself free of him. I heard him laugh, and in my agitated state, the sound took on a sinister connotation. But when he spoke, his voice was almost pleasant. "Whoa," Hugh said. "Where's the fire?"

"I—"

He gazed down at me in bemusement. "Are you all right?"

Even in broad daylight with the pine boughs stippling the sunlight, Hugh Asher's looks rendered me speechless. Everything about him, from the casual but elegant attire to the way he carried himself, was so excessively perfect.

Once again, I searched for the flaws, and this time they were easy to spot—a faint tinge of yellow beneath the jawbone where a bruise had almost faded and a scab above his left eyebrow where the skin had been split.

He'd been in a fight recently, and the thought was so incongruous as to take my breath away. My mind shifted at once to Thane's cut temple, his bruised knuckles. Had he and Hugh fought?

I tore my gaze from his face. "I was just coming up from the studio. I thought I heard something in the woods."

He looked past me down the path. "Probably a deer. Could have been a coyote but they don't normally come out until dusk."

Like ghosts.

"I'm a city girl," I tried to say lightly. "I'm not used to the wildlife around here."

"It does take some getting used to."

The way he stared down at me made me increasingly uncomfortable, and I had to wonder why he was there. Had he come to observe me, too?

"How's the restoration coming along?" he asked, still in that pleasing cadence. But no matter how agreeable or personable he seemed, I had no wish to make small talk. I really just wanted to go home, and I glanced longingly toward my car.

"Fine."

Still he lingered, but I didn't think he was as relaxed as I'd first thought. There was something about him, some tension or excitement that made his eyes overly bright. "When I was a kid, we used to play hide-and-seek up on that hill. Not a game for the faint of heart. It could get a little hairy after dark."

"I can imagine."

"There are places up there where you could hide and not be found for days. If ever."

Like the laurel bald, I thought with a shiver. "Speaking of the cemetery...I should get going," I said, latching onto the first excuse I could think of.

"I won't keep you. But you'll have to come to dinner soon. Maris has gone away for a few days and it gets dull in that big house with just us three men."

"I'm sure Luna will be more than happy to accommodate," I said, surprising myself as much as him.

He lifted a brow, eyes gleaming in amusement. "I think Father may have underestimated you," he murmured.

"What does that mean?"

Something dark flashed across that handsome face. "You really don't know, do you?"

"I have no idea what you're talking about. If you'll excuse me...I have work to do."

I brushed past him and headed toward my car. This time, I did glance back, but Hugh Asher had vanished.

Twenty-Five

❧❧❧

That afternoon Thane came by to see me. I let Angus out the back door, and he prowled the yard while we sat on the steps in the sunshine. Neither of us talked much at first. I was too preoccupied and disturbed by what I'd heard at Catrice's studio and by that brief clash with Hugh. I still couldn't understand why he thought Pell Asher had underestimated me. *You really don't know, do you?*

Thane leaned back, elbows propped on the top step as he looked out over the glistening surface of Bell Lake. I followed his gaze. The uninitiated would never guess at the darkness that lay beneath that silken shimmer, but my time with ghosts had given me nothing if not sufficient imagination to envision that sunken necropolis with its overturned monuments and encrusted angels. I could picture Freya down there, too, floating among the headstones.

I turned back to Thane. "Can I ask you something?"

He shrugged. "Sure." His eyes were very clear and very green in the sunlight, but like Bell Lake, his secrets were hidden beneath that placid surface. In the short time I'd known him, I'd detected ripples of some underlying disturbance. Flashes of some deep-rooted anger.

"Why did you tell me about the flooded cemetery that day on the ferry? Were you trying to scare me away?"

He smiled, but his face remained impassive. "Not at all. I only meant to entertain you with a little local color. I figured a cemetery restorer would appreciate a good ghost story. Was I right?"

"You have no idea."

"See? I knew it." He closed his eyes, basking in the sunlight.

"It's funny to think about that conversation now," I said. "I'd never set eyes on you or this place, and yet you already knew so much about me."

"Not enough." He smiled teasingly. "Tell me your deepest, darkest secrets."

"I wouldn't know where to start."

"How about your childhood? Or your teenage years? What were you like in high school? Did you have a lot of boyfriends? Were you popular?"

I gave him a look. "Hardly."

"Late bloomer?"

"You might say that." A ghost had haunted the hallways of my school, making it impossible for me to participate in extracurricular activities after dusk. Not that I would have wanted to, anyway. By the time I entered high school, my reputation as a loner had become local canon. Rather than reinvent myself, I had embraced the solitude, retreating with my beloved books to the sanctuary of Rosehill Cemetery. "I grew up in a graveyard. You can imagine how popular I was."

He grinned. "Were you teased?"

"Not really. I was pretty much just ignored."

"Were you lonely?"

I hesitated. "Yes, sometimes. But being alone was all I ever knew. And in some ways, my childhood was idyllic. At least…for a time." Until the ghosts came.

"That's more than most people can say."

I glanced at him curiously. "What about you? I can't imagine that you were ever an introvert."

"No, not an introvert. I had too much to prove. Too much to live up to."

"Because you were an Asher?"

A shadow flickered across his face. "Because I wasn't an Asher."

"Was it hard when you first came here to live?"

"Yes, but I survived. It was eat or be eaten at Pathway Academy. And at Asher House."

"That doesn't sound very pleasant."

He squinted into the sun. "It is what it is. Survival of the fittest."

That made me think of Catrice's hawks, and my mind turned once again to that troubling conversation I'd overheard. I wrapped my arms around myself and shivered.

"Cold?"

"No…just someone walking over my grave."

"Cheery thought."

"Can I ask you about your stepfather?"

"Edward? What about him?"

"What was he like?"

Thane considered the question for a moment. "He

wasn't like Hugh or Grandfather. He had the Asher charm, but he was quieter. More introspective. At least that's the way I remember him."

"What did he do? For a living, I mean."

"I have no idea. He tried any number of things, but he always seemed to fall back on his trust money."

Was that bitterness I heard in his voice? I didn't think so. More like resignation. He'd done more to restore the family's holdings than either Edward or Hugh, his grandfather had told me. And yet he still had to fight for his place.

"He wanted to break free of the Asher shackles," Thane said. "He just never quite managed."

"What about you?"

"I'm not imprisoned. I like what I do."

"And what is it you do, exactly?"

"I guess you could call me an overseer. The Ashers made their fortune in timber and mining, but these days, it's mostly a matter of managing the investments, dwindling though they may be." He paused. "I do understand why Edward left, though. Grandfather can be overbearing. Sometimes it's hard to take."

"Like trying to end your relationship with Harper?"

"Like trying to play God," he said grimly.

"Do you think Edward was involved with Freya?" I asked.

He lifted a brow in surprise. "Where did that come from?"

"I don't know. I'm just curious."

He shrugged. "Given his reaction to her photograph, I'd say it's a safe bet they had some sort of relationship, and I can't imagine Grandfather being too happy about it."

"Do you think he broke them up?"

"Does it matter? It was a long time ago and they're both dead now."

"I know, but I find all these relationships fascinating. Freya and Edward. Edward and Bryn. Wayne and Luna. Luna and Hugh. It's all so—"

"Incestuous?"

"I was going to say entangled."

"That's the nature of a small town," Thane said. "Especially one as isolated and insular as Asher Falls."

"You've never considered moving?"

He frowned. "Why would I move? This is my home. This is where I belong."

I thought about the familiarity I'd felt in those woods, and I pulled up my legs, hugging them to my chest as I rested my chin on my knees. What an odd, scary place this was. So much dark history. So many lingering emotions bubbling beneath the pastoral façade. Yet here I was and here I would remain because I couldn't leave without knowing the truth. Without finding my place.

Lifting my gaze to the highest summit of the mountain ridge, I listened for that whisper. That telltale ripple through the trees.

Beside me, Thane caught his breath, and I turned to find his eyes on me. He looked pale and unsettled, though I hadn't seen or heard anything to disturb the calm setting.

"What is it?" I asked sharply.

He reached out as if to touch me, then let his hand fall away before he made contact. "My God," he whispered. "Who are you?"

Twenty-Six

A shiver ran up my spine at his stunned look. "What are you talking about? You know who I am."

"It's like seeing—"

"What?" Something inside me started to quake, and I tried to glance away, but the intensity of his gaze held me.

He searched my face. "The way you were staring up at the mountains just now…your expression…" He trailed off. "This is crazy."

"What is? Please, just tell me." But already I could feel myself withdrawing into my own head. For all my preoccupation with truth and destiny, I was terrified of what I might learn here, terrified of how it would change me. I sensed a connection to whatever waited for me on that mountain just as surely as I'd felt a suffocating tie to that hidden grave.

There was a reason I saw ghosts. It wasn't happenstance, and it couldn't be heredity because I was adopted. So what was I? Where was my place? Why, after all these years, had I been led here to Asher Falls?

He shook his head, as if trying to free himself of something unpleasant. "It was just one of those strange moments. Déjà vu or something."

"Your reaction seemed more than déjà vu. You were genuinely upset."

"No, not upset. Just…surprised." He tried to laugh it off, but his voice sounded strained. "Sorry if I freaked you out. I'm seeing things, I guess. Like you did that day at the laurel bald, remember? You thought for a moment I was someone else."

"I remember."

"We concluded it was lack of sleep. The mind playing tricks." He was trying very hard to convince himself. Who had he seen just now when he looked at me? *What* had he seen? "You called it something that day."

"A waking dream," I murmured.

"A waking dream. Yes, that's exactly how it felt. Well." He glanced at me. "That was interesting."

"You're not going to tell me about it?"

"No, I think we should just let it pass," he said. "Moving on…"

But we both fell silent, as if entrapped by the heavy weight of our secrets. The shadows lengthened at the edge of the woods, and the sunlight on the steps was dappled now, filtered through the branches of the evergreens. I felt bone-weary from all the physical labor at the cemetery, and yet an odd restlessness gripped me.

Suddenly, I thought of that vision I'd had at the falls of the couple naked and entwined at the water's edge as creatures looked on. As the very earth seemed to pulsate with dark, unspeakable passion….

I shuddered violently.

"What's wrong?"

My cheeks colored as I glanced away, but he leaned forward, taking my chin in his hand to gently turn me to face him. "I'm sorry if I upset you just now. I don't even know why I said that."

"It's not that. I was thinking about something you said after dinner the other night when we were going through those pictures." Not exactly what I'd been thinking about, but I could hardly tell him the truth. "You said there was a certain eccentricity about Luna and Bryn and Catrice. You called them witches. What did you mean by that?"

"It was just a joke, but there's always been an air of mystery about them," he said. "An element of mysticism. Somehow they've managed to thrive while the rest of the town languishes. But I suspect that's more a matter of smart investments and good genetics than witchcraft. Despite the talk."

I glanced at him. "What talk?"

"The usual small-town gossip mixed with mountain folklore.

"There's an old rumor that the Daughters of our Valiant Heroes was once a coven."

I glanced at him, startled. "I thought it was a historical society."

He shrugged. "Like I said, it's an old rumor."

The breeze had a distinct chill now. "Why didn't you say anything about these rumors when we were at the falls looking at the *Drudenfuss?*"

"You already seemed a little spooked. And it's no big deal. A town like this breeds superstition and gossip, especially when it comes to those three women. They've always been close, always a little different and now that they've reached a certain age with no families to speak of—"

"What about Sidra?"

"Ah, yes. Sidra."

"Why do you say it like that?"

He was silent for a moment. "Sidra is a bit of an enigma herself, in case you hadn't noticed."

"She is different," I agreed. "But I like her. I think she has an old soul. She seems much more mature than other girls her age."

"Little wonder, given her condition. She was born with a severe heart defect. The doctors didn't think she'd live past her twelfth birthday, but somehow she's managed to defy the odds."

I thought of the girl's pale complexion and those guarded eyes. She looked fragile, but I'd always sensed an inner strength. Now I knew why. I also wondered if her condition had something to do with her ability to see ghosts. But that wouldn't explain my situation. There was nothing wrong with my heart. I'd always been the picture of health.

"Where's her father?" I asked.

"He died years ago. Suddenly, as I recall. I don't remember too much about him except that he had money and he was a good deal older than Bryn." Thane watched the water for a moment. "Why all the questions about Luna and her cohorts?"

"Is that how people around here refer to them? Luna and her cohorts?"

"Just a figure of speech. Anyway, why all the interest?"

I hesitated, still considering how much I should tell him. "Something happened earlier and I've been trying to figure out what it means. I saw Catrice in town and she asked for a ride home. Then she offered to give me a tour of her studio. She never said a word about anyone else being there, but Bryn and Luna were in another room. And then I saw Hugh coming up the path to the studio as I was leaving."

"So?"

"Why didn't she mention that the others were there? Why did Luna and Bryn stay out of sight? Don't you find that odd?"

"I take it you do."

"Very odd. I had the distinct impression that they had all gathered at the studio to…observe me."

"To observe you," he repeated. "That's—"

"Disturbing. I know."

"And maybe a little paranoid," he suggested. His tone was light, but I had a feeling he meant it. I did sound paranoid.

"Why would they want to observe you?" he asked in a cautious tone, as though wanting to placate but not encourage me.

I hugged my knees tighter. "I don't know. But it's not my imagination. Something strange is happening to me here, Thane. I have this awful feeling…this premonition…" I looked past him to the mountains. "You must feel it, too," I said in a half whisper. "It can't just be me."

He glanced away. "What do you think is happening to you?"

"I don't know, but it has something to do with the flooding of Thorngate Cemetery. And Freya's death. Maybe even Wayne's attack and that hidden grave in the laurel bald. They're all connected somehow. There's a design here, some bigger scheme, and I know it sounds insane, but I can't shake the feeling that I've been brought here for a reason."

"You *were* brought here for a reason," he said. "To restore a cemetery."

"But think of the circumstances." A hint of desperation crept into my voice. If he hadn't thought me paranoid before, he certainly would now. "The donation that brought me here was made anonymously. Why? And why restore Thorngate *now* after years and years of neglect? Why hire *me* when there are other restorers in the state with far more experience?"

"Your credentials are impressive," he reasoned.

I shrugged.

"Why else do you think you were brought here?" he asked softly. "You've never been to Asher Falls before, have you? You don't have family here."

"I don't know why. But there's a tie. I know it." The breeze blew a dead leaf against my leg, and it clung for a moment before tumbling away. "Remember that day at the falls when I told you I felt a vibration? It was strong, like the pulse of an electrical current, but you couldn't feel it because it was coming from within. It's like this place, this land…even the mountains are calling out to me, and something inside me is responding."

An emotion I couldn't name flashed across his face before he rose and put out his hand. "Let's take a walk."

Angus followed us down the stepping-stones, but he wouldn't come out on the wooden walkway. Instead, he remained on solid ground, keeping watch while we strolled to the very end to gaze down into those murky depths.

As the sun slipped toward the treetops, the shade

from the forest deepened the shoreline to black. I leaned over the railing, peering through the shadows and algae, straining to see the headstones and monuments of that watery graveyard. If I stared long enough, would I see Freya's ghost float to the surface?

"Have you ever been down there?" I asked Thane. "To Thorngate, I mean. It seems like something an adventurous kid would want to see."

"I did dive down there once," he admitted. "I was maybe twelve or thirteen at the time."

"What did it look like?"

"Visibility is pretty limited. There's a lot of sediment and debris. I didn't see any graves or headstones. No coffins or bones, either," he said with a grin. "But there was a statue…an angel. It was tall and still upright and it seemed to appear out of nowhere right in front of me. There was just enough light shining down through the water that for a moment, she looked alive. It was… unnerving to say the least."

"What did you do?"

"Surfaced and got the hell out of there." The grin flashed again.

"You've never gone back down?"

"No, but not because of the angel." He rested his arms on the railing and stared out across the calm water. "It seemed intrusive somehow. Disrespectful. Like I was disturbing their rest." He slanted a glance. "Feel free to call me crazy."

I tucked a strand of hair behind my ear. "I'm the woman who feels phantom vibrations, remember?"

I saw a smile in his eyes and something darker. Something that made me tremble in anticipation as he put his hand over mine on the railing. "About those vibrations. Maybe it's not the land you're responding to."

I glanced away.

"Do I make you uncomfortable?" he asked.

"Yes, because I think you're somehow a part of this."

"That's ridiculous. There's no grand design to all this, Amelia. There's no such thing as destiny. What you feel is what you feel. You just have to trust it."

I thought about the girl he'd wanted to marry—Harper—and wondered what she'd been like. Pell had said she was unstable. A danger to herself and to others.

Like Devlin's family, she'd died in a terrible car crash. But her ghost hadn't lingered. For whatever reason, she didn't haunt Thane. I wondered if that was his doing or hers.

I could feel his warm gaze on me. Shakily I said, "This is hard for me."

He nodded. "I understand. You still have issues with that detective. No one knows better than I do how hard it is to let go of memories. But the past is no place to live your life, and sometimes the best way to move on is to move on."

"And if I'm not ready?"

"Then you're not ready. I won't push you. But I won't go quietly away, either."

"You won't have to. Once the restoration is finished, I'll be the one to go away."

His eyes darkened as he stared down at me. "Charleston isn't so far."

Wasn't it? At the moment, my beloved city—and my beloved Devlin—seemed a million miles from me. "Why me?" I asked softly.

He stroked a knuckle down my cheek. "Why not you?"

I closed my eyes on a shiver. "Ivy once told me that you would never choose me...an outsider."

"She said that?" He sounded annoyed. "Ivy's a troubled girl. I don't think she has much family support. Her father is some high-powered attorney in Columbia and her mother is always traveling. Half the time, Ivy is left on her own. Poor kid's starved for attention. That's why I've tried to cut her some slack. But she knows nothing about my choices. Or anything else about me, for that matter."

"But there is a caste system in this town. Sidra told me earlier that she's not allowed to visit Tilly Pattershaw's house because Tilly isn't one of them."

His hand dropped away, and I could sense his irritation. "She's probably just parroting what she's heard her mother say. Bryn's an insufferable snob."

"No. Catrice said something like that, too." I glanced down at the blisters in my palms and thought of Tilly's burned hands. "She said that Freya was always trying to fit in where she didn't belong. I suppose that's why she turned up in all those pictures. She wanted to be one of them."

He sighed. "You do realize you're sounding a little obsessed."

"Yes."

He watched me for a moment. "Why does this stuff matter to you so much? It's ancient history."

"You said the other day that you have a responsibility to find out who's buried in that hidden grave because it's located on Asher property. I feel a similar responsibility to Freya."

"But why? You never even knew her. And she's been dead for years."

I thought of her ghost wavering at the end of the pier, right where we stood now, and I felt something well inside me, that deep sadness that wasn't my own but had somehow become a part of me. "I don't understand it myself, but I feel driven to find out what happened to her. To find out why no one will talk about her death."

"That's just the way it is around here. Folks tend to mind their own business."

"Even when it comes to dog fighting and hidden graves," I said bitterly.

"When it comes to anything."

I stared down into those gloomy depths and envisioned Freya's ghost. I could see her in my mind, dressed in her burial finery, hair blowing in the breeze. If I found out what happened to her, would she be able to rest? Would she leave me in peace?

Or would she come back at every twilight to feed on my warmth and energy so that she could sustain her presence in the world of the living?

Either way, I had to know.

Twenty-Seven

After Thane left, I stayed outside to watch the sunset. As late afternoon drifted toward evening, the air and light shifted, and the scattering of clouds across the western sky turned bloodred. Dusk dropped and I felt, not a vibration or even a ripple, but a waiting stillness. A held breath....

And then she was there as I somehow knew she would be. Freya's ghost.

Her shimmering form appeared to me a split second before Angus growled a warning. I didn't turn toward her, of course. I couldn't discard my father's rules that easily. So I sat there quaking in that abnormal chill as I watched her from the corner of my eye.

She floated up from the lake, pausing on the stepping-stones as if some invisible barrier kept her from coming any closer. As I tracked her in my periphery, I talked soothingly to Angus, but he wouldn't settle down. He paced in front of me, hair bristling in agitation.

"It's all right," I soothed. "We're perfectly safe here."

Perfectly safe. Was there even such a thing?

A few steps and we would at least be on hallowed ground. That was the one rule that hadn't changed since my time with Devlin. My sanctuary had yet to be penetrated by ghosts. I had to believe that Freya's spirit wouldn't be able to breach my refuge, either.

But instead of retreating into the house, I turned my head slightly, pretending to gaze out over the lake. The first thing I noticed was her demeanor. She wasn't staring up at me as she'd done on that first night. Nor did she challenge me as she had on the second. I didn't feel her confusion or her anger or any other emotion. She was just…there, suspended in that strange in-between time when the glow of the sunset lingered even as the moon started to rise. Trapped in that eerie light, she hovered motionless until I looked at her. And then slowly she lifted her head and impaled me with her ghost eyes.

My heart tripped, and the air expelled from my lungs in a painful rush. There was no wind to speak of, but I felt the icy bite of a draft down my spine, the bristle of fear at my nape. Now I was desperate to retreat, but I couldn't move. I sat frozen in terror, frozen in time as those nebulous tentacles reached out to me, connecting for one split second my mind to hers. In that fleeting moment of illumination, everything around me and inside me went very still, and yet the silence teemed with imagined noises. With moans and whispers and a million hellish sounds that threatened to blend at any moment into one very real scream.

I saw her in my mind but not as a ghost. Gone was that ethereal façade, the otherworldly beauty of her specter, and in its place was the grotesque death mask of her corpse. She hadn't perished in a tragic fire. She'd been murdered, her throat slashed from ear to ear. And as she lay prone on the ground, eyes open and sightless, I could see the outline of a pregnant belly through her bloody dress.

It happened in a heartbeat, that vision. As the breeze swept up from the lake, it was already starting to fade. But I remained in the grip of that terrible paralysis, unable to move, barely able to breathe. My fingers had automatically gone to the stone at my neck, and I clutched it frantically, trying to summon the protection of Rosehill Cemetery. Not just for me, but for Freya and her unborn child.

She was fading, too. I could see through her now, all the way to Bell Lake where mist swirled and writhed over the surface. Below, the bells started to ring as the dead began to stir.

The ghost turned toward the water, tilting her head as if listening to the phantom tolling. She looked back once, over her shoulder, and then she was gone.

I remained on the steps as the mist coiled over the lake. My disregard of the rules was reckless and stupid, and yet there I sat.

It was almost as if I was daring Freya's ghost to come back. I didn't understand my behavior. What was happening to me here? How could I be so drawn to and repelled by the same bizarre place?

Go home, a little voice prodded. *Forget about this town. Forget about restless souls and Freya's murder and that hidden grave in the laurel bald. Forget about Pell Asher and Luna Kemper and poor Tilly Pattershaw, with her wounded birds and burned hands.*

Forget about that presence in the mountains, those odd vibrations and the bells that toll for the dead beneath the lake. Forget that you have a connection to Asher Falls. Forget that you were ever here.

I drew a breath and slowly released it. But I couldn't forget because now I knew that Freya had been murdered. I might be the only person other than the killer who did know. And no matter how many years had passed, justice would have to be served. Maybe that was why I'd been brought here.

Angus had been lying at my feet, but now he got up and trotted down the stepping-stones. He was too close to the water's edge. Too close to the mist. My heart started to pound in trepidation.

"Angus, come back here!"

He looked up at me and whimpered, his tail working furiously, but he didn't obey and I didn't want to go get him. Already the fog rolled toward the shoreline. The spirits would soon rise. All those restless souls reaching out for me....

I shivered and called to him again. "Angus! Come, boy! Time to go in!"

Another mournful look, another whimper and then he began to paw frantically at the exact spot where the ghost had disappeared.

Dear God, what had he found? And did I really want to know?

Reluctantly, I got up and walked down the stepping-stones, my gaze on the lake, on that creeping, swirling mist.

"What is it, Angus?"

The offering lay on one of the stones.

I had almost expected to find a puddle of blood, but

what she'd left instead was a rose and a bud, both severed from a thorny stem.

As I bent to pick them up, the rose started to wither.

Not surprisingly, I couldn't sleep that night. I lay wide-awake for hours, contemplating Freya's murder. She'd been pregnant when she was killed, and for whatever reason, she wanted me to know that she and her unborn child had been buried together in that hidden grave, not in the cemetery as Thane had said. Which begged the question, who was buried in the Thorngate grave? Who had perished in that fire?

And who had been caring for that hidden site in the laurel bald? The killer?

Luna's voice drifted out of the darkness. *Someone knows*. Had she been talking about Freya's murder?

The questions went on and on, and as I lay there wide-awake, I tried to think of possible suspects. As much as I wanted to pin the blame on Edward—someone already dead—I had a very bad feeling that the murderer still resided in Asher Falls. After all these years, they must have thought they were home free. Then I'd found that hidden grave. I'd started to ask questions about Freya, and now I'd made myself a target.

Angus whimpered in his sleep, the sound a manifestation of my own anxiety. It was only from total exhaustion that I finally drifted off, but my mind still wouldn't rest. Visions swirled in my head of Freya and her unborn baby. Of someone lying in wait for her at the falls.

And then the whole dream shifted and I was in Thane's arms in that same glade. I could feel the mist on my face as we lay entwined by the pool. I could feel my heart pounding even in sleep, and my whole body pulsated with the need to have him deeper, deeper inside me. I clutched at him frantically, my nails leaving marks on his back, and the pain seemed to excite him. For a moment, he didn't look altogether human, but something savage, something beautiful, something not quite of this world.

"Soon," he whispered. His mouth found my breast, and as I responded to his rhythm, the creatures stirred. One by one they crawled from their holes to stare down at us. Not ghosts this time, not the Others that had been awakened by Devlin and me, but abominations that belonged neither to the living world nor to the realm of the dead.

A wind blew down from the mountains, rippling leaves and carrying night scents, and the half-beings began to howl. Or was that noise coming from me?

I tried to push Thane away only to realize that he was already gone. I was alone in the glade, shivering in the mist from the falls. I drew my knees to my chest and wrapped my arms tightly around my legs. Never had I felt so lost, so alone. So afraid.

I glanced up and saw someone gazing down at me from the top of the cliff. Not Ivy this time, but Luna....

Eyes gleaming like a cat in the moonlight, she lowered herself over the edge and slunk headfirst down the cliff. Then came Bryn and Catrice, and the unholy trio formed a circle around me as I buried my face in my arms.

I felt lips in my hair, a breath on my neck and the trail of icy fingers down my spine. They lifted me to my feet, touching and crooning as they dressed me. I looked down to find that I had on Freya's burial frock.

Through the diaphanous folds, I could see the swell of my belly, could feel the vibration of a second heartbeat inside me....

My own gasp woke me up. Heart still pounding, I clutched my flat stomach. It took a moment to realize that I'd been dreaming. *Oh, thank God.*

The room had grown colder while I'd slept, and I pulled the covers to my chin as I pushed myself up against the headboard. Angus wasn't in his makeshift bed, but instead had gone over to the window to stare out. He glanced around when he heard me stir, but then his head whipped back to the glass, as if he'd spied something in the dark that he needed to keep an eye on.

"What is it?" I whispered as I slipped out of bed.

I padded over to the window to look out. I saw nothing at first, but then at the very edge of the forest, my gaze lit on a shadow, deeper than the others, with a distinctly human shape. And I started to tremble.

Someone—or some*thing*—watched the house.

Twenty-Eight

Angus and I returned to the cemetery the next morning. The day was cloudless and so warm and peaceful I could hardly believe all that had transpired since I'd last been there. I now knew that Freya had been murdered, and she and her unborn baby were buried in the laurel bald.

But what could I do with the information? Going to the police was out of the question, and I wasn't equipped to launch an investigation on my own. My interest in Freya and the hidden grave had already aroused suspicion, and I was being watched. From here on out, I had to be very, very careful. Until I could figure out how best to act on the ghost's revelation, I had to continue the restoration as though I knew nothing. And as badly as I wanted to return to the hidden grave to look for clues, I didn't dare go into the laurel bald alone. It was too remote. Too confusing. *There are places up there where you could hide and not be found for days. If ever.*

As I made my way through the gravestones, I kept

an eye on the mausoleum. With my back to the gate, I relied on Angus to alert me if something—animal, human or otherwise—came up the road or through the woods.

Armed with clippers and a machete, I attacked the overgrowth near the fence with a vengeance. Kudzu had crept in from the woods and had a choke hold on some of the monuments. The elongated stems curled around tree branches and entangled with briars, making the grove nearly impenetrable.

As I worked, squirrels foraged in the underbrush and birds twittered from the treetops. Despite everything that had happened, I began to relax. Like Papa, I loved working with my hands, and I found nothing more satisfying than uncovering overgrown headstones and markers.

But as I chopped deeply into the thicket, a feeling of claustrophobia overtook me. The vegetation was dense and insidious, and the harder I worked, the more entangled I became. Vines wrapped around my arms and legs and half-inch thorns stabbed through my jeans. As the flora closed in on me, the silence deepened. It was troubling, that quiet. I heard nothing in the underbrush now, and the birds had all flitted away. The only sound was my labored breathing and the swish of the machete.

A shadow passed over the sun, and as my head came up to track a lone hawk, I caught a whiff of something dead, something rotting.

I told myself an animal had crawled into the thicket and died. But suddenly I remembered the smell that had seeped through my open car window that day on the hill when I'd passed the old man in the overcoat. He'd had an animal carcass in the wagon, but I remembered thinking that the smell might have come from his own decaying flesh.

As I lifted a hand to my nose, a vine caught my arm and a thorn tore through my shirt. I pressed fingers to the scratch and brought away blood.

There was something strange about that thicket. Something unnatural. I tried to fight my way out, but vines snaked around my ankles. As I bent to free them, another twisted around my neck, and suddenly I was yanked off my feet. Before I could utter a sound, I was being dragged backward into the thicket as brambles ripped through my clothing and tangled in my hair.

I tore at the snare around my neck, tried to dig my heels into the ground to slow the momentum. Frantically, I clutched at the briars, oblivious now of the pricks. Inch by agonizing inch, I was being pulled into the heart of the copse....

Angus was barking. The sound seemed a long way off. We were so deeply inside the thicket I could see nothing now but shadows. Nothing but darkness. The smell of rotting flesh grew stronger. I heard a rasping breath, and an image came to me of something not quite human towing me through the bushes....

Oh, God, help me...someone help me, please....

Hands closed around my ankles. I felt a vicious tug and then another. Someone was pulling me back toward the edge of the thicket, and for a moment I was locked in a terrifying tug-of-war. The noose around my neck snapped, and I heard something that sounded like a squeal. Then silence. I lay still for a moment before I began to kick my way free.

"Stop thrashing, girl! You'll tear your skin to ribbons."

Tilly?

She was beside me, lifting my head. "Can you walk?"

"I think so…"

"Get up, then. Hurry!"

I felt it then, that awful wind. That dank chill that seeped down into my bones, down into my soul.…

"It's coming," she whispered.

She handed me a machete, and together we whacked our way out of the brambles. Angus ran back and forth at the edge of the thicket, his bark as agitated as I'd ever heard it.

"Angus, run!" I screamed, and, taking Tilly's hand, we tore after him, dead leaves swirling at our feet.

Fishing the remote from my pocket, I unlocked the SUV, and we all jumped inside. As I reached to start the engine, a crow landed on the hood and then another. The sky was suddenly black with them.

"What's happening?" I asked fearfully.

"Don't mind the birds, girl. Just go!"

I turned the ignition, pressed the accelerator and the car shot forward as the crows filled the cemetery, landing on headstones and monuments and swarming down upon that formidable circle of Asher angels.

We flew down the hill. Tilly rode up front with me, and Angus was in the back, head thrust over the console between us. I turned onto the main highway without slowing, and Tilly said, "Ease up, girl, before you get us all killed!"

I let up on the gas and flashed her a glance. "What was back there?"

Her gloved hands lay still in her lap. "I don't know."

"But you must have seen something."

"You were all tangled up in them brambles. That's what I saw."

My voice rose in desperation. "Something was *there*."

"Carry us to my house," she said calmly. "You've got blood all over you."

"I don't care about that."

"You will care if infection sets in."

"Tilly—"

"My house, girl. After I tend to them scratches, I'll tell you what I know."

She was silent the rest of the way to her home, and I was in so much pain I didn't feel like talking. All I wanted to do was crawl into a tub of ice water to relieve my inflamed skin.

"Lie down here," she said as she led me into a bedroom, and I stretched out on cool sheets.

"What about Angus?"

"I'll put him out back."

"He might run away. I'm worried about him going into the woods."

"He won't go into the woods." She pressed me back into the pillows, and I closed my eyes.

She left the room for a few minutes, then came back smelling of fresh herbs. She placed a moist, cool cloth on my face, then gently peeled back my shirt and treated the scratches on my neck and arms.

"What are you putting on me?"

"An old remedy my mama taught me. You rest now, girl. Give that pokeweed time to draw the fire out."

"But—"

"Shush. You rest and then we'll talk."

I closed my eyes. It was so cool and quiet in that little bedroom. I could hear Tilly puttering around in the house, and the birds were chirping outside the window. Such comforting sounds. So soothing. That terrible burn from the scratches began to subside, and I let myself float. I felt very safe here.

I must have fallen asleep almost at once. When I woke up, the noonday sun slanted through the window, and I lay there for a moment, still drowsy and drifting in that in-between space. Then I remembered where I was, and I sat up in bed. The cloth that Tilly had applied to my face was dry now, and I peeled it away. The flesh was still irritated, but much less inflamed. Her mother's remedy had done the trick.

Swinging my legs over the side of the bed, I sat on the edge as I buttoned my shirt and looked around. It was a sweet little room with blue willow plates decorating the pale walls and brightly colored birdhouses hanging from the ceiling. A patchwork quilt lay folded at the end of the bed, while homemade scatter rugs warmed the scarred wooden floor.

The room was pleasant…but oddly impersonal. No photographs adorned the nightstand, no lipsticks or perfumes cluttered the dressing table. And yet I somehow knew the room had been Freya's. Where were all her belongings? I wondered. Her adolescent keepsakes? Then I remembered that she'd been dead for over twenty-five years. She would remain seventeen forever in the ghost world, but here time had marched on. Tilly had probably put away her things a long time ago.

A little porcelain sparrow sat alone on a shelf above the pine headboard. One of the wings was broken off, and I wondered why Tilly had kept it. Maybe it was symbolic of her work with injured birds. Or, more likely, it had been a gift from Freya, and now Tilly displayed it in a place of honor over her daughter's empty bed.

Did she have any idea that Freya had been murdered? How could I possibly keep something like that from her? And yet what good would the truth do her now?

It was a terrible dilemma, and something twisted inside me as I stared at the bird. In some cultures, sparrows were believed to carry the souls of the dead, but I didn't want to dwell on death at that moment, let alone murder, so I moved to the window to stare out. We were in the middle of the woods. I could smell the evergreens even through the glass and a whiff of spice now and then that lingered from Tilly's remedy.

Turning from the window, I reluctantly left that little blue sanctuary and went in search of her.

She was out on the back porch working on a wounded mourning dove.

I glanced into the cage. "What happened to it?"

"Broken wing," she said, and I thought of the little brown sparrow in that little blue bedroom.

"Is it going to be okay?"

"God willing."

The injured wing had been fastened securely to the dove's side with gauze, but the healthy wing lifted in agitation as those tiny black eyes tracked me. I kept my distance so as not to create undue stress.

"You look a good sight better," Tilly said as she replenished the minuscule food tray in the cage.

"I feel better. Thank you. I don't know what I would

have done if you hadn't come along when you did. You seem to always be coming to my rescue."

She said nothing to that, and to cover the awkward silence, I glanced around the cozy porch. I saw more bird cages at the far end, an old-fashioned porch swing and a comfortable rocker for keeping vigil. Outside, dozens of birdhouses were mounted on posts, and the treetops were alive with chatter and flitting bodies. I walked over to the screen to peer out. Angus saw me and came trotting up, whining to get in. "Tilly, why were those birds in the cemetery?"

"Let's sit, girl," she said as she moved to the other end of the porch. She took the rocker, and I sat down on the swing.

"You always seem to know when I'm in trouble," I said. "How was it you happened to be in the cemetery this morning?"

"I came to see about a job. I heard you needed help."

"Who did you hear that from?"

"Do you need help or don't you?" she asked bluntly.

"I'm always in need of an extra pair of hands, but I can't afford to pay much, I'm afraid."

"I don't need much."

I glanced around the homey porch and the lush backyard. The spider mums were blooming, and I could smell rosemary through the screen. "Your place is very peaceful," I said.

"It's home."

I settled back against the swing, one hand clasping the heavy chain. "Can we talk about what happened in the cemetery?" I asked. "Something was there. I know it."

Her head dropped back on the rocker, and she heaved

a sigh. "I don't have all the answers you're looking for, girl. All I know is that it's old. Older than the mountains, I reckon. Maybe it's been there from the beginning of time waiting for a chance to come through."

"Is it a ghost?"

"Not a ghost, though it be with them on the other side. Some call it Demon. Some call it Beast. I call it Evil. Pure evil."

My knuckles whitened where I clutched the swing chain.

Her eyes met mine, and I saw something hard and glittery and determined in those faded depths. Something that might have been edging toward crazy. "It has dominion there, but here it has to work through the weak, feeding on their fear and their hate and their greed."

"That's why you said I should be afraid of what's inside me," I said shakily.

She nodded.

"How do you know all this?"

"I can feel things," she said. "I can sense things. Ever since I was a little girl I could always tell when something bad was about to happen. My mama could, too. People feared us for it."

"That's what brought you into the woods the other night and to the cemetery today. You weren't looking for a job. You sensed I was in danger."

"I knew from the moment you set foot in Asher Falls you were in danger. Everything changed when you came."

"How?" I asked fearfully.

Her gaze went to the yard. "I've lived here a long time. I've seen things in these woods, heard things at

night that can't be explained. Not naturally, anyway."
Her face darkened, and I glimpsed that hint of insanity
again, though I had seen and heard the same things.

"I always knew this place was tainted," she said.
"I could feel it in the wind when I first came here. It
got so I was afraid to go outside after dark, and I was
never that way back home. But I knew something was
out there...watching and waiting..." She trailed off and
drew a breath. "When the water rose over the cemetery,
it got worse. Animals started acting up. Strangers came
to town to walk the streets at night. People turned on
each another. Those who could left this place. Those
who stayed learned to watch their backs. And some
embraced Evil."

"Embraced it how?"

She put a gloved hand to her heart. "They let it in
because it allowed them to do bad things."

Like murder? I wondered. "How is it different now
that I've come?" When she didn't answer, I said desperately, "Please, tell me, Tilly. Why am I here? What
does it want from me?"

"It wants you, girl."

An icy chill gripped my spine, and I could feel my
eyes go wide with fear and shock as my heart flailed.
"Why?"

"You're special and you don't even know it yet. You
walk both sides of the veil, so that makes you dangerous. It fears you, so it seeks to control you."

"How?"

"By getting inside you. By allowing you to do bad
things."

My breath caught at the look on her face. "And if I
resist?"

"It'll try to weaken you by using those around you." She leaned in, her eyes blazing with the fervor of an old-timey preacher. "Stay away from Thane Asher, girl. You hear me?"

"Why? What does he have to do with any of this?"

"The Ashers be in league. Have been for generations." Her eyes glittered madly. "How do you think they came by all that money and power?"

"But Thane wasn't born an Asher."

"No matter, girl. He covets what he can never have. That makes him susceptible to Evil. That makes him dangerous to you."

I tried not to shiver. "I don't believe it."

"You best heed what I say and stay away from him. Thane Asher is not for you."

"Why don't you let her decide that for herself?"

I hadn't heard him come up, and when he spoke through the screen, it was all I could do not to jump. He opened the door and stepped up on the porch, a large paper bag in each hand. He took them inside without a word. When he came back out, his gaze raked over us. "I put the groceries on the table," he told Tilly.

"I laid out your preserves in the usual spot," she said.

"I'll collect them before I leave."

I had a feeling they'd had this exchange many, many times.

He came over to where we sat. "You've known me since I was a kid, Tilly." I could tell he was angry, but his voice remained calm. "We've been friends for a long time. You know I would never do anything to hurt Amelia."

She lifted her chin. "I've always thought the world of you. Still do. But I've made no bones of what I think of your granddaddy. Your uncle, too. And them leeches that hang all over him. Bad news, the lot of them."

Thane's eyes flashed. "What do they have to do with me?"

"Like it or not, you're a part of that family."

"Is that reason enough to condemn me?"

Her mouth thinned stubbornly. "I've said my piece."

"And that's it?" His whole demeanor hardened as he turned his gaze on me. "Can I have a word with you?"

"Will you excuse me, Tilly?"

She looked as if she wanted to say more, but she rose and went into the house.

Thane opened the screen door, and we went out into the yard.

"Good God," he said, when he saw me in the sunlight. "What happened to your face?"

I was still trembling from everything that Tilly had told me. *You're special and you don't even know it yet.*

It was an effort to turn those thoughts aside. "I got caught in a briar patch."

"Again? Are you okay?"

"Tilly fixed me up. They hardly hurt at all now."

"You need to be more careful." He picked a sprig of rosemary from the bushes by the porch and tucked it into my hair. "To ward off witches," he said with a smile.

I shivered at his touch. "Thank you." I glanced back at the house. "Tilly sure has strong feelings about your grandfather."

Thane shrugged. "A lot of people have strong feelings about Grandfather. I'm sure Tilly has her reasons."

"She shouldn't take it out on you, though."

"She never has before. I guess you're special."

I said sharply, "What do you mean?"

"Tilly's always kept to herself, but it seems she's taken you under her wing and she feels protective. Maybe you remind her of Freya."

"Maybe." I glanced away. "Do you think Tilly knew about the baby?"

Thane had been looking up into the trees, but now he spun to face me. "What baby?"

Too late, I realized my mistake. I knew about Freya's unborn child the same way I knew about her murder. But I had no way of knowing if her pregnancy had been common knowledge. I suspected she'd kept it secret for as long as she could.

"I was thinking of the marker on the hidden grave," I said. "The rose and bud that signify a mother and child burial."

"Freya's buried in Thorngate. I already told you that."

No, she's not. "But I haven't been able to find her grave. I've looked all over the cemetery, so unless it's in the middle of that briar patch, it's not there."

"It's there," he insisted. "I used to see Tilly bringing flowers at least once a week."

"You spent that much time at Thorngate?"

"I loved it there as a kid. It could get pretty lonely at Asher House, so I roamed the countryside. That's how I met Tilly. I came across her place one day and I've been helping her with the birds ever since."

I was silent for a moment.

He gazed down at me. "Why the look?"

"It's just…you're not at all like you presented yourself on the ferry that first day."

"How did I present myself?"

"You know exactly the impression you made. You deliberately let me think you were a shallow, aimless man with nothing better to do than bide your time until your grandfather died."

The green of his eyes dazzled in the sunlight. "How do you know that's not the real me?"

"Because I've seen you with Angus. And now I've seen you with Tilly. Whether you'll admit it or not, you have a kind heart."

"For some people." He put a hand to my face, stroked a thumb down my cheek, and I thought to myself that, despite Tilly's warning, this could be a turning point. I could do nothing and let the moment slip away, or I could take a step, even a tiny one, out of the past and into the present.

His other hand came up, and he cupped my face, searching my eyes. I could smell the rosemary on his fingers, and I closed my eyes to draw it in.

Gently, he tilted my head so that he could examine the scratches on my cheeks. "You really should be more careful," he murmured.

"I'll try to be."

"Tilly might not be around next time."

"She's around right now, though."

"Does that bother you?"

I glanced toward the porch. "I wouldn't want to upset her."

"I don't want to upset her, either."

But we both knew that he was going to kiss me whether Tilly approved or not. Whether he was dangerous to me or not. He threaded his fingers through my hair, and I exhaled slowly, trying to calm my racing pulse. My hands fluttered to his chest as he pressed his lips against mine. I could feel his heartbeat against my palms. The vibration stirred something inside me, and I pulled away quickly before I had time to respond.

"Not here."

His gaze deepened. "Where?"

Tilly's warning hammered in my head. *He covets what he can never have. That makes him susceptible to Evil. That makes him dangerous to you.*

I put a hand to my temple, trying to block her voice. "I don't know. I can't think…"

"Tonight," he said urgently.

"I can't. I'm meeting Sidra at the library."

"Afterward."

"I have to pack. I'm going home to Charleston this weekend."

"I'm coming by," he said. "You can send me away when I get there if that's really what you want."

"Thane—"

"I just want to see you before you go," he said. "I want to make sure you're coming back."

"I've barely begun the restoration. Of course, I'll be back."

A shadow darkened his features. "Will you see *him* while you're there?"

Devlin. I drew an unsteady breath. "No. That's over."

Angus brushed up against the side of my leg, and I reached down to pet him, glad for the diversion.

Thane watched us together. "What will you do with Angus while you're gone?"

"I'll take him with me. Why?"

He pulled me back into his arms, and I didn't resist.

"I was hoping I might persuade you to leave him here. That way you'd have to come back to me," he said against my lips.

Twenty-Nine

❧❧❧

I drove into Asher Falls late that afternoon to meet Sidra at the library. She was behind the counter when I came in and lifted a finger to her lips, then pointed to the office door to let me know that Luna was still around. I nodded and went back to the records I'd been sorting through the day before. I was leafing through one of the research books when she came to get me.

"Luna just left," she said in a hushed voice.

"What now?"

"This way, but keep away from the windows, okay? The library is supposed to be closed. If anyone happens to glance in, I don't want to be seen."

"Won't they just assume you haven't left yet?"

"Maybe. But I don't want to take any chances. Luna would be very angry if she knew you were here after hours."

"Then maybe we shouldn't be doing this."

"No, it's fine. Just stay behind me, okay?"

The clandestine nature of our rendezvous both worried and excited me. Why so secretive? I wondered.

Luna's silver tabby was stretched out on the desk in her office, and he watched with suspicious eyes as we came through the door.

"What's that cat's name?"

"Whisper. Don't mess with him," Sidra warned. "He's a biter."

His baleful eyes tracked me as I crossed the room to the framed photographs on the wall. To Freya's ghost. Now I knew why she looked so angry.

I felt Sidra's gaze on me and turned.

"It's through here." She pointed to the narrow, arched door. Then, extracting a skeleton key from an ivory box on one of the shelves, she inserted it into the ornate lock and opened the door.

As I moved across the room, my gaze fell on the cabinet where Luna kept an assortment of treasures. The blown-glass figurines, the antique pocket watches and that collection of oddly shaped knives....

"Is something wrong?" Sidra asked.

I tore my gaze from those blades. "No, everything's fine." I followed her into the dim little room, the only natural illumination spilling in from an octagonal window near the ceiling. Sidra turned on the light, and I glanced around curiously at the crowded bookcases, then walked over to peruse some of the titles: *Animatism in Polynesia. Belief and Practice. Magic and Religion. The Sleeping Giant.*

"Why are these books in here and not outside?" I asked.

"I don't know. My mother has some of the same titles at Pathway."

"Does she keep them under lock and key?"

Sidra paused. "No. But she keeps other things locked up."

"Such as?"

"I don't know. I've never been able to find the key."

I thought of that secret door in Catrice's studio and shivered.

"So what did you want to show me?"

"You asked about those symbols carved into the cliff at the waterfall."

"Yes. You told me I wouldn't find any information about them at the library."

"That's not entirely true," she said and lifted her eyes.

I followed her gaze and gasped. The *Drudenfuss* had been perfectly reproduced on the ceiling of Luna's secret room.

"It's like the pentagram in *Faust*," Sidra said. "Mephistopheles was able to enter the study because one of the points was left open."

"And in order for him to leave, the pentagram had to be destroyed." I remembered what Thane had said about the Daughters of our Valiant Heroes and the old rumor that it was a coven.

"What do you think it means?" Sidra asked.

"Maybe it doesn't mean anything. The story is just a fable," I said, but my mind had gone to those knives in Luna's office and now my heart was racing.

"What if it's not? Just a fable, I mean? Shouldn't we destroy it?" she asked anxiously.

I glanced at her in surprise. "Destroy public property? We could get in a lot of trouble for that. Not to mention, we're not even supposed to be in here."

"I know, but…"

"But what, Sidra?"

"Nothing.

She looked very small in that room, and very, very frightened. "Is there something else you want to show me?" I gently grilled. "Or tell me?"

Her eyes went wide. "Someone's coming."

"Are you sure? I didn't hear anything."

"Shush." She pulled the door closed with a slight click and turned off the light. A moment later, I heard Luna's muffled voice through the wall. Someone was with her, and from the intimate laughter, I thought it must be Hugh.

In the muted light, I saw Sidra lift a finger to her lips. I nodded. We could do nothing but wait. Unlike the library, the room had no air shafts to magnify voices, but I had a pretty good idea of what they were up to. I was sure Sidra did, too.

Something drew my gaze upward. Instinct, perhaps, or a slight sound that barely registered. The gray tabby, perched on top of a bookcase, stared down at us. He must have slipped into the room when we first came in. He blinked slowly as he got to his feet and stretched. And then he meowed.

Sidra spun toward the sound. Then her head whipped back to me. We stared at each in horror for a moment as I pressed my ear to the door.

"Hush," I heard Luna say.

"What is it?" Hugh asked.

"I heard something."

"There's no one here but us."

"No, I heard a meow. It was Whisper."

I held my breath in the ensuing silence.

"He's probably down in the basement chasing rats. Shall I go look?"

"That's very noble of you, but no. Stay here with me. We haven't much time."

"What do you mean, we haven't much time? Maris won't be back for days."

"I'm not worried about *her.*"

I heard him laugh softly. "You shouldn't be worried about the other one, either."

"You're a fool *not* to worry," she said. "You know why he's brought her here."

"It'll never happen."

"How can you be so sure? I've seen them together."

"Have you been spying on them, too?" he asked with a chuckle. "You always did like to watch. Shall we call Bryn and Catrice over? We could have a party like in our younger days."

My gaze shot to Sidra, but she was still watching the cat.

"What's the matter?" Hugh taunted. "A little competition never bothered you before. Of course, you are getting older. Is that a gray hair I see?"

I heard something that sounded like a slap.

He said angrily, "Why you vicious little witch."

Now it was Luna who laughed. "Yes," she said. "I am, aren't I?"

During the whole of their conversation, I'd kept an eye on the cat. Now I let out a breath as he stretched and settled back down for a nap.

I moved my ear away from the door, not wanting to hear what might come next. But the rendezvous seemed to have run its course. The office door slammed, and I waited another moment, then said, "That was close."

"Too close," Sidra said. "We should probably get out of here. It'll be dusk soon."

Dusk. My scalp was already tingling as I followed her into Luna's office. She locked the door, returned the key to the ivory box, then took my arm. "Hurry!"

But it was too late. As we passed from Luna's office into the library, I felt the all too familiar chill of a ghostly presence.

Thirty

Her grip tightened on my arm as she pulled me through the library, the wooden floorboards moaning beneath our feet. I felt a chill breath at my neck, the brush of something cold against my arm, and I tried not to shiver.

We went through the front door, and Sidra locked it behind us, then turned toward the street. I went very still as I heard her draw a shaky breath.

Twilight was upon us.

"They're coming," she whispered.

I understood then her urgency, the fear that shadowed her crystalline eyes and trembled at the corner of her lips. I felt her nails dig into my arm as I looked up and down the street. Pale faces appeared in every window. Diaphanous silhouettes drifted through doorways. Everywhere I looked, *ghosts.*

And with them came the mist, chilled from the murky depths of Bell Lake.

"Don't look at them," Sidra warned.

I couldn't move. I stood there bracing myself against

the death-frost as the entities hovered all around us. A frigid hand sifted through my hair, another slid up my spine. Out of the corner of my eye, I saw a ghost child clutch Sidra's hand as another hovered behind her and a third stared down at us from where he perched on a tree limb. The poor little Moultrie boys that Tilly had mentioned on the pier that day.

Clasping Sidra's other hand, I pulled her with me into the street.

"You feel them?" she whispered. "You see them?"

"Yes."

"It's not just me, then."

"It's not just you."

Her voice quivered. "We should go."

"Where?"

"To the clock tower. It's hallowed ground."

We crossed the square among those floating phantoms, that endless parade of grasping souls.

Sidra gripped my hand, and I was glad for the warmth, glad not to have been alone when I made this discovery. Asher Falls no longer belonged to the world of the living. It was a ghost town, just as Sidra had warned me on that first day in Luna's office.

The chill faded as we entered the clock tower. There was very little light, but I had the impression of iron grillwork and tiled floors as we made our way up the spiral staircases. The higher we climbed, the tighter the passageway until we reached the very top where long narrow windows gave us a 360-degree view of the town.

I stood at one of those windows gazing down. The pavement glistened beneath street lamps as the mist moved through town. Moonlight shimmered through the live oaks, silvering the Spanish moss that streamed like an old woman's hair in the breeze. The town was very quiet, the sidewalks empty of the living.

"Where is everyone?"

"No one comes out after dark."

I turned anxiously. "Why? They can't see the ghosts, can they?"

"It's not the ghosts. They're afraid of each other." Her back was to one of the windows, and the spill of moonlight washed out her face and darkened her eyes. She looked ethereal, otherworldly. Almost…ghostly.

And I was suddenly very frightened as the chill of her words and Tilly's seeped through me. *Those who could left this place. Those who stayed learned to watch their backs.*

I took a step toward Sidra, searching that pale profile. "You didn't just want to show me the hex sign, did you? You wanted me to see the ghosts."

She turned. "I had to know you could see them, too," she said desperately.

"Why?"

"Because I've never met anyone like me." Her eyes fluttered closed. "You can't imagine how lonely I've been."

Oh, I could.

"How long have you had this…gift?"

Her wan smile struck a chord. "Since I was five. That's my earliest recollection. I went into cardiac arrest. When they brought me back, I saw a ghost in my room. He stood at the side of my bed gazing down at me. I think he was waiting for me to die so that he could take me back."

Goose pimples prickled. "How did you know about me?"

"The same way you knew about me," she said. "There's a look in your eyes, a certain way you carry yourself. As if you're constantly on guard."

Because I was. "Why did you deny seeing Freya's ghost in that photograph?"

"That's what we do, isn't it? We deny it even to ourselves."

I moved up beside her at the window, staring down at that pale, writhing legion. "Have they always been here?"

"No. Not like this. I think some must have come through when the cemetery flooded. Maybe it opened a doorway. Every time I get sick, more gather around my bed. But there were never this many..." Her gaze dropped to the street. "They try to talk to me sometimes, especially the children. I think they want to tell me that my time is near."

"Don't say that."

"I've already been to the other side," she said. "I think you have, too."

"I've never had a near-death experience."

"Maybe you have and you just don't know it. Maybe you belong to the other side as much as you belong here. Maybe you're an in-between just like me," she said.

"An in-between?"

"A living ghost."

I shuddered violently. "There isn't such a thing." But even as I denied it, Tilly's words were already clawing at me. *You walk both sides of the veil, so that makes you dangerous.*

"Why do you think there are so many of them now?" Sidra demanded.

"You said a door had been opened when the lake flooded."

I saw a flash of pity in her eyes. It reminded me of the look on Papa's face the first time I saw the old man's specter in Rosehill. Her voice lowered to a whisper. "They're here because of you, Amelia. They came when you came."

Everything inside me went very still. With a trembling hand, I clasped the stone at my neck.

"You know it's true, don't you?" she said. "You've always known. You belong to them."

Thirty-One

I left Sidra in the clock tower and drove home to
Angus. He had to go out, and I stood shivering on the
steps, encouraging him to hurry. Mist swirled over the
lake, but the bells beneath were silent. I wondered if the
ghosts had already returned to their graves.

Dark thoughts plagued me. *You belong to them.*

You're special and you don't even know it yet.

No, no, *no.* I belonged *here.* I was alive, not a living
ghost, not an in-between, not some restless abomina-
tion who walked on both sides of the veil.

It fears you, so it seeks to control you.

I couldn't stand to think of it any longer, so in desperation, I forced my mind back to Freya. Had she been
killed by someone whose baser instincts had taken control of them? Someone whose deviant pleasures had
driven them to savagery? Someone who had painted a
hex sign in a secret room?

Was her killer out there even now watching me?

Hurrying into the house after Angus, I showered and
changed into my only dress and then restlessly paced

as I waited for Thane, my mind churning. I was still pacing, still denying, a few minutes later when he rang the bell. He knew at once something was wrong. Taking hold of my arms, he turned me to face him. "What is it?"

I cast an uneasy glance toward the window. "It's this place. I'm suffocating here."

"This house, you mean?"

I nodded, but it wasn't just the house. It was the lake, the woods, the town. It was Tilly's warning, Sidra's terrible claim and the murky details of my birth. All of it bore down on me like stones heaped upon a grave.

He searched my face. "Let's get out of here, then. Maybe go for a drive."

Go back out into the dark, into that mist? Into those ghosts?

"It's late…"

"It's not late at all," he said. "The moon's barely up."

"I know you mean well, Thane, but I'm not fit company tonight."

"But you're all dressed up." His gaze took me in, and I shivered. He was dressed in jeans and a leather jacket, looking darkly handsome and mysterious. When I hesitated, his voice lowered persuasively. "Come on. It'll do you good to get out."

As I stared up into his green eyes, I realized how badly I wanted to go with him. I wanted it more than anything because I was tired of being alone. I was tired of always being on guard. All I wanted at that moment was to feel like a normal twenty-seven-year-old woman who could love and be loved. Not someone who could see ghosts. Not someone hunted by Evil.

"We don't have to go anywhere special," he said.

"We'll just take a drive. Besides, there's something I want to show you."

A warning bell sounded in my head despite my baser desires. Tilly had told me to stay away from him, but if I allowed myself to believe that Thane was dangerous to me, then I had to believe the rest—that Evil stalked me and only me because I walked on both sides of the veil. It feared me, so it sought to control me.

If I mentioned any of that to Thane, he would probably think me crazy. And I wondered if he might be right.

"What do you want to show me?" I asked.

He smiled down at me. "You'll just have to trust me."

Still, I hesitated. I shouldn't go. I knew that. My place was here, sequestered on hallowed ground, shackled to what remained of my father's rules.

"Come on," Thane urged softly.

There was a time when I would have continued to resist, but the bleakness of the coming years hounded me as I felt myself drowning in loneliness.

"I can't be gone long," I said.

His grasp tightened as he stared down at me. "I'll bring you back whenever you want."

Against my better judgment, we went out into the evening, and I tried to keep my guard up against the ghosts, perhaps even against Thane. The moon hovered just above the treetops, and an owl called from deep within the woods. The night seemed dark and primal. Full of danger and promise, and my heart raced in anticipation.

Thane put his arm around me as we walked to the car, and I leaned into his warmth. He was alive and vital. Nothing haunted or ghostlike about him. I could almost hear the beat of his heart in that quiet. The throb of blood through his veins.

We settled into the car, and he smiled again as he started the ignition. I lay my head against the seat and stared out the window as we drove through the evergreens and through the encroaching shadows that shrunk the outside world to that which could only be seen in our headlights. When we reached the highway, Thane turned left, making me wonder if we were going to that cliff-top mansion. I had no desire to see Pell Asher tonight. Not with Tilly's warning still echoing in my head.

I turned to stare at Thane's profile. He drove fast, taking curves with a reckless abandon that both unnerved and thrilled me. I welcomed the adrenaline rush. It made me feel alive. "Where are we going?"

A dark glance. "You'll see."

We drove on, the shadowy countryside flying like dreams past my window. And then he slowed and nosed the car up the hill toward the cemetery. We ascended through the cedars, and he pulled to a stop at the entrance. There was no mist up here, no willowy forms gliding through the headstones. The graveyard seemed almost surreal in its stillness. A dreamscape aglow in moonlight.

But something lurked. In the distance, the mountains were a hovering darkness.

"Why did you bring me here?" I asked.

Thane had been staring out the window, too, but now he turned, his gaze seeking mine. We were sitting very close in his sports car. Cocooned from those mountains and the evil that swept down with the wind. At least…I wanted to believe so.

"I told you once that the cemetery was designed to be viewed in moonlight, remember?"

"Yes."

"Don't you want to see it?"

Did I dare? It wasn't as if I'd never gone into a cemetery at night. As a child, I'd often played in my grave-yard kingdom by moonlight. But Thorngate wasn't Rosehill. It wasn't a sanctuary. Something had whispered to me in the mausoleum, attacked me in the briar thicket. That same something had come after me at the hidden grave and again in the woods. But Tilly was right. It wasn't the cemetery that was afflicted. It was me.

Thane's hand brushed my shoulder lightly, and I shivered. "Well?"

I nodded, and we got out of the car. He took my hand as we walked through the graves and passed side by side through the lych-gate. I caught my breath as I lifted my gaze to the angels, to those eerie, incandescent faces. They stared now, not at the sunrise, not at the mountains, but at the moon gliding up over the treetops. Snakeroot and yarrow shimmered in the underbrush, and I could see the spangle of dewdrops on the leaves from a lingering dampness.

Something shifted in the air, inside *me,* and I stepped into that circle of angels, lifting my own face to the sky, turning and turning, eyes closed, arms flung wide, the way I had as a child in Rosehill. Embracing the night. Embracing my difference. Unharnessed from the remnants of Papa's rules, the loneliness faded, my fears melted, and I let myself fly.

It began as a low hum. I didn't even notice it at first. Wouldn't realize until later that the brief moment of liberation had probably invited it into the ruins of that white garden, into that withering moonscape. Or had it been there all along?

The hum grew and grew until something inside me began to respond, and I felt that strange pulse, that primordial heartbeat that pounded down from the mountains and up through the ground, hammering its way into the core of my very being.

Thane touched my arm, and my whole body thrummed like a plucked wire that had been strung too tight. I had never felt so attuned to the night. I'd never felt so alive.

Backlit by the moon, he stared down at me, a mesmerizing silhouette that embodied my secret desires, all my dark dreams. Those visions came back to me now, the entwined couple at the falls, straining and gasping, the woman's head thrown back in wanton abandon as she rode him. I couldn't see their faces, even when he turned her, even when he rose up behind her, and the night creatures began to howl. I had a sense that it was Devlin and his dead wife, and a part of me wondered if Mariama had somehow managed to invade my thoughts even here in the mountains, even here with Thane, or if the insidious evil that Tilly spoke of had found my weakness.

It was only a fleeting worry because already my arms were winding around Thane's neck as he drew me close and pressed his body against mine. He kissed me, again and again, his tongue weaving a trail of black magic that lured and enthralled and seduced.

We sank to our knees in the circle of Asher angels, in the remains of that romantic white garden, and I skimmed my hands down my sides, lifting my dress as I lay back, drenched in starlight.

I no longer wondered or cared about the consequences of my actions or the desecration of a place I would have once revered. There was nothing in me now but need, a greedy, grasping hunger. Thane's hands were all over me, strumming and stroking, his mouth hot against mine. I tangled my fingers in his hair, pushing him down, down, down until the feather of his lips on my thigh evoked a shudder, until the dart of his tongue within drew a moan.

My cries mingled with the primitive sounds in my vision, those carnal screams that called forth the creatures, the half-beings, those terrible atrocities that crawled up from the underworld to slink through the door that could never be closed.

As Thane brought me to the very edge, the night came alive with sound and motion. With moans and whispers and shadows creeping from the woods and flitting through the treetops. Moonlight animated the statues, and I could feel those sightless eyes cast upon us now as those stone lips whispered my name over and over, an incantation that stoked my frenzy.

Thane yanked off his shirt and moved over me, and for one breathless moment, he didn't look like Thane at all, but something dark and beautiful and otherworldly.

A familiar medallion dangled from his neck—a painful reminder of my time with Devlin. I tore it away with a vicious jerk, and I heard the sharp intake of his breath as though I had ripped something up from his soul. I sensed a hesitation, a withdrawal, but I would have none of it. I pulled him back to me, arching violently into him as my hand went to his face and I sank my nails into his flesh.

He reared back with an oath.

I'd broken the skin. The ooze of crimson both frightened and exhilarated me. I reached up and touched a fingertip to the blood, drawing a deep shudder from Thane.

A breeze trembled through the trees and a distant howl brought his head up. "What was that?"

"It's coming," I whispered.

He scrambled to his feet, his gaze scanning the darkness as I rose more slowly, in the grip now of a strange lethargy. The wind picked up, thrashing branches and whirling dead leaves underfoot. I turned instinctively to the mausoleum and could have sworn I saw a silhouette squatted and hunched on the rooftop, pale eyes gleaming, the tails of a coat flaring in the wind. And then a rasping laugh sawed through the trees.

I gasped.

Behind me, Thane said urgently, "We should go."

We didn't run back to the car, but neither did we tarry. All the way home, I trembled, staring out the window as a terrible acceptance settled over me.

Thane walked me to the door, but he made no move to hold or kiss me. Why would he?

"Something was out there," he finally said. "You felt it, didn't you?"

My gaze went to those claw marks on his face, and I shuddered. "Yes."

He turned to the woods. "It wasn't just out there. It was in *me.*" He lifted a shaking hand in front of him. "It was in you, too," he said.

I nodded.

"What was it?"

"Tilly called it Evil."

To my surprise, he didn't question it. Instead, his eyes rose to the mountains. "Even as a kid, I knew this place was different. I sensed a darkness. It was like a spider always trying to creep inside my head. I told myself it was just my imagination or a nightmare. A waking dream," he said. "Even so, I would never allow it in. But something changed tonight and I *wanted* to let it in. I welcomed it." A tense pause. "I know I sound crazy."

"I almost wish you were," I said weakly.

"Why?"

I drew away from him. "Because it wasn't you that let it in. It was me."

Thirty-Two

❧❧❧

I slipped from bed that night, and I went to stare out at the darkness. The moon was still up, shimmering on the lake and silvering the edges of the pines. As I gazed up at those distant peaks, I had the strangest feeling of déjà vu, but the source of that familiarity came to me almost at once. I could see my reflection in the glass, and it reminded me of all those stone angels—all those up-turned faces—gazing toward the mountains. Watching and waiting just as *it* had watched and waited for aeons.

It had always been there, Thane said. Scratching at his mind like a spider. An evil as old as the mountains. A darkness that stirred the dead and unleashed unspeakable desires.

Asher Falls is a ghost town.

I'd had only an inkling of what Sidra had meant that first day in the library. A mere suspicion until the tolling of the bells had awakened me. And then I'd seen the diaphanous forms in the swirling mist. I'd witnessed those phantom hands reaching out for me, felt a presence in the wind, heard that terrible howling, and *still*

I remained in Asher Falls because I had a sense of destiny here. Like it or not, I was connected to this terrible place.

I moved away from the window, then glanced back, my heart jumping. Was Freya's killer out there at the edge of the woods?

I watched for the longest time, but nothing stirred. It was just a tree or a shadow, I told myself. Angus was already sleeping peacefully at the end of my bed. If anyone or anything had been about, he would have roused to sound the alarm.

Or so I wanted to believe.

I climbed into bed and curled up under the covers, but I didn't want to fall asleep. I intended to lie there and wait out the darkness. But my eyes soon grew heavy, and I kept drifting off only to startle awake every few minutes. During those short naps, my sleep was filled with the strangest images. I dreamed about Devlin and Mariama. About floating with ghosts and destroying hex signs.

And I dreamed about being back at the falls stretched out on the ground as faces hovered over me, and those in-between creatures crawled out of their holes to stare down at me. I felt something wet on my neck, and my fingers came away bloody. Someone said softly, "It's done," and then I heard a baby cry in the dark.

I woke up with tears on my face. I had no idea why that dream disturbed me so much, but I refused to close my eyes for the rest of the night.

Rising at dawn, I packed up the car and Angus, and I caught the first ferry. It was raining when we left, the kind of downpour that seemed portentous, as if it could wash the whole doomed town right into the lake. I stood under the cover, protected from the slash of rain as I watched the mountains slowly recede. But I didn't feel a sense of relief until sometime later when we drove out of the deluge and headed east, straight into the sun.

The light streaming through the windshield was warm and healing. A weight lifted. I plugged in my iPod and hummed along to some music as we left the foothills and entered the gentle rolling countryside of the Piedmont.

Angus watched the passing scenery with avid interest, and I cracked the window so that he could feel the wind in his fur. At that moment, I wanted nothing more than to just keep driving until we reached the coast. I didn't want this feeling of lightness to ever end for him or for me.

I stopped for gas and a quick breakfast in Columbia, and my euphoria held until I approached the Trinity exit. And then the questions resurfaced. My need to know where I came from so that I could understand my place in this world and the next. I didn't want to be a living ghost. I didn't want to be hunted by Evil. I wanted to be normal.

The original plan was to drive straight through to Charleston, but instead I made the turn to Trinity and headed for Rosehill Cemetery, the place where I had seen my first specter.

The white bungalow where I grew up hadn't changed much over the years. It was shaded by hundred-year-old oak trees that kept the house cool and dim even in the summer months, making it a pleasant refuge for Papa after hours of working under a baking sun. The front porch had always been my mother's domain. She and my aunt had spent many an hour out there sipping sweet tea and gossiping as the scent of roses drifted up from the cemetery.

My bedroom window looked out on Rosehill. The view of the graveyard never bothered me even as a child, even after my first ghost sighting, because Rosehill had always been *my* refuge, and the hallowed ground had always protected me. Even after all these years, I still felt safe and at peace there as I never had anywhere else, even my own sanctuary in Charleston.

A layer of dust had settled on the concrete porch. Before my mother got sick, she would sweep that floor at least once a day. It was almost an obsession with her. Dirt—especially the grime Papa and I tracked in from the cemetery—drove her crazy. My aunt called her a persnickety housekeeper, to which my mother had once replied that it was a shame Lynrose had never learned to run a vacuum as well as she ran her mouth. My aunt had gotten a kick out of that retort. She loved to get a rise out of Mama, and I so envied their relationship, that constant banter. No one had ever been able to make my solemn mother smile the way her sister could. Not Papa. Certainly not me.

The house was all closed up, which was unusual. Papa would never have locked the front door unless he planned to be away for some time, so I didn't think he was working in the cemetery or out back in his work-shop. The whole place had a forlorn air, as though no one had been home in days.

I suppressed a momentary panic as I fished the key from a flower pot and let myself in. Papa had probably driven to Charleston to spend some time with Mama. He must have missed her terribly during all the months she'd been gone. They'd been together for a long time, and though neither was openly demonstrative—I couldn't remember having ever seen them hug, much less kiss—I had to believe something more than habit kept them together. Something more than secrets, too.

I left Angus on the porch and went inside. The quiet of the house unnerved me. I took a quick walk through the downstairs just to reassure myself that nothing was amiss, and then I climbed the stairs, peeked into my old bedroom and continued on to the far end of the hallway where I opened the door to the attic stairs. I flipped the light switch and went up without hesitation. I'd never been afraid of the attic. It had been a favorite haunt of mine on rainy days when I grew bored of the family photo albums. Mama had kept a lot of her dresses from high school formals up there, and I had loved going through all those old trunks. She and Aunt Lynrose had been quite the belles, despite the family's middle-class status.

Papa stored his keepsakes in a metal bin. It was always kept locked. *Always.* I'd been curious about that container since childhood, but it never occurred to me then to try and pick the lock. Now I shoved any qualms aside and used a hairpin to slide open the tumblers. If there was a secret in this house about my birth, it would be in that locker.

Inside was the usual paraphernalia that a man of Papa's age and stature would have accumulated over the years. Service medals and framed citations from his time in the army. A pair of boots. An old pocket knife. A cigar box of photographs.

The most efficient way to conduct the search was to take everything out. I did so quickly and carefully,

arranging the items in order so that I could put everything back exactly as I found them. I hated going
through Papa's things. He was a private man, and ri-
fling through his treasures and memories was a viola-
tion that I likened to the desecration of a gravesite. But
I didn't let a guilty conscience stop me. I kept right on
looking because I knew I wouldn't rest until I found
something.

I had almost given up when I happened upon a little
blue box tied with a white ribbon. I assumed it was another medal or perhaps his wedding cuff links.

But, no.

Nestled against a bed of cotton was a shard of brown
porcelain. I would never have known what it was, let
alone the significance, had I not seen that little brown
sparrow in Freya Pattershaw's little blue bedroom.

However he had come by it, Papa had stored that
broken wing amongst his most prized possessions.

Thirty-Three

～⊙⊙⊙～

I called ahead and made an appointment for Angus at a veterinarian clinic convenient to my house in Charleston. I stayed with him for the exam and shots and then left during the grooming to run errands. When we showed up on my aunt Lynrose's veranda a few hours later, we were both freshly bathed and looking our best.

My aunt lived in a narrow two-story house built deep into the lot, as was the custom in the historic district. She'd bought the house years ago before the real estate market exploded and could undoubtedly net a small fortune if she chose to sell it. She never would, even though she was forever complaining about the taxes. I loved the house and the shady street she lived on. It was very quaint and charming. Very old South.

Her eyes widened when she opened the door and saw me through the screen. As always, she was dressed elegantly in off-white linen slacks and a wheat-colored tunic embroidered with flowers. I caught a whiff of her perfume through the door, and it took me right back to all those summer twilights when I had sat at that open window listening to her and Mama.

A hand fluttered to her heart. "Goodness gracious, girl. I wasn't expecting to find you on my doorstep. Why didn't you tell us you were coming? I'd have made lunch. Or ordered out," she said with a wink. Her gaze dropped to Angus, and her eyes widened even more. "What in the world is *that?*"

"My dog. His name is Angus."

"*Your* dog?" She gave a delicate shudder as she came out on the porch. "Good Lord, what happened to the creature?"

"He was in a dog-fighting kennel. Then they turned him loose in the woods to starve."

"Oh, dear." She gave him a tentative pat. "I suppose you'd better take him around to the back. Your mama's in the garden. Take care you don't frighten her half to death with that…with Angus. I'll go pour us some tea."

She disappeared back into the house, and I motioned for Angus to follow me down the porch steps and along a narrow path that led through thick beds of fountain grass already sprouting cotton-candy plumes. Mama might keep a perfect house and set an elegant table, but my aunt had been born with a green thumb. The back garden was spectacular this time of year with the last of the summer roses mingling intoxicatingly with the tea olives, all encased in boxwood hedges that wound along stepping-stones and low brick walls shimmering in the afternoon light.

My mother reclined in a green-stripe lawn chair with an open book on her lap. She sat very still, head turned into the cushion, and I thought she might be asleep. I watched her for a moment, a pain in my heart at the sharpness of her cheekbones and the gray tinge to her complexion. Like my aunt, she'd always been very thin, but now she looked gaunt, and I could see new lines in her face and a tremor in her hand as she roused to turn a page. Months of chemo had taken a toll, but she was still the most beautiful woman I'd ever laid eyes on. As sick as she was, her wig was perfectly coiffed, and I could see a pale pink sheen on her lips. She wore a floral skirt and a pretty blue cardigan even though the day was hot and humid.

I said, "Mama," very softly and she looked up with a start.

Then she smiled in a way I'd seldom been accorded, and it made me very happy that I'd come.

"Amelia! How long have you been standing there? I didn't even hear the gate."

"I came in just now." I went over and knelt beside her chair. She lifted her hand to brush the hair back from my face. It might have been my imagination—or wishful thinking—but I thought her cool fingers lingered for a moment. Then she spotted Angus, and like Lynrose, a shudder went through her.

"Amelia Rose Gray, what on earth?"

"His name is Angus. I found him in the mountains and I'm keeping him."

She lifted a brow. "Well, of course, dear, if that's what you want. You have your own home, your own rules." She paused. "Poor thing looks like he's been through the wringer."

"You could say that."

"He has my sympathies."

Angus, bless him, was on his best behavior. He didn't growl or bark or try to encroach. He hung back, sensing

Mama's reticence. Even when she put out a reluctant hand, he didn't come forward to nuzzle. Instead, he retreated to a spot beneath the angel oak and watched us warily.

"Lyn said you'd been out of town. You had a restoration somewhere?" Mama asked as I settled down in a nearby lawn chair.

"Yes, ma'am. She didn't tell you where I was?"

A frown flitted across her brow. "She may have. I don't remember if she did."

I was just about to tell her myself when Lynrose came out the back door with the iced tea. "You should probably get that dog some water, Amelia. It's a hot day even with the breeze. I can feel a storm brewing. You feel that air? Thick as molasses...."

I left her going on about the weather as I filled a bowl from the water hose and took it to Angus. By the time I rejoined my mother and aunt, they'd moved on to a new topic.

My aunt handed me a glass of tea. "I was just telling Etta about an acquaintance of yours I ran into the other day. I was standing in line at the grocery store when I heard someone behind me mention that she grew up in Trinity. Well, naturally, I had to strike up a conversation. Turns out she was a grade or so behind you in school, but she said the two of you had crossed paths just a few months ago."

"What's her name?"

"Ree Hutchins. Do you remember her?"

I took a sip of tea. "Ree? Yes, I remember her. She came to see me about Oak Grove Cemetery."

My aunt looked stricken. "Oh, Lord. She wasn't involved in any of that terrible business, was she?"

"No. She was interested in the history of the cemetery."

"Oh. Well…she was with a very good-looking young man. Hayden something-or-other. She said he was a lawyer."

"He's also a ghost hunter," I said.

A brow arched. "You don't say. He seemed so normal."

"I'm sure he did," I murmured.

"Anyway, Ree told me about some of the awful things that went on at that mental hospital where she worked. Abuse, illegal testing, patients admitted under false names by wealthy families who just wanted to forget about them. It was all over the news last spring. I'm sure you saw it. I don't remember all the particulars but someone was murdered by a doctor—Farrante, I think his name was. He was quite famous, and apparently his grandfather before him had conducted all sorts of gruesome experiments at that place." She shook her head. "Blood will tell, as they say."

As my aunt prattled on, I kept glancing at my mother. Her head had fallen back against the cushion, and her eyes were closed.

"Mama, are you okay?"

She smiled faintly. "I'm a little tired. Would you think badly of me if I went in to rest for a little while?"

I set my glass down. "Of course not. Can I help you?"

"No, dear, I'm fine. It's just…I don't have much energy these days."

"It's that blasted chemo," my aunt grumbled as she helped Mama to her feet. "Well, never you mind. We'll get you all settled in for a nice nap."

"I'm perfectly capable of turning down the covers

myself, Lyn. Stay out here and visit with Amelia. I feel terrible deserting her when she only just arrived."

"Don't worry about that. We can visit later," I said.

"Will you stay and eat with us? We'll go out somewhere. I wouldn't subject that poor dog to Lynrose's cooking."

I smiled. "That would be nice."

"Now, you hush up," my aunt scolded good-naturedly. "I haven't heard you complaining lately about my cooking."

"Because I have no appetite," Mama countered.

"Are you sure you don't want me to come in with you?" I asked.

"No, you two have a nice visit. I'll join you later."

After she disappeared inside, I turned to my aunt. "Oh, Aunt Lyn, she looks so frail. Even more so since I last saw her, and that was only a week or so ago."

"She's had a bad few days, but the doctor is still optimistic with her progress. Setbacks are to be expected."

"I guess. But she just seems so…I don't know. *Old.*"

My aunt's eyes flashed. "Don't you dare say that to her!"

"Of course, I won't! And, anyway, she's still beautiful."

My aunt's eyes grew misty. "The prettiest girl at the dance. Always was."

I reached over and patted her arm. "You've taken such good care of her. She's so lucky to have you."

"I'm lucky to have her, too. If anything happens, I don't know what I'll do without her—"

"Don't say it."

"I know. I know. She's going to pull through this."

My aunt lifted her chin defiantly. "I'm going to make sure of it."

"Aunt Lyn, has Papa been here this morning? I drove by the house on my way in and the front door was locked."

"He may have gone into town for something. You probably just missed him."

"Does he ever come by to see Mama?"

"You know Caleb. He lives in his own little world. Just like you. Two peas in a pod, Etta used to say." I saw a shadow in her eyes before she glanced away, and for a moment, the air quivered with something unspoken. I didn't know why, but I felt a momentary panic. I took a sip of tea to calm myself.

"Does Mama know where I've been working?"

My aunt traced a bead of condensation down her glass. "Didn't you tell her?"

"No, I called here before I left, remember? I told you that a job had come through and I would be working out of town for a few weeks. Mama was resting and you said you'd let her know. But you didn't say anything to her, did you?"

She shrugged. "I don't know. I have a lot on my mind these days. We all do."

"Every time I called this past week, she was always resting or napping. You never let me talk to her."

"Never let you? What a thing to say. As if I would deliberately try to keep you from talking to your mama."

"Maybe you didn't want her to know that I was working in Asher Falls."

"Why on earth would I be concerned about that?" But her fingers had tangled in the string of pearls at her throat.

"It's true, isn't it?"

She said, almost angrily, "You make it sound so manipulative and sinister. It wasn't like that. I didn't want her upset, is all. *I* knew where you were, and if anything happened, God forbid, we could always reach you on your cell phone."

"But why would it upset her to know that I was in Asher Falls? What happened up there, Aunt Lyn?"

She was on the verge of another denial. I could see it in her eyes. Then she seemed to deflate, and her eyes filled with tears. "Oh, Amelia, why can't you just leave it be?"

"Leave what be?"

"I knew nothing good would come of you going up there to that place. If I could have found a way to stop you, I would have."

"Aunt Lyn—"

"It was all such a long time ago. Best forgotten, I say."

I reached over and took her hand. "Don't I deserve to know the truth?"

She took my hand in both of hers and closed her eyes on a sigh. "Of course, you do. But I never wanted to be the one to tell you."

"Tell me what?"

She dropped my hand and smoothed back her hair, as if trying to soothe her emotions. "It's not my place. And I don't really know all the details, anyway. Your papa's always been so secretive, but that's his way. Keeps everything bottled up inside. If only he and Etta had been able to talk it through. But…" She let out another breath. "That's all water under the bridge now."

I watched her anxiously. "I have no idea what you're talking about."

"I know you don't." She was silent for a moment. "Has either of them ever told you how they met? They don't talk about it much."

"I know they met here in Charleston."

She nodded absently. "Your father was one of the caretakers at St. Michael's, and Etta spent a lot of time in the gardens there, especially in the days leading up to her wedding."

"But she and Papa weren't married at St. Michael's."

"I don't mean her marriage to your papa. Etta was engaged to her high school sweetheart before she met Caleb." She pressed a hand to her heart. "They were such a handsome couple. A perfect match. Everyone said so, and Etta, bless her, bought into the notion that she was destined to lead a fairy-tale life. I guess that's why she was so devastated when he left her. Not at the altar, mind you, but close. He broke it off the day before the wedding, and Etta was inconsolable. You can imagine the humiliation. And there was Caleb, in love with her from afar. He was a comfort to her and a balm to her shattered pride. They eloped a few weeks later."

I sat in stunned silence. I'd never before heard the details of my parents' courtship. The hasty marriage didn't sound like either of them to me. They were both so cautious and reserved. So…restrained.

"What does any of this have to do with Asher Falls?" I finally asked.

"I'm coming to that." My aunt seemed to muster her thoughts as she idly picked at a loose embroidery thread on her tunic. "Your mama and papa…they lived up there for a while."

I almost gasped. "In Asher Falls?"

"It was a long, long time ago. Caleb hired on with a stonecutter that summer. He loved the work, but Etta hated living in the mountains. She hated that place. Said it was oppressive. It did things to her, played with her mind. She tried to tough it out, but she missed her family. Missed Chaa'stun. So she came home. Eventually, Caleb quit his job and followed her. They reconciled, but things were never quite right. I've heard people say that the hardest thing in the world is to live with someone you don't love. But I've always thought it would be far more difficult to live with someone who doesn't love you."

"You don't think Mama ever loved Papa?"

"In her own way, I guess she did. But he was never going to be the love of her life and he knew it. That's hard on a man. Hard on his pride. Understandable, I guess, that he would turn to someone else."

"Papa had an affair?" I could hardly imagine such a thing.

"That was Etta's suspicion. There was a woman in Asher Falls... I never knew her name. She had no family, no husband or children. She worked as a midwife, I think. I guess she and Caleb were both lonely. Something happened between them. Etta knew, but she put it behind her and she and Caleb never spoke of it. She had other worries by then. Other heartbreaks. So many devastating miscarriages. Years passed and they moved to Trinity. Etta eventually gave up on the notion of having a family. Maybe it was for the best, she said. They were getting too old, anyway. Too set in their ways. And then one night seventeen years later,

Caleb was called away. When he returned home, it was in the dead of night. With you."

My heart was pounding. "Where did he get me?"

She shuddered. "From that awful place."

"Asher Falls?"

"You were such a tiny thing and so upset. You cried and cried for days."

"Why?"

"You'd been through some trauma. I don't know any of the details of your birth. I'm not even sure Etta knows everything. But whatever happened the night your papa brought you home...whatever he found in that town...changed him."

By this time, my aunt had worked herself into quite a state. She sat wringing her hands, which was not at all like her. Mama was the high-strung one. Lynrose had always been her rock.

It was strange, but the more agitated she became, the calmer I grew. I felt almost detached, as if we were talking about a stranger or someone I barely knew. "Who is my mother? My birth mother," I clarified, because no matter what happened, no matter what I found out, the woman who had raised me would always be Mama.

"I never knew and that's the God's honest truth." She bit her lip. "But Etta and I have always had our suspicions. You see, the woman we think Caleb had the affair with, the midwife... She had a daughter."

"How do you know?"

"Your mama found a picture among Caleb's things once, long after he brought you home."

I shook my head in confusion. "And the girl..."

"Was Caleb's daughter. Your mother."

"But if that girl was my mother, then Papa—"

A tear spilled over and ran down her cheek. She wiped it away with the back of her hand as she nodded.

That moment was very surreal, and I knew later on, I would never be able to describe it. The snapping together of those puzzle pieces. If everything Lynrose suspected was true, then the man I had always known as my adoptive father—my beloved Papa—was in reality my biological grandfather. That was why we could both see ghosts. I had inherited my ability from him.

My mind flashed back to that first sighting in the graveyard and to the look on Papa's face when I asked him about the ghost. There had been regret and pity in his eyes because he had known what my life would be like from that moment on. The years of loneliness that faced me.

I looked down at my clasped hands. The knuckles had whitened. "What about my biological father?"

She shook her head.

I thought about the porcelain wing I had found in Papa's treasures and suddenly I knew it was true. Freya Pattershaw was my mother and Tilly, my grandmother.

"Why did no one ever tell me any of this before?"

"Because those memories are still too painful. And because…" She trailed off on a whisper.

"Because why?"

My aunt reached over and clutched my arm so tightly, I winced. "You can't utter a word of what I'm about to tell you. Promise me you won't tell another living soul." Her nails dug into my flesh, and her face had gone as ashen as my sick mother's.

"Aunt Lyn, let go! You're hurting me."

Her grip eased, but her brimming eyes held me enthralled. "The night he brought you home…your papa was covered in blood."

I had an early dinner with my mother and Aunt Lynrose before heading back to my place on Rutledge Avenue. I hadn't said a word to my mother about any of my aunt's revelations. I would never risk upsetting her when she needed all her strength to battle the cancer. Somehow I'd managed to put on a mask and playact my way through the meal.

But now that I was alone in my own garden, my mind returned time and again to that conversation. Papa was my biological grandfather. That somehow felt right, even though I was still in deep shock. He'd always seemed so old to me. White-haired and stoop-shouldered for as long as I could remember. Mama was older, too, but she had the kind of grace and beauty that wore well with age and seemed timeless.

I sat in the swing, lost in thought, as Angus became acquainted with his new home. It was a cool, breezy night, one that made me think of summer's end. Of lost love. Of Mama and her high school sweetheart. Of Papa and Tilly Pattershaw.

Inevitably my mind turned to Devlin. I wallowed for a moment, and then I tucked those memories away.

And now it was Thane Asher who occupied my thoughts.

When I arose the next morning, I knew I had to talk to Papa before I went back to Asher Falls. *If* I went back. I'd promised Thane that I would return, but if I really was the target of evil, then I had no future with him. I had no future with anyone. My loneliness—once an old friend that had sheltered me from the real world—was now the enemy, a monster that threatened to swallow me whole. I searched for an end, no matter how dire, but now I couldn't trust my own thoughts. Maybe the evil was still inside me.

I almost expected to find the house closed up, but Papa's truck was in the driveway, and when he didn't answer my knock, Angus and I walked down to the cemetery to look for him.

The scent of fading roses drifted on a mild breeze as we wound our way through the lush trails of ivy and creeping phlox. I found Papa working on the angels, the collection of fifty-seven statues that commemorated those children whose lives had been lost in an orphanage fire at the turn of the last century. It had taken Papa years to restore the memorials, and as I moved among them now, I couldn't help but compare those sweet, pensive faces to the hubris of the Asher angels. But I didn't want to think about those arrogant, upturned visages that watched the mountains. I didn't want to dwell on what had happened between Thane and me in that dreamy circle. Time enough later for brooding.

Papa glanced up as I approached, then went right back to his work.

"You don't seem surprised to see me," I said.

"Your aunt called." His voice had thinned in the past year, and his face was even more weathered than I remembered. But the passing years hadn't diminished his quiet dignity or his distance. He was right there before me and yet he seemed a million miles away.

"You know why I'm here, then."

"Yes, child."

I drew a trembling breath. "We have to talk, Papa. No more secrets."

"Those secrets were meant to protect you, Amelia."

"I know that. But the only thing that can protect me now is the truth."

Silently, he gathered up his tools and put them away. "Let's sit a spell," he said, and we sank to the ground, facing the angels, our backs to the gate. When Angus padded over and plopped down at my feet, Papa leaned in absently to rub his head.

"That's Angus," I told him.

"Where did you get him?"

"In Asher Falls," I said, and I saw him shudder. "So many strange things have happened to me there. I felt a connection from the moment I arrived, and I'm only now starting to understand why." I paused. "Who am I, Papa?"

"You are my Amelia," he said quietly. "And I love you more than life itself."

My eyes filled with tears. He'd never said anything like that to me before. After the ghosts came, he'd withdrawn into himself, never showing me the slightest affection, and for years I was left wondering what I had done. But now to hear the tremor in his voice, that desperate sadness in his eyes…it was too much. I had to look away.

So many questions lingered, but I wouldn't ask him about his time with Tilly. That belonged to them. I didn't condone what had happened—I was fiercely loyal to my mother, after all—but I could understand it. Two desperately lonely people with their secrets— Papa with his ghosts and Tilly with her premonitions.

Drawing my legs up, I laid my cheek on my knees. "What are we, Papa?"

"In the olden days, we were called caulbearers. Babies born behind the veil with the ability to see beyond the real world into the spirit world. Nowadays, it's considered an old wives' tale, but it happens every generation or so in our family."

"Was Freya born behind the veil?"

"Yes. And she had Tilly's ability to sense things. She was an extraordinary child, I'm told."

I glanced at him. "You never knew her, Papa?"

He stared out over the graveyard so that I couldn't see the desolation in his eyes. "She was my daughter, my only child, but I never saw her alive."

My heart quickened. "Have you seen her ghost?"

"I saw her corpse." And the sorrow in his voice brought a fresh sting of tears to my eyes.

I dug the little broken wing from my pocket and handed it to him. "I found this in your things. I shouldn't have taken it."

His fingers closed around the bit of porcelain, and he clasped it tightly as he told me his story, how he had not seen or heard from Tilly since he'd gone back to my mother. He hadn't even known about a baby until Tilly had called one night seventeen years after he'd last seen her and told him just enough to send him flying back to Asher Falls where he'd learned that Freya, his only child, had been murdered.

"Did Tilly know who killed her?"

"She never told me. I guess she was afraid of what I might do. But she had a vision of her child's death. That's what guided her to Freya."

"She found the body?"

He nodded.

"But if she knew Freya was murdered, why didn't she go to the police? Why did she let everyone think that her daughter had died in a fire?"

"Because she didn't want anyone to know about you."

"Why?"

"You were born after Freya was murdered."

My heart started to hammer. *"After?"*

His eyes grew distant. "The girl had snuck out of the house to meet someone that night. Tilly didn't even know she was missing until she woke up from a dream. That dream led her to the laurel bald where she found a fresh grave."

"Freya's grave."

"And yours, child."

The shock of his words stole my breath even though I must have already intuited the truth. That was why I'd been so overcome at the gravesite. Why that terrible suffocation had pressed down on me. I had been buried there with my murdered mother.

Angus had sensed it, too. That must have been how he found the grave. As impossible as it seemed, he must have picked up my scent, not my mother's.

I tunneled my fingers through his fur, and he turned, dark eyes gleaming as he nuzzled against me.

"The grave was so shallow the dirt barely covered the body," Papa said. "She hadn't been there long. Only moments. Her skin was still warm, and Tilly prayed that she might still be alive. But when she unearthed her, there was no heartbeat. No pulse. The only thing Tilly could do was try and save the baby."

I had been buried alive, I thought in horror. I had

been born to a dead mother. No wonder my life was so strange.

"You weren't breathing, even when Tilly peeled away the veil. She resuscitated you. She blew her breath into your lungs and brought you back from the other side."

Brought me back from the other side.

An icy hand grazed my nerve endings.

"And then she gave me to you," I said softly.

"Yes, but before I took you home, I had to see my child. I had to give her a proper burial so that she could rest in peace."

My poor, young mother hadn't been able to rest, but I wouldn't tell Papa. I wanted him to have that solace.

At least I now knew why he'd been covered in blood when he brought me home. "You've been caring for her grave all these years."

"It was all I could do for her."

"But, Papa, why did you bury her north to south? Surely it wasn't because—"

"I didn't want her facing those mountains," he said harshly.

I caught my breath. "You felt it, too." The wind, the dankness. That awful howling.

"Yes, I felt it. So did your mother when we lived there. So did Tilly."

His gaze moved to the angels. "It was there when you were born. It was with you on the other side. Tilly sensed it that night. There was a terrible struggle, she said."

I thought of that day in the cemetery when she had tugged me out of the briar patch.

"You fought hard, Amelia. You battled your way back, but even as you drew your first breath, Tilly knew it wasn't over. She was afraid for you. Afraid it would come for you. She knew she had to get you out of Asher Falls. She thought you would be safe with me."

I hugged my knees. "Why did you shut me out, Papa? Why did you turn away when I needed you the most?"

He looked old and defeated, indescribably weary. "I was afraid the ghost we saw that day had been sent to watch over you. I was afraid the evil had found you and it would use my devotion to you—my weakness—to somehow get to you."

I couldn't stop shaking. Angus sensed my agitation and whimpered. "All this just because I came back from the other side?"

"And because the power it could wield through you on this side would be very, very strong."

"Why?"

"You are the last of the Ashers," he said.

I buried my face in my arms, succumbing to a storm of emotions. "Who is my father?" I asked fearfully.

"Edward Asher."

"Was he evil? Was he in league like the others?"

"I don't know. But his blood runs through your veins, so your ties to that place are strong. That's why you were lured back there."

"But why now?"

"The rules kept you safe," Papa said. "But you broke them, and now that the door has been opened, you're vulnerable. Those closest to you are the most dangerous because it will try to use them to weaken you. It will lie and trick and deceive you. You mustn't let it. And you must never, ever return to Asher Falls."

I lifted my head. "If it fears me, then there must be a way to defeat it. I can't live like this, Papa. I can't live with the loneliness. Sometimes I think I'd be better off dead."

"Don't say that! Don't even think it."

"Then help me destroy it."

"You still don't understand, do you?" He turned away quickly, but not before I'd seen that same look of pity and regret in his eyes.

Thirty-Four

❧❧❧

Angus and I returned to Asher Falls that afternoon. I didn't tell Papa because I didn't want to worry him. But I had to go back. I had to find a way to protect myself. I had to close that terrible door, and if it could be done at all, it would be in the place where I had been born on the other side.

A weight descended the moment we entered the foothills. It was raining, and I wondered if it had poured the whole time we were away. The lake looked swollen, and the ditches were overflowing. The deluge subsided as we drove off the ferry, but the sky remained gray and bleak. For the first time, Angus turned away from the window and settled down in the front seat, resting his snout on the console. I put my hand on his head and felt the bristle of his hair.

"I know," I murmured. "I feel it, too."

The oppression. The weight of those mountains bearing down on us.

I heard a crack and looked up to see a boulder crashing toward us. It hit the highway directly in front of the car, releasing a shower of rocks and gravel that pelted my hood and windshield. I was so startled, I swerved too sharply and almost lost control of the wheel on the wet pavement. Righting the vehicle, I pulled to the side of the road to catch my breath and settle my nerves.

The boulder had been close. Too close. A very dark omen.

I wanted to believe it was just bad timing, but I had a feeling it was more than that. I had been warned.

"It's coming," I whispered and Angus whimpered.

I had decided on the drive back that if anyone could help me, it would be Tilly. I headed straight for her house, but the dirt road through the woods had washed out, and I had to park my car and hike most of the way on foot. Halfway there it started to rain again, and I was soaked and miserable by the time I stepped up on her porch. She didn't answer my knock, so I went around back to see if she might be working with the birds. The feeders and houses were empty, the trees disturbingly silent. I might have taken the quiet for another omen if I hadn't realized the bad weather had chased the birds away.

Angus huddled under the porch as I climbed the steps and opened the screen door. "Tilly?"

No answer.

I moved across the porch and tried the back door. It opened silently, and I stuck my head in, calling out her name.

Still no answer.

I pushed open the door and moved into the kitchen. "Tilly? Are you in here? It's me, Amelia."

I stopped just inside the door and looked around.

Nothing seemed out of place, but I'd only been inside the house once before. I might not notice if a chair had been moved or a cupboard rearranged. Something was different, though. I could feel it. Sense it.

"Tilly?" The echo of her name in that silent house was eerie and foreboding. I made myself move out of the kitchen and into the living room. Nothing out of place in there, either, except for a pair of muddy boots at the front door where Tilly had undoubtedly left them.

I walked down the tiny hallway. The front bedroom door was open and I peaked inside. It was small and sparsely furnished with an iron bedstead and an oak dresser. I saw myself in the mirror, face pale and drawn, eyes wide with fright. Yes, I was frightened. Fear had an icy grip on my spine as I inched deeper into the house.

In the bathroom, I found blood splotches in the sink and bits of glass on the floor.

My every instinct screamed for me to get out of the house, quickly, the same way I'd come in. But I couldn't. Not until I found Tilly. She could be lying hurt somewhere. She could be—

A sound froze me in my tracks. My hand flew to my chest as if I could quell the panic that accelerated my heartbeat and drove the air from my lungs.

Someone was in the house, and I didn't think it was Tilly. She would have answered me when I called out.

The wood floor creaked as someone slipped down the hallway toward me. I didn't dare move for fear of giving myself away. But I couldn't just stand there. I needed to find a place to hide.

The creaking stopped. Not as if the footsteps had moved away but as if someone had paused in midstride because they'd heard a sound or sensed a presence. And now they waited with suspended breath on the other side of the wall.

I lifted a foot, and the screech of the floorboard drew a cringe. Out in the hallway, a shadow crept along the wall.

A moment later, Catrice appeared in the doorway, and we both screamed.

"Amelia!" She clutched her sweater around her.

I stood there trembling. "What are you doing here?"

"I was in town. I saw you drive through and I followed you." She glanced around anxiously. "Tilly isn't here?"

"I thought your car was broken down."

Her gaze darted away. "I…just got it fixed."

Her nervous demeanor confirmed what I had suspected all along—that our meeting in town that day hadn't been coincidental at all. I doubted she'd even had car trouble.

"Why did you follow me?" I asked sharply.

"I have to talk to you," she muttered. "I just hope—"

"What?"

"I'm so worried about Tilly."

"Why?" When she didn't answer, I grabbed her arms. "There's blood in here. Do you know something about that?"

Her eyes widened. "Blood? Are you sure?"

"Of course, I'm sure. See for yourself if you don't believe me. But first, tell me why you're looking for Tilly."

She looked distraught as her gaze flitted around the bathroom like a frightened bird's. "I never thought it would come to this. You have to believe me."

"Come to what? Is Tilly in some kind of trouble?"

Her brown eyes filled with tears as she nodded. "I'm afraid she might be."

"What kind of trouble?"

"Bad trouble. I think she's in danger."

"From whom?"

Catrice closed her eyes. "From Freya's killer."

My heart jumped. "Who killed her?"

"It could have been any one of us," she whispered. "We were all there that night. And we'd talked about doing it before. Luna said we needed an offering and Freya was so easy to manipulate."

"An offering…for what?"

"It was just talk, a stupid game," she babbled. "I never thought anyone would go through with it."

"But someone did."

"Yes."

"Who was there?"

"We three girls, Hugh and Edward. Freya had told Edward earlier that she was pregnant with his baby. He was in shock. We all were, especially considering that she was almost ready to deliver. She kept to herself so much and she had such a small frame that no one suspected. And why would we? Who would ever dream that he would be so careless with someone like…with an outsider? Luna was furious because she'd always planned to have the first Asher grandchild. Hugh wasn't exactly thrilled, either. And poor Bryn. She was the most devastated of all."

"Why?"

"She was crazy about Edward. She would have done anything to get his attention, and there he was, sleeping around with someone like Freya Pattershaw."

"And you?"

She drew a trembling breath. "Oh, yes. I had my reasons, too. I wanted to fit in just as badly as Freya, so I went along with the game. And all these years…" She glanced down at her hands. Her fingers had curled back as though the joints were afflicted with arthritis. "I should have come forward a long time ago but I didn't have the courage. I've been such a coward."

"It's not too late. You can still make it right. Catrice…who killed her? You must have some idea."

"I swear I don't know," she said desperately. "Don't you see? That's the way we planned it. None of us would know…except the killer. We lured her up there and then we scared her into running off. It was like a game of hide-and-seek. We split up and searched for her. Whoever found her first…" She trailed off. "We would all be complicit, but only one would have blood on their hands."

"But what about the fire?"

"That was just a cover. We all panicked when we realized…when Freya never turned up, so Luna went to Pell. She convinced him that Edward had killed Freya. Naturally, he took care of everything. The fire, the funeral arrangements. Everything."

"How did Tilly burn her hands?"

"Somehow she got word of the blaze. A lot of people had gathered to watch the building burn, but no one tried to do anything to help. When Tilly got there, she tried to get Freya out. That was hard to watch because Freya was never inside. She had already been killed when Pell had the fire set."

And Tilly knew that. So why had she rushed into that burning building?

"Wouldn't it have made more sense to put Freya's body in the building?"

"That would have given the killer away because no one else knew where the body was. And we promised ourselves we'd never tell a living soul. We'd just forget what had been done. Forget about Freya." She touched a hand to her forehead. "But someone must have seen. They dug up the body and delivered Freya's baby. It had to be Tilly. No one else could have done it."

I pictured that lonely grave in the laurel bald. Freya's grave. My grave.

"If Tilly knew Freya was in that grave, why would she try to get her out of a burning building?"

"Maybe she was already unhinged. Or maybe…" Catrice had gone very pale. "Maybe she knew that was what we would have expected her to do. Maybe she didn't want us to know that she'd found the body because she was afraid for you. She burned her hands trying to protect you."

I went very still. "You know who I am?" I asked in a strained voice.

"You have a certain way of turning your head…a certain way you smile. I see Edward in you."

"Who else knows?"

"Luna, Bryn and Hugh. Pell, of course, because he's the one who brought you here. You're his last hope of producing an Asher heir. You and Thane."

I stared at her in shock. "What do you mean?"

"He arranged to have you brought here so that Thane could seduce you."

"No. That's not true. He wouldn't have anything to do with that."

She looked at me with pity. "It is true. But Pell selfishly put you in danger because the fact that you're alive proves Freya didn't die in that fire."

"Thane didn't know," I said numbly.

She put a comforting hand on my arm, but I jerked away from her.

She searched my face. "Don't you understand?" she asked softly. "He'd do anything to solidify his position in that family. I think he might cut off his right arm for the chance of giving Pell Asher a grandson."

I thought of Tilly's warning about Thane. *He covets what can never be his.* And I thought about that night we were together in the cemetery, how the evil had found a way in through his weakness.

Terror washed over me at what might already have been done. "I'm calling the police."

"You can't," Catrice said. "Not the local police. Wayne is too afraid of the Ashers to help us, and it'll take too long for the state police to get here. Or even the county patrol. They'd have to come across on the next ferry because the back roads will be flooded by now. In this weather, it could take hours for them to get here." Her gaze slowly lifted. "We're completely isolated."

Thirty-Five

I don't know why I headed to the laurel bald, to Freya's grave, but I had a strong sense that Tilly had gone there. Maybe I'd inherited her uncanny intuition, or maybe I could somehow hear her calling out to me. Maybe it was Freya's ghost that guided me. I only knew that the pull was too powerful to ignore. And I knew of no place else to look for her.

It was raining again by the time Angus and I reached the cemetery. As I charged through the woods with my mace and a handful of tools—make-do weapons— I'd grabbed from the back of my car, I told myself it was foolish to think that I could save my grandmother single-handedly. Or that I could trust anything that came out of Catrice's mouth. By her own admission, she had helped plan a murder. And yet…what choice did I have? Freya was lost to me forever. I didn't want to lose Tilly now that I'd only just found her.

As Angus and I crested the hill, I tried yet again to call the state police, but I still couldn't get a signal. I thought about calling Thane, but what if Tilly was right? What if he'd been in league with his grandfather all along?

The thought of his deception cut like a knife, but I didn't have time for self-pity. Later, I could look back and dissect our every conversation, searching for clues and nuances that might have given him away. But now was not that time. Not with Tilly's life on the line. She'd brought me into this world, and she'd never once hesitated to protect me. How could I not do the same for her?

I scrambled down the overhang, and my heart started to pound as I approached the grave. *My* grave. Angus was acting very strangely. He sniffed the leaves and pawed at the ground, and I thought perhaps he'd picked up my scent. But when I called his name, he whirled with bared teeth and feverish eyes.

My stomach tensed as I watched him warily. "Angus? What's wrong, boy?"

He answered with a low growl, and I drew back on a gasp. What had come over him?

He crouched and circled as I stood frozen, Papa's terrible warning thundering in my head: *Those closest to you are the most dangerous because it will try to use them to weaken you.*

"Not you, Angus," I whispered.

He continued to circle, hair bristled, until I had no choice but to slowly back away. He returned to the grave then, but he kept his agitated gaze on me. He didn't try to approach or attack. I wondered if he only meant to scare me away.

The rain was still coming down, and I could hear the steady drip on the leaves. And something else. Something familiar and instantly alarming. A splintering sound…

I couldn't identify the noise, but I knew—somehow I *knew*—that the killer was just beyond the overhang, just beyond my line of sight.

I remembered something Catrice had told me once. The three of them—she, Bryn and Luna—were like blood sisters, and they knew these hills like their own backyard.

And what of Hugh? Could he be out there searching for me, too?

Like Freya before me, I had been drawn into their dastardly game, but I couldn't let myself think about my birth mother's gruesome end or the horrifying way I'd come into this world. I couldn't think about Thane's duplicity or Angus's betrayal. I had to keep a clear head—

A silhouette appeared at the top of the overhang—black-clad with ax in hand—and I turned with a gasp, plunging recklessly through the bald. I almost expected Angus to lunge after me, but he stayed at the grave, watching over something that I couldn't see.

Limbs whiplashed my face and yanked at my hair as I ran blindly, driven by pure terror and the memory of Freya's ghost. I kept up the pace until the mountain laurel thickened, the branches becoming so tightly entwined I could barely claw my way through. Any light that might have shimmered through the rain clouds was completely obliterated by the low-hanging canopy, and I was soon hopelessly lost.

Emerging into a tiny clearing, I bent to rest, hands on knees, as I tried to catch my breath and corral my racing heart.

Lifting my head, I listened for sounds of pursuit, but all I could hear was the relentless patter of rain and the buzz of mosquitoes around my face. No, that wasn't quite true. If I listened closely, I could hear the waterfall in the distance. I tried to orient myself to the sound, but I'd strayed too far into laurel hell, and now I'd lost all sense of direction. A more effective trap, I could hardly imagine.

I hunkered in that little clearing, wet and trembling and petrified of what waited for me somewhere in that maze. If the sameness of the landscape befuddled under the best of circumstances, navigating that solid wall in a full-blown panic appeared hopeless. I found myself turning in a slow circle, searching for some clue that would lead me to Tilly. To safety. All around me, the skeletal forms pressed in on me, the grasping branches like disembodied ghost arms reaching for me from the mist.

Then over the rain, I again heard a cracking sound, rhythmic and steady, and now I knew what it was. The killer was using the ax to hack a path through the tangle of limbs, and the noise was getting louder as the hunter closed in on the prey. There was no need for stealth. I was already cornered.

Hand to heart, I strained to pinpoint the direction. It was coming from my right, I thought. No, to the left. No…right….

As if tugged by a string, my head moved back and forth. Thoroughly disoriented by that treacherous labyrinth, I found myself momentarily paralyzed, terrified of fleeing straight into danger.

Curling my hand around a knotty branch, I clung as if to a lifeline. I heard nothing now. No chopping, no footfalls, no ragged breaths other than my own. In that bated silence, my fingers tightened convulsively around the brittle limb as I imagined the killer's hand gripping the ax.

And at that precise moment, when I could have used every advantage, every scrap of cover, the rain stopped. New sounds came to me suddenly—the distant trill of a loon, the muted rush of the waterfall.

I could hear breathing now, too, a sharp inhale-exhale as if my scent had been caught. The killer was right there. *Right behind me.*

Dropping to my knees, I scrambled up under the branches. The rhododendron—a dense, stunted nightmare—was now my ally.

My lip had been split, and I pressed the back of my hand to the pain, trying to relieve the throbbing pressure. I tasted blood and thought again of Freya. I didn't want to meet the same end. She had been young, pregnant and desperate—easy prey. At least I had the advantage of knowing the game.

Huddling beneath the branches, I pictured the killer in the clearing, patiently waiting for the quarry to take flight. I didn't move even to tuck back the hair from my eyes. I hardly dared to breathe. I was concealed for the moment by the screen of leaves and limbs. All I had to do was keep still. The killer would have no way of knowing which way I'd gone. After that initial mad flight, I'd learned a valuable lesson. The trail of broken twigs had led straight to me. From now on, I wouldn't make it so easy.

The killer was moving around in the clearing now. I could hear the scrape of branches and the shallow, rapid breaths that came from excitement. I peered through the snarled branches until a form took shape.

I made no sound. I was sure of that. But all of a sudden the ax slashed down through the twisted limbs right above me. I didn't scream. I barely even gasped. Something more than fear drove me now. Instinct for survival, yes, but also anger. Anger at what had been done to my young mother. Anger at being hunted like an animal. I wouldn't succumb to fear or panic. I bit down hard on my sore lip, and the pain gave me a spurt of adrenaline.

On hands and knees, I crawled through the endless tunnels of tree trunks as the ax chopped at the branches above me. I felt the blade graze my shoulder, and I went flat, propelling myself forward on my stomach until I was safely out of reach. I could move faster underneath the canopy, and I almost expected the killer to ditch the ax and come in after me. But miraculously, the sound moved away from me, and I realized I hadn't been spotted, after all. The killer fanned out around the clearing, trying to flush me out.

Now that the rain had stopped, sound carried surprisingly well, and I heard the thrash of another body moving through the bald. The killer heard it, too, and reversed course making a beeline toward it. I wanted to call out, not just for help but as a warning. But what if someone had come to help the killer? If I gave away my position, I would be a sitting duck beneath that canopy.

I waited until the sound of the chopping faded, and even then I didn't ease back into the clearing. Instead, I stayed on all fours and began a long, miserable crawl through that thicket. The feeling of isolation and impending doom sapped my energy and destroyed my will, but I forced myself to go on. I had no choice. The canopy had tightened, and the only way in or out was on hands and knees.

At some point, I thought I heard the hack of the killer's ax coming closer, but it may well have been my imagination. It was dark beneath those branches, and with no sense of direction the mind began to play tricks. I heard my name called, softly, furtively, and I had to catch myself from responding, so great was my need for human contact.

What if I never got out? What if I died in here, all alone without seeing my mother or my aunt or my papa ever again? Without finding Tilly—

I cut off those insidious thoughts. I couldn't lose control. I had to stay focused. There must be a path somewhere, an animal trail that would lead me to the edge of the thicket.

On and on I crawled. My knees were raw and bleeding, and I was in torment from a thousand scratches. After a while I began to hallucinate. I could see glowing eyes deep within the laurel tunnels, and the ground beneath me trembled, as if in the aftermath of an earthquake. Worst of all, I heard the whisper of my name, and I thought that it was Thane. His voice was so real to me that I once again started to call out. But reason interjected, and I realized that it was only my imagination or some terrible trick. Even if he was there, he might be in league with the killer. He might even be the killer.

Amelia...can you hear me? Amelia...answer me....

"Thane?" I said his name aloud into the wind, but he

didn't respond because he wasn't really there. No one was. Not even the killer.

I was all alone in my own private hell.

I lost all sense of time as well as direction. I had no idea how long I'd been crawling through that maze, but it must have been hours. The canopy was so solid, I couldn't see the sky to gauge the time of day. There was no way to follow moon, stars or even the mountain peaks. It really was a damnable web, and for all I knew, I'd been crawling around in a circle.

Energy flagged and I stopped to rest. Drawing my bloody knees up to my chest, I wrapped my arms around my legs and sat there wet and trembling and demoralized. I don't think I was even frightened of the killer at that point. I might even have welcomed the sound of the ax hacking a path toward me because at that moment, anything would have been preferable to that utter seclusion.

I knew that I would have to somehow rally and keep moving, but for a moment, I allowed myself to flounder in hopelessness and self-pity. I probed at the scrapes on my knees and wiped blood and rain from my face. The scratches from the laurel bark were far more painful than the surface cut left by the ax, but the idea of that blade slashing down through leaf and stem drew a very deep shudder.

Still I sat there. I couldn't make myself go any farther. It wasn't like me to give up, but I had nothing left in me. No energy, no hope, not even the anger anymore. The thought of remaining there until a wild animal picked up my scent or until I died of starvation was not without appeal. All I wanted was to just…sit there.

And then through that dense foliage, a sound came to me, and I discovered that I wasn't quite as apathetic as I'd thought. Something was coming, and my head jerked up to register both sound and direction.

Whoever it was—whatever it was—stayed low to the ground and moved quickly. A scent came to me then, that of a rotting corpse, and even as fear exploded, I again tried to tell myself it was just an animal carcass. Something had died in the bald, and the wind had shifted so that I only now got a whiff.

But that scrabbling sound…

As my gaze scoured the tree trunks in front of me, I caught the dart of something down one of the tunnels. It was only a flash, a shadow, but in that brief instant, I saw the flare of a coat. Or was that wings?

The idea of something not quite human stalking me through that godforsaken warren brought me to my feet, and I plunged irrationally into the thicket only to run up against an impenetrable wall of limbs.

Teeth chattering from cold and fear, I once again dropped to my knees and scrambled down one of the burrows.

I could hear it behind me. Then in front of me. Then off to the side. Whichever way I turned, it was always there. And that smell… Oh, God…that smell…

Panic spiraled out of control, and my breath came in sobs. Twigs snapped directly over me as if the thing had climbed to the top of the canopy and crawled above me. Heart pounding, I stopped and looked up. I could see nothing, hear nothing. But that fetid smell crept down through the branches and gagged me.

Fear flailed anew, and I turned to clamber through

one channel and then another. Twigs and leaves rained down on me as the thing kept pace with me.

After a moment, I realized that it wasn't keeping pace at all. Rather, it seemed to be herding me. It stayed just ahead of me, causing me to turn this way and that in a futile attempt to escape.

The worst part was…I didn't even know if it was real. Maybe my mind had broken down completely and the thing had been sprouted by fear, panic and insanity.

I glanced up again, saw a pale eye leering down at me through the branches, and it was all I could do to choke back a scream. A shriek would undoubtedly bring the killer, and I couldn't be certain my otherworldly stalker hadn't been dredged from the deepest, darkest corners of a mad mind.

Maybe the *killer* wasn't even real. Maybe everything that had happened in Asher Falls was just a nightmare….

I kept going, babbling under my breath, "It's not real, it's not real, it's not real."

The rain was still coming down. On some level, I'd been aware of the drum on the leaves all along, but now when I looked up, the drops pelted my face, and I realized that the blind had thinned. Light seeped through and I could see nothing in the trees above me, hear nothing in the underbrush all around me. The thing was gone and with it, my panic. I closed my eyes for one brief moment and let the chill of the rain revive me. Then I rose on shaking legs and stumbled forward.

The edge of the thicket beckoned.

Thirty-Six

❦

As I stumbled out of the bald, the rain slacked. It seemed like a sign, and I felt almost giddy with relief. I could see mountain and sky and, through a break in the rain clouds, a sliver of moon. The air was fragrant with evergreen, the cool darkness now a welcome cocoon.

But I still had no idea where I was. None of the landmarks looked at all familiar, and after a momentary reprieve, panic resurfaced. I'd found my way out of the maze, but I was still lost. And I was still being pursued by a killer, someone who knew the area *like their own backyard.* I couldn't stand there forever and wait to be found. I had to get moving.

I started to climb, picking my way through the trees and up a steep, rugged incline that quickly stole the reserve of my energy. The going was slow without a flashlight, the path treacherous with fallen branches and slippery stones. I had to stop once to remove a pebble from my boot, but the damage had already been done to the tender tissue in my heel, and I had to bite back a cry of pain and frustration.

Somewhere above me, I could hear the muted sound of rushing water and thought I must have come out of the bald on the back side of the waterfall. If I followed the base of the cliff, I would eventually arrive at that arched opening, and from there I could find my way back to the cemetery and my car.

As I knelt to relace my boot, I heard what I thought was the distant rumble of thunder. But in the next moment, the whole mountain seemed to shudder, and an avalanche of pebbles and stones rained down upon me. Scrambling for shelter beneath a rocky ledge, I huddled there until I was sure the rock slide had run its course, and then once again I began to climb.

Even though I'd never been on this side of the hill, I was starting to get my bearings. The ground leveled out, and a crude path ran along the foot of the cliff. The going here was a good deal easier, but I had to keep constant vigil because I was more or less in the open. The sound of the waterfall grew ever louder as I limped along, and just ahead, I spotted what I thought was the arched entrance to the glade. My heart started to race because, for the first time in hours, I knew exactly where I was. With any luck, I could be back at the cemetery within half an hour.

A hawk took flight from the top of the cliff, and I spun to track it against the gloomy sky. What had startled it from its roost? I wondered uneasily. And then as I slowly turned back to the path, I caught the bob of a flashlight coming across the meadow still some distance away.

I darted off the path and flattened myself against the rock, but with the moon peeking from the clouds now, I was completely exposed. For a moment, I considered turning back, but then I remembered that Thane had told me there was another way up to the top of the cliff. If someone had been up there just now and startled the hawk, I might have already been seen. They might be on their way down even now, and in my present condition, I could never outrun them.

My only hope was to find a place to hide, but even with the hunters closing in on me, I hesitated to enter the glade. I remembered all too well that feeling of being penned in, the almost suffocating claustrophobia. The scars on Wayne Van Zandt's face.

But I was already hemmed in with someone approaching from the meadow and, for all I knew, someone already behind me on the path. There was nowhere to go but inside the arch.

Even so, I might still have resisted if I hadn't heard Angus bark in distress. The sound was muffled, as if he were a long way off.

"Angus!" I called in a loud whisper. "Angus, where are you?"

An answering whimper came from the depths of the cave.

Careful. It could be a trick, a little voice warned me.

Easing through the archway, I said his name softly, *"Angus."*

As I scoured those rock walls, I felt eyes staring back at me from every crack and crevice, saw the dart of shadows along the shelves and ledges. The place seemed alive in the moonlight.

"Where are you, boy?"

As I moved across the clearing, I heard a faint noise outside the arch, the softest of footfalls. My mind raced frantically. I couldn't hide in the cave...it was a dead end, another trap. Thane had said it ended a quarter of a mile in.

I whirled as the footsteps drew closer.

Then once again, my gaze scaled those walls, treacherous enough in daylight, but by darkness, it would be a suicide climb....

I imagined the ax hacking through my flesh, and I turned to scramble up the wall, fear and desperation unleashing agility I never knew I had. Even in the dark, I managed to find handholds and footholds, some of them crumbling away into nothingness as I climbed. I was almost to the nearest ledge when I sensed, more than heard, someone enter. I scurried up as silently as I could, hoping that by some miracle of miracles I wouldn't be made. Pressing myself against the wall, I glanced down into the glade.

From my vantage, I could see Luna clearly as she moved into the center of the clearing and flung her arms wide, head tilted to the mountains, turning and turning, calling the evil just as I had in that circle of Asher angels.

Gone was her lush hair, the luminous skin, the voluptuous figure that the years seemed hardly to have touched. The mask had slipped yet again, revealing a face and body that were wrinkled and withered.

She held the flashlight in one hand and in the other, something that shone in the moonlight. It was one of the curved knives I'd seen in her office. Perhaps the same blade she'd used to slit my young mother's throat.

Eyes open now, she continued to turn in a slow circle, scanning the walls. Lowering her arms, she started back toward the arch, and for one breathless moment, I thought she might have given up. The relief left me light-headed as I pressed my cheek against the cool, wet rock.

Then I heard a whimper.

Luna stopped, turned, her gaze going back to the cave. Even in the moonlight, I saw the tilt of her lips, could almost hear the rush of adrenaline through her veins as she caressed the knife blade.

My heart was still pounded, but not in fear for my own safety.

I rose on the ledge, sending an avalanche of pebbles down into the glade. She looked up, and I could see moonlight gleaming in her eyes.

"There you are." Her tone was so casual she might have been inquiring about the weather.

I flattened myself against the wall, trying to meld into the stone. My gaze lifted, gauging the distance to the top of the cliff or even to the next ledge.

"I wouldn't try it if I were you," she said as she walked toward the base. "If you keep still, I won't hurt the dog."

I stared down at her from my ledge. "Why should I believe you?"

"What choice do you have?"

"You killed Freya," I accused.

Luna shrugged. "She was a nuisance just like you."

"Why am I a nuisance?" *Keep her talking,* I thought. Keep her engaged until I could figure a way out.

"You're very draining, Amelia."

"What do you mean?"

"Look at me. Look at my face. That's your doing."

"How?"

"Everything changed when you came. The wind, this mountain…even the dead."

A cold breeze swept over me, and I thought again of Emelyn Asher's corpse. "How do you know that's my doing?"

"Oh, it's you. You've somehow fed on our energy. You've somehow usurped all my power." Her eyes glittered dangerously. "And I mean to have it back."

I thought I had scaled the wall with relative ease, but she came up like a panther. Within moments she'd climbed above me on the wall, and as she jumped down to the ledge, I turned and leaped to the next. The edge of it crumbled beneath my boots, and I hovered for what seemed an eternity before I found my balance and dug my hands into the tiny crevices in the wall.

"I'm Pell Asher's granddaughter. If you kill me, he won't make it go away this time. He'll come after you."

She merely laughed. "Do you really think I'm afraid of an old cripple? He only *thinks* he's still in control."

I sensed someone moving above us, but I didn't dare take my eyes off Luna.

"If I'm such a threat to you, why did you bring me here? Why did you put me in the Covey house?"

"Oh, that was all Pell, and I admit he still has a few tricks up his sleeve. I had no idea you were alive. I thought the old fool merely wanted to restore the cemetery before his time came. That would be like him. It was only after you arrived that I figured it out. As for the Covey house…" She gave a low laugh. "I can only assume he thought it would keep you safe until the deed was done."

The deed was done….

I shuddered.

"Once you produced an heir, he would have had no more use for you. Not with your unfortunate lineage.

No doubt he would have taken care of you the same way he handled Harper and Thane's mother."

I inched back. "What does Thane's mother have to do with this?"

"He thought if he eliminated Riana, Edward would come back to him. So he arranged a hit-and-run. Poor thing never knew what hit her."

I tried not to succumb to the horror of her words as I clung to the rock wall. I wanted to believe the gap between my ledge and hers offered a modicum of protection, but I knew better. She was toying with me now. She had me right where she wanted me, so she could afford to take her time.

"Did Edward know?"

"He must have suspected, but there was nothing he could do. He did manage to have his revenge, though."

"How?"

"He committed suicide, and had his body cremated before Pell could claim him and bring him home."

I remembered what Thane had told me once about Edward. *He wanted to break free of the Asher shackles. He just never quite managed.*

"If he hated Pell that much, why would he leave Thane with him?"

"He didn't leave Thane. Pell took him. Edward was too weak to fight him." She thumbed the moonstone at her throat. "That's your family, Amelia. That's your legacy. That's who you are. Not that it matters now…."

The *Drudenfuss* was right above us, the open end over Luna's ledge, a closed point over mine. I don't know what I hoped to accomplish. I suppose I was still acting purely on instinct and adrenaline, but I grabbed a loose stone and began to chip away at the closed point, trying to blunt the end.

"No!" Luna screamed.

She leaped the distance between the shelves, easily clearing the edge. But there must have already been a fissure in the rock—or perhaps I'd created one—because I heard a crack that sounded like a gunshot. Even so, she might still have saved herself if Angus hadn't appeared in the shadowy recesses of one of the crevices. He growled viciously and lunged. Caught off guard, Luna stumbled backward with a stunned cry. For the longest moment, our eyes clashed, both of us frozen, and then her hand shot out to clamp onto me and we were free-falling.

Somehow, I grabbed onto the ledge, feet dangling, and clung for dear life. A split second later, I heard a thud as her body hit the ground, then a great roar—the flap of a thousand bird wings as a murder of crows descended into the glade.

I heard Thane call out to me as he climbed down to the ledge.

He stood over me. "Take my hand!"

Even with the rock crumbling away beneath my fingertips, I hesitated.

Something flared in his eyes, anger...hurt....

It was gone in a flash as he grabbed my arms and pulled me up. The shelf was already giving away. Angus darted back into the cave, and with a heave, Thane propelled me up the wall. I climbed without hesitation, groping for holds.

The birds had gathered over Luna's body, and I heard

her scream. As I reached the top and turned to give Thane a hand, I caught a glimpse of Tilly standing at the edge of the cliff, gazing down into the glade.

Thirty-Seven

"Tilly, Tilly, are you all right?" I rushed toward her.

"I'm all right, girl. Are you?" she asked anxiously. She looked tiny standing up there on that cliff. Tiny but stalwart.

"I'm fine. I was just so worried about you. I went by your house and saw all that blood in the bathroom.... I thought the worst."

"I had one of my spells and dropped a glass. I nicked my finger and didn't take time to clean up the mess because I knew you were in trouble. I had to come looking for you."

"But...I was looking for you. When Catrice told me what happened to Freya—"

Tilly's eyes went cold. "Where did you see the Hawthorne woman?"

"She followed me to your house."

"You let her into my house?"

Her tone took me aback. "I didn't let her in. She just showed up there."

"I should have planted more rosemary," Tilly mumbled.

I looked at Thane. He stood off to the side, allowing us our reunion. He looked tall, dark and handsome in the moonlight. Stalwart in his own right.

"What did that woman want?" Tilly asked.

"She said she was worried about you because my being alive proved that Freya didn't die in the fire. Oh, it's a long story," I said on a breath. "You know most of it, anyway. She told me you were in danger and we couldn't get the police here fast enough, so I came to... rescue you," I finished lamely.

Her eyes darkened as she gazed up at me. "That was a mighty foolish thing to do. You could have been killed."

"So could you. But it doesn't matter now. We're both safe. And I know everything," I said softly.

She took my hand and squeezed it, then turned her attention to Thane. "How did you know she was up here?" she demanded.

He turned, and I caught a glimpse of the scratches I'd left on the side of his face, reminding me all too vividly of the darkness that had enthralled us both at Thorngate. The same darkness that had been Luna's downfall.

"I saw her car in the cemetery," he said. "I went all through the laurel bald calling her name, but she never answered." Was that a hint of accusation in his tone? I wondered.

"What would you have done if you'd found her?" Tilly demanded.

"Whatever it took to save her life."

"Even if—"

"Yes."

Tilly nodded. "Well, you did save her, didn't you?"

Suddenly, there was a knot in my throat, and I couldn't speak. I looked at Thane, but he wouldn't meet my gaze.

Tilly grabbed my arm. "Come away from the edge of that cliff, girl. It feels like it's about to come down."

She was right. The rim was eroding even as we spoke. I heard a distant bark, and my heart sank. Angus was still in the cave. If the walls came down, he'd be trapped.

I whirled back to Thane. "You said there was a path somewhere. Can you show me?"

"This way."

We went down at a breakneck speed, and when we rushed through the arch, my gaze went to Luna's body. Then I turned quickly away. Tilly had no such compunction. She shooed away the birds and stooped to yank the silver chain from the corpse's neck. I saw the glow of Luna's moonstone as Tilly held it up to the light.

"You shouldn't touch the body," Thane warned. "We'll need to get the authorities up here."

Tilly said nothing. She continued to stare at the moonstone as if bewitched.

I tore my gaze away and screamed for Angus.

"I've been through that cave dozens of times," Thane said. "I never knew it connected to the other caves. If Angus found a passageway, then he can surely find his way out."

And at that precise moment, he bounded out of the cave and rushed to me, nuzzling his cold nose against my hand. I was still puzzled by his earlier behavior, and I didn't want to believe that darkness had somehow entered him. If he'd meant me real harm, he would have followed me into the laurel bald. Instead, he'd chased me away from the killer and maybe away from himself.

Tilly's eyes were lifted to the cliff now, to the *Drudenfuss* with the newly damaged point. I saw her lips move, but I couldn't hear what she said. Then she flung the moonstone toward the star, and as it shattered against the rock wall, the earth trembled.

"Get out!" Thane grabbed Tilly and pulled her out of the clearing as the ledges gave way and crashed to the ground.

A few minutes later, we were hurrying through the woods to the cemetery. Thane had taken the lead, and it was all Tilly and I could do to keep up with him. He'd said very little, and his silence was starting to worry me. He'd heard what Luna had said about his mother and Harper, and as I watched him put distance between us, I knew he was headed for Asher House.

I left Angus with Tilly and went after him. I'd seen enough of his temper to worry about what he might do if Pell actually admitted to his crimes. So I ran after him through those dripping woods, and when we got to the cemetery, I went straight to his car and climbed in.

Thorngate was softly aglow in the tenuous moonlight. I could see the Asher angels towering above the other monuments. Proud, defiant, almost godly. I shivered as I recognized some of my own features in those faces now.

Thane slid behind the wheel and slammed his door. "What are you doing?"

"I'm going with you."

"You don't even know where I'm headed."

"To see your grandfather," I said. "But shouldn't we call the police first?"

"We can't. There's no signal."

"How do you know? You didn't even try."

"I tried earlier. The nearest towers have been taken off-line due to the flooding. We'll call the police from Asher House."

"But that's not why we're going there, is it?"

He ran a hand through his wet hair. "You should just go home with Tilly. This won't be pleasant."

"I don't think you should confront him alone."

"I won't kill him if that's what you're worried about. Although I think I could with very little effort."

I put my hand on his arm. "He's not worth going to prison over. And what if this isn't you? What if you've let it in again?"

He started the engine and turned the car without a word.

As we reached the main highway, the moon disappeared and the countryside darkened. I could barely see the outline of the pine trees against the tapestry of mountain and sky. Raindrops splattered the windshield and strained the already-full ditches.

Thane drove fast despite the wet roads. I turned to study his profile. His anger was a tangible thing, an unwelcome passenger that goaded a flirtation with danger. He took a curve that made me catch my breath and clutch the seat.

He slanted a glance. "You heard me looking for you in the laurel bald, didn't you? Why didn't you answer me?"

This wouldn't be pleasant, either, I thought. "I was afraid."

"Of me? Why?"

"Because of something Catrice told me."

"What did she say?"

Absently, I rubbed a hand up and down my arm. "Do you remember that day I gave her a ride home? I told you I thought they'd all gathered at her studio to observe me. And I couldn't shake the feeling that I'd been brought to Asher Falls for a reason."

"I remember."

"That same day, when we were sitting on the back steps, you looked at me as if you'd seen a ghost. You said that you must have had a waking dream because for a moment I looked like someone else."

He frowned at the road. "What about it?"

"Who did you see when you looked at me?"

A pause. "Edward."

"So you did know."

"I guessed. You had this faraway look in your eyes and you held your head a certain way. For a moment, you were his spitting image."

"Do I look like him now?"

"Maybe not at this particular moment, but I've noticed the resemblance before. That day in the cemetery when we were talking about the angels…one of the faces reminded me of you. But I never thought much about it until later and then I started to put two and two together. Your uncanny resemblance to my stepfather. Your insistence that you'd been brought to Asher Falls for a reason."

"You didn't know that day on the ferry?"

"I recognized you from a picture in the paper," he said. "But I didn't make the connection to Edward until later. Why?"

"Catrice told me that you knew. She said you were in league with your grandfather, that he had brought me here so that you could seduce me. Because I was his last hope to continue the bloodline."

His face looked pale and grim in the dash light. "And you believed her?"

"I didn't want to, but I was scared. Tilly was missing and Catrice had just told me about Freya's murder. It was a lot to take in and I wasn't thinking clearly…." I trailed off. "Surely you can understand how her accusation might have given me pause."

"What did she say?" His voice was very tight, very controlled.

"I already told you—"

"I mean exactly. Word for word."

"She said that you would do anything to solidify your position in the Asher family. That you'd cut off your right arm to be the one to give Pell Asher an heir."

"I see." He was still staring straight ahead, speaking very softly. "There is a certain plausibility in that, I don't deny. But for you to think that I would hurt you… that you would hesitate to take my hand on the cliff…" He drew a breath. "That's hard to accept."

"I'm sorry." I turned back to the window, watching the night shadows fly past me. "But maybe it's all for the best."

"Why?"

"Because of who I am."

Another pause. "This is about the other night, isn't it? You said you were the one who had let it in."

"It seems it all started on the night of my birth. Freya Pattershaw was my mother."

"So Freya and Edward…?"

I faced him, my gaze going again to the marks I'd left on his cheek. "There's a lot I still don't understand, but this place is very dangerous for me. And I'm dangerous to the people who get close to me. Whatever is out there…whatever you and I felt that night…it's coming for me."

"How do we stop it?" he asked, the dangerous edge in his voice making me shiver.

I closed my eyes. "I don't think we can stop it."

Thirty-Eight

❧❧❧

As we came around a curve, the police flashers took me by surprise. Obviously, someone had managed to get a call through. Then I wondered if there'd been a bad accident. Not unusual in this weather. But as Thane slowed, I saw the yellow hazard lights on barricades that had been pulled across the road.

He rolled down his window as one of the policemen approached.

"What's going on?" Thane asked.

"Flash flood washed out the bridge," the officer said, water rolling off the brim of his hat as he bent to glance inside the car. "You won't be able to get across tonight. Creek's too high."

"We need to get up to the house," Thane said. "My grandfather is an invalid."

"He's not up there alone, is he?"

"I don't know if anyone is with him or not. That's why I need to get up there."

"If the rain stops, the water should recede in a few hours. At least by morning."

Another cop approached. "What's the problem?"

"No problem," Thane said. "We'd like to get home, is all."

"Not going to happen tonight. You try to go across now, you'll get swept downstream. My advice is to find someplace warm and dry and wait it out. And keep away from these bluffs. We've got reports coming in from all over the county of mudslides. People claim they've seen boulders the size of cars crashing down on highways. You get enough rain and sooner or later these ridges will start to cave."

"Thanks." Thane reversed the car, turned in the road and headed away from the barricades. As soon as we were around the curve and out of sight, he pulled to the shoulder.

"Why didn't you tell them what happened?" I asked anxiously.

"Because I didn't want to get waylaid with questions and statements. I'm going up to the house," he said. "You can tell them after I'm gone or you can go home and wait for me. Do whatever you want."

"But…how do you intend to get across the creek?"

"There's a foot bridge about a half mile downstream. I'll go across there."

"Thane, that's crazy. Why don't you just wait until morning to talk to him?"

"It's not about that." He tapped a restless finger on the steering wheel as his gaze searched the darkness. "I know it's crazy. I could kill him with my bare hands after what I heard tonight. The man took everything from me. But I don't have it in me to leave him up there in that chair."

"What are you going to do? Sit up there with him

until the storm passes? With everything you found out tonight? That's a terrible idea. And what if the flooding gets worse? You could be trapped for days."

"Which is why I have to get him out. There's an old four-wheel drive he used for hunting. If things get too bad, we'll come downhill in that."

"But you heard what the cops said. The water's already too high. You won't be able to get across even in a four-wheel drive."

His eyes glittered angrily. "Then I'll bring him down as far as I can and carry him the rest of the way. I don't expect you to understand. I don't even understand it myself." He fell silent. "Just go and let me do this."

I glanced back. I could see lights twinkling in Asher House, and I could imagine Pell Asher up there, master of his kingdom, as the hillside crumbled around him. I hated myself for it, but I didn't have it in me, either, to leave him up there. "I'll go with you."

"No," Thane said adamantly. "It's too dangerous. Just take the car and go back. This doesn't concern you."

"Yes, it does. And, anyway, if no one else is up there, you'll need my help. You can't get him down that hill by yourself, and you know it. So let's just go." I opened the door and got out. He came around the car and took me by the arms, staring down into my rain-soaked face.

"Are you sure about this?"

"Yes. Let's go and get it over with."

The surrealism of that whole night would strike me later, and I would replay the events in my head over and over trying to make sense of what happened. Why I agreed to put my life at risk for a man who had never shown me the slightest regard until he'd needed something from me. A man who had destroyed lives and been all too willing to cover up a young woman's death in order to protect his son and the Asher name. A man who had flooded a cemetery and opened a terrible door. A man who had invited evil into this town and into my life with wide-open arms.

And yet there I trudged, head bowed against the torrent. Without rain gear we were drenched to the bone, our shoes caked with mud. I felt weighed down from that mud and from the storm and from my own bleak thoughts. I was glad when Thane picked up the pace, and I had to concentrate on keeping up with him. All around us, the woods were dark and gloomy. Over the drumbeat of the rain, I could hear my own ragged breathing, not so much from exertion, but from nerves and pent-up emotions. Too much had happened too quickly. I felt pummeled and assaulted from every direction.

Thane glanced over his shoulder. "You okay?"

"I'm fine." I moved up behind him, my gaze going now and then to the light at the top of hill. I imagined again Pell Asher at that window, regal and defiant and unrepentant even as he reaped the bitter fruits of what he had sown.

Thane pointed ahead. "The bridge is just down there."

We slipped and slithered our way down the treacherous bank, and my heart jumped when I got my first look at the bridge, nothing more than a few wooden planks and a flimsy guardrail. The water was only a foot or so from the bottom, and as we walked across in single file, the icy spray made me catch my breath. I didn't want to consider how easy it would be to lose my footing and get swept away by the swirling foam or bashed against the rocks. So I concentrated on not slipping.

Once across, we scrambled up the bank and headed over the rocky hillside to the road. The going should have been easier on the tarmac, but the incline was steep and we were climbing into the wind, so even here the trek was a struggle. I was anxious to have this over and done with so that I could go home to a hot bath and a warm meal. This hellish night needed to be behind me.

As we approached the house, I heard a pop that sounded like gunfire.

I caught Thane's arm. "What was that?"

"I don't know."

As we stood gazing up at the house, another crack sounded. And then another. I had a momentary image of Pell firing down at us from one of the upper balconies until Thane said, "Jesus. The house must be shifting off the foundation. The beams are snapping."

He took my hand, and we sprinted up the drive and across the lawn. Two cars were parked in front.

"Bryn and Catrice are here," he said. "I wonder if they're waiting for Luna."

"They're in for a surprise, then," I said grimly.

The steps had separated from the porch and the whole structure seemed to shudder as we leaped across the gap.

Inside, the sounds of the storm mingled with the creaks and moans of centuries old timbers. Rain poured through the roof and seeped down walls to puddle on floors that had already buckled from old leaks. The power flickered, and I could hear an electric sizzle as fissures appeared in the ceiling and water dripped from light fixtures. Thane and I stood in what had once been an elegant and opulent foyer and stared in amazement as the house started to come apart at the seams.

Then Thane called out to his grandfather—my grandfather—as we searched the rooms one by one. The house creaked and moaned like a living, breathing entity, and I could feel the weight of some dark emotion pressing down on us.

"If you see a pentacle, destroy it," I said.

"You have my word."

A ceiling tile had loosened, and a steady stream of water poured down upon the long mahogany table where we had sat at dinner and I'd told them about the hidden grave in the laurel bald. That seemed like a lifetime ago.

"Grandfather!" Thane shouted

"We're in here!" Hugh called back.

They had all assembled in the parlor where we'd had drinks only a few nights ago and where, even then, Pell had been scheming.

He'd rolled his wheelchair to the window just as I had pictured earlier, and he didn't turn when Thane threw open the double doors.

I followed him into the room and heard a gasp. Shock and fear fleeted across Catrice's face before she glanced away. Bryn looked defiant and angry. Hugh, at the fireplace, stared morosely into his drink.

"Where's the staff?" Thane said. "We need to get them out of here. The house is coming apart."

"They left hours ago," Hugh said. "It's just us."

"Why are you still here?" I asked.

"Where else would we go?"

"Someplace safe."

He shrugged. "We've always been safe here."

"Not anymore," Thane said.

Catrice took an anxious step toward him. "We tried to leave earlier, but we waited too long and the bridge washed out. How did you two get up here?"

"On foot."

"Then you're stuck just like we are."

"Not quite," Thane said. "I'm taking Grandfather down in the four-wheel drive."

Hugh's head came up. "The four-wheel drive? It hasn't been started in years. The battery will be dead."

"I took it out for a drive not too long ago," Thane said. "The battery is fine, so we're leaving. I don't care what the rest of you do."

"But you can't just abandon us!" Catrice cried.

"You can come with us," Thane said. "But I should probably warn you first that the county sheriff's deputies at the bottom of the hill will likely have heard what happened by now. You all have a lot to answer for regarding Freya Pattershaw's murder, so you might want to prepare yourselves."

"If you'd just keep your mouth shut, none of this would have to come out," Bryn snapped.

"It'll come out once Luna's body is recovered," he said.

Catrice buried her face in her hands and turned away.

Hugh downed his drink.

Bryn glared at me with utter contempt. "Luna was right. You're a threat to us all. None of this would have happened if you hadn't come here."

Thane crossed the room in a flash and grabbed her arm. "Don't blame Amelia. You all brought this on yourselves. And I intend to see that every last one of you is charged as an accessory to murder." He turned to Pell. "Including you, old man."

Pell didn't even bother to turn.

Thane walked over to the window and stood over him. "You had my mother and then Harper murdered because they dared interfere with your grand plan."

Pell gave a dismissive wave. "Gutter trash, the pair of them."

Thane's jaw clenched. "You dare say that to me?"

Pell's head jerked up. "How dare you take that tone with me? You'd be out on the streets if not for my kindness."

"Kindness? You killed my mother and my fiancée and you call it a kindness?"

"Edward was better off without her. She kept him from his home and family for years. *She made him hate me.*"

Thane's expression was passive now, as if the old man's rage had somehow calmed him. "That wasn't her doing. That was all on you." He leaned in, twisting the knife. "You should have heard the way Edward spoke your name… I've never heard such loathing."

"Shut up!" Pell screamed. "You shut your mouth, boy. What I give I can just as easily take away."

Thane straightened. "And you never let me forget it, did you? But if I was so inconsequential, so beneath the Asher name, why take Harper from me? Why did you care who I married?"

Another indifferent wave. "That girl was nothing but trouble. She would have made your life miserable."

"So you had her killed?"

Pell Asher paused, something sly fleeting across his face. "I never said that, did I? The girl's still alive."

My gaze shifted to Thane and I saw his disbelief a split second before an explosion of white-hot fury made me take a step toward him. Before I could reach him, he jerked the wheelchair around so that Pell had to face him. "What are you talking about? Answer me!"

"You heard what I said. Harper Sweeney is still alive."

Thane reeled back as though he'd been struck. "You're lying. Her body was identified. There was an autopsy, a funeral. She can't be alive. Not after all this time. I would have known."

"You know nothing," Pell said in disgust. "You accepted everything I told you without question. A real Asher would have insisted on seeing the body for himself."

Thane gazed down at his grandfather, breathing hard, hands balled into fists at his sides. "I don't believe you. I don't believe any of this. You had her killed and now you're trying to cover your tracks."

"She was no use to me dead, but alive..." Pell's gaze slid to me.

"You could use her for leverage," I said.

His eyes glinted approvingly.

"Leverage for what?" Thane demanded.

"To make you do whatever he wanted." I stared down at my grandfather. "Isn't that right?"

His smile made my skin crawl.

"We're not your possessions," I said angrily. "You can't control what we do or how we think or who we choose to be with."

"I already have," he said.

"If she's still alive, then where is she?" Thane asked quietly. The hush in his voice worried me more than his temper.

"Someplace where you'll never find her," Pell said.

"Where is she?" Before I could stop him, Thane lunged and grabbed his grandfather by the neck. Catrice screamed and I heard Hugh swear. He was suddenly at my side, trying to help me pry Thane from the old man's throat.

"Thane, stop it! Let him go!" I cried.

It took a moment for my voice to penetrate, but then Thane's hands dropped and he staggered back. His eyes were wild, almost demented.

"Get him out of here!" Pell shouted, his hands clutching the arms of his wheelchair. "Leave now, all of you! I need a moment alone with my granddaughter."

"Like hell you do," Thane said. He was gradually starting to regain control. "I'm getting Amelia out of here. This whole place is about to slide down the mountain."

"Asher House has stood on this land for over two hundred years," Pell said imperiously. "And it'll be here long after you and I are dead and gone. Now get out."

"It's okay," I said to Thane. "Let me talk to him."

After the others had gone, I stood in front of his chair. I wouldn't give him the satisfaction of kneeling.

"Where is she? You can't keep him from her. You have to tell him," I pleaded.

"Are you that anxious to send him into the arms of another woman?"

"I care about him. I want him to be happy."

He sneered. "How noble."

"Don't you see what you've done? You've taken everything from him. Even his peace of mind. He'll never stop looking for her."

"He won't find her."

"Then why tell him at all? Just to torment him?"

Pell reached for a book on the table beside him. It was the leather-bound volume he'd been holding the first night I met him. He traced the emblem on the cover with his fingertip. "I've watched the two of you together. The attraction is palpable. But you won't let it happen, because you can't let go of the past. You can't forget about that Charleston cop."

I gasped. "How do you know about him?"

"I know everything about you, my dear. I've kept track of your every move for years." He handed me the book. "Take a look."

I thumbed through the pages in horror. He hadn't been kidding. Every stage of my life had been meticulously photographed and cataloged. I saw pictures of me in Rosehill Cemetery. Pictures of me with Papa. Pictures of me with Devlin. I looked up, trembling.

"You're the last of the Ashers," he said. "The bloodline depends on you."

"What does that have to do with Harper?"

"You hold the key to her freedom."

I clutched the book. "What do you mean?"

"On the day you produce my first grandchild, Harper Sweeney will be set free. Not a moment sooner."

I said on a ragged breath, "You make it sound as if you're holding her somewhere, but I don't believe you. You're bluffing. Even you can't be that unspeakably cruel."

"You said yourself that you care about Thane. You

want only his happiness. Or were those words empty?" he taunted.

"You think you can play God with people's lives, but you're wrong."

"We're Ashers," he said. "Here, we *are* God. We've always been one with this land. You know what I'm talking about. You've felt it. It's already there inside you. Accept it."

"Like you did? Like Luna did?"

"Luna." He all but spat her name. "Good riddance, I say. The other two parasites can meet her in hell for all I care. But you…" His hand reached out to grip my arm. I tried to move away, but his grasp tightened until I could feel the pressure of his bony fingers through my wet sleeve. "You have more power than the lot of them. You have the chance to start a new dynasty."

I wrenched away. "No, thanks."

His eyes hardened. "The legacy won't end with you, girl. Your children and your grandchildren will be Ashers. They'll be drawn to this place just as you are. They'll be connected by blood and by land just as you are. They'll feel it in the wind as Ashers have for generations. And one of them *will* embrace it."

I shivered. "And if I don't have children?"

"You must, for Thane's sake and for Harper's. And for your own. It's your destiny."

Thane appeared in the doorway. "We have to go."

I looked down at Pell Asher.

Silently, he turned back to the window.

Thane brought around the four-wheel drive, and I climbed in beside him. We both turned to stare at the façade of the house, and my gaze lifted to the upper balcony where I had seen Pell Asher staring down at us the night Thane kissed me. He had known who I was even then. He must have been so pleased that his plan appeared to be working.

I clutched the book to my chest. "What about the others?" I asked.

"It's their choice," he said. "Stay here or face the police."

"That's not much of a choice."

"It's more than they deserve."

And no sooner had he said the words than the power line running into the house snapped, and the live wire danced across the wet pavement in front of us. A moment later, the windows in the house exploded.

The hillside gave way beneath us. The truck shifted sideways, and I gripped the seat in terror as Thane fought the wheel and we thundered down the drive. I glanced back just as the house separated from the foundation and started to slide.

"Thane…"

He glanced in the rearview mirror. "I see it."

"Can you go faster?"

I knew we could outrun the house. That wasn't the problem. It was the idea of that house—of Pell Asher—pursuing us down the hill.

"Hold on!" Thane yelled a split second before we slammed into a boulder that had landed in the road in front of us. I flew toward the windshield only to be yanked back painfully by the seat belt.

Thane reached for the ignition and tried to restart the vehicle. It wouldn't turn over.

The house loomed behind us.

"Oh, God…"

"Jump!"

We bolted from the vehicle and scrambled across the wet hillside. By the time we reached the creek, the rushing water had flooded the footbridge. The flimsy structure swayed and creaked, and the water sucked at our feet. I clung to the guardrail—and Grandfather's book—and didn't draw a breath until we were all the way across.

And then we turned in unison to watch Asher House collapse at the bottom of the hill.

Thirty-Nine

❧❧❧

Hours later, Thane, Tilly and I stepped from police headquarters into a glistening, deserted town. We'd been there for hours answering questions and giving statements to the two state police detectives who had commandeered Wayne Van Zandt's office. Wayne had gone off to join the search-and-rescue team, but not before I'd noted a satisfied gleam in his eyes when he'd heard about Luna. I wondered if we'd ever know the truth about what had happened to him at the falls. Maybe his amnesia was a blessing.

Thane had been questioned first, and while Tilly and I waited, she cleaned up my scratches and doctored the superficial cut on my back with antiseptic she'd plundered from a first-aid kit. I asked her about my mother as she worked. She reminisced softly, and I could see Freya clearly in my mind, so lonely and tragic and desperate to fit in. A girl who had once found solace in a graveyard.

"What about Edward?" I asked.

"I won't talk about him," Tilly said.

"Why not?"

"Maybe he didn't have a hand in what happened to my girl, but he didn't do anything to help her, either."

"I think he must have been a weak man," I said. "And probably terrified of his father." And of the evil, perhaps.

"That don't make it right."

"I know." But a part of me wanted to believe there'd been some good in my birth father. I didn't want to think of Pell as my only Asher legacy.

Tilly put her gloved hand on my shoulder. "Don't dwell, girl."

"I won't."

But, of course, I would. How could I not?

"Did you know that Luna was the killer?" I asked Tilly.

"I knew they were all involved, but she's the only one I dreamed about."

"But you kept it to yourself. All these years you knew…"

"I had no proof. And besides…I didn't want anyone finding out about you."

"You burned your hands to keep me safe."

"I did what I had to do." She closed the first-aid kit and set it aside. "I'll give you some remedy when we get home," she said.

"Thank you."

She sat down beside me.

"Why did you take the necklace off Luna's body?" I asked.

"It had a drude's foot on the back," she said. "I meant to destroy it."

"Like the one on the cliff?" I asked anxiously. "It had an open point?"

She nodded.

"There's another one at the library. Sidra showed it to me."

"Tell me where it is."

I glanced at her suspiciously. "Why?"

She clasped her gloved hands in her lap. "You ask too many questions."

After we dropped Tilly at her house, Thane and I sat out on the back steps of the Covey house for a while. It was a quiet night now that the rain had stopped. There was no mist to speak of. No hovering ghosts. Just moonlight dancing on the lake and sparkling from the wet treetops.

"How can the night be so beautiful after everything that's happened?" I asked in wonder.

"Maybe it's over," Thane said. "Grandfather is dead. Luna's dead. Hugh, Catrice, Bryn…they're all gone. Maybe they took the evil with them."

I very much wanted to believe that, but living with ghosts had made me cautious.

Still, the air had a lightness I hadn't noticed before. The breeze felt different, too. Soft and cool and fragrant.

A shadow intruded. "I'm worried about Sidra. She shouldn't be alone tonight."

"She's with Ivy."

"How do you know?"

"One of the detectives mentioned it."

"Because you were worried about her, too," I said.

He shrugged. "She's just a kid. It's hard losing your mother."

Even a mother who had been dead when you were born, I thought. But I was lucky because I still had Mama.

"What will you do now?" I asked Thane. "You don't even have a house to go home to."

"Don't worry about me. I'll make do."

"You can always sleep here if you need to."

He stared down at me for a moment, and I wondered what he was thinking. "Thanks."

I looked up at the mountains, where starlight glittered over the peaks. Something unspoken lay between us. We hadn't yet had a chance to talk about Pell's revelation. "Do you think he was telling the truth?"

"About Harper? I don't know. I'm almost afraid to believe."

"He can't be holding her somewhere against her will," I said. "Not after all this time. Even Pell Asher couldn't get away with that."

"There's an alternative. It's possible she left on her own." He paused. "Whatever the reason, if she is alive, I have to find her."

"I know."

"But it doesn't change how I feel about you," he said quietly.

"It will, though. Eventually, it would have to."

He rubbed the back of his neck. "I don't even know where to start looking. Asher House is gone and with it whatever clues Grandfather might have kept there."

I took his hand in mine. "Then sift through the rubble. Do whatever you have to do, Thane. Just find her."

I thought of everything Pell had told me earlier, but I wasn't yet ready to share that conversation with Thane. Pell's machinations only complicated matters.

"Someone else must know," I said. "He didn't engineer that accident alone. He paid people off…the cops, the coroner, maybe even his attorney. You have the Asher fortune behind you now. You can make them talk."

Thane shrugged. "Who knows what provisions Grandfather made in his will? Besides, you're the true Asher. You have a legal claim to the estate."

"It's yours. I don't want any part of it. This place…" I trailed off on a shiver. "Better you have Pell's legacy than me."

"Meaning?"

"Maybe you can do some good here."

I saw the ghost of a smile. "Restore it, you mean."

I looked out over the lake where a mist had started to rise. "If it's not too late."

"It's never too late," he said, and kissed me.

I didn't expect to rest at all that night, but it was one of those times when the body ignored the mind and I drifted off quickly. Thane had left some time ago to join the search-and-rescue team. I'd made him promise to come back when he needed to sleep, though.

I don't know how long I'd been out when I heard Angus get up and trot into the hallway. I had no idea of the time, but moonlight still shimmered through the bedroom window. I lay very still, listening to the quiet, until Angus whined to go out.

"Seriously? This time of night?" I muttered.

He whimpered again, and I dragged myself out of

bed, slipping a sweater over my nightgown as I padded down the darkened hallway and into the kitchen where he stood waiting at the back door.

I peeked out the window. There was mist on the lake, but no ghosts.

Pulling my sweater around me, I crossed the porch and pushed open the screen door, then followed Angus down the steps. He ran to the edge of the woods and barked excitedly as if he'd treed something in the shadows.

"What's out there?" I asked with a shiver.

He ignored me, but I knew he hadn't gone far. I could still hear him barking. Then I could have sworn I heard a voice and a moment later Angus fell silent.

Alarmed, I started toward the woods only to freeze when I saw a shadow emerge. I thought it was Sidra at first. She wore a dark hoodie pulled low over her face and I called out to her before I realized that the silhouette was too tall for Sidra.

"Ivy?"

She pushed back the hood and let her dark hair fall around her shoulders as she crossed the yard to the porch.

Instinctively, I backed toward the steps even though I had no reason to fear her. "Where's Sidra?"

"How should I know?" she said sullenly, but there was an edge of excitement in her voice that worried me.

"Isn't she spending the night with you?"

"Then I guess she's home asleep."

"What are you doing here?" I asked in confusion.

"I came to see Thane."

Now I felt a trickle of real fear between my shoulder blades as she moved in closer and everything Thane had said about her came rushing back. *There've been some incidents.*

"He's not here," I said, trying to keep my voice even.

"I know. I watched him leave."

"Where were you?"

"Over there." She gave a wave toward the woods where I'd last seen Angus. Where was he?

"I saw the two of you together," she accused. "I saw you kiss him."

I drew a breath to calm my racing heart. "It's not what you think."

"It's exactly what I think!" Her sudden explosion of temper rocked me. Her eyes narrowed as she took a menacing step toward me. "You've been after him from the moment you showed up in town. I told you to leave, didn't I? I told you he would never choose an outsider. Why didn't you listen?"

"Ivy—"

"We belong together," she said. "He knows it, too. He just can't admit it because of what my father would do. But as soon as I turned eighteen, it won't matter. No one can stand in our way, least of all *you.*"

"Ivy, listen to me," I said firmly. "Where's Angus? What did you do to him? Did you hurt him?"

"God." She rolled her eyes, suddenly looking very young in the moonlight. "That stupid dog is the least of your worries. But, no, I didn't hurt him. I gave him a tranquilizer, just like before."

"What do you mean, just like before?" Then something clicked in my foggy brain. "You're the one who set those traps in the clearing."

"It had to be done," she said. "You weren't going to leave on your own."

It was eerie how clearly I could see her in the moonlight. The gloss of her dark hair. The contemptuous curl of her lips. The gleam of madness in her eyes.

Thane was right. Ivy *wasn't* like other girls. She was lonely and needy and because Thane had probably shown her some kindness, she'd spun a fantasy that had eventually become her reality.

If she lived in another town, she might have outgrown her infatuation. But here in Asher Falls…who could say if Evil had played on her weakness? Who knew if even now she was driven by a rage far greater than her own?

A wave of terror washed over me because now I understood. There would always be someone greedy and power-mad like Pell and Luna, someone lonely and needy like Ivy, waiting to invite Evil in. It wasn't over. So long as I remained in Asher Falls, it would never be over.

I drew a shuddering breath. "What kind of tattoo do you have on your ankle? A pentacle with an open point?"

She glared at me in the moonlight. "I warned you, didn't I? I told you to go home that day you gave us a ride. You should have listened."

I glanced down where a curved blade, much like the ones I'd seen in Luna's office, now glinted in her hand.

I eased farther back and felt the porch steps against my heels. I could try to fight her off. I was strong. I'd had years of physical labor to build up my muscles, but the knife gave her the advantage.

I began to sift through possible scenarios in my head. I couldn't get on the porch without turning my back on her. I might be able to outrun her to the woods, but once inside the trees, she'd know the terrain far better than I. And I felt certain she'd set traps all over the place.

The only other means of escape was the lake.

I stood with my back to the porch, facing down the stepping-stones. If I could make it to the water, I could lose myself in the mist....

She advanced on me even as I calculated my chances. I heard something in the woods, the trample of brush near the tree line, and I thought of Tilly. Ivy heard it, too. She whipped around, and in that split second that she was caught off guard, I bolted for the lake, keeping my balance on the slippery rocks only by some miracle. The mist crept over the pier as I sprinted toward the end, my bare feet thundering on the wooden floorboards.

I'd had some hazy notion of making it to the boat, somehow unmooring and launching toward the far shore. But I could hear Ivy behind me, and as I reached the end, I ducked under the railing and slid into the lake.

Stunned by the chill, I went under, my arms flailing in panic. I fought back the terror and as my head broke the surface, I had a new plan. I'd swim out a few yards from the pier and head toward the near bank. But the mist had condensed, and I found myself disoriented. I put out a hand, trying to find the pier, but I'd already drifted away from it.

I glanced around. Nothing in any direction but that white, floating wall. It was almost as if the mist had thickened to give me cover, but the notion was hardly a comfort.

I heard Ivy's muffled voice calling to me, and I swam out several yards, letting the haze and that silence swallow me. My breath was already ragged, my limbs numb from the cold. The cotton nightgown was weightless, but the thick sweater felt like an anvil on my shoulders. Now I didn't have the strength to drag it over my head.

For what seemed an eternity, I listened to the silence. I heard something scrape against the wooden pilings and then a wave lifted me. I thought at first Ivy had jumped into the water, but then I realized she'd launched the boat. I heard the lap of water against the oars, and I kicked away from the sound and circled back around to where I thought the pier should be.

My shoulder bumped up against one of the pilings, and I put out a hand to balance myself only to find the side of the boat. A light came on in my face, and as I pushed off, she swung an oar. The blow dazed me, and I sank like a stone in the water.

Down, down, I drifted. My arms floated over my head. Moonlight shone through the water and I could see Thane's angel reaching out for me as the bells called me to the fold. There were other angels, too, alabaster faces veiled in algae. The bottom of the lake was strewn with broken wings, with toppled monuments and exposed coffins, and deep within a forest of wavering reeds, the statue of a child beckoned. The underwater garden was eerily beautiful, and it came to me that I might already be dead. Maybe that was why I could see everything in such detail—the Gothic spires of the mausoleums, the half-buried headstones. I could even see some of the names: FOUGERANT, HIBBERD and, etched into three tiny markers, MOULTRIE.

And then everything grew gray and hazy, as if I'd drifted too far. Now there was nothing but shadows and ghosts and those half-beings that belonged to both worlds and neither world. Abominations with gleaming eyes and primal faces.

One of them detached from the shadows and I recognized him. It was the hideous creature from the cemetery. The one who had slithered under the fence like a snake. The one who had crawled like a spider into the bushes. Only now, in this realm, he didn't seem hideous at all, but ancient and wizened.

We were no longer underwater, I realized, but in some strange dreamscape. He stood in front of the entrance to a great cave or tomb. I could see nothing behind him but darkness, a black void from which the smell of death emanated. The odor clung to his clothes, his skin, but now I was more intrigued than repulsed. Who was he? *What* was he?

When I tried to move around him, he glided in front of me, coattails flapping, as if to keep me from entering. Lifting a gnarled hand, he motioned for me to go back. But I'd glimpsed something in the tomb behind him. Something beautiful and glowing. The fragile aura of a ghost child.

Was that Devlin's little girl?

She beckoned desperately and my desire to go to her was nearly irresistible.

Suddenly I was being pulled from the other direction and I found myself once again in a fierce tug-of-war. The guardian stepped aside then, as though he could no longer guide or protect me. As if the decision had to be mine.

When I reached for that tiny hand, a claw shot out from the tomb and curled around my wrist. For one brief moment, I stared into the monstrous countenance of something ancient, smelled the fetid breath of pure evil....

Even as I thrashed and tore at the arm clamped around my neck, I felt myself swathed in something warm and peaceful. Like a baby being cradled in her mother's arms.

To this day, I'm not sure how I lasted so long underwater. Maybe I didn't. Maybe I really did cross over. But the will to live is a powerful instinct, even for someone born on the other side. Even for ghosts.

I never remembered breaking the surface or the resuscitation. My first recollection was staring up into three pale faces.

Later, I would learn that exhaustion had driven Thane back to the Covey house, a dream had awakened Tilly and a suspicious Sidra had followed Ivy out into the night. As the three of them converged on the lake, Ivy had fled.

Their faces floated above me now, and when they spoke, their voices were like distant echoes.

"Amelia, can you hear me?"

"He brought you back, girl."

And Sidra's cold lips against my ear, "I saw your ghost."

I looked past them to the end of the pier where Freya wavered in the moonlight, and I somehow knew that she'd helped Thane pull me back from that abyss. And now she'd come to say goodbye.

Forty

The sun was shining when I left Asher Falls the next day. I hated to abandon Thorngate before it was completed and I was sorry to leave Thane when he needed me the most, but it was too dangerous for me in that town. Acting as executor of his grandfather's estate—soon to be *his* estate—Thane had released me from my contract and promised to hire a new restorer.

He and Tilly and Sidra had all come down to the dock to see Angus and me off.

Tilly took my hand in both of hers. "Keep safe, girl."

"I will, Grandmother."

Her eyes glistened as she glanced away.

Sidra looped her arm through Tilly's. She would be staying with her for a while, and I liked the idea of her in Freya's little blue bedroom. That somehow seemed right to me. And Thane would be nearby in the Covey house. That seemed right to me, too.

After we'd said our goodbyes, Thane walked with me to the ferry.

"So this is it," he said. "Full circle."

"I'm worried about Sidra," I said. "I don't think Bryn's death and Ivy's arrest have really sunken in yet."

"Maybe the funeral will help," he said. "I'll be there to look after her."

"And Tilly?"

"Of course, I'll look after Tilly." He bent and scratched behind Angus's ear nubs. "And you take care of *her*," he said to the dog.

"He will."

Thane straightened. "Are you sure you're okay to drive?"

I brushed a hand against the mark near my temple left by the oar. "It's just a bump and a bruise. No concussion. I'm fine."

"Still, I wish I could convince you to stay. At least for a few more days. I don't like the idea of you being on the road alone. It's too soon."

"You know I can't stay," I said softly. "It's too dangerous for me here."

"Yes, I know."

But I wasn't just running scared. I was going home where I belonged. We both understood that. We each had unfinished business.

"Thane…I need to tell you something your grandfather said to me about Harper…."

"I heard." Anger flashed across his handsome face. "Don't take this on yourself, Amelia. He had no right."

"I wish there was something I could do."

"There is. Go back to Charleston and find a way to be happy. That's what I want for you."

"I want that for you, too."

Thane tucked a strand of hair behind my ear. "Maybe if we'd met before…"

"Maybe. But things happen for a reason. And we'll always be connected. You saved my life. You brought me back from the other side."

His eyes were very green in the sunlight. As lush and deep as a Carolina marsh. "If you ever need me…"

My throat tightened. This was harder than I thought it would be. "I'll miss you."

"This isn't goodbye," he promised. "I'll see you again." He smiled then, bringing us truly full circle. Only this time, I knew that behind that deceptively charming smile was a complex man, one who cared very deeply. One who would move heaven and earth to find the woman he still loved.

A little while later, I stood at the rail and watched the shoreline recede. Thane towered over Tilly and Sidra, and I knew that I would always remember him that way. Not as an Asher. Not as a pawn in his grandfather's cruel game. But as the protector of strays.

Farther down the shore, I saw a shadow emerge from the trees, coat flapping in the breeze. Was he real or had I dreamed him? Was he a guardian or a watcher like the old white-haired ghost of Rosehill Cemetery? Whoever he was, *whatever* he was, I had a feeling our paths would cross again someday. He was there one moment, gone the next, and I turned to face the other shore as we inched our way home.

Halfway across Bell Lake, my phone dinged, alerting me to an incoming text.

My heart quickened as I opened the message from Devlin.

It read simply: *I need you.*

* * * * *

REQUEST YOUR FREE BOOKS!

2 FREE NOVELS FROM THE PARANORMAL ROMANCE COLLECTION PLUS 2 FREE GIFTS!

YES! Please send me 2 FREE novels from the Paranormal Romance Collection and my 2 FREE gifts (gifts are worth about $10). After receiving them, if I don't wish to receive any more books, I can return the shipping statement marked "cancel." If I don't cancel, I will receive 4 brand-new novels every month and be billed just $21.42 in the U.S. or $23.46 in Canada. That's a saving of at least 21% off the cover price of all 4 books. It's quite a bargain! Shipping and handling is just 50¢ per book in the U.S. and 75¢ per book in Canada.* I understand that accepting the 2 free books and gifts places me under no obligation to buy anything. I can always return a shipment and cancel at any time. Even if I never buy another book, the two free books and gifts are mine to keep forever.

237/337 HDN FEL2

Name _____ (PLEASE PRINT) _____

Address _____ Apt. # _____

City _____ State/Prov. _____ Zip/Postal Code _____

Signature (if under 18, a parent or guardian must sign)

Mail to the **Reader Service:**
IN U.S.A.: P.O. Box 1867, Buffalo, NY 14240-1867
IN CANADA: P.O. Box 609, Fort Erie, Ontario L2A 5X3

Not valid for current subscribers to the Paranormal Romance Collection or Harlequin® Nocturne™ books.

Want to try two free books from another line?
Call 1-800-873-8635 or visit www.ReaderService.com.

* Terms and prices subject to change without notice. Prices do not include applicable taxes. Sales tax applicable in N.Y. Canadian residents will be charged applicable taxes. Offer not valid in Quebec. This offer is limited to one order per household. All orders subject to credit approval. Credit or debit balances in a customer's account(s) may be offset by any other outstanding balance owed by or to the customer. Please allow 4 to 6 weeks for delivery. Offer available while quantities last.

Your Privacy—The Reader Service is committed to protecting your privacy. Our Privacy Policy is available online at www.ReaderService.com or upon request from the Reader Service.

We make a portion of our mailing list available to reputable third parties that offer products we believe may interest you. If you prefer that we not exchange your name with third parties, or if you wish to clarify or modify your communication preferences, please visit us at www.ReaderService.com/consumerschoice or write to us at Reader Service Preference Service, P.O. Box 9062, Buffalo, NY 14269. Include your complete name and address.

AMANDA STEVENS

31400 THE RESTORER   ___ $7.99 U.S. ___ $9.99 CAN.

(limited quantities available)

TOTAL AMOUNT	$ _____
POSTAGE & HANDLING	$ _____
($1.00 for 1 book, 50¢ for each additional)	
APPLICABLE TAXES*	$ _____
TOTAL PAYABLE	$ _____

(check or money order—please do not send cash)

To order, complete this form and send it, along with a check or money order for the total above, payable to MIRA Books, to: **In the U.S.:** 3010 Walden Avenue, P.O. Box 9077, Buffalo, NY 14269-9077; **In Canada:** P.O. Box 636, Fort Erie, Ontario, L2A 5X3.

Name: _____
Address: _____ City: _____
State/Prov.: _____ Zip/Postal Code: _____
Account Number (if applicable): _____
075 GSAS

*New York residents remit applicable sales taxes.
*Canadian residents remit applicable GST and provincial taxes.

MIRA | HARLEQUIN®
www.Harlequin.com

MAS0412BL